ARIZONA SUNSET

THE BEGINNING OF THE O' BRIAN FAMILY SAGA

RAIN TRUEAX

Arizona Sunset
Arizona Historicals Book 1

Copyright © 2013
Rain Trueax

ISBN: 978-0-9898075-0-0
Paper Back

Reformatted 11-2017

Prepared and presented by
Seven Oaks
Monmouth, OR
113017-404

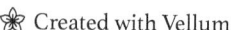 Created with Vellum

INTRODUCTION

<u>ARIZONA SUNSET</u>

In Arizona Territory, 1883, a woman's options were limited by her social status, which Abigail Spenser resented. Despite her father's wishes, she planned to remain a spinster to avoid another man ruling her life—right up until she saw a way out.

Was it safe? Who asks that question when an exciting option appears? Maybe she should have.

Sam Ryker had grown up in a brothel at the back of a saloon. He was tough, a gunslinger, and if not legally an outlaw in Arizona Territory, bordering right on it by rustling cattle south of the border to sell to rich Arizona ranchers. He didn't see any chance for more than a quick death—right up until an option was presented to him. One he maybe should have denied but that wasn't his way.

Put these two combustible personalities together on Sam's ranch, where life rode a precarious edge, and a marriage begun for all the wrong reasons couldn't possibly work—not when each sunset might be Sam's last. A logical woman wouldn't stay with such a man—would she?

Arizona Sunset is an adult, western romance about finding a new way—when we follow our heart.

CHAPTER 1

Tucson, Arizona Territory-- June 1883

She leaned against the wood frame door, arms crossed over her chest. Dust devils, kicked up by a faint breeze, whirled up the street. The sun blazed onto the land with an intensity that attempted to suck the life from all living things. She shifted her gaze to the distant mountains, a hazy purple, their outlines jagged against the intense blue of the sky. Somewhere up there, they said it was cool. She'd have to take their word for it as her world allowed no such escapes.

In the office behind her, the uneven clicking of Martin Matthew's typewriter indicated he was struggling with the report for her father. Loud voices carried up the street from one of the string of saloons that began at the corner of Congress and Meyer Streets. Apparently, she thought with a cross between amusement and disapproval, there were a few activities that weren't affected by heat.

A woman's voice rang out with joy—most likely coming from one of the bawdy establishments north of Congress, the Tenderloin, which no gentle woman was supposed to know existed. As

to why it was called by such an odd name she could only specu-
late because she could never ask anyone apt to know.

Farther away she heard the steady beat of a blacksmith's
hammer, a horse's nicker. A heavily loaded wagon lumbered past,
accompanied by the clip clop of hooves, muffled curses of the
driver, and squeak of the springs. The heat put man and beast in
a foul mood... well, except for those in the Tenderloin.

"Abigail, I could use help on this." Martin's whine didn't
improve her own mood. She moved farther onto the boardwalk.
Holding her dress away from her skin, she wished for the
hundredth time since April that she could wear the loose cotton
blouses and skirts of the Mexican women. At this time of day,
they would be down along the Santa Cruz, their colorful laundry
stretched across bushes while they chattered and enjoyed the
shade of big, overhanging cottonwoods.

Changing one's station in life, however, was not an option.
She sighed. A woman was born where she was; and from that
time on, important decisions were taken from her control. She
washed clothing along a river bank, or she wore clothing ill
suited to the climate. Little of it mattered what the woman
wanted.

Martin's complaints penetrated her thoughts. Why on god's
green earth, not that there was much of that in this land, was it a
threat to his manhood for her to go outside for a few moments?

She heard his chair squeak as he rose from it. She waited.
"What are you doing out here?" he protested as he squinted at
her against the glare of the sun.

"Nothing, Martin. Absolutely nothing."

"You should come inside."

"It's not cooler."

"Abigail, ladies do not stand on boardwalks."

"How do you know?"

When he had no answer for her, his irritation grew and
turned his face pinker. It wasn't as though she should blame him
for what he was. He was doing what was laid out for him also.

She wondered if he thought he was going to be able to grow a full beard and mustache. The scanty fuzz on his face seemed rather sad. Was he fond of his starched shirts and tidy ties. Perhaps he was as trapped as she. Did he even think of such things?

Despite what she knew had to be a mutual lack of attraction between them, she had begun to believe he was the man her father hoped she would marry whenever he, instead of hinting, became more direct. Of course, she would be expected to approve the convenient arrangement.

She was not a pretty woman. Beyond marriageable age, she had no prospects to change that. The fact that she wanted no prospects was beside the point. She had spent twenty-five years obeying her father's dictates; and with such a opportune marriage, she could continue to take care of him, merely adding a husband and any children that might be immaculately conceived.

Most of her life was controlled but that marriage would not happen-- not to Martin Matthews, nor any demanding, unappreciative male creature. She didn't know how she would escape the trap that had sprung closed on her long-deceased mother and, so far as she could tell, the spirits of all women; but she would find a way.

Martin's eyes reflected nervousness as he glanced down the street and back at her. "I must insist you come into the office."

"No."

"No?"

She smiled, raising her eyebrows. "No."

He glared. "I cannot accept that, Abigail."

"I don't see what you can do... other than tell on me."

He opened his mouth like a fish; then shut it. She expected more arguments, but he swung on his heels and headed into the office. The footsteps did not stop at the front desk but headed straight for her father's inner sanctum. She resisted the laugh. He was going to do it. He was going to tell on her.

She turned her gaze to the street where she noticed men coming out of the Pedrales Bar. They were roughly garbed, laughing, their boisterous voices and crude words carried on the heavy air.

If she hadn't known that to go into the office now would make Martin believe he had won, she might have ducked inside when she saw several of the men mount their horses and wheel them up the street, a route that would take them past her.

A tall man, garbed in black, strode from the cantina, cast a laughing comment behind him, and gave a quick running leap to vault into his saddle. The whole movement had been like that of a big cat. She found her attention held by the grace of the man's seat on a large black horse that showed its spirit by rearing up, then settling down under a sure hand on the reins.

In seconds the man had wheeled his horse and was heading up the street at a fast canter. Abigail pressed herself against the wall. She could not explain the mix of emotions-- repulsion and fascination-- in equal parts. She didn't turn her gaze away even when she saw his head turn toward her. He wouldn't see her, wouldn't notice a mousy woman like her even if he had, but she felt a surprising apprehension.

A heavy gun belt hung low on his hip. That gun identified him as clearly as her stiff dress and bound hair would identify her. He was a gunman; she was a spinster.

Startled, she saw him wheel his horse to an abrupt halt in front of her. Good Lord. His black shirt was open almost to his waist and she saw through the opening a bare chest. Good god. She should look away, but she couldn't tear her eyes from him. He took his hat from his head, ran a muscular forearm across his forehead as he turned and looked straight at her. No gentleman would have done such a thing; he would've pretended not to see her. Not that she had any reason to suppose such a man would be a gentleman.

Their gazes met and then to her shock, he looked her up and down, giving her a clear view of an angular face. Beneath his bold stroke of a mustache and heavy beard, she could not tell if he was smiling. She sensed for one wild moment that he was considering coming toward her, saying something, but he settled his hat onto his head and kicked his horse into a gallop, leaving a cloud of dust and hundreds of tiny dust devils in his wake.

In moments, he was at the head of the other men. Like the pack of wolves they resembled, they raced, yelping for the outskirts of town-- woe unto the human or beast in their way. She watched until the desert haze swallowed every sign that they had passed. Only then did she go into the office.

"It's about time," Martin snapped, his expression disapproving. "Don't you ever consider the consequences of your actions? Didn't it occur to you men such as those could kidnap a woman, carry her off into the desert, and she'd never be seen or heard from again?"

Abigail laughed with genuine amusement. "I think they could do better than me if that was their intent."

He ignored her logic. "Who would have to save you if you were kidnapped?"

She realized then that he must have seen the men coming from the bar, and it explained his own quick retreat.

She sighed. "Martin, are you reading dime novels again?"

"Tucson is a dangerous place. There was another killing last night, and I don't read dime novels."

She smiled and walked to his desk, pulled out a side drawer, and revealed his hidden stash. "Let's see what do we have here? *Bat Masterson in Dodge, Sam Bass Races Destiny.*"

Martin, his face flushed, slammed the drawer before she could read more. "You are no lady," he snapped.

"Oh, I definitely am a lady, Martin," she retorted still smoldering over the limitations that placed on her life. When she saw his hurt expression, she regretted ridiculing him. The poor little man was also caught in his own limited world. His books were probably his escape. "I'm sorry, Martin. I shouldn't have made fun of your choice of reading material."

"You're sorry?"

"It was unkind of me."

"I shouldn't have demanded you come inside either. I was officious." His tone told her he had decided to be magnanimous. She wasn't at all certain that she didn't prefer him overbearing. For a moment Abigail considered finding something else for which to apologize. It was too hot for such games. Better to leave it that he'd bested her as she turned to her ledgers.

As she struggled with the numbers she was supposed to be organizing and tallying, she found her thoughts going to the gunman who'd stopped and for a single moment had become part of her boring life. She remembered her feeling of fear, something she didn't experience often. Despite her denial to Martin, she had felt something dangerous swirled around that man. She just was not sure what.

Foolishly she wondered what he had seen when he watched her for those few seconds. Had he actually seen her? Had he really considered coming toward her as she had sensed?

Ridiculous thinking. She knew what she was-- a plain woman, one who would be old before her time, would never have lived. She knew her own lack of beauty all too well. Her face was a pleasing enough oval if it had been softer of line, but instead she had prominent cheekbones, a stubborn chin, none of the roundness that was so favored in the great beauties of her time.

Her eyes were brown, not a clear blue or unusual violet, and worst of all was her nose. She sighed. Her nose was not that delicate button that graced her friend Priscilla's face. Nor did she possess her friend's delicate, finely tinted porcelain skin.

If she had one characteristic that might be considered beautiful, something a reckless gunfighter might even notice, it would be long, brown hair. She was proud of its thickness, the auburn highlights in the brown, but its very virtues were also its untidy sins. The thick unruliness forced her to wear it pulled into a bun where only intense efforts kept it in a semblance of order.

Abigail had never cared that she had no physical beauty. After all, what difference did it make to be comely when a woman didn't desire a husband? She had never cared until that gunman had looked at her. Foolishly, for one stupid moment, she'd wished a man had seen her as beautiful.

She drummed her fingers on the desk. What was wrong with her? She had always taken pride in her strength. Although tall for a woman, another mark on the debit side of the ledger, she could work longer and harder than women trained to be decorations. In one area Abigail had fought against the rules of her culture. She had ordered a special leather skirt enabling her to ride Belle astride. Not for her were the ridiculous skirts with weights sewn into their hems to keep the skirts down when riding sidesaddle. Oh, she could do it. What would be the point when it was so much more pleasurable to feel the horse between her knees? She kept her hours of riding to evenings and early mornings to avoid criticism reaching her father. Those hours of riding had had yielded a strong body, long lean legs, well-muscled arms.

She had a good mind, capable of doing the accounting for her father's Wells Fargo office, leave at five to go home, manage his household, and still help in the evening with a church bazaar. She had all the skills desired in a woman of her station. What did any of them mean?

Interrupting her personal inventory, she realized Martin was talking to her. "What is disturbing you so much?" he asked, obviously not for the first time. He left his desk to hover over hers.

"It's hot."

"Always wickedly hot in June." Martin sat in the chair in front of her desk. "Why don't you go home early?"

She looked up at him-- surprise, mingled with suspicion. "I have work to finish."

"It will wait for tomorrow, Abigail."

She managed a faint smile. "You're right."

Now it was his turn to show surprise. He recovered and gave her a grin. "Would you consider going with me to Carrillo's Gardens tonight? I think the coolness of the lake might be refreshing. Perhaps the amusements would take your mind from the heat."

What was this about? Martin had never asked her to go anywhere. Although she had guessed her father's intentions regarding him, she'd never been certain as to Martin's own. One invitation didn't give her that answer, but it did mean she had best tread carefully.

"Thank you for the thought," she said with a smile, "but I feel you are right. The heat is bothering me. I don't feel up to going anywhere tonight."

"Did your father mention I will be there tonight for the repast?"

She remembered. Not difficult to do since Martin dined with them most evenings. She gathered the files she'd been working on and placed them in a stack to deal with in the morning. "I'll see what Serafina has planned."

"Something special, I hope?"

"I wouldn't count on that. You know Serafina."

"Perhaps you might suggest--"

Abigail shook her head. She would never consider finding fault with whatever Serafina prepared even if it was frijoles every night. She herself could heat water for tea and had little interest in doing more. If she offended Serafina, she didn't know where she'd find such a congenial cook. Besides they were finally over-coming the language barrier. Between her smattering of Spanish and Serafina's slowly growing English vocabulary, they might someday manage a real conversation.

Martin shrugged as he gave a grimace. "She does fix delicious enchiladas."

Outside in the heat, Abigail took long, quick steps, grateful the house she shared with her father was a few blocks from the center of town. Although not by any means one of the mansions of Main Street, nor constructed of the more recently fashionable brick or lumber, the Spenser house was spacious, well-appointed, and situated in a prosperous neighborhood. Large cottonwood trees shaded the dirt-covered front yard and part of the modified Victorian facade.

Walking in the gate, she sighed at her flower bed. As it had in the four summers they'd lived in Tucson, it was shriveling, making the yard more pathetic than if she'd stuck to the bare soil her father preferred. Only the roses were still attempting to bloom, except what was that bug putting holes in the leaves?

Jacob Spenser thought it foolishness to put money into anything that didn't have the potential of making money. Abigail hadn't minded not having a grassy yard, few attempted such a foolish thing in the desert, but she had insisted on the flower bed, something she remembered her poor mother always planting. Neither the elements nor her father had been able to dissuade her, but every summer the hot Tucson summer tried again.

Walking into the foyer, Abigail took off her bonnet and put it over the mahogany hall tree. It took the usual moment for her eyes to adjust to the dark interior. She glanced around the parlor, assuring herself that Serafina had indeed dusted as she'd promised. The room was furnished with quality, somewhat ostentatious, furniture from the East. A circular Victorian sofa took up one wall. A marble-topped table stood in front of it, flanked by two Hepplewhite chairs that had been her grandmother's, upholstered in deep blue velvet. Flocked wallpaper adorned the walls. Although everything was very proper, probably beautiful to some, it represented more of her ordered life.

Serafina, wiping her hands on a dishtowel, came out from the kitchen, a smile on her round face. "Buenos dias, señorita. You home soon."

Abigail smiled. "I wasn't getting much done this afternoon."

"*Qué necesita?*" Abigail could see her search for the words in English then smile as she shrugged. "You want?"

Abigail smiled as she decided what her cook had asked. Then came her own struggle for the right Spanish words to respond. "*Nada. Está bien.* I will wash now. Do you need help with our meal?"

Serafina shook her head, as Abigail had known she would. Nothing caused more friction between the two women than Abigail in the kitchen.

"*Bueno*," Serafina said, heading for her kitchen. "I bring... *agua*."

"*Gracias*." Abigail walked up the narrow stairs to her room, grateful for the thick adobe walls that made the house almost pleasant even on a day where the outside temperature had to be well over one hundred. If they had lived in a wood-framed home, she would have been sweltering with the heat and humidity. The adobe, with its thick walls, was made of this land and for it. Her father might have ordered the addition of the Victorian trims to give the home more prestige, but the comfort came from the earth.

In her bedroom, Abigail wrestled with buttons and fabric, that adhered to her sweaty skin, as she pushed her dress up and over her head. She tugged loose petticoat ties and stepped from all three. When she was down to her chemise and drawers, she stood in front of her floor mirror and stared at her reflection.

Serafina's knock with water and towels interrupted her frustrated evaluation. Told that her father and Martin had also come home early and were already in the parlor, Abigail managed thanks and a faint smile before Serafina closed the door, leaving her alone. On an impulse, Abigail wriggled from her undergarments and turned again to the mirror. She felt a surge of guilt as she stared at her naked body-- the sins of the flesh.

She remembered the pastor's preaching on Sunday, had even then felt it to be directed at her. Perhaps the narrow minded man was right about the dangers of hidden desires, how it led to rebellion. One step out of line and you were over the edge. Well, that was all right. She felt in rebellion. Against him, against her father, against all she had been taught.

What was wrong with being aware of her body, of her own skin and curves, the soft womanly places that were hidden from all, usually even herself. She watched in the mirror as her hands stroked over the fullness of her breasts, down the line of her hip, to her flat belly. She felt scandalized but unwilling to stop. What was she hoping to find? She had no idea. But something. Definitely something.

Feeling mutinous, she walked naked to her wardrobe and looked at her dresses, selecting the lightest cotton on the rack. She shook it and fresh underwear out, just to be certain no scorpions or spiders had taken up residence, then dressed, this time with a light chemise and only one petticoat.

CHAPTER 2

Abigail walked into the parlor where Martin and her father were talking. Martin looked up. "You are lovely this evening," he said surprising Abigail and apparently, from the expression on his face, also her father.

"Thank you."

Her father nodded but said nothing as he looked at her critically. She saw the moment he realized she was slimmer than usual and had guessed the reason. She smiled at him, ignoring his look of paternal annoyance.

As the two men resumed their talk, Abigail found her mind drifting to forbidden fruit--the stranger in black. Was the gunman so fascinating because he had ridden free and wild from town? No one would dare question his shirt being open to display a muscular chest – lusty though it might be. As she thought of his gaze meeting hers, her body grew warm with a different heat.

"Abigail can take care of that," she heard her father saying and looked up wondering what he'd committed her to this time. Before she could ask, Serafina interrupted to tell them their meal was ready.

Seated at the mahogany dining room table set with an

ornately flowering Spode china, Jacob Spenser bowed his head for the grace. In her impatient state, his words seemed to go on forever. Though the food was flavorful, Abigail found herself picking at it.

"Are you ill, daughter?" her father asked as she put down her fork.

"No." Not from any actual disease anyway.

When they had finished eating, she picked up the plates and carried them to the kitchen where Serafina was wiping the counters. "*Usted a casa*, Serafina," Abigail said relatively sure she had mangled the words. "I can clean up tonight." Serafina's eyes widened with surprise and Abigail understood why.

"For pity's sake, I can wash a few dishes," Abigail protested. "Go home to Alfredo and your little ones." Serafina smiled, her eyes darkened to almost a black and Abigail didn't have to guess why. She'd seen the dark-haired, handsome husband who'd given Serafina four children; and if the increasing roundness of her abdomen was any indicator, a fifth before Thanksgiving. Although the whole family was crammed together in a small adobe house on the edge of Tucson, several generations in the dwelling, Abigail envied the woman on many levels.

"I made a..." Serafina struggled a moment for the word, then pointed to the pierced, tin-fronted cupboard. Abigail peeked inside and saw fruit tarts.

"They look delicious." She guessed dried peaches. "*Gracias.*"

Serafina took off her apron, but frowned. "*Seguero?*"

"*Si.*" Heavens, one would think she'd never washed a dish in her life. She smiled then, aware she hadn't washed many, but it would be a more welcome task tonight than listening to Martin and her father discuss business.

When Abigail walked into the dining room, Serafina's apron tied around her own waist, her father and Martin both looked up with what appeared to be guilty expressions.

"What are you doing?" her father asked as she picked up the serving dishes.

"I sent Serafina home. Would you like dessert now?"

"Perhaps in a bit," her father said with a smile. She went back into the kitchen, humming tunelessly as she scraped the plates, washing them in the hot soapy water Serafina had readied. She smiled at her pleasure in the simple task. She wondered, with only a smattering of interest, if she might like other household chores. Unlikely. This was pleasing because she had chosen it. It was part of taking control of a tiny part of her life.

With the kitchen clean, she walked out onto the back porch. The sun was almost gone. The crimson and purple grew on the horizon stretching high into the sky. Glancing north she saw the mountains bathed in a pale purple light, washing out details and leaving the raw bone of their spine etched against the horizon.

A gentle breeze was blowing from the Catalinas. She thought of the stranger who'd ridden that direction. Had he been going into the mountains? Maybe he was on his way out of Arizona. She wasn't going to see him again, whatever his destination. Why did he haunt her thoughts? Why did she care who he was? So far as she was concerned, gunman or outlaw, he was beyond the pale-- a moment, a fantasy that would flit through her mind now and then to be replayed until she forgot the colors, the feelings.

Three houses away, she heard children playing in the alley. Laughing, they threw a ball, purposely making each other miss, then chortling at the joke. Children found pleasure so readily, except had she ever? She didn't remember playing. Even before, but especially after her mother had died, there had always been the concern she might dirty her dress, skin a knee or catch some dread disease.

Back in the house, she saw her father and Martin had settled into the parlor, a chess set between them on the small table. "Now would you like dessert?" she asked as she looked over her father's shoulder at the chess pieces remaining on the board. As usual, it appeared her father was winning. She suspected Martin didn't try very hard to make it otherwise.

"Perhaps later," her father said, staring at the pieces, his hand hovering over a knight. Abigail was tempted to suggest he move instead his king's bishop, but she knew her suggestion wouldn't be appreciated, so she moved to the small pianoforte, running her fingers over the rosewood cabinet. In a melancholy mood, she started with *Barbara Allen*, then a few folk songs before she tried for something more uplifting and switched to Stephen Foster.

"That was beautiful," Martin said when she rose from the bench. "I think I have you in checkmate, Sir," he said then to her father.

Abigail looked over with surprise to see the sullen expression on her father's face and Martin's quiet satisfaction. Something was changing-- some undefined balance of power in the home. "I am going to bed," her father said, rising from the gaming table. "I'm a bit tired." He smiled at Martin then kissed Abigail on the forehead before he headed up the stairs.

When he had gone, Martin grinned. "I'd enjoy that sweet now, if you don't mind." She gave him a questioning look. "Dessert, Abigail." He touched his sparse mustache with a finger.

As he ate the tart, she kept him company at the table.

"Very nice, Abigail," Martin said when he finished.

"I would say thank you, but of course, I didn't make it."

"You may still say you're welcome."

She nodded agreement as she rose from the table. In the kitchen, she washed the dish and fork in the cool wash water

"We've known each other some time." He watched as she rinsed the plate.

She didn't like the sound of that, so said nothing.

"You must have sensed my growing admiration for you."

"Martin, I..."

"Abigail, I cannot think of a better way to say this. Would you do me the honor of becoming my wife?" He took the towel from her hand and turned her to face him

"I never expected this."

"Surely you are not surprised by my proposal."

"I am... We haven't..."

He frowned. "You mean I haven't properly courted you." He twitched the end of his mustache. He smiled then, the smile confident, taking away any concern she might have felt at hurting him. "I would like to do so," he said, nodding his head. "I think we might start Sunday with a picnic."

"No," she said, shaking her head.

"No picnic?"

"No courting. I don't... We haven't... I can't believe you even want me as your wife."

"We are imminently suitable. We like the same kind of work, the same sort of home. I wouldn't disturb the pattern of your days. I would be happy to move in with you and your father."

Her eyes widened. "You make this sound like a business proposal, Martin. What about love?"

His smile was condescending. "Love is a much over rated basis for marriage. Far more important is suitability."

"Martin, I want..."

He interrupted. "Few marriages among civilized people are enjoined for reasons of love, my dear." His tone had become one of patience. "Ours would be begun on more honest emotions."

She wondered what those were. She felt the urge to squelch him and any possibility of desiring to marry her but saw the uncertainty in his face again. She didn't have it in her to immediately tell him no. He meant well... she thought.

"I need time to think about this."

"Of course, I understand." His tone said he didn't. Had he been expecting her to leap into his arms? She suppressed a wry smile. Definitely he had not been expecting that. His own were folded over his chest, his expression anything but lover like. If Martin was suffering a disappointment, it was more one of planning than emotions.

"We could talk about it... Monday. I would like the week-end to consider."

"We could talk about it tomorrow."

"No, I want to think about what you've said.... Alone!"

"All right. You don't need to raise your voice." Leaving he kissed her fingers. She suppressed her desire to pull her hand away. If she had had any doubts, they were gone at her feeling of repulsion at his touch. She would not marry Martin, no matter how much pressure was brought to bear.

Walking up the stairs to her room, Abigail shuddered at the thought of sharing a bed with him, well with any man. Marriage would doom her to years of living a role, of pretending, of being what everyone else thought she should. Being a spinster was acceptable although she recognized the pressure she would be under if her father disagreed.

She undressed and lay on her bed, the heat still making sleep all but impossible. She should have been considering how to refuse the proposal, but the image she could not put from her mind was not of the fair Martin but rather a dark-haired man on a black horse. She was angry at herself for daydreaming about a man she would never see again. A man she would never *want* even to know.

The man on the black horse was forbidden fruit. Every logical bone in her body told her he was cruel, ruthless and dangerous, probably very like the wolf he and his pack resembled. It was why she had felt the surge of fear. He was not a man for a gentlewoman.

Every rational line of thinking told her all of that, while something else deeper argued that she had felt something in that brief moment. It was something she'd never experienced in the whole of her life. Lying awake longer than usual, trying to blank images from her mind, it seemed hours before she fell into a deep sleep.

An Indian woman stood back in the shadows in a grove of aspen trees. Snow was on the ground. She was watching men of her tribe as they advanced with bows in their hands, arrows at the ready. Beyond a pack of wolves was running but one stopped and approached the men,

17

standing as though waiting. The men drew back their bows and two arrows struck the wolf, one in the chest, the other the loins as it fell. The men walked toward it, satisfied, they then left the clearing.

The woman moved toward the wolf. She understood it had been killed to protect the tribe, that the village needed this ritual for its safety. Perhaps the wolf had agreed to be the sacrifice. When she saw the wolf was not dead, she began to tend its wounds. As she applied the poultices and remedies she knew, she understood she was going against the good of her tribe. She did it anyway.

It was a shock when the body of the wolf morphed into that of a man. He was not appreciative of her efforts on his behalf but lay still as she tended him. Finally she realized she had done all she could but her efforts were not enough to heal him. He had the power to heal himself, but she was unsure he wanted to do so. The dream ended.

In the morning, when Abigail awoke, she lay in bed trying to put the pieces of the dream together. It had been so vivid, as though she was the woman. She had never dreamed such an odd set of images, never imagined such a thing in her waking hours.

Yes, she did remember talk from some of the elders that men and women could do this changing of their form. There was the fear that witches regularly did it. She believed none of it. If the dream was a message, to what?

Dressing for church, she put the questions aside. Silly dream. Hardly worth wondering at deeper meanings for such things. That's what her father always said. What the pastor would say. She would tell no one of it. It had no meaning.

"Are you ready?" Priscilla Wesley asked as she swooshed into the hallway.

"Nearly." Abigail ducked into the kitchen and picked up the picnic basket.

As the two women walked out the door, Priscilla said, "I saw Pastor Ryan eyeing you again this morning at services. Whatever is going on there?"

Abigail made a face. "Most probably he thinks I'm doomed to hell."

Priscilla gave a wicked laugh. "That wasn't the look."

"You are a gossip. You'd be the last person I'd tell if there was anything to tell."

"Then there is something. You know you can trust me. I'd never tell a soul," Priscilla promised, crossing over her full-bosomed chest.

"Cilla, you've never kept a secret in your life."

Priscilla gave a short laugh. "I have too. I'm sure I have." She frowned. "Well, maybe I have." Her face grew more animated. "Tell me, Abigail. There is a secret. I know it."

"Not in the least, but well... there is something. After the service, he asked me to dine with them."

"Them? He and his sister?"

"He could hardly ask me without including her. They do live together."

"I thought he was interested in you in more than a spiritual sense."

"Cilla, if you thought something like that, why didn't you warn me? Then I would have been prepared."

"I assumed I was wrong as usual." Priscilla frowned. "Did he tell you her first name?"

Abigail grinned. "No." It was a point of humor between them as neither had ever heard Pastor Ryan's sister called anything other than Miss Ryan, even by her own brother.

When they crossed the street, Priscilla dragged on Abigail's arm. "I want to stop by El Tiradito."

"You can't be serious. You know it's a waste of time."

"How can you know for sure? I must do this."

"You want to make a wish there?"

Cilla's face got the mutinous expression that Abigail knew meant arguing was pointless. "It's about more than a prayer. It's about knowing something also."

"If it is a prayer, it's at an occult shrine."

"Occult is just a word."

Abigail quit arguing with her as she thought about the wishing shrine situated at a year-round spring. El Tiradito had been visited by believers and skeptics for over ten years. The story surrounding it was romantic and tragic, as were many of the most intriguing Mexican myths. This one involved a love affair that ended tragically with a young man being killed, then buried below what later became the shrine. Abigail doubted anyone was buried there or the truth of the myth. She also didn't think it hurt anything for those who went there with requests—about as likely to work as prayer. Not that Pastor Ryan would agree.

"So what are you going to ask for?" Abigail asked.

"If I told you, would it come true?" Cilla quieted her voice as they neared the shrine. Lit candles, rosaries, crucifixes and bits of cloth were fastened to the adobe enclosure. If a candle continued burning through the night, it was believed it was a sign the wish would come true.

"My dear friend, this isn't like blowing out a birthday candle. Besides, you can't believe in this sort of thing?" Abigail hushed her own voice at least partly because an old woman, a shawl almost covering her white hair, was kneeling in front of the small structure and gave her a gimlet eyed look.

"And if I do?" Priscilla pulled a candle from her shawl. She knelt and lit it, closing her eyes.

Abigail looked at the shrine wondering if it did have some kind of magical powers. If so, from where might the enchantment come? A catastrophic result on love could fix someone else's problems. She resisted a sarcastic laugh. For what would she wish if she believed in such? Nothing could be wished into existence. She had prayed when her mother grew sick and what good had it done.

Wishing for freedom, for adventure, for forbidden fruits, none of that would bring her what she wanted—if she even knew what that might be. Would a wish bring the dark gunman into her life? She remembered how he had looked, what she had felt in that moment when their gazes seemed to lock. He had been a handsome man even under the beard. Would she want to conjure a reckless love like that into her reality? No, that was not for her. Wishes were for children or naive adults, not practical women.

When Priscilla rose, she met Abigail's skeptical expression with a benign expression of her own. "What can it hurt?"

Abigail made a dramatic shudder. "Perhaps wishes are dangerous."

Priscilla laughed. "I will risk it."

"What we wish for sometimes has another thing connected. Something we may not have considered."

"Maybe I would want the other thing too." Priscilla laughed even though she received another stern look from the old lady. They walked down toward the Santa Cruz, finding a place in the shade of the cottonwood and willow trees where the water ran almost a foot deep and the grass was thick. Up river they could hear the soft strumming of a guitar, perhaps a lover courting his intended. Farther away children laughed. They spread their own blanket and sat looking at the reflections on the water.

"Martin asked me to marry him," Abigail said, when she could resist telling Priscilla no longer.

Priscilla was silent for a moment. "When?" Her voice was small.

"Friday night."

"What did you tell him?"

"I didn't." She looked over at Priscilla and frowned. "What's wrong?"

"Nothing."

"Don't tell me that. We've been friends almost four years now. I know better."

"Let's eat." Priscilla opened the basket, poked around and pulled out a drumstick.

Abigail realized she'd been blind. "Was it Martin? Is he what you wished for?" She should have realized it sooner. Every time Martin was around, Priscilla grew shy and quiet, laughing at his jokes but never saying a word. God, did Cilla have any idea how shallow he really was?

"You already said the wishing shrine was foolishness. Anyway it doesn't matter."

Evidently, she did not. Abigail considered if trying to tell her would help. "Whatever the case, I won't be a factor in it. I only waited to turn him down to spare his feelings."

"Why would you do that? He's a handsome man. He'd make an acceptable husband for any woman."

"Acceptable, Cilla," she laughed. "What a word for deciding on a yes when a man asks you to marry you. I not only do not love Martin. I... well to be honest, barely can stand him."

"But if he loves you..."

Abigail laughed. "Love. Martin didn't bring up the word. I am not sure he's capable of loving anyone but himself, but if he is, it's not me." She pulled out a hard crusted dinner roll.

"Your yes or no won't change anything. He doesn't see me."

"And why do you think that?"

"I'm fat."

Abigail looked at her critically. Priscilla's figure was full breasted with rounded hips but nothing fat about it. "Don't be ridiculous. You are voluptuous, not fat."

"I am, and I especially am compared to you." She grimaced. "Look at you. You can eat anything you want and you stay wasp-waisted. I watch everything I eat and..." She laughed then. "Actually, I guess I watch it the most just before I eat it."

"Cilla, you're the beautiful one."

"You are jesting."

"Not at all."

"You are so slender. I'd give anything to have your exotic features."

Abigail felt shocked. "I'm not even pretty."

"Not pretty, but beautiful. Are you telling me you don't know it?"

"My nose is too large."

Priscilla snorted. "Its shape is fine and delicate. I saw a drawing of a woman like it in a book about the ancient Romans."

"You can't say you see me as beautiful."

"Everyone does. Your figure is perfect. Not an ounce of fat... Unlike mine." She looked down with disgust.

"I admire you, and you're telling me you admire me?" Abigail shook her head as she finally got it. "We're trained from girlhood to want and admire what we don't have."

"Oh my. I hope that's not why I admire Martin."

"That's a dangerous thought," Abigail smiled, considering her own forbidden fruit.

"I think I did read an article in *Harper's Bazaar* that said that was exactly what women do. Do you want to read it?".

"Not a chance. I've read too many articles telling me what I ought to look like, think like, and be like. I'm swearing off all such magazines—well I might still read Father's *Good Health*."

Priscilla laughed, her eyes gleaming with humor. "For heaven's sake. That's the worst. I thought I was dying for a whole week after reading one of those articles." She dug for a roll in the basket. "The description of the symptoms, everything fit until I forgot about it, and the symptoms went away."

Abigail laughed. "Father does seem to have constant litany of physical complaints."

"None of this solves my unrequited desire for Martin. I wish..."

"You must think about this a bit longer, Cilla. Perhaps get to know him better before you... Well whatever the case, Monday I'll tell him no." She shook her head. "You know, it was the most unromantic proposal you ever heard anyway. He made it sound more like a merger than a marriage. Martin has no interest in me as a woman."

"How do you know that?"

Abigail wasn't sure, what it meant, how she even knew the truth of her words. Most likely she'd never understand what a man could feel for a woman, the things he could make her feel.

She had felt something in the fleeting stare of the gunman, except that had been only a fantasy.

She wished for that moment that she had had the courage to make a wish as Priscilla had done. Did she have the courage to bare the secrets of her heart to even herself? But wishes were for children, for foolish women, for those who still dared to dream. She was not such a woman.

CHAPTER 3

Abigail had planned the words to tell Martin she would not marry him and was about to open the conversation when the outer door slammed open and Silas Jensen burst through. "Where's he at," he wheezed. He looked then at Jacob Spenser emerging from his office. "Spenser, today's stage from Nogales was held up."

Jacob Spenser stared at him. "Held up?"

"Jesus H. Christ, you goin' simple on me, Jacob?"

"Just we haven't had such a thing happen for over a year."

"Like that means we cain't never have it happen again?" The old man wheezed.

"It makes no sense. There was no reason. No gold aboard."

"You figure I got the answer to that. Damnation, I don't know what the..." He stopped and looked uneasily at Abigail suddenly remembering the presence of a lady. "Who the blazes knows what they was after."

"Surely they didn't touch the mails."

Silas shook his head. "You ain't listenin' to me. They robbed the stage, took it all. Donnor was killed, guard bad wounded, they don't figure he'll make it." Silas sunk into the chair in front of

Abigail's desk. "They took the horses too, just left the stage there with the dead and dyin'. Wounded shrieking for mercy most likely." Silas did have a flair for the dramatic.

"Then how did..."

Silas interrupted. "Tarnation, you going to let me finish tellin' this? Frank Smith was heading into town. Come on it after it only a bit after it happened."

"He saw the miscreants then?"

"Nope, saw nothing or so he claimed anyways. You know how folks are. Don't want to know nothin'."

"This is horrible." Jacob stared at his hands, then at Silas. "Everything gone?"

"Thought I jest told ya that."

"The mail? The Wells Fargo shipments?" Jacob asked, his voice failing. "And the sheriff is..."

"That drunk. He's doing nothin'. It's as usual Marshal O'Brian what rode out."

"This... this is horrible." Her father sank into a chair, his face white.

Abigail went to him, putting her hand on his shoulder. "I'm sure the marshall will find the bandits, recover everything."

"Not likely," Silas retorted. "Remember that rainstorm south of town? Well it woulda wiped out any tracks. Not gonna find nothin'."

"I should go down there," her father said, heading for the door. Then he was gone, Martin trailing behind. An hour later they were back. Their disappointed faces told the story before their words could.

"It is unfortunate, Father," Abigail said as the two men sank into chairs, "but we've had robberies before. It is tragic that the driver was murdered, but that happens too sometimes."

"Not like this."

"The guard didn't make it," Martin said.

"No one to identify the bandits. There were no passengers," her father moaned. "The guard said, before he died, that there had been two, masked, of course. They'll never find them. Tracks will be wiped out by that storm. Silas was right. Men like that fade into the hills, until they sneak out like the jackals they are."

"Logically they'll drop the mail when they realize there's nothing of value in the bags."

Jacob shook his head. "Maybe. Or maybe they already dumped it somewhere." He groaned again. "Or maybe this is related to something else."

"Like what?" Abigail asked.

"I personally insured part of that shipment. Maybe they are actually attempting to defraud me."

"Personally? Defrauding?"

"The shipment that was lost was more important than it might seem on the surface--land deeds, old grants for a big *estancia* south of us. They were being readied for a court case. Their owners were extremely concerned for their safety." He groaned. "Maybe someone wanted them stolen. Perhaps the insurance was a way to get money from me. Lord, I just don't know." He sunk his head into his hands.

"I am confused. Why would you personally insure anything?" she repeated shaking her head. "Isn't that Wells Fargo's responsibility?"

"I thought I could make some extra money from it. Offer a better rate. At the time, it seemed a safe way to multiply my funds."

"You didn't mention that to me," Martin remonstrated.

"I didn't see a reason to... I have been having a little trouble making ends meet with the railroad taking some of our business. I didn't want to concern you two. I just hoped we could use this to expand our own shipping line." He looked up. "Do you know what this means?"

She shook her head.

"I insured it for ten thousand dollars."

"Father!"

"The potential reward was great. The penalty now is greater.

We don't have ten thousand dollars." He moaned. "I never thought it would be a risk. It didn't seem like a risk. After all, no gold was scheduled to go out. Shipments come through all the time. Why this one?" He put his hand over his chest. "Lord have mercy, I think I'm having a heart attack."

Abigail had her doubts about that, but she sent Martin for Dr. Hadley who confirmed her diagnosis of emotional stress.

"Go to bed, Jacob. It will seem better in the morning," then he added in a more ominous tone, "and quit fretting, you'll give yourself apoplexy."

Abigail's father groaned and glared at the doctor, then at Abigail. "I am ruined. They're going to sue me, you know."

The doctor put his hand on his shoulder. "Jacob go home and to bed."

Jacob groaned but agreed, heading for home and leaving Abigail to drum her fingers on her desk. "We have to do something," she said to Martin.

"The marshal is going to do all that can be done. What can we do to add to it? Leave it to professionals, Abigail."

She had thought her day was bad enough that she was supposed to let her one and only suitor down gently, that her one and only real friend was waiting to hear the words she hadn't yet said; now she was needed to figure out a way to get her father out of his dilemma. Instead of having less bindings and tightness in her life, her borders were narrowing.

"This is not good but not as bad as your father fears right now." Martin's tone was probably meant to be soothing but instead annoyed her with its pious sound. "It will all seem better tomorrow."

"We have to do something, Martin. I just don't know what. From the sounds of things, the professionals do not have options to do anything. Nor does Marshal O'Brian have a reason to care as much as we do."

"It's his job."

"But he won't lose it over it. We need to... well give the thieves a reason to return the mails."

"Highly unlikely."

"That would be true as things stand. But what if we can give them a reason?" She rose to pace the room. Her heels the only sound as she turned over her idea over in her mind.

"Nobility of spirit?" His voice reeked of cynicism.

"I was thinking something more practical. We offer a reward."

"Are you crazy, Abigail?" he sputtered. "There is already money lost. This would just toss more after it."

"The reward must be of sufficient value to tempt someone to claim it but not so great that they will question the mails true value to us and ask for more."

"How much?"

She considered that. "Suppose we leave that vague and just say—handsome reward?"

Martin laughed. "I might not be a detective, my dear lady, but I can see a flaw in your logic."

"What?"

"How does this man bring in the mails without also facing the law? Only the robbers are going to know where that shipment is."

She thought a moment. "We could ask for information on the recovery. No questions asked for information which leads to recovery."

"Hmmmmm." He smiled and rose to walk to her side, taking her hand before she'd realized his intent. "It's possible it could work, I suppose."

She pulled away and sat again behind her desk. "It has to work, Martin because if it doesn't, I think Father is right, we're not only ruined in this town but with Wells Fargo. I don't think they'll like his taking on a separate insurance that way. Could you go down to the printers and have say... fifty posters made up."

"Of course, uh... I know this isn't the time to ask for an answer to my proposal, but it might reassure Jacob if he knew we had formed our own alliance."

There was no easy way to say it. "No."

"No?" Martin frowned. "What do you mean no? If you think this is a bad time to ask you--"

"That's not it. I just can't marry you, Martin."

"Don't be ridiculous. Of course, you can."

Whatever she might have hoped, it was obvious now that love her or not, he was not going to take this well. This was about male ego. She tried anyway. "I'm not the right woman for you. I'm stubborn, can be truculent, as you well know. I don't have the feminine skills. We wouldn't suit."

He stroked his mustache, his gaze not leaving her eyes. "I shouldn't have asked you again now. We can discuss this when things are calmer." He managed a laugh. "First I propose in a kitchen and now after a robbery. What can I be thinking?"

"My answer isn't going to change," Abigail said. "I hope we can be friends."

The expression on Martin's face hardened. "You know, Abigail, your chances for making a more fitting alliance are non-existent. You're not getting any younger and..."

She laughed. There was no way to restrain it. "I know, Martin. I know everything you're going to say, but don't you see that the wrong *alliance* would be worse than none."

He stared at her; then he stomped toward the door, anger in the tilt of his head. "I'll take care of the reward notices."

Abigail said nothing to stop him as she supposed he'd hoped. When he had gone, she remained sitting in the chair, not thinking of him or his proposal but instead of the plan she had set in motion. It might never work. He was doubtless right, but they had to do something.

The morning dawned with the hint of the heat to come in the

intense redness of the desert sun. Abigail, wearing a simple white blouse and dark blue skirt, poured herself a cup of coffee as Serafina retrieved the milk from the pail on the back porch where it had been refilled by the milkman on his nightly rounds.

"*Señorita es* no uh good," Serafina observed, beating up a batter for pancakes.

"I didn't sleep well."

"Ah, me neither. Juanita, she sick. Mucho crying."

"How old is Juanita now?"

"Almost a year."

Even knowing that Serafina had her mother living with her to look after her children, Abigail considered how hard it must be for her to leave every day to work at the Spenser home, especially when her baby was not well.

"I don't know much about babies, but it seemed to me my mother dosed me with cod liver oil for just about everything. You must hate leaving your children."

Serafina shrugged her ample shoulders as she put a dab of lard into the hot pan. "It is the way."

"The way again." Abigail sighed, then looked at what Serafina was doing. "Don't fix me anything this morning."

"You must eat, señorita."

Abigail shook her head as she refilled her coffee cup. "Are you happy, Serafina?" She tried to remember the correct words in Spanish. *"Feliz. Eres feliz?"*

Serafina smiled at her effort and made one of her own. *"Yes."*

"Life can be so complicated." She had no idea what the word would be in Spanish and knew Serafina couldn't possibly understand what she was trying to say.

"Señorita not happy?"

"I don't know." Abigail walked to the window. The birds were noisy and colorful as they seemed to be everywhere in the big tree that shaded the house. They chittered and jumped from branch to branch. They seemed happy, but was that an illusion like so much of life?

Abigail's father walked into the kitchen, slumping into a chair at the long table. He sipped the coffee that Serafina placed before him, not even bothering to grunt a thank you.

"How are you feeling, Father?"

"How do you think I'd feel? I'm a ruined man." He stared at his hands on the table. "Have you read the *Star's* version of this yet?"

"Well, they will write about it, of course. It's news, but they won't know about the complication for us."

He shook his head. "I am simply put-- ruined."

To distract him from his pointless lamenting, Abigail said, "Martin is going to make reward posters. We will have them posted throughout southern Arizona. If the posse doesn't find the mails, perhaps the posters will bring someone around with information."

He looked up, then sighed. "Probably already buried or burned. And why would anyone bring in such things? It would be tantamount to admitting they robbed the stage."

"We'll allow them to deal with us privately. Since there was no money on board, they might be more interested in profiting from their robbery than you think. They will at least want to know the amount of a reward."

"If such men can read," he grumbled. "I was such a fool. Ruined myself and your prospects as well."

"My prospects?"

Serafina put a small stack of hotcakes in front of him and he buttered them, then added syrup. "Eggs also, please... uh easy over," he said not looking up from his plate. "A woman without a dowry is not marriageable."

Abigail laughed. "That's archaic. Besides I am not looking for a marriage."

A quick knock at the door and Priscilla, dressed in a pink swirl of ribbons and soft cotton, rushed into the kitchen. "I came too early," she apologized, sitting at the table.

"You like?" Serafina asked her gesturing toward the stove.

"I shouldn't... Rose fixed me a big breakfast." She sniffed the air and put up one finger. "They do smell good. Just one, please?" She smiled and then looked at Abigail. "How is everything?" She emphasized the last word.

"As we'd discussed," Abigail answered with her one genuine smile of the morning and most likely of the day.

Abigail's father pushed back his plate and looked at her but said nothing. He rose. "I'll go on down to the office."

"How did he take your rejection?" Priscilla asked as soon as he was gone.

"Want I should clean?" Serafina offered.

"With your baby sick at home, absolutely not. You take the day home, Serafina."

Serafina shook her head and frowned. Abigail reached for an apple and took a bite as she considered. She knew Serafina needed the money. She wished for the hundredth time that they communicated better. "Come back after lunch" she ordered. "Father will not mind."

Serafina looked at her and then smiled. She took off her apron and hurried out the door before the *patrona* could change her mind.

Priscilla sighed, returning Abigail's thinking to her other problem. "Was he miserable at your refusal?"

Abigail shook her head as she chewed. "Martin feels nothing for me. I would guarantee that. He made up his mind what was the wise thing to do, and when I told him no, it became a challenge, made me appear to have more value."

Priscilla's mood improved as she considered that. "So what I need to do is intrigue Martin enough to ask me something, tell him no, and he'll want me next."

Was it that simple? Abigail had no idea, but she had reached the point where she knew very little about what worked and didn't, and so she smiled and nodded.

~

It was nearly a week later when Abigail looked up from her desk as a stranger entered the office. Clad in ill-fitting and dirty clothing, she could smell him almost as soon as she saw him. He wore a gun tied to his hip and a slouch hat, which he didn't remove as he walked to her desk. "Mr. Spenser here?" The stench of cheap liquor was heavy on his breath.

"He's out," she said. "May I help you?"

"Who're you?"

He looked her up and down, at least as much as he could see from where she sat behind her desk. She didn't trust the look in his eyes. "I'm Miss Spenser."

"I need to be talkin' to a man here. Then maybe I can help you folks."

"In what way?"

"Seen the notice about you folks lookin' for some mail bags off a stagecoach. Might be I know somethin' could help if I knew how much it'd be worth to me."

She was glad her father was gone for the morning because the days since the robbery had been hard on him. False hopes wouldn't help his fragile state of mind. "I will get Mr. Matthews." When she came back from the inner office with Martin, the stranger was slouched in the chair in front of her desk.

"Whatever you know," Martin said, "out with it. We have no time for deceptive miscreants."

"What?" The man frowned.

"Cheats."

"Oh." He glared at Martin. "Ain't nobody callin' me a cheat to my face."

"He didn't mean that," Abigail said. "Please just tell us what you know."

The stranger eyed her. "Might be I seed something. Maybe some folks buryin' leather bags. Might be about the right size for mail bags."

"Might be?"

He smiled his jagged smile. "Might be for the right reward."

"Where might you have seen all this?"

"South of here, but north of the Santa Ritas."

"That's a ways from the stage route." Martin twisted the end of his tiny mustache. "What makes you think there's a connection?"

"Could be," the stranger snapped, "I'll just forget the whole thing. Ain't heard nothin' yet to make this worth my while no ways." He got out of his chair and headed for the door.

"Wait!" Martin cried. "We need some kind of proof."

"Ain't got none."

"Bring the mails here and..."

"You figure I'm a little teetched in the head?"

"You can't expect a reward for some words which might be all lies?" Abigail said.

"Wal, Missy, I'll tell you where it's at-- after I see the color of your money. What you fixin' to pay?"

"Nothing without something specific and the mails in our hands."

"We could ask the marshal to discuss this with you," Martin said his voice rising with his nervousness.

The man laughed with what could best be described as a cackle. "You take me for a fool, pretty boy. "No law. I seen how yore Mr. Lawman would figure a thing like this. All right, I'll meet you half way with it. First what's it worth?"

"We had discussed a thousand dollars," Martin said.

"Not enough."

"Look mister," Abigail said, "we don't even know you have information."

"Won't neither if it ain't worth more'n that."

"All right," Martin grumbled. "The most is two thousand, and considering you are selling us nothing but information, that's likely too much."

The man considered. "Half the reward up front."

"Not a chance," Abigail said. "You'd get drunk and we'd not see you again."

"Such a distrustful gal. All right, might be it's worth two thousand to take me away from my... business."

"Of course, we'll also bring the marshal since you didn't steal it," Martin said.

He snorted. "Not a chance. Marshals like getting back loot and blamin' some innocent soul. I seen yore marshal in action a time or two. He'd nail me-- even me bein' innocent and all."

"We appear to be at a stalemate," Abigail said.

The small man rubbed his bearded chin. Abigail waited, glad that finally Martin did the same thing. After a moment, the stranger whistled. "Tell you what-- I'll trust you enough to take you there, if you bring the money with you, pretty boy."

"And you kill me as soon as we ride into the chaparral." Martin shook his head. "I don't think so."

"Martin," Abigail said, taking his arm. "You and I need to talk about this--privately." She looked at the stranger. "Would that be all right, Mister-- Uh, what did you say your name is?"

He grinned. "Reckon I didn't say."

"Will you wait while we talk this over?"

"Reckon." He sat in the chair while Abigail led Martin into her father's office.

"I refuse to go with him," Martin snapped as soon as they'd closed the door.

"I wasn't going to suggest you go alone."

"Well then, what?"

"We both go."

"Absolutely not," he exploded. "That's worse than my going alone."

"It has to be this way. I don't think he'd hurt a lady." She didn't believe that for a second, but it was the only argument she could think of that would give Martin sufficient reason to agree to her plan. One of them had to go. She couldn't go alone and Martin wouldn't. So they had to go together. "Two of us can keep a better eye on him, and who else could we trust to go with us?"

"Your father would never permit it." Martin dug for reasons.

"He won't know."

"How would you keep him from knowing?"

"I go for horseback rides all the time."

"By yourself?" Martin said, his voice showing how scandalized he was at the thought.

She shook her head. "Of course, by myself. Heavens Martin, you'd think the Apaches were raiding the desert right outside Tucson looking for victims."

"No, but I hear they're camped the other side of Sentinel Peak."

"Peaceful ones."

"This isn't safe, Abigail. I won't allow it."

"I've been out frequently and never even been insulted by anyone." She didn't add that she made it a habit to ride toward Fort Lowell, picking well-traveled routes. Her confidence came from knowing Belle was one of the fastest horses in the territory. Although this would be a completely different situation, it seemed the right answer.

"I don't like any of this," Martin said, opening and closing his mouth like a fish. "I..." He groaned.

"We'll return before supper. The Santa Ritas are not that many miles. How long can it take us to get down there and back? On the off chance we have to camp, I'll arrange with Priscilla to spend the night. She won't worry like Father would if I don't make it until the next morning."

"And would she approve of you spending the night out with a gentleman?"

"Knowing it was you, I doubt she'd worry." Abigail knew she was right but not for reasons Martin could guess.

"I don't know whether to be insulted or complimented by that," he muttered.

"I just mean she knows we're friends and nothing more."

"That wasn't what I have been hoping for." He sighed but followed her into the office, where they again faced the stranger.

"You need to give us something more to establish your good faith," Abigail said.

"What?"

"Describe exactly what the bags looked like and be more specific about where you saw them. The Santa Ritas cover a lot of land."

He rubbed his chin. "Then you give me a twenty dollar gold piece before we go to show *your* good faith."

"How drunk will you be tomorrow morning?"

He grinned. "That ain't going to even keep me drunk tonight."

Abigail took a breath before she reached into the cash drawer for the gold piece. "Now your turn," she said without handing it to him.

He described the bags until there could be no doubt they were the correct ones. "They're buried northwest of Mt. Fagan. You know that country?"

"Well enough," Abigail said, though she'd never ridden that far. "All right then, we'll meet you just before daybreak down where Stone crosses the Santa Cruz."

He rose from his chair and claimed his gold piece.

"You might consider using some of that for a bath," Martin sneered.

The little man glared at him. "You're pretty smart, ain't you pretty face. Well, the desert has a way of cuttin' a man down to size. Might be you'll be wantin' to reconsider going with me tomorrow."

"Might be I already have." Martin scowled at Abigail. "Might be I don't have any choice."

CHAPTER 4

Prepared for the possibility of one night on the trail, Abigail packed blankets, a heavy coat, extra canteens of water, food, extra bullets, and in the pocket of her leather jacket, a loaded .38 revolver. Her hat was wide-brimmed to protect her from the sun and her leather skirt was divided. In addition, she wore high boots to protect her from mesquite thorns and ocotillo whips.

She walked from the house before first light taking care not to awaken her father. When she returned, she hoped it would be with good news.

At the stable where Belle was kept, she saddled the mare, her thoughts on the ride ahead and the strange little man. Whatever his name was, and he never had said, he was one of the lone wolves that roamed the desert beyond Tucson, men with no creed, no values other than to protect themselves and to make money off anything, which fell their way. She wouldn't trust him, not for a second, and she was glad her gun would be with her. She had never anticipated shooting a man; but if she had to, she was a good shot.

The sky was still black with a pale pink horizon building to the east as Martin rode up to her. "Abigail, what are you wearing?" he asked trying to see better.

"Stick to what matters, Martin."

He glared. "I still think we're making a mistake." He spoke in a hushed voice, which seemed apropos; even though there was no one near to hear them.

"It's what we must do. Did you bring a gun?"

He patted his hip and she almost laughed at the gesture. Martin with a gun seemed silly. She realized it was equally so for a spinster to be carrying such a weapon. They were an unlikely pair to be heading off on such an adventure.

They waited a few moments on the banks of the Santa Cruz before the stranger arrived, never stopping as he headed south. Even at such an early hour, a few of the

Chinese, who farmed the banks for produce for the city, were already in their fields, their voices carried on the dawn air.

Soon they had gone beyond the farms, the Indian encampments, passed San Xavier mission, and were heading south on the old road that cut along the Santa Cruz river through the surrounding chaparral to Mexico. None of the three talked as they rode; and for that, Abigail was grateful. She always enjoyed her early morning rides, but never more than when she was alone to observe the denizens of the desert before the heat of a summer day drove them underground.

The land that ringed Tucson was harsh and raw filled with things that had thorns or teeth, a land that demanded much and yielded little except to those powerful enough to wrest it away. For some it sapped their strength, left them disoriented and afraid whenever they traveled beyond the town.

Abigail understood the dangers in a land where one mistake could mean death. There were the Apache who for centuries had had ruthlessly ruled this land, riding wherever they would, taking what they wanted. Raids by them were still not unknown. Living to the south of Tucson were the more peaceful tribes, those who lived within the chaparral, ate the fruits and seeds from the desert, made their homes from the desert plants.

For Abigail trips, into the land of the tall saguaro, the short, fat barrel cactus, the long, whip-like ocotillo, the endless arroyos, the craggy mountains, always made her heart beat a little more quickly, her eyes see more clearly, and her mind whirl with thoughts of what was and what had been.

As with so many limitations on her life, her trips had not been as frequent as she would have liked, nor has she dared venture far because of the human wolves who occupied the more isolated reaches. They were men who had come seeking a sanctuary from civilization-- gold hunters, outlaws, wild, reckless men who preyed upon others given half a chance. She recognized she was riding with such a man, but she felt prepared and strangely excited, ready for this moment. It could be the only such freedom she would ever know.

By the time the sun was well up in the sky and the heat settled over the land, they were at the edge of the valley. A haze hung in the air, dust clinging to the air. In the distance, probably as far away as Mexico, Abigail noted the formation of thunder-heads. The storm might never come this far north, it was still early for the steady storms of the monsoons, but if one did, it would do more soak them. Out in the open as they were, it would present the danger of being struck by lightning, followed by possible cloudbursts leading to flash floods, as arroyos, normally dry, would fill with fast moving water.

A small lizard skittered in front of her horse, but Belle paid it no mind, keeping to her steady gait as they veered from the main trail, heading toward the mountains. Not long after stopping to water their horse and take a short break for themselves, they began to climb through brushy oak-lined hills skirting the west flank of the Santa Ritas.

The stranger whistled through his teeth, a grating sound that began to play on Abigail's nerves. He would turn once in awhile and look at her, but he said nothing. He obviously had used none of the gold piece for a bath. She wondered if he ever bathed as she concentrated on staying upwind.

It seemed they'd ridden all day, but the sun said it was still late afternoon when the stranger reined in his horse. He smiled and pointed to a place under a large spreading oak. "Told you I could bring you. Where's the reward?"

"We don't have the proof yet," Martin said with his first words in hours.

The stranger grinned and rode forward. Abigail grasped her revolver and took a deep breath as she urged Belle to follow, Martin right behind her. She had seen the fear in Martin's eyes, the shaking of his hands. It might be better if she stayed between the men.

Dismounting and digging with his hands in loose dirt, the little man buried his hands in the soil. Abigail watched him; then saw on the horizon a rider disappearing over the ridge. She remembered then that there had been two outlaws robbing the stage. Was this a trap?

The little man jumped up from where he'd been burrowing. His eyes were angry.

"What is it?" Abigail asked, pointing her gun through the jacket pocket at him.

"It was here, but it ain't now."

"There was a horseman over there." Abigail pointed. "You had a partner, didn't you?"

"Twern't him. Don't think there was no rider." He narrowed his eyes, not looking toward where she pointed but at Martin and her. She saw the moment his expression changed, at the same time his hand reached for his revolver. Out of the corner of her eye she saw Martin reining his horse around, kicking it in the side. The impact of the little man's bullet caught him, and he reeled in the saddle, falling to the ground, his horse racing off.

Belle held steady as Abigail yanked her gun out, pointing as she pulled the trigger. She saw as her bullet hit the man. His eyes looked at her with surprise. He frowned and fell to the ground.

Sitting in her saddle, in stunned silence in the eerie aftermath of such violence, Abigail felt confused, unable to think what she should do. Was Martin dead? No, couldn't think that. First she had to deal with the man she had shot. What if he was alive? Should she try to save his life, or shoot him again?

She dismounted, never taking her eyes from the still body. As though in a dream she dropped Belle's reins to ground tie her, then knelt and felt of his throat. No pulse. She had killed him. She gagged at the thought. No, she couldn't be sick. She had things to do.

She went to where Martin lay curled on his side, his eyes closed. There was blood on his hair. She felt for his pulse and determined it to be strong. She put her gun into the pocket of her jacket, threw it over her saddle, and took her canteen back to Martin. When she started to kneel at his side, she realized they were no longer alone in the clearing. How could she have forgotten that other man?

She ran toward her horse and gun. Before she could reach them, a horseman had swooped her up with a long, hard arm. Although she couldn't see the face of the one who'd captured her, there were six men on horses now ringing her--hard, rough looking men.

She kicked out at the man, his horse, anything to force him to drop her. She heard a deep masculine laugh. It increased her efforts to free herself. She bent and bit the hand that held her, her teeth sinking deep into the soft flesh between thumb and finger. In another moment she landed on her knees. Like a cat she leaped to her feet and ran for her horse. The man who had held her was quicker as he flung himself from his horse and put his hard muscled body in front of her. He was a solid wall, stopping her so abruptly that only his strong hand kept her from bouncing back so hard that she would have landed on her posterior.

"Looking for something?" he asked, white teeth flashing in a swarthy, bearded face as he turned and delved into her coat for the gun.

She reached for it, desperate beyond clear thinking. A tall man, he easily held it above her grasp and laughed again. "Don't think I'm that much of a fool, lady. I saw what you did to that one." He gestured with his thumb toward the body.

She didn't know if it was the cool grin on the rugged face or his words, which infuriated her more. She only knew she was too angry to be frightened. "Give me my gun," she demanded.

He shook his head. The other men, who hadn't dismounted, laughed. One of them yelled, "I'd be glad to help iff'n you need." Another added, "She too much for you, boss?" "

The tall man laughed. "Maybe so. We'll see." He eyed her a little warily, then glanced down at his hand, which was bleeding from her bite. "Hope you haven't been foaming at the mouth, Ma'am." He chuckled at her thinly suppressed rage.

She knew, not knowing at what moment she'd recognized the truth, that she'd seen him before, that he'd filled her dreams for nights since. He was the man in black, who was no longer a dream but now a living nightmare. She chastised herself for having romanticized an outlaw. Had a wish gotten through at the shrine despite her skepticism?

Martin's groan diverted her thoughts from herself, and she backed away from the tall man and ran to where Martin lay. There was blood on the side of his head, matted into his hair. His eyes opened and looked at her. "Wh--what happened?" he asked, his voice cracked.

"You were shot," she said, her own voice none too steady. She realized then the darkly garbed stranger had knelt beside her as he bent and parted Martin's pale blond hair away from the wound.

Martin cried out with pain.

"Sorry," the man said. "Need to see if it went deep." Long, finely shaped fingers probed the bloody crease. "Just a graze. Don't amount to much."

Martin groaned again. "Not much? I've been nearly killed."

The stranger laughed. "No where near, boy." He glanced at

Abigail. "There's a deserted cabin near here. Reckon it'll do to get him under cover."

He rose and signaled one of his men. "Get the horse that ran off. Looks like he's grazing over there."

"What about burying him?" Abigail asked, gesturing toward the man she'd killed.

"No time."

"But he needs a Christian burial."

White teeth flashed again in that bronzed and bearded face. "He a Christian?"

"Well, I don't suppose so."

"Then he doesn't need a Christian burial."

"Martin and I should stay here," Abigail said, uncertain of what was safe, but surely riding with men such as these wouldn't be. "We could do the burial."

"You can't stay alone, and we're not hanging around," the tall man said, his tone telling her there would be no arguing with his decision. She nodded and mounted Belle, wincing as Martin was helped onto a horse in front of one of the men.

They rode south. She couldn't guess at the distance. Maybe five miles-- miles that passed for her in a daze. She'd killed a man. She was riding with what had to be outlaws. There was no reason for honest men to be out here or behave as these had. Martin was wounded. Her thoughts went in circles, settling nowhere. Then they were reining in the horses, and she followed suit in front of a deteriorating adobe building.

The men dismounted, one of them helping the tall man with Martin, easing him from the horse, then carrying him through the door. The rest of the men remained outside, drinking from canteens and slouching back to wait. Judging from the looks on their faces, their curious gazes, Abigail decided the safest place for her was in the shack with the one they called boss.

The interior was dim; dust covered everything. Along two sides of the room were built-in bunks. It was on one of those they had laid Martin who moaned. A small lizard scurried under a broken chair. It disappeared through one of the many holes in the floor. Abigail shuddered as she ran into a spider web and wiped it from her face.

"Get a canteen and the whiskey, Joe," the tall man ordered. The man who'd helped him carry Martin disappeared back outside.

"You can't think to have an intoxicant at a time like this," she reproved.

He grinned; then bent over Martin. "I figured it for disinfectant, but if you'd like a nip, that's up to you." He checked the wound. "Hardly bled at all." He turned to face Abigail. "Got anything for a bandage?"

She looked down at her leather skirt. No petticoats there. "Would my handkerchief do?"

He looked at its size. "Maybe." He took the canteen Joe brought him and first helped Martin to drink from it, then ripping the cloth in half, used part to clean the wound, then pulled the cork from the whiskey bottle with his teeth and poured a little over the wound.

Martin let out a yelp and glared up. "That hurt!"

"So does infection." He made a pad of the other half of the small handkerchief and using his own scarf tied it in place. He rose then and turned to face Abigail.

In Tucson, even at a distance, she'd been struck by his power; up close it was enough to cause her to back up a step. He looked to be a handsome man, even with his face half covered by a thick beard. His lips were sensual. He had defined cheekbones and intense eyes set beneath expressive brows. His hair, a heavy lock of which had fallen over his forehead, was black, worn long on his neck.

She found her gaze drawn past the dark face, down the strong neck to the rest of his body. His shirt as before was open enough to reveal a muscular chest, oh god and a ridged abdomen. He was pure masculinity.

Embarrassed that she'd given him such a thorough perusal,

she brought her gaze to his eyes and found them looking at her. The irises were a deep, clear blue rimmed with black, the expression in them bold as he gave her the same kind of inspection to which she'd just subjected him. When his gaze reached her eyes again, the expression in them was impossible for her to read.

She sucked in a breath as he looked past her to the other man and said, "Get out."

The man chuckled but left with no argument. Abigail closed her mouth and moved to put the rickety table between him and her. There was no place to run, so she straightened her spine and met his gaze.

"You in the habit of biting men?" he asked his voice husky.

"If they grab me."

He smiled crookedly and held up his hand which was still had blood on it. She thought of the other blood she had spilled that day and grimaced.

"You did it. You fix it."

She clenched her jaw. "I don't know anything about doctoring."

"You going to go around shooting and biting men, you better learn." He righted one of the chairs and sat on it, laying his hand out on the table, palm up. His gaze met hers again, and he waited.

"You don't have to do that," Martin moaned from where he lay.

The man smiled. "You shut up before I throw you to my wolves." Martin shut up. The man looked back at Abigail.

She took a deep breath as she looked at the callused, well-shaped hand and studied the wound. She supposed the same sort of treatment he'd given Martin would be appropriate, so she washed out the injury, sickened at the blood, the bite marks on his flesh, but determined to do what she could now that she had begun. When she felt she'd cleansed the area sufficiently, she reached for the whiskey bottle. "This will hurt," she warned.

He nodded. When she poured the whiskey over the open wound, his expression didn't change, nor did his hand move. She found herself being the one to wince, the one who wanted to moan, but he didn't reveal by so much as a twitch that she hurt him. She untied her scarf and wrapped it around his hand. When she'd finished, she stepped back, too aware of him as a man to be comfortable standing near.

"What are you going to do with us?" she asked.

"There'll be a posse soon," Martin put in.

"There will, huh?" the man said. He glanced at Martin, then to Abigail. "What're your names?"

"Abigail Spenser," she said, "and Martin Matthews."

"Abigail," Martin protested. "You should have told him nothing."

"You shut up," the man ordered keeping his gaze centered on Abigail. "So what am I going to do with you?" he asked repeating her words.

"Just let us go. There's no posse."

"Maybe, maybe not."

"Really. We won't cause you any trouble."

He smiled. "Well, Abby, I've never known a beautiful woman didn't cause a man trouble and as for him." He gestured toward Martin, "His kind shoots men in the back."

"I beg your pardon," Martin said, shutting up again when the man grinned at him with a smile that was anything but friendly.

"Sam," a huge man yelled, popping his head in the door.

The man called Sam cut him off with an angry glare and a quick curse. "I told you to stay outside and keep watch." He glanced at Martin, whose eyes had now closed, then took Abigail's arm and pulled her toward the back door. "We'll talk out back."

He walked Abigail to a grove of trees behind the shack. When he stopped, he pulled out a small sack of tobacco and rolled a cigarette as she watched. Leaning one broad shoulder against the tree, he lit the cigarette, taking a long drag on it before he looked at her. "Well, you've got a sharp mind, what do you think I ought to do with the two of you?"

"Let us go."

He grinned. "You've seen us. A body is lying in that grove of trees."

"I shot him."

"And who would believe that?"

"I would tell them."

"Sure you would. Besides, they'd have made up their mind before they saw us."

She considered. "We won't cause you any trouble or say anything about meeting you."

His smile widened. "Even if you meant that, your friend would make you out a liar as soon as he gets someplace safe."

"Then there's nothing I can say to convince you. Are you going to kill us?"

"It's one thought." He threw the barely smoked cigarette down and ground it out with the toe of his boot. Before she realized his intentions, he had his hand on her arm, pulling her against him. His other hand reached down and took her chin, turning it up until she was looking straight into those clear blue eyes. For a long moment their gazes held, and it was for her as it had been those seconds in Tucson. Some sort of invisible force drew her to him, made her want to look into those eyes forever.

"There are others." Bending his head, he put his lips against hers. She could taste the tobacco, feel the hardness of his lips. The kiss was at first gentle; then he put his arms around her, the flat of his hand against her back and pulled her tight against his body. She felt the hardness of his muscles, the sinewy strength in his arms as he held her. He lifted his head for a moment before he kissed her again, and this time his tongue teased at her closed lips.

Instinctively, she opened her mouth to him. Then frightened at her response, she bit down.

He pulled his head back. "You are a biting little she devil," he said, but he didn't set her free. "What'd you do that for?"

"I didn't invite you to kiss me."

"Lady, with a mouth like yours, you just say hello, and you're inviting me."

She pushed against his chest, feeling the rock hard muscles under her hands but no give in his stance. When he didn't release her, she kicked out with her boot, attaining some satisfaction when she heard him grunt. So it was possible to hurt him.

Then she heard the loud voices from around the shed. "Boss, there's dust in the air. Buck says a bunch of riders coming this way."

He cursed. "How far off?"

"Maybe seven miles northwest. Buck saw 'em looking for sign, but it won't take them long to find ours if we're what they're looking for."

"All right." He looked down at her with regret in his eyes. "Well, lady, looks like this is it."

"Leave us here. We can ask those men to help us get to Tucson."

His smile was cynical. "You think you'd be safer with them?"

"I don't know who they are. Do you?"

"There is no posse coming after you, is there?"

She shook her head. "No." Her father wouldn't miss her until the morning, if then depending on what Priscilla told him.

"Then out here no big bunch of riders is safe for us or you."

"What are you going to do with us?"

A heavy-set man came around the cabin; he looked at Abigail then the man he called boss. "Shall I kill these two?" he asked. "They seen us here-- too near that dead man."

The tall man looked down at her, and Abigail realized how easy it would be for him to order their deaths. No one would know.

Without looking at the big man who'd just offered to commit murder, the man she now knew was Sam said, "Get ready to ride. I'll meet you out front."

"What about the mail bags?" she asked, hoping she could deflect his thoughts from murder.

"That what was buried there?" he asked.

She nodded. "We offered a reward for them. I know you didn't steal them." She knew no such thing, but she decided she had to play a game here, a game for hers and Martin's lives. "You could have the reward if you restore them... To this point, you've done nothing wrong."

"If you think that, you really are green to the way of things."

She tried again. "We won't say anything about having seen you." He appeared undecided. She sucked in a breath. "Take us with you then."

"Oh that'd be smart." He chuckled.

"You can't really kill us... can you?"

He smiled. "Taking you would be pretty stupid. Your friend is a back-stabber and you... you lady are pure trouble." He walked away from her, leaned against the tree, arms crossed over his chest and stared at the ground in thought.

"I wouldn't cause trouble."

He laughed but didn't look at her. "Kidnapping a woman in this country gets a man hung. That's trouble enough in my book."

"It would not be kidnapping if I went willingly."

His head snapped up. Those beautifully rimmed eyes watched her, the expression in them impossible to read. "Willingly?"

"Leave Martin here with water and his horse. You said he wasn't badly hurt. He can't identify you anyway. He's delirious."

"And you?"

"I'll go with you."

His look was penetrating. "What for?"

She hadn't expected that. "Must I have a reason?"

"For something like this... Would be a good idea."

Was he teasing her? She met his gaze. He could snuff out her life if he chose. He probably had killed. What would one more be to him? For that matter, she now had taken a life. A life for a life. Maybe she deserved to be killed, but she wanted to live and she wanted something even more. Something to which she couldn't find words.

She could justify asking to go with him to save her life. She could imagine going to get the mails. If he hadn't stolen the bags, it was a good guess that he or his men were the ones who had moved them. She knew deep in her heart that her reasons for asking to go weren't as simple as any of that. It was insane, complex. "I want to go. Isn't that enough for you."

"You're crazy."

"I could cook for you," she said, lying.

He laughed. "Clean house too, I suppose."

"Of course." How hard could housecleaning be?

He shook his head. "I don't much like the idea of hanging from a tree. The question is would you be worth it?" His blue eyes seemed to darken to almost a black as he smiled.

No man had ever desired her, never even tried to kiss her lips. This man had kissed her with a passion she'd never imagined. He showed, by the expression in those clear blue eyes, that he wanted more. "I don't know." She knew little about pleasing a man, nothing about a man like this one.

She could see him thinking, had no idea what he would say. Would he kill her? Take her? Use her then discard her?

"You'd cause me nothing but trouble."

"Then the answer is no?" She sucked in her breath. What had she expected? An old maid, a spinster, she had nothing with which to tempt such a man.

"I didn't say that." She waited. "You'll likely be what gets me killed, lady, but I will take you." His smile was barely discernable, his eyes darkening with his thoughts. She wondered what they were.

"What's your name?" she asked.

"Sam Ryker."

"Are you already in trouble, Sam Ryker?"

"You having second thoughts already?"

"No." It was her turn to smile. "Just I wanted to know what I'm getting into."

"Define trouble."

"Are there any arrest warrants out for you?"

"Not in this country."

"When we go, you'll let Martin live. Leave him his horse."

"I could."

A skinny, bearded man poked his head around the corner of the building. "Sam, we got to get out of here."

'I know, Ollie. Get her horse ready."

"What fer?"

"She's going with us."

You nuts, boy?" the older man asked.

Sam Ryker grinned. "Probably. Get it." He turned to Abigail. "We have to ride for it. You understand that?"

"Why? If you've done nothing wrong."

He shook his head. "In this country, just being where I am is something wrong. Having a wounded man in the cabin, a woman beside me, a dead man in that clearing, that's enough. There'd be no questions."

"I don't believe that." There was something more to this group approaching.

"Believe it or not. It's how it is." He handed her a canteen. "Leave this for him."

"I'll also tell him I'm going with you of my own accord."

He laughed. "Not that he'll believe you."

"Perhaps but I'll tell him anyway."

Abigail walked into the small shed and found Martin had fallen into a restless sleep. She tried to wake him, then realized he had the nearly emptied whiskey bottle beside him. She wouldn't be able to tell him anything. She worried about leaving him this way. There was no way of knowing who the approaching men were, whether they would offer Martin help or even see him, but Samuel Ryker had said Martin was not badly wounded. When he woke, he should be able to ride home on his own. She could do nothing more for him. Her life was going another direction. Her chance had come, and she was taking it.

When she came out of the shack, the fat man was on his horse, looking down at her. "You are loco, boss. There's lots of dames. Why this one?"

"Shut up." He looked at Abigail. "You ready?"

She nodded.

Sam handed her the reins to her horse. "This is going to be some ride," he said with that faint smile she couldn't interpret.

She mounted without help and within moments, they had all ridden from the clearing, leaving behind a cloud of dust as they spurred their horses into a run, heading south.

CHAPTER 5

F rom the time they left the cabin, she had no clear idea of
what directions they rode. She saw no further sign of
whoever might have been following them. They headed up one
arroyo, down another, over a ridge, behind a rocky knoll, then
toward the setting sun, again away from it. Even though she'd
ridden often in the past, she wasn't a seasoned rider like these
men and soon her whole body began to hurt, muscles she'd never
known she had ached.

Only after dark did they pull their horses to a halt in a grove
of live oaks by a little stream. She had the feeling that even then
the only reason they'd stopped was to spare the horses, not
themselves.

Horses, she thought as she dismounted. She didn't care if she
never got on another horse in her life, not even her beloved Belle.
Unfortunately she was sure in the morning she would have no
choice but to remount. She let Belle drink from the small stream,
and then pulled her away before she drank more than was good.
She loosened the saddle, tethered her where she could find what
dried grass there was.

The darkness, the feeling of isolation added to her surge of fear as she thought about being alone with these men, men who most likely were outlaws. What had she been thinking? Would Sam Ryker have her, then pass her from one of his men to another? She'd seen the look in the eyes of several of them and wondered if that was what they were expecting. Had they taken women before like her? It had been her own idea to come, but what exactly had she entered into? She shivered as she stood in the shadows, watching as they lit a small fire, laid out their blankets and began eating hard biscuits. They never looked at her.

She knew Sam wasn't with the men. Where had he gone? Without him, who would protect her? Why did she expect he would protect her?

From out of the darkness, Sam came and stood beside her. He handed her a hardtack biscuit, some dried jerky, and a canteen. "Eat," he said, then added with a grin, "I won't suggest sitting just yet."

"Thank you." She chewed on the hard fare, washing down the food with tepid water from the canteen.

"You and your men didn't rob the stage, did you?" she asked when she'd finished.

"I told you I wasn't wanted for anything."

"But is that because you haven't done anything illegal or because you haven't been caught."

He grinned. "Good question. Time for us to talk."

She looked over at the men watching them, their own conversations quieted to listen. Possibly they were as curious as to Sam's intentions as she was.

"I fixed a place in the rocks," Sam said.

So soon. So soon she would be called to face whatever he had in mind for her. "In the rocks?"

"I said to talk."

It didn't matter what he said. She knew whatever he wanted to do to her, he could. She had chosen this path. She had wanted freedom from the life she had been living, the one spread out for her future. Now there was a price to pay. There was no one to help her. She felt so exhausted that she could barely think, but her wits would be all that could protect her as she followed him into the darkness.

Sam Ryker led the way to where he'd laid out two blankets--side by side. She looked at them nervously, and then at the small fire he'd built. "Lie down," he said. She suppressed the urge to run.

"Don't be looking like a jackrabbit every time I say something to you," he ordered, then evidently realizing the ridiculousness of such a command, rephrased, "I won't do anything you don't want. I just thought lying down might feel better to you than sitting. You have to be worn out."

She tried to smile and did as he'd suggested. She was exhausted emotionally and physically, but she propped herself on one elbow. That seemed less suggestive than lying flat.

"How come you were out here?" he asked, when he'd sat on a rock across the fire from her.

"Just what I told you. Trying to retrieve stolen mail bags."

"So they sent a woman?" His smile was sardonic. The flickering flames highlighted his face, likely leaving hers mostly in shadow.

"Nobody sent me." She felt defensive.

"Mail isn't usually that important. It gets lost, so what?"

"I work for my father in a Wells Fargo office. All shipments are important."

She saw the flash of white teeth. "Put me in my place."

"I didn't mean--"

"Sure you did."

She looked toward her hand, studying her fingers. "Did you rob that stage?"

"I thought you said earlier you didn't think I had."

She nodded still not looking at him.

"I did not rob any stage."

"But you did dig up the bags."

He chuckled, and the sound drew her gaze up and to his face.

The planes of his cheeks were highlighted by the firelight, his eyes hidden by the dark shadows. "We were camped near-- waiting for someone and saw the weasel with another of his kind. Buck watched them bury something. One went east. The other toward Tucson and yeah, we got it. Since we were stuck waiting anyway, it gave the men something to do for them to keep an eye in case anybody else showed up. It was a hunch, but it paid off." His smile broadened a bit. "Maybe."

"You must have known the bags were stolen. Why did you keep them?"

He shrugged.

"If you return them now, you could have the reward."

"Reward?"

"There is a financial reward for the return of that mail. It's why... the weasel was taking us there."

He grinned. "There is huh? So that's what the whole thing was about. Reward money. Knowing the kind of man you were dealing with, I'm guessing you had to bring the reward with you, didn't you?"

"Some of it. Martin took care of it," she lied.

He laughed. "You'd never trust a man like him with anything. No, if it went with you; you have it, and since I have you, I have it."

She glared at him. "It would hardly be right to take a reward without giving back the mail bags."

His laughter deepened. "What kind of man do you think I am, lady?"

"A gentleman, I would imagine," she said lying again.

"Well, I'd look at that reward like manna from heaven. A little something extra along with the real reward."

"Manna?" She looked up, surprised.

"Figured me for a heathen who wouldn't know a word like that?"

"No."

"Yes, that's exactly how you figured. Well, I've had people read me out of the Good Book."

"I'm glad to hear that." It was some small comfort.

"Don't count on it much. I didn't believe a word in it."

"Oh... So, where does that leave us?"

"Who knows. I saw you in Tucson, didn't I?"

She closed her eyes against the memory. "Yes."

"And you saw me."

"You know I did."

"You watched me."

"A gentleman wouldn't mention that."

"I thought we'd settled that."

She realized the direction he was taking the conversation, and it was nowhere she wanted to go. She attempted to parry the conversation to her intentions. "Do you still have the stolen bags? It's important to get the mail... and everything back to their rightful owners."

"What did you think when you saw me?" he asked, not to be diverted. She wished she could see his face but wasn't sure she could have read his thoughts any better if she had.

"Why do you ask?"

"The usual reason. I want to know."

"I thought..." She could never tell him what she'd imagined about him, the dreams that had followed those fleeting glances. "It's none of your business." She felt her cheeks flush and was glad it was dark. In flickering firelight, it would be difficult to have seen her involuntary reaction.

He tossed his Stetson down and lay beside her on the other blanket. He folded his hands under his head. "Maybe maybe not," he said with a slow smile.

"About the mail..."

"You wanted that pretty bad to come out into this country alone like you did."

"I wasn't alone. I was with Martin."

"Oh yeah, good old Marty," he said, curling his lip. "You were on your own whether you knew it or not. So what's in those bags that matters so much and don't try to palm me off with some duster about it being a grandma's precious letter to her little grandson."

"You won't believe what I tell you. Why should I keep repeating the only answer I have?"

He turned on his side and looked at her hard. The moon was rising, a full moon that illuminated the ground to the point of turning everything including his face, a ghostly silver. With the almost supernatural aura surrounding him, she felt as though she was seeing something more than a man. Was she seeing his soul or perhaps his fate? It made her shudder.

"What's the matter?" he asked.

"Nothing. Will you send back the mailbags? I think you should."

"Why?"

"They might be bad luck for you."

He laughed. "You're funny."

She shivered. "I have never thought so."

"So far they've been good luck as I see it. Besides if I did that, you'd be gone in a flash."

"You don't know that."

"Yes, I do."

"But..."

"Don't ask again. Right now they're not with us anyway."

"Where are they?"

"Somewhere safe. Carrying them around would be like asking for a rope around my neck. Bad enough I have you. I am not ready to go to hell just yet."

"I would explain."

"What could you say? You don't know who took that mail. You and I both know deep down inside you're not sure it wasn't me and my men."

"You think I lie?"

"All women lie."

There was no point in arguing with him. "Is the mail somewhere safe?"

"You do have a single track mind. When we need it, we can get it. For now though we'll head for--" He smiled, "Don't reckon I ever told you where we're heading, have I?"

"No."

"So, you maybe figured you'd just keep riding with me and my wolves forever. Is that about the size of it?"

"I never thought beyond leaving the shack," she admitted, pulling a blanket around her as the night air began to chill.

"You afraid?"

"How could I not be?"

He reached out to run his finger along her jaw. "You shouldn't have asked to come."

"I know that, but..." She shivered at his touch not knowing if she wanted to run or move closer for more contact.

"So now you want to know what I'll do with you." He put his hand to her neck, lightly holding her, his fingers playing with the tendrils of hair that straggled down her back.

"It is naturally of some interest to me, yes." She felt a nearly irresistible urge to bend her head, to clasp that rough hand more tightly to her, to know his touch over more of her skin. She could feel the gentle, soft as a feather touch all the way to her toes.

To her disappointment, he released her and lay back. As he stared up at the sky, all she could see was his profile, a strong one although the bearded chin made it difficult to determine what his face might look like under that cover.

"I've been thinking on that. I want you to marry me."

It took her a moment to respond. She had expected something but not that. "You... you are proposing you and I marry?"

He nodded but didn't look at her.

"Why?"

"Does it matter why? It's what I want. Is the answer yes or no?"

She felt so shocked that she couldn't think clearly. Of all the possibilities, she had not considered that one. "I barely know you."

"You came with me."

He had a point. That had been about as foolish a thing as she could imagine doing. Marrying him would top it.

"What are my choices?"

His laugh held little humor. "You mean will I rape you if you say no?"

"No." But it was what she wondered.

"There is no joy in raping a woman. The pleasures between a man and woman are only there if both share them."

"So then?"

"What did you think you were coming with me for?" She didn't want to face that question. What had she thought? What could she tell him? He didn't wait for an answer. "What do you want me to do with you now?"

That didn't seem much safer to answer. "I don't know."

"You won't marry me?"

"I didn't say that." She realized to her shock that she didn't find the idea repugnant. She had never wanted to be married to anyone. How could she even be considering marrying a complete stranger, a man she met as she had this one? But maybe this was the ideal one. She could marry him then easily get a divorce given the situation. It would protect her from ever having to marry another man. The stigma would never leave her.

Her own motivations acceptably settled to her satisfaction-- at least when she was not willing to delve more deeply into them-- she turned her mind toward wondering why he would suggest such a thing. Why would he want to tie himself to her? Was this all a joke or did he have a need for a wife that he hadn't told her?

"Well?"

"How could we be married? Where would we be married if... if I decided to accept your unorthodox proposal?"

"I thought on that. The mission."

"You don't mean a Catholic mission?"

He nodded.

"Well, it's not my church."

His smile showed little humor. "You weren't thinking of having Daddy give you away, were you?"

"Of course not."

"Well, then it's as good a place as any. It will do the job. I know the priest."

She wasn't sure she would feel married to be wed by a priest, maybe one who barely spoke English. But then she hadn't planned on staying with this marriage; so what difference would it make who did it. She wracked her brain for what she could remember of Catholicism. "Don't they post banns or something?"

"Maybe for believers, but they can marry others. He'll marry us," he said, his voice hardening, "unless you want to go home instead."

"Could I?"

"I didn't kidnap you. You have freedom to leave if that's what you want."

"You mean it's marriage or going home?" She could hardly believe what she'd heard.

"Make up your mind by morning. If you want to leave then, we'll figure out how to do it." He began unbuttoning his shirt.

"Wait! What are you doing?" she asked, horrified as she watched him strip off the shirt and lay it beside him.

"What does it look like?"

"You can't be undressing."

"I could be," he said with another faint smile. He unfastened his gun belt laying it on the shirt.

"But we're not married yet."

"I remember." He used the toe of one boot to push off the other, then repeated the process until his boots were stacked beside his shirt.

"You can't... Well, you just can't." She was awed by the powerful muscles in torso and arms that the moonlight revealed, sharpened by the contrast of shadow and light. She'd had no idea men had so many angles, so many ridges of hardness. She looked up then and saw the amusement in his eyes.

"Unless it'll disappoint you too much, that's all I'd planned to take off," he said, grinning, pulling his gun from its holster, and then rolling over.

She couldn't believe he could go to sleep, but within moments his even breathing suggested that was exactly what he'd done. She supposed he was more used to sleeping on the ground than she, but still shouldn't he have lain awake worrying about everything, wondering if he'd done the right thing in asking her to marry him? Shouldn't he be concerned about that band of horsemen who might even now be following them?

It almost made her mad when she heard his breathing quiet to the point she knew he was deep in sleep. She had never heard a man breathe so lightly and she had to wonder if he was alive. She looked to be sure his chest was going up and down. Well, impossible or not, he was sound asleep, not dead, and she was the one who was going to lie awake and fret over all that had happened, all that was yet to happen.

She debated her choices. If she rode north in the morning, she was unlikely to ever find those mail bags for her father. Her father had claimed he would be ruined. She didn't know if it was an exaggeration, but for sure he would suffer a financial setback. Her own reputation was already in tatters by this night with a border renegade—whether anything had actually happened to make that a ruination a fact.

More importantly than any of what should have been her obvious concerns, there was another fact. If she left in the morning, she would never see Sam Ryker again, never taste his kiss, feel his arms around her, see those beautiful, darkly rimmed blue eyes. She would return to life as it had been-- a bit besmirched, but her days would go on the way they had been.

No, she wasn't about to do that. She had felt restrictions on her life. She had accepted others' rules, regulations. She had let their fear be hers. Her father depended on her, but that dependence had been selfish, had kept her at his beck and call.

Well, if she married Sam Ryker. What would that do? What

possible reason could such a man have for offering her marriage? She had no answers. Perhaps, as with all the men she had seen, he wanted a slave to do his bidding. Clean his home, wash his clothes, and cook his meals. She smiled with amusement. If that were so, the man was in for a bit of a disappointment. She could not imagine he wanted her be his wife because he desired her. A man who looked like him could get any woman he wanted. Why would it be her?

As questions swirled, she had no answers. She was foolish to keep trying to figure it out. This was her chance. Where it would take her, she didn't know. She did know as clear as the sliver of the moon above that if she said no to it, she'd never see Sam Ryker again.

So, she could choose to take a risk, a big one or she could return to life with her father, to life as it had been, and wither up to be the old maid she had claimed she already was. Just the taking of the risk would change her forever in ways she only barely grasped.

When she slept, she didn't know, but she woke with the first rays of morning light to realize she had curled herself against Sam's side, tucked her head onto his muscular chest. At first she felt a sense of rightness followed immediately by one of panic. She had to get away before he woke and saw her.

She tried to inch away, but his arm tightened. She looked up then into his eyes. Too late.

"Let me go," she ordered.

He smiled. "Uh uh."

"You have to."

"Eventually. I like this. I never woke up with a woman in my arms. Feels good."

"I can't believe that."

He bent toward her, put his nose against her hair. "Never said I wasn't in bed with a woman, not that my past would be of any interest to you, but I've not gone to sleep with one. Your hair smells sweet, like lilacs."

His touch, the conversation was so personal, too personal. "I need to--" Oh my, it was about to get more personal. As though he understood without her asking, he said, "Over behind that bush. Nobody to see."

He rose then and headed for the small stream. When she returned from tending to her personal needs, she saw him kneeling on the bank, splashing water on his chest and arms.

He was beyond beautiful, the muscles sculpted like something by a master artist. Words didn't do justice to what she saw and again she had to wonder why such a magnificent creature would want to marry a plain mouse like her. He could take her sexually if he so chose. That wasn't the reason for a marriage. What was?

He looked up then and saw her. Rising, he shook off water droplets. "What have you decided?" he asked, his voice giving no clue to his thoughts.

She almost asked about what. Her thoughts had been so carnal that it took her a moment to remember that he'd left her with a decision. "If you still desire it to be, I will marry you," she said. She knew there had never been a decision to make.

"All right." He grabbed his shirt and gun belt. "I've got to talk to my men. Then you and I'll head for the mission." He slipped on his shirt and buckled the gun belt to his hips.

"You... need that?"

He smiled. "I always need that."

"With your own men?"

"They're a pack of wolves."

She felt a shiver of fear.

"Don't worry. They won't hurt you." He put up his hand to still any further objections. "You stay here, 'til I come for you." As an afterthought, he reached into his saddlebag and pulled out her gun. "Keep this with you from now on."

She swallowed her fear as she watched him stride away. If they killed him, how long would she live?

CHAPTER 6

Returning to face the men, Sam didn't expect them to like what he was about to do. He had heard the grumbling last night, known they resented his unilateral decision to bring her along, but it didn't matter.

From the moment he'd seen her in Tucson, he'd thought about her, about those high cheekbones, delicately boned face, the large dark eyes, that full, passionate, meant-to-be-kissed mouth, and a sweet woman's body that a man could only dream how many places he could find pleasure, giving her pleasure back.

He remembered thinking, as he'd ridden out of Tucson that day, about the kind of woman she represented. He had known no women like her. The reason he had never slept with a woman is because any woman he'd have had sex with was not the kind to be trusted. Oh, he had seen women like her from a distance. She was the kind who made a man's house into a home, who gave him something to work for, to want to come back for.

He'd known with his fleeting glimpse of her in Tucson that a man could die for a woman like her, and die happy, but a man like him would have no chance of getting her for himself. She'd have shook the dust from her skirts if he'd dared brush too close, but then fate had delivered her into his hands. He wouldn't voluntarily let go.

He tried to quiet his mind, steady his hand, forget how soft her body had felt curled against his as he'd lain there since waking before dawn, not moving for fear of losing that softness. Now, he had to harden himself, make himself back into the man who could hold his wolf pack in line, who could bend their will to his own.

"Where's that woman?" Buck Russell snapped as soon as he saw him.

Sam pulled out his tobacco bag and rolled a cigarette. He sealed the paper, struck a match, lit the tip, and drew in the smoke before he let his gaze travel from one man to another. Only Joe smiled with a nod and no concern on his face. Ollie, his foreman, was worried, uncertain about what this would mean for himself. Buck Russell's gaze challenged him. "How was your ride last night? Any chance you going to be sharing?"

Sam dropped his cigarette with regret, grinding it out with his boot before he moved forward, his fist lashing out with a blow hard enough to set Buck on his butt. The big man sat there, rubbing his jaw and glaring up at Sam. "Didn't mean nothin'."

"Then you should've kept your mouth shut." Sam let his gaze travel over the other men. "Anybody else got nothing to say, spit it out."

"Don't like a woman traveling with us. They're bad luck. This won't bring good to any of us." Sam had expected that from Snake Bill, who had acquired the nickname partially for his liking of snake skins but more for his personality.

"She'll be traveling with me. Not us."

"Same thing."

Sam shook his head. "No. It isn't. Do I need to teach you the difference?"

Snake shook his head and looked away.

"Anybody else got concerns?"

68

Only Ollie dared confront him. "What are you thinkin'? Bringing a woman like her along with us. She's different, don't you know that?"

"And so?"

"When they realize she's gone, they'll come chasing us. Men get strung up for taking a woman like that one."

"Only under some conditions."

Ollie snorted. "Don't know which ones they don't."

"Marriage being one."

The older man's eyes widened and no one else said a word. Finally Ollie managed, "You marrying her?" When Ollie saw the look in Sam's eyes, he swallowed, cutting off a plug of chewing tobacco and stuffing it into his mouth. "You're as blind as a post-hole if you think marrying a woman like that one is going to keep her."

"She'll leave you right out of the gate," Buck agreed.

"Thanks for your good wishes," Sam said.

"Good wishes don't do a fool, no good," Snake jeered.

Sam let his gaze move around the men, lingering longest on Rock Thompson. If anyone had the nerve to go toe to toe with him, it would be the quiet, big man. He was several inches taller than Sam, outreached him, and outweighed him by thirty pounds. This time though Rock glanced at him, then shrugged, looking away. It would take Rock awhile to work through what he thought about anything.

"Any of you want to split off, that's fine with me," Sam said. "You can collect your pay at the ranch. If you stay with me, you'll treat my wife with dignity." He raised his eyebrows expressively. "Got it?"

Ollie spit into the ground at his own feet, just missing his boots. "It's your funeral."

"Exactly." He walked to the remuda and snagged first his stallion, Satan, named for his color and disposition, then her mare, tightening the saddles on them both. Satan attempted a couple of quick nips at him, but gave up when his nose was slapped hard.

As Sam walked through camp, leading the two horses, Ollie was the only one who had the nerve to question him. "What's the plan?"

"We split up. Two by two. Everybody pick a different way to the ranch. We might not be followed, but if we are, I don't want any of you leading them there. Got that? I'm taking the woman to the mission."

"You figuring you can talk Father Marcos into marrying you?"

Sam smiled coldly. "Eventually."

Abby had braided her hair into one long, thick braid. She was sitting waiting when he returned. She looked up with questioning dark eyes, but she said nothing as he told her they would ride a few miles with the others, then split away. She petted the nose of Belle, talking to her softly.

"She your own horse?" Sam asked, noting the tender care.

"I bought Belle three years ago."

"She's a nice little mare."

She looked skeptically at his own big horse, who was balking at Sam's tying his bedroll onto the back of the saddle. "Which is more than I can say for that monster you ride."

"Satan's all right."

"Satan? You named a horse Satan. Whatever were you thinking?"

"That it fit him." Satan was living up to his name as he shied away when Sam put his foot into the stirrup. Used to the behavior, Sam vaulted into the saddle, then put up with a couple of perfunctory bucks before Satan settled down to accept his position--under the rider—if not forever, at least temporarily. He smiled at Abigail as he thought the situation might not be so different with her. "Ready?" he asked, giving away none of his thoughts... he hoped.

"He is spirited," Abigail said, mounting Belle.

"That's one word for it," Sam agreed.

The others caught up with them a few hundred feet down the

trail. Sam rode for a mile or two, then reined up his horse, the others followed suit as Ollie kneed his mount next to Sam. "What's up?"

"A break," Sam said leaning over the pommel of the saddle, the saddle leather creaking as he stood in the stirrups. He pointed to a small herd of cattle grazing contentedly in a meadow along the creek. "Round 'em up."

"You aren't going to--to steal them, are you?" Abigail asked, as she watched Sam's men ride down into the creek bottom and begin gathering the cattle.

"Rustle is, I think, the word you want," Sam said with a grin, "but no. We're just going to move them a ways." In moments she saw the plan as running horses and cattle hooves along the creek bottom muddied the water, leaving a mix of tracks that would be difficult to separate if anyone had been trying to follow them.

Sam's horse shied as Ollie pressed his mount too close. Satan didn't like the more lowly horse's presence and attempted to nip at him to establish who was boss. Sam jerked on the reins, pulling him back in line. Riding his horse never came easy. He wondered with dawning self-doubt if that would prove true of his relationship with what was to be his bride.

"You're making a mistake taking her," Ollie repeated.

"Could be."

"Let her go."

"I'm not forcing her."

"Take her back. She'll bring you and us nothing but bad luck."

"You're listening to Snake."

"Nah, I just know women and that one is trouble. She'll never be satisfied with nothing as it is."

Sam chuckled. "You worried she's going to spoil your happy home life?"

Ollie snapped out a few choice epithets.

"I know you figure you're my mama, Ollie," Sam said with a wry smile, "but it's time to cut the apron strings."

Ollie's scowl deepened as he looked back at Abigail who was looking woebegone. "She don't belong with the likes of you."

Sam said nothing. He saw the split ahead in the mountain and signaled the men to him. "This is where we separate. Remember to watch your back trail. When I get to the ranch, I want to only find you there." In moments they'd all ridden in different directions.

Sam and Abby rode in silence. His thoughts were only marginally on the creeks they crossed, the country they had to traverse. He was not letting himself think about the woman nor what he was doing. The decision had been made. He wouldn't consider the stupidity of it nor the illusion that he was once again allowing to build in his life even knowing the futility. There was only one possible end to such reckless dreaming.

When the sun was high in the sky, he suggested stopping. They watered the horses; then sat on a log to eat the sparse food he had with him.

"Why did you return my gun?" she asked.

"Was it a mistake?"

"What do you think?"

"I think in this country, man or woman needs a gun. If you want to use it on me, go ahead."

"Why would you suggest such a thing?"

"Just watching how you're holding it in your pocket right now."

She frowned. "Touching the gun just now was a nervous reaction, not an intention to shoot you."

"Well, just make sure that nervous reaction doesn't cause a twitch in your trigger finger. Might be you'd shoot yourself."

She took her hand out of her pocket. "I know how to use a gun."

His smile was only half amused. "I saw."

"I didn't want to kill that man."

"Never figured you did, but you did right. In this country, if you pull a gun, use it and make the first shot a good one. A bluff won't cut it." Chewing on the hardtack, he studied her face. "Were you in love with that man?"

"Martin?" she asked, a frown putting a little crease between her brows.

He nodded.

"He'd asked me to marry him."

"You said yes?"

"I obviously said no or I couldn't have said yes to you."

"What do you think you said yes to?" he asked.

There was a long silence. "What should I expect?" she asked not giving him the answer he wanted.

"You said you'd cook for me, keep house. What else?" He wanted to pull her into his arms, wanted to crush her against his chest, but he couldn't hold a woman like her that way. How could he hold her?

"What else?"

"What are you going to promise when you marry me? That you'll kill me some night when I don't do what you want? Run out your first chance?"

"If you thought that, why did you ask me to do it?"

Good question. He wasn't willing to give her the answer to that just yet. "How long will you be with me?"

"Whoever knows something like that?"

He wasn't satisfied but managed a shrug, handed her the canteen, then after she'd taken her drink, took his. He'd wanted a good woman, wanted a woman who would side him. He knew you didn't get any of that by pressuring one into marriage, but he didn't know how to go about it any other way. She would never have even stepped out for a walk with him in town. Now he had her, but what did he have?

Abigail watched with disapproval on her face as he pulled cigarette makings from his pocket, rolled one and lit it. "You're smoking again," she said all but holding her nose.

He took a long, satisfying drag on the cigarette. "Looks that way."

73

"It's a dirty habit." Her tone indicated her disapproval as much as her words. He supposed he should have expected as much. Good women didn't approve of a whole lot in life from the little he'd seen of them.

He nodded. "Does that mean the wedding's off, baby?" he asked, having just about decided maybe he'd be better off if it was. She was all but holding her nose. Not exactly the response he desired from her, but he wasn't about to give up the cigarette. Nothing was working as he wanted. Ollie was right. He had made a fool of himself in taking her.

She got up from the ground, walked to the horses, and petted the nose of Belle. "Smoking is a bad habit."

"Most likely," he said, leaving the cigarette dangling from his mouth as he knelt to pick up the canteen and food sack. "And most likely it's not the only one."

She harrumphed. He looked away, but not before noticing the way her breasts pressed against her shirt, good sized nipples was his guess. His body hardened.

"So, are we going to the mission or not?" he asked, rising, not removing the cigarette from his lips.

She scowled at him. Her thoughts frustrating her. Why did he have to ask? Why couldn't he demand? He could leave her some ground to pretend, at least to herself. Of course, this was all happening for the mail bags, the important deeds; yet, she wouldn't doubt with enough persuasion she could talk him into telling her where those were without marriage or from the sounds of it anything else.

She heard an unusual bird sound from the tree and looked up to see a brightly colored red, black and white bird, almost parrot like. "That's a pretty bird," she said-- any distraction to avoid the moment of truth.

He glanced to the small oak tree. "Trogon."

She snapped her head around to look at him. "Trogon?"

He narrowed his eyes, looked again at the bird. "Elegant Trogon. A male. They're the colorful ones."

"I've never seen a bird like it."

"I've just seen them in the mountain canyons of southern Arizona and Mexico."

"I've never even heard that name."

"So you didn't expect I'd know it either, or... did you think I lied about its name?" She could see she had offended him.

"I... uh no, I know you wouldn't... about that."

He dropped his cigarette to the dirt and ground it out, then looked at her, those blue eyes so intense. His lashes were thick making his eyes seem almost to be outlined by kohl. "So, Abby, where do we go this morning?"

"You'd really let me go home?"

He nodded.

She felt irritated. She didn't want to have to admit even to herself that she was choosing this. "You're no gentleman," she said finally, having decided one thing for sure--a gentleman wouldn't have put her in such a spot.

He laughed. 'You got that one. So what's it to be?"

She glared at him. "I said I'd marry you." The next thing would be him insisting she ask him to marry her.

"You don't look like a happy bride," he said, tying the food bag to his saddle.

She groaned. "You want a smile. Here. Here's a smile." She forced a wide one onto her lips and didn't know whether she was pleased or irritated when he laughed.

"Well," she said, "this is hardly going to be a typical wedding, one of the more unusual probably in the annals of time."

"In the what?"

"In forever," she snapped.

He smiled, that strong, blatantly male face dangerously close to her again. She wished she could look at him and not find her toes curling, her belly tightening. She wished she could look at his chest and not remember it uncovered. Wished she wasn't wondering what lay beneath the pants.

"If you don't look a little more satisfied when we get to the priest," he said, mounting Satan and doing a battle for control before he could finish, "he won't marry us."

"What do you mean?"

"We're not Catholics. He's not going to like it at best. Father Marcos is a good man, as far as his kind go. He'll do it if he thinks it's what you want. If he doesn't, it's forget it."

"Oh." She mulled that over. She didn't want to forget it. Crazy as it seemed, she wanted to see this wedding through, even though she had no idea what would happen afterward. She forced a smile on her face. "Will that do?"

He laughed. "You look like a squirrel who just ran across a polecat, but yeah, if that's the best you can do, it'll have to be enough." He shook his head as he gigged Satan in the side and headed off to the west, satisfied that within a moment she'd catch up with him.

"Aren't you concerned I'll ride off?" she asked as she pulled her mount even with his.

"What for?"

"I mean... I could run away."

He nodded. "You could."

"Don't you care if I do?"

"I told you I won't force you into this."

"Riding off with a man alone pretty well did that," she said. "I couldn't hold my head up in Tucson if I went back now." She knew she didn't care about any of that, but he couldn't. She decided a little guilt for him was in order.

"For what it was worth, I offered you my name," he said, not looking over at her.

"I... know." She felt like crying. This wasn't the way it was supposed to be when she got married, and yet how many women found it any different? Women married for money, position, because they had to, convenience. She'd even read of mail-order brides, who had come west with no idea what kind of man they'd be marrying. How many women were wed for love or passion? At this point, she wasn't sure where her own reason for a wedding would fit among the various possibilities, but she was determined to go ahead with it. He wouldn't dare back out now.

"How far is this place?" she asked, still sore from the long ride the day before.

"Maybe twenty miles."

She suppressed her groan.

In the late afternoon, they crossed the Santa Cruz River and rode into the settlement. Sam told her a little of its history as they rode. Although not as impressive as the showier San Xavier up near Tucson, the little mission was lovely with its soaring design, quiet, peaceful setting that belied its history. It had been occupied and abandoned several times due to Apache depredations. Father Marcos had moved in officially or otherwise and re-established it--at least for a time. The Papago camped around the fringes helping with the restoration work and attending services, their children receiving classes in a small structure alongside the mission.

As they rode into the central courtyard, Father Marcos, a man of middle years, garbed in a plain brown robe, walked out to greet them, urging them to dismount and come into the living quarters. Abigail managed a smile as she was introduced to the balding missionary; then he turned to Sam and the two spoke fluent Spanish with no attempt to stop and translate for her. She was feeling sorry for herself and abandoned by the time they turned and looked at her.

"He wants to know if you want to marry me," Sam said.

Abigail smiled as she met the small priest's concerned eyes. "Sí," she said, nodding with what she hoped was an emphatic manner.

Father Marcos's grin broadened. "I no think Sam ever marry. "You *muy bonita*."

"*Gracias*," she said grateful for her sporadic attempts to learn Serafina's language. Father Marcos patted her hand, then nodded.

Soon he and Sam were engaged in another conversation, which lost Abigail until Sam took her hand and put it on his arm, leading her into the dimly lit sanctuary. She had assumed they would wait, eat, perhaps get married in the morning, but she saw that was not how it was to be.

She would be married in a dirty, leather riding skirt, torn blouse, boots, her hair straggling out of a braid and to a man she barely knew, other than that he was probably some kind of desperado. She was to be married by a priest who spoke barely any English. Well at least she wasn't doing what was expected by her society. How that was going to benefit her-- on that she couldn't predict.

She shook her head at her own foolishness, but as the priest said the words, when he looked toward her, she nodded, smiled, and said, *sí*. In moments, Sam bent to a kiss that barely brushed her lips. The priest laughed and patted Sam on the back as he smiled again at her. Sam signed the certificate before handing it to her. With her own name, she finalized the deed.

"Father Marcos would like us to eat with him." Sam looked at Abby questioningly. She was nearly starving, having eaten little for two days. Anything the priest might offer would be very welcome, and she nodded her agreement. Besides, she felt nervous at the thought of being alone with her new husband. Would he immediately expect husbandly rights? He'd said he would not force her, but it was not force for a man to have sex with his own wife.

After they'd eaten a light meal of potatoes and roast lamb, the priest again made Sam an offer which he translated for Abby. "He invited us to spend the night here."

She looked up at him with a feeling of panic. Even though she was exhausted, she said, "I'm not ready for bed."

"I'll sleep on the floor tonight," he reassured her.

She swallowed. "That wouldn't be right."

He grinned. "When I share your bed, it'll be because you're begging me to."

"Begging?" She lifted her eyebrows.

"You will want me to be there so bad that you can't do anything but beg." His voice was husky, little above a whisper.

"You are pretty confident of yourself."

"About some things." He turned to the priest and accepted the lodging. He then told Abigail he'd play a little chess with Father Marcos, but she could go on to bed.

Moments later, Abigail was ushered by an Indian woman into a single room with a dirt floor and adobe walls, a simple flat roof, furnished with one double bed and a dresser upon which set a candle, a basin of water, and a pitcher. The windows had no glass in them, but they did have wooden shutters she could close. To do so would make the room stifling hot. She opted instead to blow out the candle, stripping down to her chemise and washing in the darkness.

Lying in bed she wondered what would her life be like in the morning. Would Sam keep to his word and not force her to have sex with him. Did she want him to keep to his word? She was torn between desire for the man, curiosity about sex itself, and the fear that the act would be painful and take her to a place from which she could not return.

How long before Sam would join her. He'd said she'd have to ask him to join her on the bed, but the floor looked awfully hard. Surely he wouldn't sleep there when he had a choice. She tucked the sheet around herself, making a little nest that would protect her only so long as he allowed it to be so.

She had drifted off to sleep only waking when the door creaked open. "Sam?" she asked.

"It's me, Abby."

She had never liked that nickname but something about the way he said it, those dark, husky tones, made her change her mind. "How... how did the chess game go?"

"He beat me. First time too. My mind wasn't on the game."

She shrank further against the wall, leaving as much of the

bed as possible for him. She heard his rustling, knew he was dropping clothing.

"There water in here?" he asked.

"The girl brought in fresh," Abigail said. He then moved unerringly in the dark to the dresser and she heard the sounds of water splashing. She imagined the water driplets rolling down his body and wondered how much clothing he'd removed. Judging by the silvery sheen of his skin, in the scant moonlight, it looked as though he'd removed everything. She swallowed hard again and tried to still her trembling.

The next sound she heard was his taking a blanket from the bottom of the bed and lying down on the floor.

"What are you doing?" she asked, leaning forward to make out the shape of his body on the blanket. .

"You begging me to join you?" She could hear the amusement in his voice.

"No."

"Then, I'm sleeping on the floor. See you in the morning."

She stared down at his still form and couldn't believe he was going to sleep on the floor on his wedding night. Did that mean he didn't desire her-- that he found her unattractive? For the moment, she forgot her own fears and her hope that he would do exactly as he had done. The question for her now was—why had he?

CHAPTER 7

Abigail and Sam were up Sonoita Creek between the Santa Ritas and the smaller mountain range when the storm clouds began to build across the valley.

"Summer rains are coming early this year," he said, pointing to the dark thunderheads building against the Tumacacoris from whence they'd come.

"You think the storm will come our way."

"From the direction of the wind, I'd put chips on it."

"I like storms," she said, "but not when I'm out in them."

"Man or woman doesn't respect an Arizona thunderstorm is a fool. No shelter here either." They were out where it was too open, no protection from lightning strikes. The trees were scrub oak and juniper, the pines spindly and of no account.

"Maybe we can outride it."

He smiled at her. "Maybe so." He spurred Satan and saw similar burst of speed from Belle. Riding hard, he and Abby headed for the pass that would lead into his valley. He realized he'd never told Abby where they were going, but he guessed maybe seeing it was the best way.

They varied the speed of their horses, giving them a respite when possible, but keeping as much distance as possible between themselves and the fast moving storm. The wind blowing behind them picked up force. Sam pulled up his horse. "You have a slicker?"

"Just my jacket."

He reached into his bag and pulled out his long slicker handing it to her.

"Use this."

"What about you?" she asked.

"I'll be all right. Not the first storm I've weathered. Put it on. We're going to get wet." Behind them he saw the flash of lightning and seconds later the first angry boom of thunder. He waited as she put on the coat, pulling the brim of his own hat down to keep the wind from sucking it away. Overhead the sky darkened, giving it the look of prematurely arriving night. "Keep low," he said and for the first time, sent her horse ahead of his. She would know where they were heading when she saw it, up and over the rise.

The rain began falling, at first not heavily, then with more force. Within moments Sam was soaked to the skin. Nothing he could do about the lightning. He'd had it hit close before, knew it could kill, but wasn't anything a man could worry about. Just how it was with life. Hit one and not another. He trusted in his luck where it came to that. Not so sure about where it came to the woman riding ahead of him.

They followed the cut between Red Mountain and American Peak and then came out into his valley. He urged the horses to pick up speed again. It was all or nothing.

At the highest ridge, already soaked and even knowing Abby hadn't fared much better, Sam couldn't resist reining in Satan for just a moment. When she realized he wasn't right behind her, she pulled her own horse to a halt, looking back at him. "What's wrong?" she yelled.

Lying in front of him was the San Rafael Valley, his valley, rolling grasslands for as far as the eye could see, year round water. Room to graze a thousand head of cattle. His ranch reached from where he had stopped to the border of Mexico and east to the Canelo Hills. He never rode over this rise and saw it but what he didn't feel a surge of pride. Even now, with a threatening storm overhead, there was something new added to it. He was bringing home the woman to the ranch, the kind of woman who could make it a home. Foolish man. He knew it, but the dream would not be denied.

"Is something wrong?" she repeated, reining her horse even with his.

"No, just wanted you to see something. In front of you is my ranch." He leaned forward and pointed to a sprawling ranch house on a small rise, dimly visible through the driving rain.

He saw the surprise in her eyes as she gaped. "Your land?" He knew she couldn't have expected he'd own anything. Or if he had, she probably figured a shack like where they'd left her old boyfriend. He pointed out the lengths of the land and saw her trying to take it all in.

He smiled as he watched her. She was so beautiful with the rain running down her cheeks, the look of amazement in those beautiful dark eyes. The flash of a distant bolt of lightning outlined her finely boned face. Her hair had come out of the braid again, straggled wet around her face, as the hat brim was unable to protect her from the driving storm. She had the kind of face that a man would never tire of looking at.

He should have ridden on, but he wanted this moment. He thought about how it'd be to continue surprising her with things. There was so much he could show her if she would let him. He did enjoy her beauty, but it wasn't all he wanted from her. She was a fulfillment of something, a dream long ago put aside and now resurrected.

Ignoring the storm, he pointed out what could be seen. "The barns are below the house. Can't see them from here. Pond's over there. A year round stream feeds it. The house is big, porch all the way around."

"It looks amazing," she yelled against the storm, "but do you think we could go there before we drown?"

He grinned at her practicality. Of course she couldn't know what he was thinking. Hell, he didn't want her to know just yet. He spurred Satan into a run as they headed out onto the grasslands, pounding across the open country, the rain and wind at their backs. Beneath his thighs, Sam felt the throb of Satan's powerful muscles as the stallion covered the ground in mighty heaving strides. Sam didn't mind the rain soaking him as it did his land. Both could use the cleansing.

As he and Abby rode into the ranch yard, he saw Ollie and Rock come out of the bunkhouse, followed by the others who then stood on its porch. Things were going to change, and Sam knew the men wouldn't like it. They had used the house more than he should have let them even before. He would have to enlarge the bunkhouse. They would now find the big house off-limits. That was for Abby.

Up until now the ranch had been mostly a front for his real business as he'd run only a few hundred head of cattle. Soon that would change. If he got his dream, he would fully stock it. Someday this would be a home, a place to raise sons and daughters.

He reined in Satan by the front of the house and had dismounted in time to help Abby down from her horse. He knew she was capable of it, but she'd also had a lot of time in a saddle where she wasn't used to it.

"This is your home?" she asked and he nodded. He saw the frown on her face and looked at the house with new eyes. It should have been painted, he guessed. There was no light coming from it. Surely she would see the potential, but as they walked up the steps to the porch, he felt a sudden unease that she wouldn't.

For Sam's purposes, that isolation had been perfect. No neighbors to ask questions. Would Abby see it that way or would she hate the loneliness, miss her friends, miss the conveniences of living in a town? His love of this place had gone beyond its being a sanctuary, a place to hide. It had represented an unnamed future, a future to which he hadn't dared put words until Abby had said she would marry him.

He opened the door for her, but didn't attempt to carry her across the threshold. She was holding herself stiffly as though at any moment she'd cry. He didn't know if he'd done something wrong or if she was just exhausted.

Lighting a coal oil lamp, he tried to see the place through her eyes. The furniture was plain, leather couches, large wooden sideboards and cupboards in keeping with the big scale of the rooms. He'd bought Indian rugs to cover the floor and he saw them as primitive, not the kind of thing she was used to. No fine antiques, no wallpapered walls, no fancy crystal lighting fixtures. It was plain and simple. The stone fireplace almost covered one end of the living room, in front of it a long, leather sofa. Along the wall with the big window was a big desk, plain, no ornamentation.

"We can fix it up," he heard himself saying, barely recognizing his hoarse voice. He had hoped he was offering her something special, but he now saw it was crude and plain, much like himself. He lit another lamp to make it seem a little brighter.

"Could we have a fire," she said, walking to the fireplace, but saying nothing about what she thought.

He went outside and brought in pine cones, firewood and kindling, within a few moments he had a good fire going, more light bringing out the corners of the room and more of the sparse simplicity that he now realized she must hate.

"I have to care for the horses," he said. "Will you be all right here?"

She looked exhausted as she turned to face him. "I should do Belle."

"I'll take care of her." He left her, unsure of what kind of words he could say that would make her feel better. It wouldn't be easy to get better furniture up here, but somehow he would do it. He would do whatever it took to keep her happy. She was a lady, the lady for whom this place had been waiting. He would keep her here somehow.

Sam went out into the storm and led the two horses to the lower barn, unsaddling and then giving each a good rubdown. He had some oats, and he poured them into a narrow trough as reward for a job well done, before he opened the gate to the lower pastures. They could stay in the shelter of the barn or eat from the meadow grass.

Back in his kitchen, Sam lit a fire in the stove and pumped up water for coffee, then set it on to perk. He thought of what he should say to her. His mind was a void, a black hole. A lot had changed when he brought her here, and yet in other ways nothing had. He was still Sam Ryker.

When the coffee was ready, he poured two cups and brought one to her. She had removed the rain slicker but otherwise hadn't moved from the leather sofa. Her eyes were on the fire. "I expect you'll want to see the rest of the house tomorrow," he said, watching as her gaze traveled past the fireplace to the high wooden-beamed ceilings. When she said nothing, he asked, "Tell me what you're thinking?"

She turned and looked at him. "How did you afford all this?"

"The usual way. I bought it."

"But how did you buy it?" Her lips were firmly pressed together, her dark eyes considering as she looked at him.

"Do you want something to eat?"

"I'm too tired to eat. I want to know..."

He interrupted. "Can we talk about all that in the morning? I'm tired tonight; so are you. Both of us wet. We need a good night's sleep."

She nodded. He didn't know what to do, how to make this right for her. It was a strange new world. She was exhausted. He wasn't far behind. He had to get her something to change into. "I'll be right back, he said and headed for his bedroom.

Alone in the silent living room, the popping of the pine logs in the fireplace the only sound, Abigail sat feeling dazed, unable to think what she should do. She wasn't actually all that wet. The slicker had done a good job protecting her blouse, just her hair was straggling around her face, still dripping water. She was cold but warming up fast with the coffee and fire. She felt frozen inside. How had Sam bought such a place? It was a virtual empire, all this land, a beautiful home.

At most she had assumed him a petty criminal, but that kind of thing didn't buy a place like this one. Had blood bought it? Had Sam killed to attain this ranch? She fingered the gun in her pocket. She'd killed a man with that gun. Nothing would ever be the same for her. If she confronted Sam Ryker now with her worst fears, would he threaten her? Would she be forced to use her gun again? Could she when it was *him*?

Tears in her eyes, she looked up as he walked into the room. He had changed into a white shirt, black pants and his feet were bare. He wore no gun, leaving him vulnerable to her weapon. He was placing himself at her mercy, and she knew, without knowing how, that it was deliberate.

He handed her a clean white shirt, by its size one of his, and a large fluffy towel. "You look like a drowned cat," he said with a smile.

She wanted answers but saw that wasn't going to happen for now. She laid the shirt over her knees. She was not about to change right in front of him. She undid her braid. Vigorously she dried her hair until it was merely damp.

"So," he asked, sitting in a large chair, "what's next?"

"Answers to my questions?"

"You do have a lot of those."

She looked at him then, seeing his tiredness, the weariness in his shoulders. How long had it been since he'd rested? She doubted he'd slept well on the floor at the mission. He had been a fantasy in her mind, and now she saw the reality--a tired man. "How long have you been away--doing whatever it is that you do?"

He shrugged. "A few weeks. Why?"

"You look tired."

"I'm fine."

"All right, I'm tired," she said. She wouldn't waste energy arguing with a stubborn man. "You were right. We will both sort things out better in the morning." Except her fear returned. Night. Where would he sleep? Where would she sleep? What would he expect now?

He moved faster than she could have imagined possible given how tired he had to be and in an instant was kneeling in front of her. He reached out a hand and ran a finger over her cheek. She felt that gentle touch all the way to her toes. "You don't need to be afraid of me," he said, his voice not much above a whisper.

"I'm not." She knew it to be a lie. She was afraid but more of what this man inspired in her than that he would hurt her.

His smile barely qualified as one. "I won't hurt you. Will you hurt me?"

"Of course not."

"We'll see about that. All right, we're both tired. Tonight you take my bedroom."

"I can't take your bed."

"Sure you can. Want me to join you in it?" He chuckled. "No need to answer. I see it written on your face."

"I am tired but I can sleep in any bedroom."

"It's the only one I know has sheets—mostly clean. You might not be ready to take me, but you will sleep in my bed."

She knew she should have argued with him, not taken his bed, but she didn't have the energy. A few moments later she found herself in the large master bedroom. It was furnished with large dressers and a big, heavy bed. On the floor were the same Indian woven rugs that he'd used elsewhere in the house. It looked masculine and right for this house, for him.

She slipped out of her clothing and into his large bed. The sheets had a male scent to them, a mix of tobacco, some shaving lotion, soap. It was a comforting scent-- one she was coming to recognize as his. She wondered for a moment how she would sleep, then knew nothing more until the sunlight was streaming in the large window onto the bed.

She dressed in the shirt he had given her and her leather riding skirt, put on her boots for what reason she wasn't sure, then headed toward where she had seen him come with the coffee. She wondered if Sam was already up, until she smelled and heard coffee perking. He stood at the window, staring out. He turned as she entered. "Coffee is almost done. Want some?"

She nodded and took the cup he handed to her, gratefully sipping the restoring brew. She looked around the kitchen, enjoying the balanced feeling of the heavy wooden counters and cupboards against the long simple table in the center of the room. Her reverie ended when she remembered she had no idea how to do much of anything in a kitchen, and she'd deceived Sam into thinking she did. She glanced around the room looking for a cookbook. How hard could it be to follow instructions? She didn't see any books though. *Uh oh* Sooner or later, she'd have to admit her lie. Preferably later.

Abigail met Sam's gaze and wondered if he was expecting her to prepare a meal. "What uh food do you have on hand?" she asked, thinking that sounded like a safe question.

"Not a lot. Salt pork, oats, flour, salt, baking powder and soda. Probably potatoes if they haven't rotted."

"Any chickens or a cow?"

"I could get some. You don't look like a woman though who'd know how to milk a cow or take care of chickens." His smile was crooked, the look in his eyes made her wonder what kind of woman she did look like to him. She didn't want to ask. Not yet.

"I've never touched a cow, but I've seen it done. How hard can it be?"

He shrugged, his gaze shifted to the window, a frown on his face as he stared through the glass.

"Is something wrong?" she asked.

"The boys are starting to get up. Reckon I better not put this off."

"Put what off? What do you mean?" She didn't like the tone of his voice.

"Nothing. Just I have to go down and face them."

"Face them?"

He smiled and again met her gaze. "Talk to them."

"About what?"

"Things have changed here. They will have some questions just like you do."

She didn't like the hard set to his lips, the darkened expression in his eyes. "You're scaring me, Mr. Ryker."

He laughed. "Mr. Ryker? Don't you think you could find something better now that you are my wife?"

She had wondered what she should call him, what she could call him. Nothing had seemed right. "Samuel?"

"Sam."

"All right... Sam." The expression in his eyes made her feel a now familiar warmth in her belly and the accompanying knotting in her heart. She heard the loudness of the voices, the laughter again from down the hill and his expression changed. Something was going on that she didn't understand. "Who are those men?"

"They work for me, but they'll be with me only so long as it suits them and me."

"Couldn't you wait and talk to them later? When they're in a better mood?"

He laughed. "No, it has to be done now." He left her for a moment, heading into the main part of the house. When he came back, his gun was belted to his waist.

"Surely you can't need a gun to talk to your own men." She swallowed hard.

He smiled and reached behind the door checking the load in a shotgun, then laid it on the table. "You ever fire one of these?"

She shook her head.

He showed her how to cock it. "Lock this door when I leave. If any of them make it in here without me, point it at them, and fire. It has quite a recoil. So be ready for that. You have two shots." He pulled extra shells from a drawer. "Reload like this," as he demonstrated.

"You're frightening me."

He nodded. "Guess so, but better you a little scared and ready for trouble than breezing around this kitchen, not knowing trouble could be on its way."

She grasped his arm. "I don't want you to go down there."

"Think maybe I oughta try to hide behind your skirts?" he suggested with raised eyebrows and flicker of amusement in those unusual blue eyes.

"Of course not."

"Then I have to go down and listen to what they want to say. I've changed things. They have the right to talk that over with me."

"Is that all it'll be--talking?"

"Sure."

She didn't like the way he said that. "Might they attack you?" she asked, feeling a cold fist clench her chest.

"I'm not expecting it--necessarily. It's just with men like these." He smiled down at her. "They're not a social club, and I'm not running things because they like my face."

She reached up before she had time to think and stroked her fingers down his lean jaw, over the rough bristle. "It's a nice face," she said, her gaze meeting his, "I wouldn't like to see it changed-- unless maybe shaved."

He smiled. "I can arrange that-- later. As to the other, don't worry. It'll likely be fine. You stay in here and bolt the door when I go out. Don't open it for anybody but me." Then he was gone, leaving her with her fears and a shotgun that scared her almost as much as what might come back through that door... or not come.

Sam knew he wouldn't need to announce himself to his wolves. They would be watching, following his progress, looking for any signs of weakness. He showed them none as he rested one booted foot on the bunkhouse front porch.

Rock lounged against the wall of the building, watching him through slitted eyes.

Sam pulled out the makings for a cigarette and began rolling one. "Any of you got something you need to say?" He knew what they were feeling, but he wanted it out.

"We don't want a woman here," Snake said, shifting from the doorway to lean a skinny hip on the hitching rail.

"You didn't really marry her, did you?" Ollie asked.

Sam smiled.

"Women are bad luck," Ollie snapped. "Cause nothin' but trouble." The others filed out of the bunkhouse, leaning against the wall, their expressions watchful.

Sam lit his cigarette. He drew in the first long, satisfying pull. "You don't like the woman. Fine. But she stays." His tone was matter-of-fact, not aggressive but brooking no room for dissent. Take it or leave it. It was the way it would be.

"She goin' with us on the next job? Maybe she will ride along with us?" Buck asked, his surly little pig eyes watching Sam but not showing any inclination to draw the gun on his hip.

"This is my place, my men, Buck. You forget that? I decide what happens when I'm ready."

"I ain't forgot nothing."

"I'm fed up to here," Rock interrupted, drawing a line across his throat, "with you calling the shots. We worked our butts off for weeks and what did we get to show for it?"

"You blame me for the deal going sour?" Sam asked smiling with no humor. He had been ready for a fight, maybe as ready as they were. He needed a release, and one or more of them was going to provide it. He wasn't eager that it be the huge Rock, but if it was, so be it.

"No... but I blame you for bringing a skirt back with you. You know somebody's going to come after her. You were wrong to bring her here, and I'm not going to take it."

"So what do you figure to do about it?" Sam asked. He flicked the cigarette into a nearby mud puddle and met Rock's gaze levelly.

"I'm not wearin' no gun," Rock said, indicating his bare hip.

"The rest of you letting Rock do your talking?" Sam asked. They nodded, muttering, "Good enough by us."

Sam unbuckled his gun belt, handing it to Ollie. He turned to face Rock. Not what he wanted for the first morning with her here, but this had to be ended or watch it grow. Men like these only understood force, and whether there was a woman as an excuse or not, a reminder became necessary now and then.

Rock approached him, his big fists clenched. He lunged forward, swinging with his left fist at Sam's face. Sam blocked, swung back, hoping to land a blow that would send Rock on the ground but received instead a solid right to his own belly, doubling him. He straightened, slamming back with a series of quick blows that drove the big man hard against the hitching rail.

For a moment they stood toe to toe, exchanging blows, some landing, some missing, but enough damage being done that Sam could feel the blood flowing from a cut on his mouth, saw the same flowing from Rock's nose.

Rock lunged forward and got his arms locked around Sam's waist, lifting him from the ground. Feeling the bite of those steel bands around him, pushing the air from his lungs, Sam knew he had to break the hold or risk having his back broken. He smacked Rock in the nose, but felt no loosening of the constriction. He grabbed the big man's ears and finally was able to draw a breath as Rock was forced to loosen his grip.

Mud slick under their feet caused Sam to slide, then go flat on his back after a blow from Rock's iron-hard fists. He lunged to his feet in time to meet Rock's powerful attack. Rock kicked, aiming for a crippling blow. Sam caught his boot, twisting and sending him to the mud. Soon they were rolling in it, pounding each other savagely.

Feeling nearly played out, his breath coming painfully, his

fists harder to lift, Sam rose, watched his man circle him and knew he had to end this fight or suffer his first defeat. That defeat would have consequences for more than him. At the thought, he felt a surge of energy and moved forward with new momentum. In moments he'd delivered two powerful blows that staggered Rock, then the third that sent his hired man to lie in the mud, unable to move.

Heaving for breath, Sam looked around him at the others. None met his gaze. He walked to Ollie and took his gun belt in nearly numb fingers. He did not attempt to belt it around his hips. This wasn't the time to show weakness, and he was reasonably sure he would be unable to manipulate the buckle for a few more minutes at the least. He only hoped, if there was more trouble, he could pull the trigger.

"Anybody got something more to say?" he asked, again letting his gaze run over his motley crew. No one said anything and Sam nodded. He was half way up the slope to the house when he heard Ollie yell a warning.

Sam spun, dropping into a crouch and forcing his hand to close over the butt of his gun, his finger to pull the trigger as a bullet from Buck Russell's gun whistled past his head. His own bullet caught Buck high in the shoulder and threw him against the bunkhouse wall.

Sam stood for a moment, watching as the big man tried to lift himself, then lay back against the wall. He walked over and kicked the gun from Russell's limp fingers regretting he hadn't killed him. A back shooter wasn't safe to have around, wasn't safe to let go.

Ollie bent over Buck, examining the wound. "Not much to it," he said spitting to the side from the wad of chewing tobacco in his cheek.

"Get him a horse after you wrap this up. Send him on his way," Sam ordered. "Rock can make up his mind if he goes or stays when he comes to, but this one goes and as for the rest of you." He let his gaze fall hard on each of them in turn. "If you stay with me, you take my orders. You don't want that, come up to the house this afternoon and collect your pay."

As he walked up the slope, he knew he had them, at least for the moment, but it would be important to keep them busy, not give them too much time to think. Wolves were rarely trustworthy for long.

CHAPTER 8

By the time he got to the house, the adrenaline that had carried him through the fight was fading, and he was hurting in more ways than physically. He was tired of fighting, tired of putting his life on the line. It never got easier, and the thought came to him, not for the first time, that there must be a better way to live.

He was on the back porch before he realized he was covered in mud and blood. He couldn't face her this way. Fighting was beyond her understanding. She wouldn't want to face the ugly reality of its aftermath. He tried to think where he could go to clean up. Before he could decide, the door swung open, and she was standing frowning at him, the shotgun cradled in her arms.

"You ready to use that?" he asked. His words were a little slurred from the cuts on the inside of his mouth. She looked like fire and a virago as she strode onto the porch, dark eyes flashing, hair waving wildly around her face, her breath coming almost as quickly as his own. If he'd thought he'd been capable, he'd have grabbed her and taken her right where she stood. Fortunately for them both he lacked the strength. She'd never have forgiven him.

"It's tempting," she snapped as she stood aside to let him

enter. He debating heading for the sink and decided he needed to sit a moment before he started the work of cleaning up.

"What happened to the man you shot?" she asked as she looked down the yard toward the bunkhouse before she closed the door, setting the shotgun down beside it.

"A flesh wound."

"You sound disappointed," she said through gritted teeth.

Although he knew she was right, he was disappointed, he didn't attempt to explain why. He watched as she went to the sink and pumped a basin of water.

He slung his gun belt over the chair beside him, taking breaths carefully as each one hurt his chest. For the moment, he felt drained of energy. He supposed he should have tried to explain what he'd done, but she would never understand. In her world gentlemen didn't do such.

She was back then. He expected her to set the water in front of him, and was surprised when she dipped a cloth in it, lifted his chin with more gentleness than he'd expected, and carefully set to work washing away mud, cleansing his abrasions and cuts.

For Abigail the whole thing had been a nightmare, the time of waiting and wondering what he would face below, then the fight, afraid to do anything for fear she'd make it worse if she ran to his rescue. She had nearly laughed at that thought. Who was she to rescue anyone from men such as these? She had to hope he knew what he was doing.

She rinsed out the bloody and dirty cloth once again as she studied his face to determine if anything needed a stitch. She hoped not. She'd seen it done, but had no interest in using sewing skills on human flesh. She shuddered. She remembered the sounds of the fight, the hearing of fist hit flesh, watching Sam knocked down and then rise to fight some more. It had been horrifying and yet something about it held her at the window, unable to turn away. Part of her had wanted to run to him, to fight for him, and part of her had wanted to run away, escape.

When she heard his step on the porch, she had felt surges of equal parts gratitude and anger. How dare he let himself be hurt? Thank God he was still upright and strong. She had wanted to scream, to tell him what his going off that way had cost her. She had wanted to grasp him to her breast and hold him tightly against her. Since she could do none of that, she doctored him, washed his face, then helped him take off his shirt and cleaned the mud from his chest and arms washing those sculpted muscles that bronzed body that had been tempting her since she'd first seen it in Tucson.

The wash basin had been emptied twice and she'd used the alcohol she found in a cupboard to cleanse open cuts before she stood back, satisfied she'd done all she could.

He had closed his eyes for some of it, his whole body relaxed as if he had enjoyed her ministrations even when she had to have hurt him. He looked up at her then. "Thank you."

"You'd better get out of those muddy pants," she snapped, exasperated at her mix of emotions, equally disgusted with herself as with him. "If you don't, they'll dry solid, and you'll have to jump in your pond to get free of them.

"You know I didn't want that fight. Didn't want to do that."

"I know no such thing." She went to the sink and pumped more water into a glass, handing it to him. "Drink this," she ordered."

"It had to be done," he said before he drank.

"That's what men always say." She pursed her lips together.

"They do huh? Well, I only say it when it's true. And In this case it was."

"You had to go down there and get pummeled?"

"It was possible it wouldn't have had to come to that."

"You had to shoot a man?"

"Once he shot at me."

She didn't want logic right now. She didn't understand this man or his world. She didn't think she wanted to. Then she remembered she had married him. Well, that wouldn't be for long. "If you didn't want a fight, why did you go down?" she asked.

She'd never known anyone like him, never had expected to. She had been thrust into a world as strange to her as that Ulysses had found on his Odyssey.

"It was now or later," he said. "Later would have been worse, giving them more time to work up their sense of being wronged."

"Worse? How could it be worse? You were beaten to a pulp; you beat another man even worse. Is he going to be all right?"

He nodded.

"Then you shot a man. How could it have been worse?"

"Well, he might have shot straighter," he said. He looked up, expecting to see a smile on her face, but instead she burst into tears. He could cope with a lot, handle many things, but a woman crying wasn't among them.

"God, I'm sorry." He wanted to comfort her and had no idea how.

"You are not," she sobbed, hiding her face in her hands. "I don't know much, but I know you're not sorry." She sniffled loudly.

"How do you know?" He suppressed his grin. It hurt his mouth and besides he was pretty sure seeing him smile now wasn't going to make things better.

"Because," she hiccupped, "you'd do it all again, wouldn't you?"

She had him there. He tried to think of words that would soothe the tears. Before he could come up with anything, she was sitting at the table, crying again, her face buried in her arms.

He put his hand on her shoulder, wishing he was the kind of man who knew the words to reassure her. He felt like a worm. He had dragged her into a world for which she was ill-prepared, for which any gentlewoman would be ill-prepared. Maybe the answer was to take her to Tucson. His dream seemed to be turning into a nightmare. It wouldn't take much for her to get an annulment.

He made himself walk to the counter. Hs body was sore and

stiff. He saw Ollie walking up to the house and opened the door before his old hand could knock.

"You all right?" Ollie asked, looking at Sam, then past him to Abby who was drying her eyes.

"More or less," Sam said.

Ollie laughed, not passing the doorway. "She clean ya up?"

Sam nodded which he saw didn't please Ollie any.

"Please come in," Abby said, sniffling and rising from the chair. "You shouldn't feel you can't come in here because of me."

Ollie looked at her resentfully but entered the kitchen. When he was sitting at the chair and Abby had brought him and Sam each a cup of coffee, Sam put his hand on the older man's shoulder. "Thanks for the head's up."

"You never figured I'd let him back shoot you, did you?" Ollie asked insulted.

Sam gave a snort. "You're prickly as a woman, old man." At Abby's snort of derision, he chuckled. "Pardon me. Present company excepted." He looked at his foreman. "How are the men taking it?"

"Little grouchin', but they'll stay quiet for awhile at least."

"Rock gonna stay?"

Ollie gave a little laugh. "Mad as a wet hen that you laid him out, but he said it was a fair fight. He'll be stayin' if you still want him."

Sam nodded. Ollie's gaze was not on him though but was instead directed at Abby as she went to the sink and stood with both hands braced against it, staring out the window. Again Sam wondered how a woman might see this place. He became more certain that he had to take her back. Sometimes a dream just couldn't be had.

Ollie rose. "I expect you two need time alone. I'll keep an eye on the boys. See you tomorrow mornin'." With that he was gone.

Sam decided he and Abby could no longer avoid discussing all the things he'd preferred to have avoided forever. I'll change," he said, "and when I come back, we'll talk."

She turned from the window, her eyes wide with surprise that he was voluntarily going to agree to talk, but said nothing as he left the room.

With some time before he would be returning, Abby looked in the cupboards, trying to find something they could eat. She knew nothing about preparing a meal, Even simple hotcakes would be beyond her unless all you had to do was add flour and water and she knew she'd seen Serafina add more ingredients than that. She would have to confess to Sam about her lie, but right now she also had to feed him.

She put a few more sticks of wood into the stove giving herself a few moments to consider her total ignorance when it came to food preparation. She remembered Sam saying he had potatoes and salt pork. How difficult could it be to peel potatoes and fry them with some salt pork? She set about finding a knife, then the potatoes.

By the time Sam returned to the kitchen washed up and in his last clean and dry clothes, the potatoes had been more or less peeled. The more being a lot of potato was in the sink with the peelings and the less meaning a lot of peeling remained adhered to the potatoes, but she did have them in a large pan and was stirring them The salt pork was frying on the griddle.

There was no way for her to hide the cloth bound around her finger but she hoped he would not comment.

"Cut yourself?"

"That's a stupid question," she said rudely, immediately wishing she could take back the words as she saw his face pale. She had said something more caustic than she'd intended. "I just meant it should be obvious."

"To somebody who isn't a dummy." He walked to the sink and pumped water into a glass, seeming to inhale it in one swallow.

"I didn't mean it that way," she said. "I'm sorry. I didn't take your apology earlier very well. Are you going to take mine more graciously?"

He managed a smile around the swollen places on his lips and cheeks. "We'll start over."

"Before or after we got married?"

"Was that a mistake?"

She managed a shrug. "Was it?"

"Maybe."

Something skittered at her feet and Abigail let out a shriek.

He was at her side almost instantly. "What is it?" He felt fortunate to be wearing boots. If a scorpion had gotten into the house, he would stomp it to bits. He was in the mood to stomp something to bits.

"Mouse," she said in a small voice.

"Mouse?" he repeated with disbelief. "Surely you've seen a mouse before."

"Of course," she glowered at him. "I just don't like them, that's all." She looked nervously around her booted feet, grateful for the first time that she was wearing her stained, dirty riding skirt. At least she didn't have to worry if the little creature was clinging to the underside of a long skirt.

Sam grabbed his gun from the table. "If he comes back, yell."

Her mouth dropped open. "You wouldn't shoot him in the house, surely?"

He smiled again, that devilish smile that, even bruised as it was, turned her insides to mush. "You want me to set a trap? I guess that'd work too."

She realized then he was teasing her and felt it doing strange things to her insides to realize that he had a sense of humor.

He pointed to the stove and she saw the smoke. "Oh no," she cried, heading for her fork and finding his hand there first. He took the salt pork from the heat and deposited it on the plate she'd readied for it. It looked more like burnt offerings than food.

Sam looked at the potatoes, which were a mix of raw and burnt too, and then he looked at her.

"I have a small confession to make," she said, looking down at her folded hands.

"I have a feeling I can guess what it is."

"When I told you I could cook, I lied."

"So I see."

"I'm sorry. I shouldn't have deceived you."

Sam had suffered a lot worse deception from women and thought if that was the only way she deceived him, he wouldn't complain. He doubted it would prove to be true. Experience was a hard taskmaster, and he'd learned his lessons on some of the hardest.

He grabbed a knife and began slicing more salt pork. His hands were clumsy still but he managed better than she had and soon a fresh batch of potatoes and pork were frying-- this time being watched and turned more carefully.

"The ranch was a disappointment to you," he said as he leaned a hip against the long, wooden counter.

"It's beautiful. How could it be a disappointment?"

"You looked unhappy when you saw it."

"I would like to know how you paid for it. You said there weren't any warrants out for you. Was that because you haven't broken any laws or because you haven't been caught?"

"This is important to you."

"Very."

"Not many men can claim to not have broken any laws."

"You are avoiding an answer."

He smiled. "You want specific denials. I haven't robbed any coaches, stolen anything I could get arrested for... in this country. Any killings I've done have been in self-defense... or defense of another."

"How many of those have there been?" she asked, trying to keep her tone level. She could barely believe she was asking any man such a question.

"Not many."

She didn't like the sounds of that. "How many is not many?"

"Abby, I am not wanted for killing anyone."

She wished she could read his expression better. Was he

equivocating? She saw he didn't want more questions, but she had one she had to ask. "Are you a gunman?"

"No."

"But somehow you bought this big ranch. How many acres are with it?"

"The Circle R is around thirty thousand acres. The north quarter has a smaller ranch within it so it's not in a block. I can draw the boundaries for you if you want to see."

"I can't grasp it. I think in terms of city lot sizes," she said, shaking her head. "I guess we're back to the same question. Do you own this all by yourself or are your men partners in it?"

"It's mine. I've had it more years than I've been riding with most of them. Ollie was with me when I bought it, but the deed is in my name."

"How did you pay for it?"

"Why does it matter?"

"I don't know if I could live someplace that had been bought with blood money, which had been gotten dishonorably, where blood was spilled for it."

"It was none of that, and any blood spilled earning it was mine." He tried to think how much he dared tell Abby about his history, about where he came from. He could hardly expect her to understand a world that would appear to her to be immoral, dirty, and seamy, and for that matter was all those things.

"But this ranch must have cost a lot of money."

He nodded. "Not as much as you might think. I worked for Marius Gray, the man who owned it. He was a wealthy man but lonely out here. His wife had left him, taken off for parts unknown because she couldn't stand the isolation. He had no children with her, maybe had considered me to be like a son. Anyway, after she was gone and he knew she'd not be coming back, he didn't have a reason to stay--so he sold it to me very cheap. He wanted me to have it for his own reasons—none he confided in me. He was rich enough money didn't matter. At the time the Apaches were regularly raiding nearby. It made an isolated ranch like this less attractive to own than it is today."

"How long have you had it?"

"Five years."

"You still haven't told me where you got the money to buy a place this size. Where you get any of your money?"

"You were wondering if maybe it was robbing stages?"

"I am asking you the answer to that."

He sighed and removed the salt pork from the pan. Testing the potatoes, he saw they were tender. "It's complicated. Could we eat first?" he asked, wishing he could think of a reason never to tell her. Even though he'd reconciled his operation in his own mind, he knew she likely wouldn't see it as he did. A cigarette sounded damned good, but he didn't want to irritate her further. He wanted... He glanced at her beautiful, animated face, the graceful way her hands moved as she ate and knew he had better not think much on what he wanted, not yet.

Having eaten and cleaned up the kitchen, they went into the parlor. Seeing the room in the daylight, Abigail appreciated even more the symmetry of the space, the way the heavy leather furniture and interestingly patterned rugs accentuated the rough hewn room. It was a man's home. It could quite easily be made into a woman's too.

Nearly two stories high with a river stone fireplace that soared the full height, the house appeared to have been created mostly with logs. It had a railing around a balcony room at one end, opposite the fireplace, with stairs that led to it. "What's up there?" she asked.

"It was going to be a library. The books are there but in boxes. After I bought this place, Marius he'd send for them; but since it's been five years, I don't figure he ever will. I didn't unpack them." He did not intend to tell her why it would have done him no good to do so. "You can do what you want with them now. Might be you'll find a few you'd like. He was an educated man."

He tried to put words to what he saw as he watched her settle into one of the overstuffed chairs. Yes, she was a beautiful woman, graceful lines to every inch of her. There was something else though, a passionate depth in her dark eyes that even as she sat watching him, looking as though she might be waiting for the church meeting to begin, even then, he could see the fire beneath the surface. Maybe it was the way her lips were so soft, lush looking, or that unruly hair which she had tied back with some sort of cloth, but it still looked ready to burst forth and cover her breasts with its many shades of brown. He looked away. He had to quit thinking like this or he'd never give her the time she needed to accept him as a husband.

He would concentrate on what he must tell her. How much of his story did she have to know? Enough to explain the owning of this ranch. There was no way to soften it.

"At the moment, I'm a trader." He smiled despite it hurting.

"Trader?"

"In cattle—other people's cattle."

"A rustler?" The word sounded revolting as she said it. "But I thought you said you weren't wanted for anything."

"I'm not. When I was in Tucson that time I saw you, I was on my way to a payoff for a herd we had delivered to Aaron Wright. You know him?"

"Didn't he just die? He was a major rancher north of Tucson." He nodded.

"I am confused. If you are not wanted for anything, how do you get the cattle, which were not yours to sell?"

"I round them up down in Mexico, bring them up here to sell to ranchers like Wright. Usually on consignment as in the contract is not in writing, but it's been settled the price and number wanted."

"Did he know you'd stolen the cattle?" Her frown deepened.

"Of course. The deal went sour. When we got up here, we found Aaron had died. His son was waiting for us. Not to pay us off but as a trap. Richard decided to have the cattle and the money. There was no winning if we made a stand, certainly no going to the law; so we ran." It still left a bitter taste in his mouth.

"They were the ones chasing you?"

"Could have been. Maybe nobody. We weren't sure. He might have been thinking it'd be best if we didn't survive to tell the tale of where his cattle came from."

"You sell ranchers stolen cattle." She had back her wet squirrel expression. He didn't find it so cute this time because he knew it was directed at who he was, something a lot more basic than smoking a cigarette.

"To men who know what they're getting. How do you think most of the big ranchers got their start around here? They don't take the risk of going down and rounding the unbranded cattle up, but they've had no reluctance to buy from somebody who's willing to take those risks. It's a rich market, and it goes both ways."

"It's dishonest."

"It's also the way business has been done in these parts for a lot of years. You think all the cattle they have, they raised on a neat little ranch with tidy fences? Most of the ranchos in Mexico have no idea how many they have as their spreads run thousands of miles. It makes it easy to pick those unbranded and move them elsewhere."

"Branded or not. You know they're not yours to take. It is rustling."

He nodded. "Yes, as well as dangerous. The vaqueros shoot first when they see a gang the size of mine."

"They'd shoot at you without finding out if you're there to steal?"

"If they asked any questions, it'd be afterward if anybody was left alive to talk. We also have to watch out for the Rurales. It's not like I waltz across there, take the cattle, and don't face a risk for what I get."

"I'm not concerned with that, but with the morality of it."

He walked to the fireplace, leaning his hands against the

heavy wooden mantle. "Cattle trading back and forth was an Indian and Mexican business before the Anglo ever got here. This ranch was nearly driven out of existence because of the raids from across the border. It's why I don't keep many cattle on it now, because if I did, I would have to stay here to keep an eye on them, or they'd be gone. Sure it's stealing, but the game goes both ways."

"It's a lot more than a game."

He nodded. "I won't argue with you. You asked what I did to pay for most of this, what I do to keep my men occupied. The whole truth is I was waiting for a meeting to arrange for the next shipment when my men saw your weasel burying the mail bags. If I named that rancher I was supposed to meet that time, you'd be shocked, because he probably contributes to your church in Tucson, but he doesn't mind getting cattle cheap from somebody willing to die to bring them to him."

"I hate the whole idea of this," she said, staring at the floor.

"I can understand that." Would she leave him now? He supposed she would. He waited to hear what she would say. He would not stop her from leaving if that's what she wanted.

CHAPTER 9

Abigail knew what she should do-- leave him. He was a criminal. Maybe not technically in this country but morally at the least. She made the mistake of looking at him then. Even needing a shave, he took her breath away. Those clear eyes, the way he levelly met her gaze, his strong lean cheeks, the faint smile almost hidden under the bristle. There was an odd tingling in her belly, deep down when his gaze met hers. She couldn't stay with him. She couldn't go. This man could teach her things about life, about the flesh. She knew that, but at what cost? Everything had a price. Some higher than she might want to pay. She couldn't let herself care for him.

"So now, Abby, you know who I am. An outlaw, a badman. You tell me who you are, lady, who you really are."

"I'm not nearly as exciting as a rustler," she said, a bitter twist to the words.

"I'm not looking for excitement."

She was stopped for only a moment. "That was obvious when you asked me to be your wife."

"What does that mean?"

"Just that a man who wanted an exciting woman would have picked one."

"And you're not?"

"That's obvious."

He laughed then. "It is?" He shook his head as he walked to her, standing a few feet behind her chair, not touching her. "That hair of yours might lead me to think there was some excitement there."

"It's nothing special."

"I have never seen hair with so many colors in it. From brown to red, and when the sun hits it, that hint of gold... Makes a man want to run his fingers through it, put his nose into it to see if it smells as good as it looks."

She rose and walked away to stand by the window.

"You act like you think I'll hurt you just by smelling your scent," he said, his voice husky.

"No... Just I don't want you to think that I'm... that we are." She snapped her jaw shut. When she turned back her face reflected her confusion.

"Oh but we are. It's just a question of when."

"You are so sure of yourself."

"No."

"Then?"

"I'm hopeful-- a hopeful man."

She sighed. "I'm a disappointment and I will be to you as I have been to everyone."

He knew that was possible, but he couldn't let her think that way. His only hope was to be positive. It was like dealing with a temperamental horse. If he let her know his doubts, he'd lose control. "You won't be."

You can't know that."

"No, I can't, but you're no delicate flower either. I knew the second time I rode up just in time to see you getting off your horse after you shot a man to make sure he was dead."

"I wish you hadn't reminded me of that. I killed a human being."

"Subhuman."

"He was a man."

"You did what was needed. It's called surviving."

"Is that what you've done?"

"All my life."

"Are you going to tell me about that life?"

"Not until I get something in exchange. Your turn. I've given you enough to have me hung twice over. I think it's only fair you tell me something at least partly revealing."

"You said you hadn't broken any laws."

"Up here," he reminded her. "So..."

She hesitated. "I don't have much to tell. Not really. I live with my father. I keep books for my father at the Wells Fargo office. That is my life."

"Mother, brothers, sisters?" He realized she hadn't made that past tense. He wondered how long it would be before she left. Everyone left.

"No one else. Just him and me. Mother died when I was thirteen. No siblings."

He didn't ask, but assumed siblings were brothers and sisters. He liked the big words she used at the same time it embarrassed him when he didn't know their meanings. He lowered himself onto the sofa.

"You live in Tucson long?" he asked, watching as she walked around the room, lightly touching the large pieces of furniture.

"A few years. We have moved a lot. He gets transferred, then we're off."

"You like Tucson?" He had to dig for every scrap of information about her and that seemed strange to him. Didn't women like to talk about themselves? What was this one hiding?

"I like the desert. Tucson is a town like any of the others where we've lived."

"You said that tadpole with you asked you to marry him, but you said no. Why?"

"I had no reason to marry."

"Yet you said yes to me."

She pressed her lips together and walked again, circling him, not lighting anywhere, showing her uncertainty in her every movement. He supposed she regretted the hasty wedding. Any sensible woman would.

"Where did you get the furniture?" she asked, running her finger over an ornate design carved into the front of a sideboard.

"Some was Marius's. That piece I found in Mexico, brought it here in a wagon."

"It was a lot of work to bring it here."

"Not that much."

"It is very right here. I like this room. A lot of furniture would look dwarfed with the high ceilings, that gigantic fireplace, but the leather and big wooden pieces seem right."

He realized she'd been giving him a compliment but was unsure how to respond. She'd indicated she didn't like how he had paid for this place. If he told her his dreams, would she use it to twist the knife?

He'd always visualized this home with a woman someday. He hadn't let himself imagine what kind of woman because that would have been taking too great a risk, but it was never going to be one like those he'd known. Still, not knowing there would ever be a woman, he'd bought things, some were still unpacked, hidden away in boxes because he'd been afraid to admit to the dream.

A woman like this one, circling him warily, she had always been beyond the pale. No, that wasn't right. He was the one beyond the pale. He'd always been outside looking in when he'd seen her kind. Even as a little boy when he'd been invited to church Christmas programs, he'd seen these women, seen the gentle touch of their hands on their own children, but they'd always looked at him as though he was something the cat dragged in, which in a manner of speaking he had been.

"What are you thinking when you get that hard, set expression on your face?" she asked, her gaze now on him at the worst possible time.

When she saw he wasn't going to answer, she asked, "Tell me about your family."

"I don't have any." He stared into the blackened coals from the fire the night before.

"Your parents are dead."

He decided to face the thing head on. There was no way to avoid it. He rose to face her. "I never knew my father. I doubt my mother had a clue who it was. She was a whore."

"Oh."

"That about covers it, I reckon. Don't suppose you've known too many real bastards, have you?"

"I don't like the word. It's not fair to label a child with a name for something that wasn't their fault."

"There are worse names." And he'd heard them all.

"I don't doubt that. Is your mother dead then?"

"Whores don't have a long life span," he said. "She got lung disease, probably made worse by too much of Dr. Jones' Elixir."

"What's that?"

His laugh was humorless. "It's a made-up name. I just meant the alcohol and laudanum women take under some kind of phony name, get addicted to, then die from."

"Oh." She did feel dumb now. She knew her grandmother had nipped from some elixir, but she'd never thought of what it must have been.

He shook his head.

"How old were you when she died?

"Four or thereabouts."

She frowned. "Who raised you?"

"Nobody really."

"But you were just a child. You had to have someone."

"I earned my keep. Annie let me do odd jobs."

"Annie?"

"She ran the house where my mother had been working when she died."

"Oh."

Yeah, he thought bitterly, *oh* about covered that too. She could never imagine what it had been like to be a child in such a setting. She would never hear from him about the innuendoes, the suggestions he'd grown up hearing, the things he'd been threatened by and finally what had been done to him. Annie had been a cruel woman, a woman who had been abused and mistreated for too many years to have a heart left in her. She enjoyed having power over someone weaker and for too many years, that had been Sam.

"I wish I knew some words that would help," she said.

"It's done."

"Is it?"

"Don't pity me, Abby."

She swallowed back tears. It was all too easy to visualize the kind of little boy he must have been. He would have had big innocent eyes, a shock of dark hair, a sturdy, sweet little boy. Who had been there to hold him when he cried, to offer him a loving touch? She saw by the jut of his jaw that he didn't want her sympathy now, would be angry if she tried to offer it.

"You are very articulate for having grown up as you did," she said finally unable to think of anything else to say.

"Articulate?"

"Well spoken."

"Marius liked to read in the evenings. I've picked up things here and there. After I moved on from Kansas, I headed to New Mexico. I worked for an Englishman there, he took in scruffs like me. Listening I learned a little about talking." He grinned. "Lucky I don't speak with an accent, huh?"

"Was the man who owned this ranch the one who taught you to rustle?" she asked.

114

"Not Marius. He was straight arrow. No, before him I had worked for a rancher east of here. He built his herd that way. When he had what he wanted, he let us go."

"You could have stayed and worked on his ranch," she reprimanded.

He chuckled. "We're wolves, lady. You don't keep them around when you're done using them."

She was silent for only a moment. "But what about now? Why don't you quit and work this place?"

He shrugged. "I might someday." He moved to the window, looking out. "I should get outside."

"Outside?"

"When I get back, I like to check on the place."

She felt shocked. "You just had a fight. You can't mean you'd go now." Then she had another thought. "You don't expect more trouble?"

"Nah, that's over for now. I just mean to check on fences, waterholes, the cattle and a herd of horses on the place. When I've been gone, I like to look it all over."

"You have cows too? And horses?"

"Not a lot but I want to be sure everything is still here." He grinned.

She felt exasperated with him and yet maybe his going was good. They could both use some time to think.

"You have questions still," he said obviously hoping she would make them short.

"Yes, but they can wait. They and I'll still be here when you get back. You can trust me to be here when you get back."

She watched as the expression flickered across his face. She saw he didn't think he could trust her; but he didn't confront it, just gave her that half smile before he strode out the door.

~

"Martin," Priscilla Wesley said, swirling into his room, a confection of lavender and ribbons, her blond hair curled into ringlets that fell from a tight little bun, "you're looking much better."

He moaned, wishing he didn't have to recover, didn't have to face the questions sure to be asked of him. When he had recovered his senses and realized Abigail was gone, he'd dreaded almost as much the questions about what had happened as the ride back to Tucson. His head had hurt as much from the whiskey he had consumed as the wound.

When he'd arrived in Tucson, Abigail's father was nearly irrational with upset, and Martin had seen the easiest way to delay questions was to faint. He had been amazed to find himself being taken to the Wesley home to recuperate. He had offered no resistance to the idea, relieved it would keep Jacob Spenser from him, and so he allowed others to have their way. Now his head ached, not so much from the wound as the upset over his situation. Sometime he would have to provide answers. He could not stay in bed forever.

Priscilla perched on the chair beside his bed. "How are you feeling?" she asked.

"Terrible. I'm confused, trying to remember... What happened to me?"

"You were shot. Where is Abigail?"

"She rode out with me, didn't she?" he asked, trying to delay his moment of reckoning yet again.

"Martin, everyone is desperate to find her. Where is she?"

"She has not returned?" he asked. He hadn't expected she would have. He tried to remember more of what had transpired at the shack. It hurt his head to think. He groaned again hoping to surround himself with a protective layer of pity. "She was with me, of course," he said. "Some men came."

"You left Tucson with several men?"

"Only one. I am confused, Priscilla. I'm sorry, I can't remember. Tell me what you know. Perhaps it will help me remember the rest."

"All of Tucson is buzzing about your misadventure. The *Star* is brimming with speculations of the most lurid sorts. Whatever was Abigail thinking to ride off with you that way?"

"She wanted to save her father's business."

Priscilla shook her head. "I thought I was the mad-cap one." She wrung out a cloth and laid it over Martin's head, her touch and the coolness soothing him. "Everyone's guessing as to what happened. They've been waiting for you to wake up. I don't know how much longer I can fend them off. You need to talk to the marshal. If Abigail was kidnapped... he needs to know where to look for..."

He moaned again, wishing he could lie with his eyes closed for at least a week. His memories were somewhat muddled, but what he did remember did not show him as having behaved well. He'd prefer not to think on it, let alone have to tell anyone else. To how much would he have to admit?

"Would you like something to eat? The doctor said you could have a light soup," she suggested, not ceasing her soothing motion. He liked the way her delicate hand looked as it lay beside his on the bed, liked the feeling of the other one petting him. He didn't want to do anything that would cause her to stop.

"Nothing now. Just tell me what's been happening."

She frowned and even that was lovely. "Nothing. Marshal O'Brian said because of the rainstorms, neither he nor his deputy could find any tracks. He cannot begin to look for Abigail until you tell him what happened."

"No backtracking?"

"The storm wiped out all traces. Everyone is desperate to find her. What do you remember?"

Hmmmmm this bore some considering. "I don't know. I was shot... I remember that. They must have taken her."

"Who are they?"

"The outlaws who shot me."

Although he was uncertain regarding details, someone had shot him. He had assumed it was the little man they had followed away from Tucson, but there had been others. Who were they? If it was the little man-- well, no matter who it was-- he was certain he had been shot while running away. That would not set well with Tucsonans to hear. But then who had to know?

"Was Abigail kidnapped?" Priscilla asked.

He had no idea where she was, what had happened to her, but he did know this whole mess was all her fault. It would be best for him if she never returned, certainly not to tell her version of what happened. "Possibly," he said. "After I was shot, it all is a blur."

"They didn't murder her, did they?" Priscilla asked, her face paling. "I can't bear to think Abigail is dead." He saw tears in her eyes.

"I don't think so. Tell me the rest. What are people saying about this?" Sweet little Priscilla, she really was being a darling. He wondered why he'd never noticed that before.

"Well, of course, people are wondering why you two went out there for. Some think you were eloping, but that wasn't it, was it?"

Had her face paled a bit more? She was so beautiful. "We were definitely not eloping."

"There are the most horrid stories being speculated upon."

"What are they saying about me? Are they accusing me of being a coward because I was responsible for Abigail, and she is missing?"

"Of course not," she said, bristling becomingly at the very suggestion and relieving his mind that at least she didn't feel he had been less than a man. "You were wounded," she said as though that excused him.

"Surely people feel I failed her." He closed his eyes again and sighed loudly. "I did too. I know I did. I just wish I could remember more of what happened."

"It will come to you."

He knew that was not the case. He liked being treated as a wounded hero. Even Priscilla would see that differently if she knew he had run. He was surprised to find how tender Priscilla's manner was. Abigail would've never treated him like this.

Priscilla looked down at her hand, then met his gaze, her own troubled. "People are so revolting. I'm afraid Abigail's reputation has been ruined." She shook her head. "If she is found, she won't be able to hold her head up in Tucson, not for months, maybe years, maybe never."

"Of course, if a man loved her," Martin said, trying to be noble, "he wouldn't let such a thing stop him from giving her his name for protection."

Priscilla smiled. "A gentleman would certainly do that."

He felt irritated and out of sorts again. He did not want to be a gentleman especially for the woman who had instigated the whole mess. He would have no choice. He had asked her to marry him, but he brightened thinking of her refusal. Still, he would not be able to withdraw his offer even though she had been debauched. He had no doubt that would have been the outcome and served her right. What wasn't right is that he be dragged into it. He had only thought her an obnoxious female before this. Now he knew it for certain.

There was a knock at the bedroom door and when Priscilla opened it, Martin saw Jacob Spenser. He wished he could lose consciousness, prayed for it to happen, but nothing saved him.

"Martin, I'm so sorry to see you in such a state," Jacob said, sitting in a chair across from Priscilla.

"Would you like me to leave you two alone?" Priscilla asked Martin, but he shook his head. The last thing he wanted was to be left with Jacob.

Jacob, unfortunately, felt differently. "Would you please?" he asked. "I'd really like a cup of tea, if you have any. I'm not feeling at all the thing."

Priscilla left, and Martin had no choice but to face Jacob. "I'm sorry," he said.

"What happened, man? What were the two of you doing out there? Where is my daughter?" He frowned then and said, "I'm sorry. I know you're not feeling well, but I have to know what happened, where she is."

"Of course, but I find the entire experience to be cloudy, very confused. We ran into a gang. One man was killed. The others... The others must have Abigail. I'm so sorry, Jacob, but I was shot very early in the whole dastardly affair. From then on, I was unconscious or... uh delirious, yes, out of my head."

"A man was killed? Who? Where? You must try, my boy. We have to have some sort of lead to have any hope to find my daughter."

"I wish I could help you... I really do."

"Why did the two of you go out alone like that and so far into the wilderness?"

"We weren't alone. We went with someone who claimed to know where the mail bags were." He wished then he'd not said that. His best approach was no information, amnesia. Probably too late for that now.

"You took Abigail out there with a scoundrel?"

On one point, Martin was certain. This was Abigail's fault, but he didn't suppose this was an opportune time to cast blame onto her. When he could delay responding no longer, Martin groaned as though in pain. "We both knew how important that insured shipment was to you. The man came to us, swore he'd never take a large group out. You had not been well. He would not let us contact the law or he would deny everything. Abigail didn't want to worry you. She insisted it would be all right." He didn't like the way that sounded and let his answer drone off. Unfortunately he could think of nothing to add to it that he liked any better.

A tall, black-haired man Martin recognized as Marshal O'Brian appeared at the bedroom door and Martin sucked in a breath wishing Priscilla had been somehow able to ward him off.

He knew he couldn't escape his day of reckoning forever, but he would have done so as long as possible.

Sitting astraddle the chair Priscilla had earlier occupied, his arms resting on its back, the marshal looked thoughtfully at him for a moment, the expression in those cold blue eyes unreadable. "Who shot you?"

Martin frowned. "I don't remember much about what happened."

"Let's start with where you were."

"We rode south, into the hills."

"Can you lead me there?"

"I couldn't get out of bed."

"When you heal up," the marshal said with a tight smile.

"I don't know that I could. I mean I followed a man. He knew where we were going. I had no idea."

"You made it here from there."

Martin swallowed. "My horse did that, I guess. I just got on him. I really don't know this country. Maybe an angel led him back."

The marshal scowled more deeply. Martin hoped he would leave him alone but no such luck. "How many men?"

"I think... Maybe ten or twelve. I woke up at one point and one of them was bandaging my wound."

"Kind of odd if he shot you that he'd fix you up."

He wished he had not said that. He wanted no sympathy for that scoundrel. "He hurt me. He poured something caustic... whiskey, I think, over the injury. It burned horribly."

"Better than infection," Marshal O'Brian said with no sympathy. "Think you could identify any of those men. Was Miss Spenser with you at that point?

"I think so. Yes."

"So they were the ones who kidnapped her?"

"I don't know... I... Everything was fuzzy... I blacked out again."

"Damn, you're not much use here. How many could you identify?"

"Only glimpses of most of them, except for the one who bandaged my wound. I do think though that he was their leader."

"How tall, what color hair, any accent?"

"Taller than you, I'd guess. I don't know. He was bearded... maybe just unshaven, I'm not sure. His hair was dark."

"That description could fit a thousand men including me."

"Of course, I didn't mean you," Martin said trying to essay a small joke but seeing from the marshal's irritation that he saw no humor in it. "Honestly, I wish I could be more helpful."

"Maybe you will," the marshal said, "as you think on it and as your *wound* heals." The tone of his voice was disdainful. Martin supposed the man had seen enough wounds to know his was not that major.

"I do remember one thing. The man had blue eyes, intense blue, not the sort of color you see often." He realized he was looking at eyes that color now. Could the men be related? Not hardly.

O'Brian rubbed his jaw. "Not a lot but something. You think on it. See if you come up with more. In the meantime, we'll send out a description of Miss Spenser. Maybe somebody will have heard or seen something down along the border."

"You've got to get her back. What will I do without my daughter?" Jacob pleaded.

"It's a big territory. She could be anywhere." The marshal rose from his chair.

"I have to do something. What can I do? I don't think I'd be up to riding with you when you go looking for her. I could offer a reward. "

O'Brian put his hand on Jacob's shoulder. "A reward might help or not. Men like those aren't loyal to much except what they can get out of something. On the other hand, once you put out a reward, you'll get all kinds of crazies trying to collect it."

"I must do something."

"I had a little girl of my own once." The marshal's expression darkened. "I'll put all I can into finding yours."

CHAPTER 10

Abigail awoke after another wonderful night's sleep. The altitude of the ranch and the setting of the house combined to provide cool nights and pleasant breezes through the rooms. Watching the morning light spread across the sky, the breeze ruffle the curtain, she lay in her bed thinking. If it hadn't been for her desire to return the stolen mails to their rightful owners, to reassure her father of her safety, she was surprised to realize she would have felt happy. There was rightness to this home that she'd never experienced elsewhere. She wondered how much of that rightness came from the enigmatic man she had married. She understood that this was a moment in time. It would not last. She must clasp every memory to her heart to remember when the day came she must return to reality. It would have to last her a lifetime.

Sam was already in the kitchen, and the aroma of coffee filled the air when she walked downstairs. His face was bruised, and he moved stiffly. Otherwise he seemed little the worse for his altercation of the day before.

Without asking, he poured her a cup of coffee. "Now," he said, "I think we need to talk."

"About what this time?"

"Cooking. You really do not know how?"

She smiled sheepishly. "I know how to make tea."

"But not coffee?"

She shook her head. "I am sorry. From the time I was out of school, I worked for my father in the office. I know all kinds of things about tallying up figures and keeping records though."

"In other words you'd be useful in my rustling enterprise, but not so much in my home."

She gave him a look and ignored his sarcasm. "I have been hoping your Mr. Gray might have left behind some cookbooks. With a little help I am sure I can manage the basic things. I'm not stupid."

He smiled. "I never once would've figured you were. Actually Ollie's done our cooking. If you want, he can do it."

"No!" Her answer was probably too sharp, but she didn't want that. She would pull her own weight. She had asked him to take her. She couldn't offer what he probably had hoped, but she would work while here. "I don't want that, but would he mind teaching me, do you think?"

"I don't know. Ollie's not much for women." He turned to the counter and scooped flour into the bowl in front of him.

"What are you making?"

"Maybe burnt offerings," he suggested with a half smile.

Her smile broadened.

At that moment he knew he would do just about anything to see that smile. It seemed to spread all across her face and made him want to kiss those full lips until they turned soft and passionate under his, until the nipples he could see under her shirt contracted into hard nubbins and her whole body was hot with wanting him. Instead, he turned to the large bowl. "I was figuring to make flapjacks."

She watched as he began dumping in various ingredients. He measured nothing and when she would ask how much of each thing, he could only shrug. "What looks right."

"That's not helpful," she complained with narrowed eyes.

The knock at the door saved him from a reply.

Ollie came through with the hulking Rock at his heels. "Rock here wants to say he's sorry," Ollie said.

"That so, Rock?" Sam asked.

The big man nodded, glancing quickly and then away from Abigail.

"I'd like to hear you tell me for yourself, not use Ollie here as your mouthpiece," Sam said.

To Abigail's mind, she thought Sam was rubbing in his victory more than needful, but it didn't appear Rock saw it that way. He nodded more definitely.

"I'm right sorry," he said then, his voice muffled and difficult to understand, and she realized why Ollie was doing his talking for him.

"All right then. I just don't want to go through this again," Sam said, rubbing his own jaw.

Rock smiled again, his smile made lopsided by swelling.

Sam then looked at Ollie. "Buck take his gear and pull out?"

Ollie nodded, looking at the bowl on the counter with interest, then at Abigail. "Uh Sam, what you doin'?"

"Looks obvious to me," Sam retorted. "You more nearsighted than you let on?"

Ollie muttered a few curses. "You been makin' a lot of mistakes lately." He gave Abigail a look. "Not killing Buck is another."

Sam nodded, not needing the reminder that he had missed his shot there. He would have to hope for the best and watch his back trail. He still could not believe he had been so careless as to turn his back on Buck in the first place. Had he done that because his mind was on Abby, on returning to her? Ollie would not always be around to yell a warning. She might yet be the end of him.

Abigail went to the stove and refilled her own cup. "Would you gentlemen like some coffee?"

Ollie looked at her with skepticism, but both he and Rock nodded, and she handed them each a cup. "Ollie," she said, "May I call you Ollie?"

The old-timer nodded again, not giving an inch of friendliness. "Yes, ma'am."

"Please make that Abigail. Sam said that you'd been doing the cooking here."

Ollie nodded again. "You wantin' me to keep on doing that?" he asked.

"Well, I suppose that will be necessary for a bit, but what I was really hoping is that you could teach me to cook."

Ollie's surprise showed on his face. "All women know how to cook."

She shook her head. "Not all."

"Wal, why the... How come you don't know how?"

"A lot of reasons. My mother died when I was young." Not that young but Ollie didn't have to know that. The truth was her mother had had little patience or interest in teaching Abigail about the homemaking arts.

Ollie looked at her with the first possible smidgen of sympathy. "Suppose I could... When would you be wantin' to start?"

"I have a few things to do this morning, but maybe for the evening meal, which I guess we'd have to start this afternoon. Is that correct?"

He nodded again, looked at Sam then. "What you gonna be doing?"

Sam considered. "I suppose we should break in that new remuda that Sandy brought in. Some of those springtails haven't ever been ridden. We're going to need them soon."

Ollie grinned more broadly. "Then, yes, ma'am. I'd be right proud to start teachin' you to cook today. Anything to keep from breaking my... uh bones out in the corral."

Abby looked with concern at Sam. "Breaking horses? That's what you're going to do, break horses? Isn't that dangerous?"

"Not when you know what you're doing," Sam said, sending a quelling glance at Ollie. "Most of them won't need much anyway."

Ollie chuckled and nudged Rock to head for the door. "We'll leave you two to argue this out. Did you tell her about the time you dislocated your shoulder--on those gentle little horses-- Sam?" With that he and Rock were gone, Ollie's chuckling and Rock's muddled attempt at it still being heard as they stomped off the porch.

"It is dangerous," Abby said, shooting up out of her chair at the table. "You cannot think this is a good time to do something like that. You're still recovering from that fight."

"The fight was nothing, and this isn't much more."

"Couldn't some of the other men do it?"

He smiled, but the stubborn set to his jaw told her he was not amused. "I don't need a mother, Abby. I had one. She wasn't much, but I don't want another. You let me take care of breaking horses. I've been doing it for a lot more years than you're giving me credit for."

"But..."

"I need some water for shaving. Is that still hot?"

She nodded and watched as he took it out onto the back porch and set the water on a wooden stand. She heard the sound of the razor being sharpened and headed out to continue the argument. When she saw he'd removed his shirt and all she could see was that perfect torso with the sculpted muscles, now flexing as he lifted his arms, she scuttled back into the kitchen to wash the breakfast dishes.

When Sam came through the door, he was again wearing his shirt. With the bristle removed, she saw a roughhewn, exceedingly handsome face. His cheeks were lean, his jaw firm and strong, a stubborn, strong face of a man who knew what he was doing in life and would give others confidence in his abilities to lead them anywhere but unfortunately with a daredevil glint in his eyes. His mouth had a humorous look, or was that sensuous?

She felt a fluttering in her belly at the thought of those lips against hers.

"Very nice," she said, wiping her hands on a towel.

He grinned. "Like it better?" She yielded to an urge to feel of his freshly shaven jaw, running her fingers along the silky, damp skin to the point of his chin. He took her hand in his and turned it over to where the palm was against his lips. He kissed the soft place at the base of her thumb, His lips were moist and firm against her skin, the sensations went clear to her belly and below.

"What else do you like?" he asked as his lips moved across her palm. The shiver in her spine traveled through her whole body.

"What... what are you doing?"

"Does it have to have a word?"

"No... but..."

"Don't give me buts, Abby. Just feel it. What do you feel?"

"Oh god." She couldn't tell him what she felt, couldn't give him that kind of power over her. She made herself pull her hand from him.

"Don't play with me, lady," he demanded his voice husky, his eyes darkened. He pulled her hard against him so that she could feel the whole, long, muscular length of his body against hers. For this one moment, she forgot about protecting herself and lifted her lips for the kiss she knew he meant to give her, the one she had been hungering for a moment earlier. She felt his mouth open against hers, his lips tease along the edges of her mouth, tempting her to open for him. Involuntarily, she heard herself give a little moan at the exquisite feel of his arms around her and his hands stroking down her back to cup her buttocks. My god, what was this?

She opened her mouth as though by instinct. His tongue entered and she felt his possession all the way to her knees. Almost frightened by the maelstrom of emotions his touch and feel were arousing, she pushed away, panting for breath.

He let her go without a struggle and sat on the chair at the table watching her. She tried to remember who she was and of what she'd thought she was capable. It was no use. Nothing had prepared her for this.

"You're a strange one."

Strange? That was right. She felt strange.

"Poor Abby. Caught up in a world you never even saw from a distance."

"No, yes... this is different."

His laugh held little humor. "Outlaw, renegade, gunman, bastard, killer. You've never known anyone like me, and you never should have either."

"It wasn't all your doing that we met. Sometimes things just happen. One day people don't know each other... the next..." She stopped unwilling to tell him of all the nights he'd been her dream, the nights she'd lain awake thinking about doing exactly what they'd done, except she'd had no experience to prepare her for what she felt at touching him. She had imagined a simple kiss, lips chastely pressing together, not this prairie fire, this restless yearning, this desire to touch his skin, to have him touch hers. Not the feeling that only this one man could ever fill the empty place within her body and soul.

"We're an unlikely combination, not a hand I'd bet much money on," he said.

"You're talking about gambling?"

He grinned at that disapproving tone, the wet squirrel look that had come over her face. "Yeah, it'd be like filling an inside royal flush to think we could ever make anything permanent out of the craziness we got ourselves into." He thought about what he'd like to fill and knew it was a good thing he was spending the day away from her.

He saw her swallow; her eyes darken. "Would you want to fill that... whatever it was."

He sucked in a deep breath and headed for the door. "I'll be back before dark."

Finishing cleaning the kitchen, Abigail decided the last thing she wanted to do was go outside and watch Sam get his neck broken. Besides, the men still weren't used to her. Better she should stay inside. She could dust the furniture, which looked as though it had been months if not forever since it had been done, then familiarize herself with her new home.

She walked into the great room with a rag and good intentions. She first looked up at the loft that had been tempting her since Sam had told her it was filled with boxes of books and headed straight up the stairs, brushing away cobwebs as she went.

Kneeling in front of the boxes, she opened the first one and smiled at seeing Nathaniel Hawthorne's *Twice Told Tales*. This was like Christmas in July. Whoever Mr. Gray had been, his tastes had been diverse and fascinating. A spider scurried away from *Essays and Nature* by Ralph Aldo Emerson which was covering *On the Duty of Civil Disobedience* by Henry David Thoreau. She chuckled when she saw *The Scarlet Letter* and under it two books by Theodore Weld, an author she didn't know. Charlotte Bronte's *Jane Eyre*, which Abigail had read three times, but knew she would enjoy again was stacked beside *The Last Days of Pompeii* by Edward Bulwer-Lytton, and a risque book by George Eliot.

Author after author delighted her as she took out the books and put them on the shelves, in something approximating alphabetical order. She smiled as she worked, thinking how pleased Sam would be when he found how many classics he owned.

Under the complete works of Shakespeare she found a book she had never read by Lew Wallace, *The Fair God*, and carried it downstairs to curl into a comfortable chair and read until Ollie was due to come up to the house for her first cooking lesson.

~

"Now, Miss Spenser," Ollie said, then corrected himself, "I mean Mrs. Ryker."

She corrected him. "Abigail, please."

"All right, Miss Abigail, I just wanted to know one thing—you really can't cook at all?" He removed his hat revealing a bald head as he rubbed it before tossing the hat onto a sideboard.

She shook her head. "I have tried a bit, but actually. No, not at all."

"Not atall. I was just wondering, was all."

"I've been busy learning other things, but I do want to learn now. At least basic things to make for supper. It is kind of you to take the time to teach me."

He acknowledged her compliment with a faint nod as he looked into the cupboard. "We been letting the supplies go down. We'll have to go to town, bring back chuck, if you're gonna to learn more than how to fry meat and potatoes."

"Chuck?"

"Grub, you know, like flour, baking soda."

"Where do you buy... grub?" she asked, thinking she might someday need to know where the nearest town was.

Ollie smiled. "Here and there."

She understood she'd receive no information that he didn't think Sam wanted her to have. She looked into the cupboard as he'd done. "I did see a few weevils in the flour."

"You'll get used to that. Just pick 'em out."

"Pick them out?" She frowned. "Isn't that unclean?"

"Now, missy, they hatched out right where they were, so it's not so bad as if you find a cockroach, now that's cause for stompin'."

"Ewwwwww." She made a face. "What will we fix tonight?" she asked, trying to erase the image of cockroaches from her mind.

"We'll keep 'er simple. I had some dried beef stashed away. With taters and carrots, we can make a passable stew."

She brightened. "How many shall we plan for?"

"What do you mean?"

"Don't you all eat up here?"

"We used to, but... don't reckon Sam'll want it that way anymore."

"I will discuss that with him, but for tonight," she said, smiling, "we should make enough for everyone. I know how unhappy the men are at having a woman here. You too, I suppose." She looked at him through her lashes.

"Well, I have figured Sam's done smarter things in his time."

"I imagine so. Anyway, I was thinking if we all ate together, got to know a little about each other, maybe it would help. What do you think?"

He grinned at her, rubbing his whiskers. "Men are going to be some scared of a woman like you."

"Why?"

"You're a lady, respectable. They ain't had much practice talkin' to such." He directed her to pick out good potatoes, then laughed. "Course, respectability's agonna get us all someday. I figgered it'd be when the preacher said the words over Sam's coffin afore it come to him though." He chuckled but Abigail did not join in. She didn't like thinking of Sam dead.

"How long have you been with him?"

He considered for a moment. "We hooked up in New Mexico. I reckon it's been nigh onto fifteen years this fall."

"He couldn't have been much more than a boy then. Did you teach him about... things?"

Ollie laughed. "Don't nobody teach Sam much of anything. He was going on forty when he was four."

"He told me a little about his mother."

Ollie glanced up from where he was sorting through the carrot barrel. "He did, did he? Well, that's good, I reckon." He squinted at her. "How much'd he tell you?"

"Just what he thought a wife needed to know, I suppose," she said, trying not to sound defensive, but apprehensive about how happy Sam would be over her asking Ollie questions behind his back.

"Wal," Ollie said, looking at her steadily, "there's wives and there's wives."

"Do we have onions?" she asked to change the subject. "It seems I remember Serafina crying when she added onions for flavoring."

Ollie's lips twisted off to the side in a thoughtful expression. "Who's Serafina?" he asked.

"She cooked for us."

He nodded. "So, she why you don't know how to cook, your old man's woman was jealous of you."

Abigail laughed. "Serafina is a cook, just a cook to my father." She smiled at the thought of Serafina and her father together in any other sense. She realized she had never questioned why there had not been another woman after her mother. It just was as it had been, but now she wondered.

"Not good enough for him or something?" Ollie asked interrupting her thoughts as he closed the lid on the carrot barrel.

"She is married," Abigail said as she picked up the paring knife.

"Don't stop a lot of folks."

"She loves her husband and has four children."

"Wouldn't stop a lot of women neither." Ollie grabbed the knife from her hand. "Not that way. You're fixin' to cut your thumb off you hold a knife that way." He repositioned it, then placed a potato in her other hand. "Here's how you go to it." He moved her hands through the steps until she began to get a feel for removing peeling, and no more potato than necessary and none of her own flesh.

"I'll get the beef," he said when he was satisfied with her progress.

Alone, Abigail stared at the potatoes, trying to remember Ollie's instructions, but thinking more of the many years Ollie's had said he and Sam had been together. Ollie's loyalty to Sam would ensure he not say things he felt damaging to Sam, but she was curious, anxious to understand this man she'd married. Did he have a mean temper? Would he turn surly when things went against him? Was she seeing the real Sam, or was he on best behavior? She knew how many women suffered because of a husband's wicked dispositions with no one to care how many times the woman was struck or beaten. Had she married a man like that? It would be better to know before she made him really angry. Not that she planned to stay with him that long anyway.

When Ollie came back, Abigail tried to think what she might say to make conversation. She had no idea what Ollie's interests might be. "Uh how long have the rest of the men been with Sam?"

"You're asking me things you oughta be askin' Sam."

That had not worked well. So she'd try direct. "I was just trying to make small talk, Ollie."

"Your husband'll tell you what you need knowing."

"So if we can't talk about Sam, how about you?"

"Me?" The old man gave her an uneasy look. "Why'd you want to know anything about me?"

"People are interesting to me. Were you born here in Arizona?"

He chuckled. "No way. I come from Missouri."

"Were you in the Civil War then?"

"I saw some of it."

"On which side? Or is that also privileged information." She smiled. Although it'd been nearly twenty years, she knew some were sensitive yet to the politics of that time.

"I fought with the South."

"For slavery?" She was not surprised. A lot of that thinking had been in various towns where she'd lived.

"Not likely." He snorted. "I fought for no big government coming along, tellin' a man how to live. I come out here to avoid that. And damn, seems like it comes along wherever I go."

"Well, the country is getting settled."

"Too damned much. Skirts come in and next thing you know

everything's changing." He gave her a sidelong look. She took no offense and smiled back.

Ollie turned to his work, putting the dried beef into a bowl, covering it with water. He poured himself a cup of coffee from the brew still simmering on the stove. She could only imagine how stout it must have been when she saw him make a face in drinking it.

"You'd rather I hadn't come with Sam, that we hadn't been married," she said, taking the bull by the proverbial horns.

"Yep. You will do nothing but hurt him."

"Or him hurt me."

"Sam won't hurt you."

She wasn't prepared to argue the point. "You are afraid I'll change things here."

"Already have," he grumbled. "Buck's gone."

"Was that a loss?"

"Maybe, maybe not, but he might still be trouble for Sam. Just like you will be."

"You look after Sam."

"As much as he'll let me."

"I don't mean wrong by him."

"Just you coming here has done that."

"I don't see how."

"You will."

She sighed. "I'm sorry you feel that way. I had hoped we could be friends, you and me."

"Can't see why you'd want that."

"Just I thought it'd be easier here for us all if we got along."

He stood up. "Wal, we'll see... Now about that stew." And he told her what she would need to do, the spices to add as it simmered. "You think you can remember all that?" he asked when he'd finished.

She nodded then shook her head.

He grinned despite himself. "I hope you do, cuz I want to go see how the horse breaking is going."

"All right... I ... I hope Sam doesn't get hurt doing that."

"Sam knows how to take care of himself." He walked to the door and then turned back. "I figured he made a mistake bringing you here, but time will tell if I was right or wrong. I hope I was wrong." With that, he was gone.

CHAPTER 11

In the afternoon with the food cooking, Abby decided washing Sam's clothing would keep her from thinking too much about what he was doing. She had hoped he would return for lunch, but although she'd heard loud laughing and yelling in the distance, she had seen nothing of the men. She supposed that meant it was all going well.

Abigail had never felt useless, a bit out of her element a few times, but here in this strange environment, she had no feeling for her role, for what she should do. She determined she would put an end to that. She got her dirty shirt, then went into Sam's bedroom, picked up the clothing on the floor and carried them into the kitchen.

She added more wood to the fire and set a large kettle of water on the stove to boil. She found washing powder in a tall cupboard. She hadn't done a lot of washes in her life, but it was a simple project and she set about with gusto, not realizing until she'd washed two pairs of pants and three shirts how hard the work was on a woman's hands. By the time she was rinsing the clothes for the second time and wringing them, her hands were reddened. Her next project would have to be finding some kind of oil or lotion.

Finding pins and hanging Sam's clothing on a line out back occupied another fifteen minutes, then she was caught in the same problem of nothing to do. With the meat simmering, Ollie had instructed her not to start potatoes and carrots until two hours before supper. The trouble was she could only guess what time Sam would return.

Feeling hot and sticky from the work, she heated a basin of water for bathing and took it to one of the unused back bedrooms. She would have to deal with which room to sleep in. Something more to discuss when Sam got in. She washed as well as she could, but other than the big shirt Sam had given her, she had to settle for putting on her riding skirt and boots. She would clean them only when she found something to change into.

At the other end of the house she heard a door open and slam, then boots on the wood floor and into the room she'd begun calling the master bedroom. She walked down the hall and waited in the great room. When she finally saw him coming toward her, she felt butterflies in her stomach, excited that he'd returned.

"What'd you do with my clothes?" he asked his voice level, but she felt an irritation in him.

"I washed them."

Surprise showed on his face. "You didn't need to do that."

"Well, I had to do something today."

"Not enough here for you?"

"There will be eventually. Just it will take me some time to find my place."

"I hadn't thought of that. But guess you are right."

"I have to stir the stew." She walked into the kitchen and he followed.

"You made a lot," he said as he watched her.

"I thought your crew might like to eat with us for at least

tonight," she said, forcing a polite tone to her voice. "Is that a problem?" The tension was unreal between them.

"No."

She sucked in a breath, feeling unaccountably irritated with him. Yes, they would have to find balance in their daily life for however long she stayed. She had no idea how to do that. This was all new for her and him too for that matter. "You would have preferred I had left your clothes lie there?" she asked.

"Just never thought on it."

"What do you want from me, Sam?"

"I'm still dirty, haven't shaved or washed, but if I wasn't, I'd show you one idea," he said with a wicked grin.

He was so appealing, a crooked little smile, those intense eyes smoldering with whatever thoughts were going through his head. She was speechless, couldn't think of a single thing to say. He reached out for her and pulled her against him. "Even though I smell like horse, do you want me to show you, Abby?"

"We can't. You can't. That is," she stumbled over the words. Her breathing was coming faster as his hands slid down her spine, cupping her buttocks. She felt him against her from chest to knee.

"I'm dirty," he said. "I ought to let you go."

"You should," she agreed, not so anxious that he do so. She liked the feeling of his muscular frame against her, of his fingers stroking down her backside. He bent and brushed light kisses along her neck. The sensations turned her insides to jelly. A yearning seemed to be building from somewhere deep within. It was exploding out through her skin, turning her hot and moist, making her want something she'd never imagined existed.

"So what shall we do now, Abby?" he asked leaning back to look at her. "I haven't done right by you," he said finally. "I dumped you here with no spare clothes, not enough food, then ran off to break horses because I was afraid to stay with you."

"I didn't think you were scared of anything."

"Wrong." His smile was bemused.

"What were you afraid of?"

"You."

"Me? How could you be afraid of me?"

The smile disappeared. "No reason."

"Well, I did keep busy with more than the washing."

"What else?"

"I went through your books," she said, smiling and ready to go onto more pleasant subjects. "You have some wonderful titles."

"That's nice."

"Come on up and look. You have an excellent collection of classics."

He walked away a few feet. "I better clean up. What time'd you figure supper?"

She was disappointed that he hadn't shared her excitement for the books. Maybe later he'd be more interested. "Two hours-- according to Ollie."

"I'll tell the boys after I get cleaned up. I don't suppose anything you washed out is going to be dry enough."

She shook her head. "I should have thought of that."

"It's all right. I have one more shirt. I like the way mine looks on you by the way."

She managed a smile. She could imagine his hands against her again; almost feel them against her bare skin. She had to stop thinking this way. Something to distract them both seemed in line. "How did it go with the horses?" she asked, pouring water from the stove into a basin and handing it to him.

"I made a good start. I can ride most anything... eventually."

Setting the bowls on the table, Abigail felt shaky. She had acted as hostess many times but never for a dinner she had cooked. Well mostly cooked. She realized strangely enough that none of her nervousness came from the fact that the men who would be sitting at the table would be considered outlaws by almost anyone's definition.

The stew smelled appetizing, but she was unsure if that was much of an indicator as to its quality. At least Ollie had returned and helped her make biscuits. They'd looked like most biscuits she'd seen. Hopefully she would be able to remember how they'd come to be the first time she did it by herself. She couldn't expect to have a tutor at her hand every time she faced the stove. She needed to find a pencil and some paper, write down instructions as it was the only way she was likely to actually be able to repeat them.

Sam entered the kitchen, a faint smile on his lips. He'd washed and freshly shaved again, but his shirt and jeans were as clean as brushing off could make them.

"You look tired," Sam said, putting his arms around her waist.

"I am a little, but mostly scared."

"Of my wolves."

"I wish you wouldn't call them that."

"I don't want you to ever forget what they are, what I am."

She didn't like thinking of him that way but she wasn't able to argue about it either. She knew so little of his world, of this world. Perhaps they were all wolves. He tightened his arms around her, then freed her and walked to the window to stare down toward the bunkhouse. "They're on their way."

She forced a smile.

"You don't have to do this."

"I want to do it."

"They're wolves, but they won't eat you," he teased.

"I know that. You're here to protect me anyway, aren't you?"

"I might be the biggest danger of all, mightn't I?" He smiled again.

She ignored that, but she knew he was probably right but not for physical danger. She also knew he would protect what was his; and for now, she was his. "It isn't being afraid of the men... It's just I've never done anything like this." She looked down at the floor.

"Done what?"

"Prepared a meal, then had somebody come and eat it."

Sam laughed, then turned to face his men as they entered the kitchen, pulling off their hats as one after another they stood at one end of the room, none of them seemingly knowing what to do next.

"Abby, the skinny little guy on the end, you already know-- Ollie Oliver. Next to him is Sandy Prescott. I figure Sandy's about--sixteen." The youth nodded. "Joe Fox is from New York. He was an artist, isn't that right, Joe?" Joe nodded. Abby wondered did any of them talk.

"Joe's always asking somebody to pose for him, drawing pictures. You could ask him to show you sometime, if he isn't too shy. And Bull Frazier, I expect you can figure why they call him that," Sam said gesturing to one of the largest men Abby had ever seen. "I've heard there's more than one reason, but we won't go into that." Sam's smile was pure wickedness, and Abby found herself flushing.

"Rock Thompson you met earlier, and the last man in line is Bill Smith. I don't for a minute figure Bill's last name is Smith and everybody calls him Snake anyway because he's always making bands out of their skins—or so it's claimed."

Sam tightened his arm around Abby's waist. "Boys, this is my wife, Abigail Ryker. You'll treat her with respect because she's a lady. I expect a few of you remember what that means."

There were nods and some curious stares, but soon all the men settled at the table, taking the napkins she'd placed beside each bowl and placing them everywhere from the neck to the lap to the floor. They then looked expectantly at Abby as she brought the heavy kettle from the stove and stood at one end of the table. She couldn't decide for what they were waiting. Something had to happen, but what?

"Since this is our first meal together. I, well, I would imagine there should be a blessing," she said uncertainly looking toward Sam. It was an unusual family; a pack of wolves, Sam had called them. She was the only female in their pack if that was so; so her responsibility was to make what she could out of this family and the men in it.

"Blessing?" Sam stared uncomprehendingly at her for a moment before he realized what she expected. He looked at the men, then bent his head. "For what we're about to receive," he said, "we are grateful. Amen."

When everyone had been served and begun to eat, Abigail took casual note of her husband's table manners and was pleased to see he would not have been an embarrassment to her if they had been seated at her father's table. It showed that somewhere down the line he'd cared enough to watch others and learn because from what he'd told her of his upbringing, no one would have set out to teach him such things.

"This is very good, Mrs. Ryker," Sandy said from where he'd ended up at her right.

"Thank you, Sandy. Ollie is teaching me to cook. Sam didn't say where you came from," she said, giving polite conversation, which had failed with Ollie earlier, another chance.

"None of us talk about where we've come from," interrupted the man she remembered being named Bill Smith--Snake. "It's not smart to ask." His tone was challenging.

"I'm sorry," Abby said, not dropping her eyes as she steadily met his antagonistic gaze. "I had no idea that was off limits."

"It's not so far as I'm concerned," Sandy said, giving Snake a scowl. "I was born in Kansas, but lost my family."

"How sad. Every one of them?"

The youth nodded. "I was in Abilene when--"

"You got any more coffee, Abby?" Sam said, interrupting. She looked up at him, wondering why he didn't get it himself; then she remembered she wanted to be the hostess at this table. It was her job to see that they all had coffee. By the time she got to the table with the coffee pot and had refilled cups all the way around, then started a second pot of coffee, she realized Sam had deliberately diverted her from hearing Sandy's story. She wondered what he was hiding. She didn't like thinking that Sam was using a youth in his nefarious dealings.

"Now then, Sandy," she said, sitting down, "you were telling me about Abilene." She glanced toward Sam and saw by the stony expression on his face that she had guessed correctly as to his attempted redirection.

"Yeah, I was in Abilene and near starving to death. Mostly eating garbage to stay alive."

She frowned. "How old were you?"

Sandy thought a moment, glanced at Sam but received no help. "Most likely I was seven or eight, but I'd been on the road a long time, kind of lost track of things."

"And since then you've been with Sam... and his men?"

Sandy shook his head. "First Sam just gave me some money, like when I'd hold his horse and stuff." Sandy's face reddened. "Sam saved me one time... From that time on everybody knew he'd look out for me, and nobody hurt me. When he left Abilene, he said I could go with him, work for him. I been with him ever since. I never been to Mexico, but Sam says soon." He gave a boyish scowl. "Course, he always says soon."

"What do you do the times they travel and you stay behind?" She was treading carefully now and beginning to wish she had let Sam have his way on not discussing any of this.

"I keep an eye on this place. Whatever Sam needs doing, mostly." It was clear from the tone of his voice that he worshipped Sam and would do whatever his hero asked.

"He's going to earn his keep now, or he's out," Snake said, eyes narrowed as he looked from Sandy to Sam. "You've protected him long enough. He's a man or a kid. Which is it?"

"You thinking of taking over here?" Sam asked, his blue eyes cold and level. Snake glared at him, then shifted his eyes to the table.

"It's true though," Sandy said. "I want to ride with you next time. You promised I could when I was sixteen. I been that for a few months now. We think anyway. You can't keep treating me like a kid, Sam."

Sensing the tensions that had been aroused by her questioning, Abby was very sorry she had not let Sam have his way on the diversion he had attempted. She couldn't undo her words, but she could redirect the talk.

"Mr. Fox, I believe Sam said you're an artist," she said, looking at Joe Fox. "What kind of work do you do?"

"I used to paint," he said, smiling at her, "until I lost my supplies and now have doubtless forgotten how anyway. Now I draw. You would make a lovely subject, Mrs. Ryker."

Abby felt as flustered at hearing herself called either lovely or Mrs. anyone. "Thank you for the compliment. Have you drawn Sam?" she asked. She knew Sam had one of the most interesting faces she had ever seen. He was handsome, but it was something more than that. An energy, a quality of beauty mixed with strength, of caring with hardness. Likely no artist could capture it.

"Whenever I have the opportunity," Joe Fox said. "Though he's been unwilling to pose for me, I have managed to catch him in action."

"I would love to see those drawings."

Fox smiled. "And I love having my work viewed by anyone and would be delighted to show you."

At that point, Abby ran out of small talk. What did one ask men who rustled for a living, especially since she violently opposed that activity. She listened to their scattered attempts at conversation but knew they were equally ill at ease. As soon as they finished, each in turn excused himself from the table. For being wolves, they had acquitted themselves quite well.

When they were all gone, Sam remained sitting at the opposite end of the table, his cobalt blue eyes on her. "Well?" he asked with a faint smile.

She felt at a loss. Then she grinned teasingly. "On a bearskin rug?"

"Huh?"

"Was that how he wanted you to pose--Joe Fox, that is?"

He smiled. "Bearskin, huh? Is that supposed to have some significance?"

She decided it might be better not going farther with that topic and began picking up the dishes. She met him midway down the table, where he had picked up half the plates. "Now you do the dishes?" he asked, suddenly looming tall and dangerously handsome over her.

She nodded. "They'd only be waiting in the morning," she said, surprised when he carried the ones he had to the drain board and began rinsing them with the hand pump.

"What are you doing?" she asked, following him.

"Helping." His eyes were amused as he looked down at her.

She frowned. "Men don't do dishes."

"They don't? How do they get them clean then?"

She gave him a look. "Well, they don't if a woman is around."

"I don't need a woman here to do dishes. There are better things." She felt his smile clear to her toes. He seemed to fill her space. His energy was all around her without their bodies even touching. It would be impossible to feel him any more completely with his arms around her than she did as they stood side by side at the counter, her washing, him drying.

"What do you think?" he asked.

"About what?"

"The men, the place here... everything. Anything." His smile was faint, the expression in his eyes intense. It made her close her own against the strength of the feelings he was evoking within her. She had to stop to think what he had asked.

"Your men are... interesting. I didn't know what it was safe to ask, especially after Mr. Smith said what he did."

"Mr. Smith won't be with us long."

She looked up at him to see that his smile had disappeared. "What do you mean?"

"I've never trusted him. I'm just waiting for him to step far enough across the line to get rid of him."

"You mean kill him?" She might have expected many reactions to her question but not laughter.

"You are a bloodthirsty little thing," he said, taking the dishcloth from her hands. "Is that what you think I ought to do?"

"Of course not." She stopped. She was constantly jumping to conclusions where Sam was concerned.

"When a man and I don't get along," Sam said, "I do what your father would do. I fire him. I give him his back pay, if he's due any, and send him on his way."

"I keep misjudging you," she said.

"You have reason. I would've killed Buck if I could have."

"But you didn't."

"I missed my shot and my chance. Now I can wait for his next shot at my back."

"He'll do that?"

"He did it once. No reason not again. Hey, don't worry about that too. He might just leave the territory, stew about the unfairness of life while he tries again in California or Oregon. I can hope for that but I won't rely on it."

"You make me afraid."

"A little afraid is good. Just don't let it paralyze you. He took her hand into his, turned it over and kissed the palm. "Make a list of what you need and I'll go for supplies in the morning, find some lotion that'll take the redness out of your hands, make your skin more silky than it already is... if that's possible."

She felt that growing warmth in her belly again and wanted to do anything to distract herself from the feelings. "Would you build a fire in the fireplace? I think it's cool enough tonight for it, and we can have our coffee in there." A few moments later they were settled onto the long sofa their cups in front of them and the flames licking up from the fire he'd kindled.

She felt nervous at being alone with him. She was so aware of his body that she nearly moved to a chair but held her ground. When he didn't say anything, she felt the need to feel the empty space with safe words. "Can I tell you about your library now?" she asked.

He smiled, looked at her over the rim of his coffee cup as he sipped the brew. She watched as he swallowed. She realized she had felt him so totally that she had swallowed with him. She closed her eyes to try and steady her nerves.

She could hear the smile in his voice. "How about instead making that list of supplies that I can take to the store."

"Ollie knows better than me."

"I was thinking of personal items."

"I can't go with you?"

"It wouldn't be smart yet."

"Why not?"

"You honestly don't know that they'll be looking for you?"

She frowned and sighed. "I need to let my father know I'm all right. He must be beside himself."

"How you going to let him know without having a posse showing up right after?"

"A letter?"

"And would he believe anything you said in it? He'd figure you'd been kidnapped, and the search would be more intensive than it most likely is now."

"I can't let him think I'm dead or who knows what he's thinking."

"You want to go back?"

She looked at him through her lashes. His expression was unreadable. Did he care? Did he want her to stay? Did any of the marriage ceremony's words mean anything to him? And then she remembered what they had meant to her. She had known from the beginning an annulment would be easy to get even if they consummated the marriage.

She had no answer to his question. Did she want to go back? She should. She hated the word should.

"Let's just forget about questions or answers... for tonight," he said with that silky tone to his voice, the one that seemed to wash over her.

"Can we?"

"Sure. Let's pretend tonight, Abby."

"Pretend what?" She felt the tingle through her body, her increasing awareness that his hand lay relaxed on the sofa only inches from hers.

"How about that we're a man and wife sitting in the parlor, watching a fire, sipping coffee, talking about the day."

"We are man and wife."

He shook his head. "Not yet, but we could be." His kiss was light and ended too quickly. "You know, I wanted you from the moment I saw you in Tucson... and it wasn't just to sit on a sofa at the end of a day."

"Wanted me back then? I don't see how that's possible."

"Why not?"

"I'm a homely, dried up woman."

He chuckled. "You are huh? Well, if you're dried up, you don't have to be. You can flow like the breezes through the trees, the river in the bottom of a canyon. You know it's in you. And homely? You have to be joking."

"Not at all. I'm not pretty one bit. I know that."

He smiled, his eyes smoky with the reflected firelight. "No, you're not. You are beautiful, with exotic, finely drawn features, eyes so dark that a man could fall right into them and never want to come out. Your face has expression in it, shows everything you are thinking from that wet squirrel look, to right now when you look soft and desirable, your body wanting things you don't even know about yet. I could teach you about all that, Abby. You want it. You know you do."

Her heart began to beat more quickly. "I'm not ready," she whispered, knowing from her body's reaction that she wasn't being honest. Physically she was ready for things she'd never even imagined but emotionally. Emotionally, she was afraid. She wanted so much but what then? Could she then ever return to the life she had left?

"I told you once you'd have to beg me to take you into my bed. I might have bent that some--begging won't be required." He took her hand in his and kissed the fingers, his lips lingering. "But I promise you, I'll never force you. It wouldn't be worth much that way."

She didn't know whether to feel glad or disappointed at his firm statement. She didn't want to be forced, but she was afraid of yielding. Not so much for the physical act itself as for what it would mean afterward. She saw by the steady expression in his eyes that he meant what he'd said. If she ever did come to him, she and he would both know it was for no other reason than that she wanted him.

"I'll need some sizes," he said, if you don't want to keep wearing what you are into rags," He grinned.

"It would be nice to be able to change. I'd sew a dress from cloth, except--"

He grinned. "You can't sew any better than you can cook."

"Maybe a tiny bit better." She smiled

"There are other things... that matter more to a man." His smile was slow and so seductive that she felt herself melt. She wondered what would come next and realized that several possibilities were occurring to her. She thought about touching his lips with her fingertips and to resist the temptation brought her hands together on her lap.

He sighed. "I'll have to get an early start tomorrow, guess I should head for bed."

That she had not expected. She looked at him, knowing her surprise showed in her eyes as he grinned. "And you aren't ready for anything more. You know it, and I see it. I don't want anything you'll regret the next morning."

She managed a shaky smile. That was true, but she didn't

want to face it. She wanted... She didn't know what she wanted and so rose as he did. She watched as he blew out the lamps; then followed him down the hall toward the bedrooms. At her door, he released her hand, which she'd barely realized he'd been holding. "I won't see you in the morning, but Ollie will keep an eye on things. I should be back by nightfall; but if I'm not, don't worry."

"Keeping an eye on things? Like me to make sure I don't leave?"

His smile vanished. "I told you if you want to leave you can. You decide on that, just tell him. Your horse is in the pasture below the barn. Ollie will take you wherever you want to go." With that he was gone. She was left to light her own bedroom lamp and to know that she'd hurt him. She thought of apologizing, but given the heat of her own feelings, the look in his eyes, she knew going to his room wasn't wise unless she was ready for more from him, and she wasn't...

Lying in bed, Abigail thought over her strange day, learning to cook from an aging rustler, entertaining an outlaw gang, and finally sitting on the sofa with Sam as though they were a married couple. She swallowed back tears. Although she had never thought she wanted to be married, never wanted to be subservient to some man, she let her mind consider how it might be if he was her husband. What if he was lying beside her right now, naked and ready to teach her all the things he knew about her body, about how to please his body?

The tears ran down her cheeks and onto the pillow. It was such an impossible dream. He was a rustler and she a spinster. Never the twain should have met and to what could it lead but more tears? There was no hope for them. She closed her eyes and let the tears flow.

CHAPTER 12

Abby, eyes still swollen from the tears of the night before, didn't hear Sam ride out in the morning, but she felt his absence in her soul. That scared her as much as her confused feelings of the night before. She dashed water in her eyes and managed a smile for Ollie when he came to the kitchen, showing her how to bank the stove for bread making. Together they put together the ingredients for loaves of bread. She worked out some of her internal frustration as she kneaded the dough into the yeasty loaves.

When Ollie had disappeared to take care of the outside chores, Abby took Sam's dry shirts and pants from the line and brought them into the house. The shirts smelled of soap and the outdoors. She brought a basin of water into her bedroom, washed herself and did the best she could with brushing off her riding skirt. She passed the remainder of the day sorting through the books, dusting furniture and watching for the dust of a horse in the distance.

She sat on the porch and watched the sun go down. A waxing moon rose over the hills to the east. Her mind was blank. She didn't try to think of what she would do nor why she missed that man so much. She thought of how she had seemed to know him the moment she saw him in Tucson. How her heart leaped when he came near her. She forced all that from her mind. She could make no choices right now. She could only sit and watch the moon, the stars, the distant hills, hear the sounds of the men laughing in the bunkhouse and then silence, except for the yodel of coyotes in the distance, that seemed so complete it enveloped her in its warmth.

Sam wasn't going to make it home before morning. She didn't know what time she knew that, but it was clear he had decided to spend the night in whatever town he had gone. Maybe he'd gone whoring—to one of those women who laughed at all his jokes, a woman who knew how to please a man. She felt her jaw clenching and forced herself to relax. She couldn't be other than she was. She would never know how to please a man. Never know the secrets of the flesh.

Back in the house, she picked up the shotgun from the kitchen. Sure Sam wouldn't be riding back this late, she bolted the doors before she undressed and slid between her covers. She lay there uneasily, still determined to not think, not attempt to plan anything. She just needed to sleep and set her mind to that.

It seemed she lay there a long while, hearing the night birds, a hawk shriek in the distance, little creatures scurrying around outside. When she slept, her dreams were filled with some kind of monster chasing her in a wooded forest. When did the monster change? Or had it always been Sam? Because it was him ravishing her, kissing her, making her body his plaything.

The sound of hooves outside woke her from her restless sleep. At first she felt relieved Sam was home. Then she knew it wasn't him. Two horses. She heard sounds of dismounting and she got out of bed, put on the big shirt she'd been wearing, grabbed the shotgun and hurried to the great room.

She heard the kitchen door rattle followed by silence, and the sounds of boots across the porch. She was frightened but surprisingly steady. Someone was opening a window. A dark shadow seemed to fill the open space. It was only when he stood, when she felt the energy of the room change that she knew it was Sam.

She made a small sound, not much but enough to alert him. He had to see her with the moonlight flooding the room and walked toward her. For a reason she couldn't understand, she didn't put the shotgun down.

He stopped scant feet from her. "Interesting view to come home to," he said.

She swallowed hard, torn between the urge to throw herself in his arms, or to throttle him for coming in like that and scaring her half to death. "What do you mean?"

"Even in the moonlight I can see you got damned pretty legs, but then there's that third leg pointing at me, looking like it'd like to blow me to kingdom come or wherever I'm heading after here." He threw his hat backward landing it squarely on the sofa and took another step toward her.

"I thought you weren't coming home tonight. I was scared when I heard two horses outside."

"One was a pack animal." He took another step. She knew she ought to put the gun down, but she didn't. He didn't order her, as he advanced toward her, each step slow and measured with no hesitation.

He only stopped when the gun was pressed against his chest. "You fixing to use this?"

"I was scared."

"Still are, I'd guess."

"Some."

"I told you if you ever pointed a gun at anyone, don't make it a bluff. Now in a minute, I'm going to take that gun out of your hands, then I'm going to put myself into them. If you don't want that, you better pull the trigger." His teeth flashed white in the moonlight. That smile told her he meant exactly what he said.

She lowered her eyes, then the gun, putting it carefully onto a stand beside her. He reached out and took her into his arms, pulling her against his body. Pressed against her stomach was his belt buckle, the soft fabric of his shirt now under her fingers. She could have pushed away but instead, she threw her arms around him. Her fingers delved into the thick hair at the back of his neck.

"When I come back to you, this going to be my usual greeting?" he asked with a chuckle.

"Which one?" His laughter deepened and she could feel it vibrate into her. "I'm glad you're safely home," she whispered against his chest.

"Lady, you've got a strange way of showing it."

"I didn't have my finger on the trigger... after I knew it was you anyway."

He smiled and then bent to claim her lips. He had kissed her passionately before, but never with such a claiming as he parted her lips with his tongue, then delved within. She felt the impact of the kiss through her whole body as she clung to him, aware that under that big white shirt she was naked and could feel his hands against her buttocks, pressing her against him, making her feel his hardness. Before she realized what she was doing, she moved her own tongue to tease his lips and enter his mouth as he'd done hers.

It was as though she melted into him as their bodies strained together. She wanted something more. His hands were now under her shirt, against her bare skin, cupping her buttocks. She wanted him to take off her shirt, to peel away the layers, to teach her all that he knew. And then she felt frightened. He would suck her into him. There would be no way to walk away if she ever let him possess her so completely, and he would possess her completely.

Her mind dazed with the passion, her body fighting for what it wanted, she forced herself to push away. She didn't expect him to so quickly step back. She felt a chill.

He smiled, his eyes smoky with his desire, his breath was coming hard. "I liked that. Did you?"

"You know I did."

"Do I?"

"I missed you."

"Good, I bought you some presents but first I'm hungry. Anything left around here to eat?"

"OIllie taught me to make bread today. It didn't turn out too badly. I could slice some for you, dip it in egg and fry it... I think there is an egg or two left."

He smiled. "Maybe you'd like to keep some chickens."

Her smile widened. "I've never had chickens, actually only seen them from a distance, but I... yes, I'd like to have chickens."

In the kitchen, he lit the lamp as she rekindled the fire in the stove. He sat in a chair at the table, his leg thrown up on the one beside him and watched her work for a moment. "I forget my head when I'm with you. I still gotta take care of the horses. Be right back." He rose from his chair and went outside, leaving the room darker and less inviting. She could not believe how his energy filled a room, filled her.

As she worked at the stove, she thought about the whirlwind of emotions that Sam Ryker carried with him. Like a vortex, he left her panting for breath. From the time he'd come home, he'd taken her from fear to anger to passion, to caring, and back through the whole range of emotions. She had been eager to see him, afraid of his appearance, afraid of her own responses. By the time he had returned bringing with him sacks filled with the food he'd purchased, Abby had fixed a fresh pot of coffee, and fried up the bread. She poured him a cup of coffee and set the plate of food in front of him.

"This looks great, Abby. Thank you," he said, taking a quick sip of the coffee before he began eating. She put away the supplies, feeling an odd sense of satisfaction at knowing she had prepared what he was eating.

"Want your gift?" he asked as he put his fork down.

"What is it?"

"Got to open it to find out." He laid a small parcel, wrapped in plain paper on the table.

She felt afraid that he'd bought her a wedding ring. She had married him. She should have a ring if she had truly been a wife. But she was not. If he gave her a ring now, she couldn't wear it. How would he feel about that if she rejected his gift?

His smile disappeared. "You won't take a present from me?" he asked, his voice coolly emotionless, but she'd already seen the disappointment.

She had no choice, so she took the package, thanked him, and managed a smile as she undid the string, then folded back the paper. She was shocked to find a silver hair clip.

"I thought women liked things for their hair. You've been tying yours back with a piece of leather. This would look prettier. If you don't like it, you don't have to keep it."

She shook her head, fought against yielding to tears. "I love it. It's a most considerate and beautiful gift. Thank you."

He reached into the saddle bag he'd put beside his chair and handed her another wrapped parcel. "Maybe you'll like this too then."

Because it was larger, she had no hesitation and opened the gift, smiling when she saw the brush and comb, also of silver. She looked up at him. "They're beautiful. Thank you. Thank you so much."

She heard a sigh of relief that she realized he'd only let out when he saw the pleasure on her face. "I wanted to buy you a dress. I'd have gone to Harshaw instead of Tubac if I hadn't been hoping there was a dressmaker there." He shrugged. "No luck though. I did buy you some boys' pants and shirts that ought to fit well enough. At least it'll give you something to change into; and when I go south again, I can find more."

She swallowed, grateful for the gifts, but not liking to hear any reference to his riding south. Surely she would be able to convince him not to return there, not to do something so wrong and dangerous; but he was tired. Tonight was not the time to argue her points. She would wait.

She half expected Sam to suggest they sleep together, but he headed for the room he had been using, leaving her alone. Later, she lay there in the darkness thinking about what she felt with him near her. No longer did the night seem filled with possible dangers. Instead it was filled with images, throbbing sensations and forbidden dreams.

~

"Are there any women living near here?" Abby asked as Sam manfully struggled to eat more than a few bites of the gummy oatmeal she had cooked.

He managed to swallow the lump in his mouth, washing it down with coffee to avoid choking. "What?" he asked when he could.

"You know, other ladies nearby. Neighbors."

Sam nearly forgot the question in the pleasure of watching her moving around his kitchen. She had worn the new shirt he'd bought her, a green plaid that accentuated her figure, defined her. He liked seeing her in things he'd bought and would be glad when the leather skirt wasn't required. He'd see to that on his next trip south. Nightgowns too, lacy ones. Nogales had a lot of shops.

Abby looked at him, her mouth open as though to renew her questioning when Ollie came through the kitchen door. Fortunately, from Sam's perspective, saving him from having to admit he'd already forgotten her question.

"You are going to have to start knocking," Sam told him as Abby poured Ollie coffee, then reheated Sam's.

Ollie scowled at him. "What fer?"

"You might interrupt us by barging in, besides, I don't think Abby likes it," Sam said, shifting the blame for his decision to Abby's shoulders.

Although it was true she would prefer a warning knock, she

didn't intend to let herself be put between Sam and his best friend. "That's for you two to work out, Sam."

He took a drink of his coffee, burned his mouth, and grimaced. "What did you want?" he asked, when he could get out the words without coughing.

"Boys just wondered when we'd finish breaking those horses."

"I have to chop wood this morning. We're almost out of kindling," Sam said. "Have them start without me."

Ollie gave him a peculiar look but finished his coffee in a few gulps and was gone with no further questions.

"Why was he so surprised by that?" she asked as she cleared the table.

"I don't usually let them handle the horses without me. Some of them get too rough. Horses do better with a gentle hand." The expression in his eyes told her it was also how he saw a man handled a woman.

"Then you shouldn't today either. I could chop the wood." She smiled as she realized how silly that sounded.

"Can you?"

"Of course.

"Have you ever done it?"

"Well, no but how hard can it be?"

"I'll chop the wood," Sam said, rising. "I like your pretty little toes just the way they are." He grinned at her embarrassed flush as they both looked down at her bare feet. Abby hadn't gone without shoes so much since she'd been a child. No, that was wrong. She'd never been allowed to go barefoot then either. She liked the feel of the smooth wood floors under her feet, liked the way it felt when her toes spread out instead of being pushed tightly together.

As she washed the dishes, she heard the sound of an ax striking wood and couldn't resist looking out the window. Sam had taken off his shirt and already his skin was slick with sweat as the ax rose and fell. As he lifted his arms, the muscles rippled down his back, his biceps tightened and expanded, then the ax would descend and the wood fall as if magically into chunks. God he was beautiful.

Abigail swallowed, sucking in a breath. She would have to be careful or she'd be finding herself in love with a man who could bring her nothing but misery. She had to remind herself that she could learn from him, but these moments were to experience, not to keep. Sam was not hers. She could never let herself forget that.

To take her mind away from the man she'd married but with whom she had never intended to stay, Abby decided to scrub the floors. She changed into the boy's pants he'd bought her, pleased that they fit loosely. Back in the kitchen, she set about doing the job much as she remembered seeing Serafina do it. The first pan of water was too full of soap, but little by little she got the idea.

Outside, she could hear Sam clumping onto the porch, stacking the firewood where it would be convenient to the kitchen. She smiled as she thought how pleasurable it was to both be working on tasks around the home, together but not together.

When the door opened, she was on her knees and looked up to order him to take off his boots.

"Take off my boots?" he repeated, his shirt under his arm, his muscular torso still gleaming with sweat.

"I just washed it. I don't want it to get dirty already."

He looked down at the floor. "Abby, I can't take off my boots every time I come in here."

"But when your boots aren't dusty and the floor isn't wet, it won't matter so much."

He grinned and obeyed. "You using that rose water lotion I bought you?"

"Well, I will. If I remember it later."

He came over and pulled her to her feet, claiming a hand, checking it for redness. "You ought to wear gloves."

"To wash a floor?" she asked with disbelief.

"Ladies should have smooth hands. I don't want yours looking like you're a washerwoman."

"Why not?"

He shook his head. "Don't know. I just don't want it." He smiled then as he ran his hands down her back and cupped her buttocks. "I like these," he said.

She frowned. "You think the men will approve?"

"I think no man in his right mind would disapprove." That thought gave him a new worry. He didn't want the men to approve too much. "Maybe you shouldn't wear them when they're around."

"Should I wear them when I meet our neighbors?" she asked. "How would they feel about a woman in pants?"

"Won't meet them," he said, heading for the pump to wash up.

"Why not? Neighbors get together. They help each other."

"The nearest family speaks Spanish. They wouldn't give much help because they still think this land is theirs."

"What do you mean?"

He shook his head to rid himself of the excess water. "They're still steamed. The original land grants were declared invalid. They didn't agree. The Montoya family thinks it's still theirs no matter what the courts say."

"That's terrible though. You mean Mr. Gray stole this land from them?"

"No, I mean there are disagreements over how valid a Mexican land grant is, especially for a family that already owns a million acres. At any rate, over fifty years ago the matter was settled by U.S. courts. The Montoyas hold a grudge."

"Oh." She didn't understand so much. She remembered then the problem in Tucson of similar land grants. Issues that the bags Sam held could resolve. She wanted to bring it up, but decided there would be better times.

"How about north of here. Surely there must be some families around that we could visit?"

"You miss other women that much?"

"I'm used to talking with friends." She thought how much she missed Priscilla. "It's just very different for me to only have men around."

She saw his jaw clench. She had again disappointed him. "It's all right," she said, putting her hand on his arm, aware of the texture of his skin, the feeling of dampness and hard muscle under her fingertips.

"The Reimers own the nearest ranch to the north. I think there's a family there, with a woman, but I've never met them."

"Why not?"

He shook his head and smiled. "Abby, I'm a rustler. I haven't had a reason to meet neighbors, and besides you don't think other men would want to know me, do you?"

"But you said big cattlemen bought from you."

"I'm the kind of man you use, not claim as a friend."

"Is that because of how they feel or you?" she asked. "Have you given people a chance to be friendly?"

His eyes were stony and unyielding. "I won't argue with you. I've got to get down and check on the boys."

"But what about lunch?"

He shook his head. "I'm not hungry." He collected his gun from the peg by the door, belted it around his hips, slung his shirt on and with that was gone. No good-bye, no quick kiss, not even a backward glance as he strode off.

"Well," she said to the walls. "He's sensitive on that one." She went back to her scrubbing, trying to reason through Sam's attitude, but she couldn't. She decided that the first chance she got, she'd find a way to ride to the Reimers and meet them, maybe invite them to supper. She was sure Sam was wrong. Maybe knowing neighbors, finding friends that were normal people, with normal goals would be good for Sam, make him see life could be other than it had been for him.

Her opportunity came sooner than she'd expected when that night Sam told her he'd be gone before first light. He and most of the men would ride the hills to the south driving the cattle into the main corrals where they would brand this year's calves.

"You really do run cattle then?"

"A few."

"Do you have to do that now?"

"I'm late this year. If I don't get them marked, they'll be picked off by the little ranchers."

She looked at him with disbelief.

"Lady," he said, "in this country a cow is a trade item. They're on the hoof, easily moved and worth money. To some, branded only makes them a little less negotiable."

CHAPTER 13

The next morning, she got up early to fix him breakfast. She was unsure if he was grateful or not, but he did eat the hotcakes she prepared. At the door, he said, "I left Sandy behind to do errands, keep an eye on things." She smiled, kissed him lightly in front of his men, and watched them all ride away. She would wait until it was a bit brighter before she took the ride she planned.

In waiting for a more acceptable hour for visiting, Abby wrote a note to leave on the table just in case Sam returned before she did. She scribbled a few words about going for a ride and hoping to meet the neighbors, then headed out the kitchen door, wearing her boots, riding skirt, her new shirt, her hat, and her gun in her pocket.

She expected Sandy to question her right to ride off and wasn't surprised when he came up to her in the lower barn as she was saddling Belle.

"Where you going?" he asked, frowning.

"For a ride. Want to come?"

"Sam didn't say nothing about this," Sandy grumbled, saddling his own horse.

"I left him a note explaining everything. I'm glad you can come because we can get better acquainted as we go."

Sandy's frown deepened as he swung onto his horse. She was glad Sam had found him, had kept him from harm because Sandy seemed like the sort of boy who would grow into a good man, despite his misadventures with Sam's gang. Time with him was what she wanted so she could give him some ideas that might redirect his goals.

"You're riding like you got some place in mind. Mind telling me where?" Sandy asked as they headed north at a gentle jog.

"I have a general idea. I am going to visit the Reimer family."

He looked more disturbed. "What for?

"Just being neighborly."

"We don't go there, not never."

"We do today."

"Sam say it's all right?"

"Did you have the idea I needed permission from Sam?"

"No."

"Then?"

"All right. Just don't see why."

"People visit each other."

"Why?"

"It's friendly. Sandy, you are wasting your energy if you continue this way and in the process ruin our beautiful morning. I am going anyway. I am not a prisoner here, am I?"

"Course not."

"Then? I am assuming their ranch house is a bit northeast." She pointed toward the low-lying ridge she had been told were the start of the Canelo Hills.

"Guess so," he said muttering under his breath.

"What'd you say?"

"Nothing."

She decided a bit of reassurance was in order. She didn't want Sandy pouting the whole day and ruining this for both of them. "I couldn't know of them if Sam hadn't told me, now could?"

He considered that. "Guess not."

"Well, then this would be all right with him, wouldn't it?" He had no answer for that. She pointed off to the west. "Look a jackrabbit. Are there many wild animals up here?"

He grew more animated as he told her about the small creatures that lived in the San Rafael Valley, the badgers, javelina, foxes, skunks, rabbits, bobcat, deer, coyotes, then cougar and bear in the hills.

"It's a beautiful place," she said. "Was your home much like this?"

"If you ever seen Kansas, you'd know better'n that. Leastwise the part I lived in. Nothing but trouble there."

"You said the other day that you had lost your whole family."

"Not much of a loss to me. I never knew my brothers. One killed in Civil War or so my uncle said. I was a lot younger. Not sure why my folks even had me They were too old. My birthin' was the end of my ma. Pa lived a few years more, just set around though from the little I remember, then cholera took him. For awhile my ma's brother took me in, but he was the mean kind. Kicked his own kids, me more than them. I ran away only to find out there's a lot like him—some worse."

"I'm sorry for all your losses."

Sandy smiled. "Folks say stuff like that, but it's the way life is, you know. Things happen. Ain't nobody's fault."

"Did Sam teach you that?"

His chuckle held no humor. "Sam's taught me a lot of things, but neither him nor me had to have someone else teach us that. We both know what it's like."

She stared at the grasslands. There was nothing to say to that. Sadness nearly overwhelmed her as she thought of the life they had known. And she had dared complain about her own problems. Her father had done his best. She thought of how he must feel now-- his losses piling up. Somehow she had to get the mails back to him.

"You help Sam a lot. Did you help him stow away the mail-bags from the last trip?" she asked with no attempt at subtlety.

He looked at her without understanding, and she wished she had never brought it up. Sandy hadn't been with them. She shouldn't have been trying to get information from him anyway. It wasn't fair to Sandy or Sam. She'd find those bags though, one way or another. They likely were on the ranch somewhere. "Never mind," she said and to change the subject. "Why haven't you ever thought of riding over to meet the Reimers?"

He looked uneasy again. "Why would I?"

"Might be young people your age living there."

He shook his head. "Don't need nobody. I got Sam and the gang." He pointed to a wisp of smoke on the air. "Looks like we're getting there."

She sighed and hoped her visit with the Reimers would go better than her attempted conversations with Sandy. As she and he rode into the ranch yard, dogs came out from under a log house and began barking, yipping at the heels of the horses. Good thing Belle wasn't skittish.

The door to the house opened and a heavy-set, red-haired woman stepped out onto a small porch. She held a rifle pointed at them.

"What you want?" she asked without a hint of friendliness.

"I'm your new neighbor." Abby tried to make her voice friendly, but didn't much like having the gun pointed at her. It didn't look like these people appreciated neighbors any more than Sam did.

"Living where?"

Abby pointed back toward Sam's ranch.

"What's your outfit called?" the woman asked, not lowering the gun.

Abby was not sure she'd ever heard and was grateful when Sandy said, "Circle R."

"I heard of it." The woman moved farther out where she could see them better. Abby could see now that although she was probably no more than in her mid-thirties, her hair was graying in front, her face lined. "Who are you then?"

"I'm Abby Ryker," Abby said, not attempting to move any closer until she saw that rifle lowered, and the dogs called off.

"What'd you want here?"

Abby forced a smile that she didn't feel. "I just wanted to get to know my new neighbors. I'm recently married."

The woman's eyes widened. "A bride?"

Abby smiled. "Of less than a month."

The rifle was lowered. "Well, that's right nice of you to come calling." She looked then at Sandy. "This your husband."

Abby laughed. "No, this is my husband's... adopted son. My husband was out working today. I thought it would be a good chance to meet you. He mentioned the Reimers lived this way, and I took the chance you might be home. I couldn't send a card ahead." She decided some humor might defuse the uneasiness.

The woman chortled, and children appeared out on the porch. "We don't stand much on formality out here. Come on; get down. I got some tea I been saving for something. Never knew what 'til now."

Abby could see Sandy was still uneasy, but he took the horses and tied them to the railing. The men of the Circle R had been isolated. Sam might not approve, but Abby meant to make her mark where she lived. Maybe there'd been a time when Sam had a reason not to know his neighbors, but the world was changing. He could change with it.

In the main room of the cabin, Abby was surprised to find well kept furniture, a nice oil lamp and a worn Oriental rug on the floor. One of the girls, who she guessed to be fourteen, told them to sit on the sofa, and her mama would be right back. Sandy took a straight chair, his eyes scanning the room, his manner showing his discomfort.

When the woman came into the room, she'd taken off her apron, attempted to tidy her hair, and had a tray with teapot and cups on it. "Sorry about out there. What must you think of me?

We don't get a whole lot of visitors though. Forgot I had manners." She smiled. "My name's Margaret Reimer."

Abby took the chipped china tea cup that was presented to her. "I am sorry if my visit is at a poor time."

"Not at all. Good time. Just my husband, Ralph, and our oldest boy rode to Harshaw for supplies. You know that man of yours been living there almost five years now, never come to see us. The time or two Ralph said he rode over that way, nobody was around."

Abby decided there was still a note of suspicion in the woman's voice and knew she was probing for information. She didn't need to see Sandy give her a telling glance to warn her to be careful in what she said.

"Sam's a hermit," she said, using the tone she'd heard women use to put their husbands down at the same time they were indicating affectionate tolerance. She decided a bit of a deception was in order. "Courting takes some time too." She smiled. "I expect you'll see more of him now."

"That's good to hear. Out in this country a woman misses other women. Need a chance to talk about those things men folk don't care much to hear. Glad your man found you and brought you to the valley. We need women and families out here."

Margaret introduced her children. Abby saw that the oldest girl, Cindy, at fourteen, had eyes only for Sandy. Likely young, good looking males were in as short of supply as women to share conversation. The other children were eleven year old Milly, George who was seven and Sarah three, watching Abby from behind her mother's skirts. Rafe, who was sixteen, was the one off with his father.

"Why don't you children shoo on out of here," Margaret suggested smiling at Cindy. "Take Sandy there and show him the creek."

Cindy smiled shyly at him, but Sandy remained seated. Clearly he was determined to protect Abby or at the least keep an eye on her.

"It will be fine," Abby insisted. "We just want some woman talk. You go with them."

He frowned but had no choice. "I'll be outside then," he said with unhidden reluctance. Abby watched as they walked across the yard. Cindy maneuvered the other children aside and was walking by the lanky Sandy.

"He seems like a nice lad," Margaret said, watching them also.

"He is. Your children are well-behaved."

"It's a struggle all the time to keep them that way. No school neither, but I do the best I can teaching them what I know."

"That must be difficult, but you appear to have done well."

Margaret nodded proudly. "Ralph helps. They can all read and do numbers. Ralph he's an educated man. Went all the way through upper school."

"A school would be nice out here."

"It's a ways off. Not many children this far out. Maybe you'll change that though," she said with a grin.

"Well, we did *just* get married."

Margaret poured tea into their cups. "Tell me about your man. Don't recall what you said his name was."

"Samuel."

"Know each other long?"

"Not a real long time."

"Ralph and I knew each other practically from the crib. Our families weren't friends or nothing, but we came from the same little town in Kansas."

"Did you by any chance know the Prescotts?" Abby asked. Margaret shook her head. "That was the name of Sandy's family," Abby explained. "He was orphaned quite young."

"Which is how your husband come to adopt him?"

"Yes."

"I feel bad to think we never went over to meet him and say howdy. How'd he happen to settle here in this valley?"

Abby hadn't thought of having to answer questions regarding Sam or the ranch. She could begin to see why Sam hadn't favored knowing neighbors. Not only was he not a conventional man, but she had not come to the ranch under the usual route. She thought on the topics Margaret had brought up and tried to decide which was safest to comment on. "You will have to come visit me also now."

"I will. When would be good?" Margaret asked, her eyes intent. Abby grinned. She liked this outspoken woman.

"Well... I am newly married. I need a little time to get my kitchen in order." She needed a lot more than a little. Like a crash course in cooking if she intended to entertain. "When Sam returns home from work, I will discuss this with him and send someone over with a date."

Margaret smiled. "I'll be looking forward to it. Real nice having a woman nearby." Little by little the two women discussed various topics, finding the places they had common ground. Abby had missed her times with Priscilla. When she saw Sandy was laughing and throwing a ball around with the younger boys, she stayed on for lunch, then helped Margaret start a pie for their evening meal. The day slipped by and before she realized it, the sun was heading downward. She had not intended to be out so long.

"Oh my," she said getting up from the kitchen table where they'd gone as Margaret had readied her evening meal, "I have to get home."

"Samuel the impatient sort?" Margaret asked with a grin.

Abby smiled back. "I haven't been married long enough to know, but I don't think he'll like coming home and finding me gone. Thank goodness I left a note."

She hurried outside and saw that Sandy and Cindy were sitting on the porch talking. Actually the girl was doing all the talking, but he was listening politely. Sandy looked up as she came to him. "We need to get home." She saw him look at the sky and realize what she had. He got the horses, tightened the saddle girths and readjusted the bridles, then brought them to Abby.

Abby looked at Margaret after she'd mounted. "I'm so glad to have met you, Margaret."

"Me too, Abby. Ride careful now, you hear." She waved as they rode off.

Heading toward home, they rode faster than they'd left, but it was still almost dark when they rode into the ranch yard. Sandy took the horses and Abby hurried into the darkened ranch house. For a moment she thought Sam hadn't returned but then saw him in the kitchen at the table, a whiskey bottle beside him on the table, no lamps lit.

She expected him to say something. When he didn't, she took the chimney from the lamp and lit it to better judge his mood. She saw the muscle in his jaw twitch, knew his teeth were clenched, his muscles taut despite whatever whiskey he'd consumed.

"I am sorry I wasn't here to fix dinner," she said as she realized he was far more upset than she'd expected.

"Why did you come back?"

"I know I'm late, but--"

"Late?" He laughed, no humor in the sound.

"I suppose you're mad because I visited the neighbors." She sat at the table across from him.

"Visited the neighbors?" he asked, his voice sounding confused. She looked then for the note and saw he'd crumbled it into a ball.

"You read the note. I didn't want you to worry."

"What have the neighbors got to do with it?"

"Sam, didn't you even read my note?"

"Sure."

"I know you didn't want me to visit the Reimers, but I didn't think you'd be this upset. Are you drunk?"

He swallowed and closed his eyes, then looked at her. "You went to the Reimers?" he repeated.

"I thought you said you read the note."

The expression in his eyes told her everything. "You didn't read it, did you?"

He shook his head, looking away.

"Are you drunk, Sam?" She looked pointedly at the whiskey bottle.

"Nope, haven't had a drink yet, but I was thinking hard on it."

"Do you drink often?"

"Sometimes. When the mood hits."

"And it was hitting now. Why?"

"Sometimes a man needs a good drunk."

"And one of those times is when your wife goes off to the neighbors?"

"I thought you left."

"If you hadn't just crumpled up my note in a fit of anger, you'd have known I didn't."

"It wasn't that."

"It wasn't? Then what was it?" She waited, thinking he'd offer some explanation, but she saw he wasn't going to. With a sudden insight she knew why he hadn't read it. "You couldn't read it, could you?"

He said nothing.

"It's why you had no interest in the books, isn't it?"

His jaw was clenched. "I can read some."

"What?"

"My name."

"Lord, I... I'm sorry. I didn't know."

"Didn't want you to. You're an educated woman."

"Not being able to read is nothing to be ashamed of."

His laugh was bitter. "It isn't?"

"Of course, not. I guess you never had schooling given how you grew up. That makes sense to me. You know, you could still learn, Sam."

He gave a snort of derision.

She decided pushing this was not a wise thing. "We need to get something to eat."

"You really went to the Reimers?"

"Yes, I did."

"Why?"

"I told you I wanted to meet our neighbors. I felt like it'd be a good thing to do for us. Having friends is a good thing, Sam."

"I don't need friends."

"It's not a matter of need. It's just nice to know your neighbors."

"God, you are green, Abby. I keep thinking I have seen it all with you, and you surprise me again."

She knew that was no compliment, and it irritated her to have him keep saying how she was so unknowing of the ways of the world. True, she had not lived out on her own as he had, but she knew something about people "People need people, Sam. It's about community. You then have someone you can count on."

"You count on anyone but yourself, and you'll be dead."

"So you keep people from getting too close?"

"It works best."

"And where does that leave me?"

His smile was reluctant. "I'm trying to figure that out."

There was no answer to that. She managed a smile of her own. "I'm hungry. How about you?" She opened the cupboard and looked around for what might be possible.

"Not much."

She gave a little laugh. "Well, I am starved." She found some biscuits and handed Sam one. "I should have left Margaret's earlier. Time got away from me."

"You liked her?"

"Yes, I did. She's a plain spoken woman. I told her we'd have them to dinner some evening."

He gave her a look. "Abby, you're not using your head. You and I are not the usual couple here. I am not the usual ranch owner in these parts."

"Well, I certainly know how it's been, Sam but..."

"If we go around other people, they're going to figure something is wrong at the Circle R. From there it won't take long to bring a hanging rope."

She wasn't ready to let this go even though she felt a surge of fear at the idea of Sam at the end of a rope. "Haven't you thought of being a real rancher someday, Sam?" She saw by the expression on his face that this was something he wasn't open to discussing. "Things change. For instance, you could learn to read if you wanted."

"I've tried. I'm illiterate."

"You're not or you wouldn't even know a word like that."

"I took care to learn that one. It had special meaning to me."

"You can learn to read, Sam. I know I can teach you. You couldn't read that note, but sometime it could be something that matters even more."

He appeared equal parts embarrassed and exasperated. "Don't you think I've tried. I've looked at books, tried to figure them out. I can't."

"Because everybody needs somebody to help them, to read to them, to show them words. You were too proud to ask for that help, weren't you? The question now is are you still?"

"What do you mean?" He didn't like the idea of her teaching him to read. It seemed to put him even further beneath her than he already knew he was. He wanted to be the one to teach her things, not the other way around. As he watched her stubborn expression, he thought of all the things he wanted to show her. But tonight was not the night. He was as tired as she was.

"I can teach you to read. Are you too proud to let me?" she asked nailing it on the head.

"It's not pride."

"Isn't it?"

He stared at her, knowing she was right. It was pride. He swallowed a chunk of it. "I could try, I guess."

CHAPTER 14

For Abigail, the days took on a soothing rhythm. She and Sam were busy with their separate activities during the day. He continued the gathering of the cattle, tallying his own, separating out the neighbors' stock, and finally branding his calves as he moved the herds onto new sections. Two hundred cattle might not be much for this region, but when they'd been running wild, it took long days to get the work done.

She spent her time learning the ways of keeping a home, figuring out a cookbook, improving her cooking, beginning to work up a garden space. The concerns she felt for her father, for returning the stolen deeds were beyond her ability to change for the time being. She hoped at some point to put together the divergent parts of her life, to let her father know she was safe, to even return the mails which she felt certain Sam had somewhere, but for now she couldn't do any of that and so she settled for enjoying her life.

In the evenings, she read to Sam, sitting beside him on the sofa, running her finger along the lines as she said the words. She enjoyed the reading and he seemed to also-- once he got past the idea it was something a woman did for a child.

She began with a book she thought he would like, *Twenty Thousand Leagues Under the Sea* by Jules Verne. And waited until she felt the time was right to go onto the next stage. One evening after dinner and the regular chapter from the Verne book, she brought out the primer she'd found among the loft books. She opened it, then looked into his eyes and saw the resistance she had expected. "You did say you wanted to learn," she said.

Those cobalt blue eyes darkened. "I do," he said, moving closer to her and looking down at the child's book, then up at her. "How about you?"

"I already know how to read, but this is an excellent introduction for you."

"You know how to read, but do you know what you do to me when you're sitting close like you are?" he asked, running his finger down her wrist to the tip of her finger. "Do you know how much I want to take this out of your hair?" He unfastened the silver clip he'd bought her, letting her hair fall free, before running his fingers through it, loosening it even further.

"This is an A," she said pointing to the letter.

He looked down at it. "A," he said seriously, then turned his attentions to her ear, his mouth taking away all her awareness of the A.

"A is a vowel," she said, her voice husky with sensual awareness. "They can have different sounds." She swallowed as she felt his lips tease along her jaw, dropping down to the hollow of her neck.

"And vowels are important?" he asked as he began to kiss her skin.

"Very." She lifted her chin to allow him fuller access to her neck before she remembered she was supposed to be teaching him to read. "You're not trying"

"Wrong. I am definitely trying." His hand firmly against her back, he pulled her against him.

"Reckon I'm interrupting," Ollie said from the parlor door,

causing Abby to jump away and Sam to curse under his breath. "The Reimer boy is out here, got something for you."

Sam rose from the sofa and looked at Abby regretfully. "You won't move, will you?"

She tried to catch her breath. Her face was flushed, which embarrassed her with Ollie looking on with such interest. "Of course not," she managed, then Sam was gone.

It seemed she'd barely reorganized her thoughts, with a firm resolution of doing their lessons at the kitchen table, when he had returned with a letter. "From the boy's mama. He's talking to Sandy but seems expects you to have an answer for him before he leaves."

Abby looked up at him, trying to see whether Sam was irritated with the arrival of the letter. His face, as usual when he wanted it that way, told her nothing. She opened the letter and read aloud.

"Mrs. Ryker. I was pleased to meet you and know there is another woman living so close. On Saturday I am having a party at our home for Mr. Reimer's birthday. We would like you, Mr. Ryker and Sandy to join us. Please no gifts, need bring no food. There'll be plenty. We're hoping to see you then. Respectfully, Margaret Reimer."

She looked up to see Sam staring at her, his expression anything but pleased.

"We don't have to go."

"But you want to." He walked to the window, leaned his shoulder against wooden trim, arms folded over his chest, and stared out.

"What's wrong?" She came up beside him, putting her arm around him.

"Nothing." She could feel the tension in every muscle.

"Tell me the truth."

"A birthday party? I can't go to a birthday party. I've never gone to anything like that."

"The Reimers are just ordinary folks, Sam. It won't be anything elaborate."

When he didn't respond, she shifted a little so she was behind him, then put both arms around him, drawing herself flat against his back. When he moved as though uneasy at having her in such a controlling position, she tightened her clasp, pressing firmly against him. She laid her head against his back, feeling the muscles contract under her cheek.

"What are you doing?" he asked. She felt him swallow, felt the strength of his body's reaction to her holding him this way.

"I'm holding you. Hasn't anyone held you like this before?"

"Maybe. Maybe not." She heard the smile in his voice. She felt heady with the energy flowing through her body. She hadn't been immune to Sam's touch for the last days, to the way he'd brush against her, his light kisses, nothing like the ones she remembered, the ones he'd given her that reached deep within and drew out emotions she had never imagined herself capable of feeling. The little kisses he'd been teasing her with were teases. She wanted more from him. She just wasn't sure how much.

She shifted her hands so they stroked up his chest, felt the hard muscles of his chest under her fingers, moving further up until she was at the collar of his shirt. She felt a desire to explore his body and felt for a button and slipped it from its hole.

"You're playing with fire," he muttered.

"Am I?"

"The boy's waiting for an answer."

"Is he?"

"Might come in sudden like."

"He's enjoying time with Sandy." She undid another button. Now she could touch his skin. She liked that. She undid the next button, continuing until she'd unfastened his shirt to the belt. It seemed like a good idea then to pull the shirt loose. She followed her impulse.

"Abby." She felt his muscles stiffen as she ran her fingers up his chest, now feeling directly the satiny skin overlaying iron hard muscle. She liked feeling the surge of the muscles as she moved down to tease one of his nipples. Her own body was reacting to touching him this way. She felt a heat growing in her loins; her breasts tingling. She wanted something. Something more.

"You trying to bribe me?" he asked huskily.

She had to stop and think what he meant, as her senses had been lit on fire just at touching him. She grinned then. "Would it work?"

"It might." He would have shifted then, would have turned in her arms, but she tightened her hold.

"What do you want?" he asked.

"Just to touch you," she whispered as she continued her exploring, losing herself in the feeling of his skin, the muscles that moved under her fingers, the sense of power as she felt him react to her caresses. She'd never known anything like this, never dreamed a woman could receive such pleasure from touching, but there it was.

He sucked in a breath as she pulled his shirt off his shoulders. She kissed his bare back. God, his body was so rawly masculine. Had anything ever been created so perfectly? She wanted to touch him everywhere. Her body grew hotter with the thoughts.

"You want to go to the party that bad?" he asked moving away from her and coldly breaking the spell.

"What do you mean?" She dropped her arms to her side.

"All that. Was it to get what you want?"

"And what do I want?"

"To go to that party, to have me go there too."

"You don't think very highly of me, Sam, do you?" She had to think about it. Had she been trying to bribe him? No, it wasn't that. Maybe it had been a justification to begin, but she had soon forgotten anything but touching. She decided to be honest. "It was an excuse. Sorry if you took it otherwise. If you don't want to go, it's all right. I will write her a reason for why we can't."

"An excuse?" He would pick up on the one part of what she had said that she'd rather he hadn't.

"I wanted to do what I did but not to make you do something else."

She could see him considering what she had said. "You want to go. I can see it. It won't hurt me. Just an afternoon, right?"

She felt unsure what to do or say. She remembered then her original belief that if she could get Sam to have a more normal life, he would not risk his life going back to Mexico. She felt a tinge of guilt at her knowledge. Yes, she was trying to manipulate him as he feared. But her motives weren't what he was thinking. "Seriously if you'd rather not, it's all right."

"I said we'd go."

"All right then, I'll write a note."

She didn't want this time with him to end, but when she looked at the expression on his face, she felt something was wrong. Did he still believe she had touched him as a bribe? She was torn as to the right way to handle this. She saw now was not the time to discuss it further. The right thing was to go to the party. Then Sam would meet his neighbors; begin to see a normal life was possible. She stopped short of thinking all the rest of what a normal life would mean for her with Sam. About what it might mean to her if they did finally consummate their marriage.

More and more she wanted that even as she knew she could not stay out here forever. This was just a moment out of her life, an interlude, but she would take something with her when she left-- a spinster's memory of a man's touch. She just had to get up her courage to let him show her the rest of what he could. Let him teach her about the flesh as she intended to teach him about words.

She watched as he buttoned his shirt. "The boys are on the kitchen porch. Paper's in that desk over there," he said striding from the room.

Abby penned a quick note to Margaret accepting the invitation, all the time her mind on the man she so little understood. Would she ever? Sealing the sheet into an envelope, she walked out onto the porch where Margaret's oldest son, Rafe, was chatting with Sandy.

Rafe looked at Abby as she handed him the envelope, then back to Sandy. "You be sure and come too," he said, grinning. "Cindy would be right disappointed if you didn't."

Sandy grunted, but Abby said, "He'll be there. You tell her."

"I can't go. It wouldn't be right," Sandy said after Rafe had ridden off.

"You were invited and besides Sam needs you to go."

He looked at her with confusion in his eyes. "Sam? Why does Sam need me to go?"

"Because he's going to hate this as much as you are, but it'll be good for both of you. You need to meet people."

"We meet people." His tone was defensive.

"Correction. Ordinary people. People who aren't going to rob you, shoot at you, or want to buy stolen cows from you. Friends. Good folks."

He gave her a doubting look. "Good folks don't want people like Sam and me around."

"Sam has taught you a lot of important and good truths, Sandy, but that is not one of them. Good people don't know you, and you're not giving them a chance to know you."

"If they knew us, they'd take a bullwhip to us. Maybe a gun," Sandy said, unsmiling and obviously believing every word he'd said.

"You met some bad people along the way, Sandy. There are also good people. You need to meet them too."

"Some things don't change," Sam said. She realized then that he had been listening to her conversation with Sandy as he was sitting at the opposite end of the porch on the rail in the darkness.

"And some do."

"Who I am isn't going to."

"Maybe you don't know who you are."

"And you do?"

"Maybe so."

He gave her a look she felt clear to her toes. That steely eyed expression had probably stopped a lot of people, but it wouldn't her. She knew it could be different for Sam and Sandy both. If she couldn't stay with him, couldn't really make her life at this ranch, she at least wanted to know he was living a good life. She would do all she knew to make that reality.

She looked at Sandy and saw his troubled expression. "You will have a good time with the Reimers. Both of you." She knew what they believed, but she would prove them wrong. She would start at the party.

～

Abby learned Sam owned a buckboard for the first time when he brought it out Saturday morning to get it cleaned and ready for the drive to the party. He'd said little to her, just gone about his work, not letting her continue reading lessons as he came in too late each night for that to be possible.

For the first time since she arrived at the ranch, she wished for a dress; but her riding skirt and blouse were presentable and clean. Her figure had always been trim, but at the Circle R, she'd worked more and used muscles in a different way, lending litheness to the lines of her body that, although not the hourglass figure popular with the magazines, at least Sam seemed to like, if that glint in his eye when he looked at her meant anything.

Knowing he liked it that way, she'd let her dark hair fall loose down her back, clipping it to her neck with the silver buckle he'd given her. She supposed as she studied her reflection in the mirror, she didn't exactly fit the picture of a lady going to a party, but she would act it.

When she walked out onto the porch, Sam and Sandy were standing near the buckboard, both wearing white shirts and dark pants. She didn't like seeing a cigarette dangling from Sam's lips, the dark expression in his eyes, nor was she pleased to see he had his gun belted to his hips. They were going to a party; wouldn't the rifle in the scabbard alongside his seat be sufficient protection?

Sam threw his cigarette into the dust and ground it out with his boot, then looked up at her. "You are beautiful," he said as she walked up to him, Sandy echoed his compliment.

"You too," she said, and then smiled at Sandy. "Both of you."

She glanced pointedly at Sam's gun, but he ignored her. "You ready?" When she nodded, he lifted her onto the front seat of the buckboard. Sandy stepped into the back. When Sam was beside her, he flicked the reins, and they headed out of the ranch yard, Sam's men watching from the bunkhouse as they left.

"I suppose they don't approve of this," Abby said.

"I didn't ask," Sam said.

"But if you had, you know what they'd have said."

Sam gave her a teasing smile. "If I starting asking, I could forget telling."

"One sign of weakness and it's all over, is that it?" She leaned a little closer to him before she pulled back remembering her irritation at the cigarette and gun.

"More or less." He cast a sidewise glance and a knowing smirk. "It works that way with horses too."

She knew he also thought it was true with women, but she'd not give him the chance to say it. "I didn't know you had a buckboard," she said, changing the subject.

"It was on the place. Grey liked nice things. I don't have much use for it."

"If you had a family, you'd have more use," she said.

"Not likely to be something I have to worry about... as things stand," he retorted.

They rode in silence for several miles. "If you're determined to have a miserable time today, you will," she said, knowing she was being argumentative.

"It won't matter what I intend. It's what will happen."

"How can you say that?"

He shrugged. "Based on experience."

"Experience?"

"I wasn't born full grown," he said, as though she might not have known that. "I've had things happen."

"Like what?"

He kept his eyes on the narrow track on front of them. "It doesn't matter. I'm going. You want this. Maybe I'm wrong."

"You will tell me tonight what you mean by all those mysterious comments."

"I will?" he asked, raising his eyebrows and giving her a slanted look.

She smiled confidently. "You will."

Sandy leaned forward. "Sounds like she means business, Sam. Maybe you better say give now."

Sam's smile was sardonic. "Or maybe I shouldn't."

To Sam's increasing unease, the Reimer ranch yard was filled with buggies and horses tied to posts. A sizeable patch of pasture had been freshly mown and was where the gathering was taking place with buckboards and horses down toward the creek. He looked over at Abby and saw the surprise on her face. "I never imagined so many around here," she said by way of apology.

He had no way of knowing from where these people had come, who they might be. Someone could know him from some of his deals. "If anyone recognizes me and this turns ugly, you never knew."

"What do you mean?" she asked, glancing uneasily at his gun. Always his innocent Abby. He brought the buckboard to a smooth stop, jumped down, and tied the reins to the brake. He reached up to assist his lady to the ground, then meeting her gaze, he reached down, untied and then unbuckled his gun belt, putting it into the box under the seat and latching it.

He saw the fear and uncertainty in her face. She obviously didn't like him having a gun. Looks like she wasn't so sure about him not wearing it. But she had been right. He saw it clearly. A gun wouldn't be acceptable among these small farmers and ranchers.

"We can leave right now," she said before Margaret Reimer walked up and gave her a hug.

"I'm so glad you could all come. Cindy's making ice cream. Maybe you could help her, Sandy."

Sandy grimaced and looked at Sam for escape from the directive, but Sam nodded to him. "Go on, have fun." He knew he wouldn't, but he could hope otherwise for Sandy.

Abby put her hand on Sam's elbow. "Margaret, this is my husband Samuel Ryker. Sam, this is Margaret Reimer."

Before they could say more than hello, a burly man walked up to them, a smile on his face. "And I'm Ralph Reimer."

When the two men had shook hands, Reimer chuckled. "Took getting married to get you over here, huh, Ryker?" Sam stared blankly at him, and Reimer laughed more loudly. "Hey, that's how marriage works, son." Reimer slapped his shoulder with enough force to require Sam to brace himself. "It's that way with the best of them. Bring a woman into a man's life, and he finds community and civilization. Without a woman, he runs like a wolf."

Sam looked at him more closely to see if there was a hidden meaning in his statement. He saw nothing but friendliness.

"Well, come on," Reimer said, taking a hold of Sam's arm. "You leave the ladies to their talk and I'll introduce you to your neighbors."

With that, Sam was urged away from her with Ralph Reimer taking him to the men. Abby felt a moment of panic. Would he be all right? She had forgotten how such affairs tended to break into male, female or child groups. She could only hope for the best and smiled at Margaret as she began propelling her toward the cabin.

"My goodness gracious, that man of yours is a handsome devil. I swear I ain't seen such a likely looking man in all my born days," she said with a girlish gleam.

Since Abby didn't think Margaret expected a reply, she didn't attempt to offer one. Before they could get to the cabin, a tall, lean man approached, blocking their way. "And who is this?" he asked Margaret, while looking steadily at Abby.

"Now, don't go looking like that," Margaret said with a chuckle, "she's married."

The man looked down at Abby's left hand. "No ring on it."

"It doesn't take a ring to make a marriage," she retorted well aware of what it did take and what was missing from hers.

"I'd put a ring on it if it was me."

"My husband and I haven't been married long."

"Where had you been hiding, beauty, that I might've missed out?"

She felt herself blush, embarrassed at being around such an assertive man. Where she had come from, men were more cautious with their compliments at least until they had met the lady. The behavior left her speechless.

Nothing stopped him as he went on. "Alas I barely missed my chance once again." The man put his hand over his heart. He sighed loudly. "It's the story of my life. Introduce us anyway," he ordered Margaret, his tone brooking no chance of disobedience.

"Abby this is Lieutenant Mark Gardiner, Ralph's younger cousin. He's stationed at Fort Huachuca. Mark, this is Abby Ryker."

The young man smiled broadly. "It's a pleasure, Ma'am. I only wish we'd met sooner. Like before you were whisked off into the bonds of matrimony." He smiled. "Tell me where they grow ladies like you as I will definitely find myself there on my next leave."

She managed to laugh at his joke. He followed them into the

cabin, then back out as they carried food to the large tables spread under cottonwood trees. "Seriously, how long have you been married?" he asked Abby when she found herself cornered by him yet again.

"Less than a month."

He groaned loudly. "Where is the lucky dog?"

Abby pointed out Sam, who she saw was watching them, his eyes dark and unreadable at the distance. His lips were set. He looked... No, he couldn't be jealous. He couldn't think she was flirting with the young lieutenant. To make sure he didn't, she said, "Come and meet my husband."

Moments later she was introducing Lieutenant Gardiner to Sam. The lieutenant smiled. "Do I know you?"

"It's possible. I've lived here awhile," Sam said. He balanced his weight on his heels; his arms folded over his chest. If Abby hadn't known him better, hadn't seen the tension in his muscles, she'd have thought he was relaxed and having fun.

"I usually don't forget a face. You live down toward the border, I hear."

Sam nodded, reaching for the makings and rolling a cigarette before he gave Abby an apologetic smile. Lighting it, he inhaled deeply, before letting the smoke out, blowing it away from the two of them.

"How long have you been in the Army, Lieutenant?" Abby asked, wishing Sam would be friendlier.

"Four years. I'm from Michigan originally."

"Is it a coincidence you came to be so near your family?"

"Yes, ma'am. You don't tell the army where to go." He grinned.

"How do you like this country?" She was seeking to find something polite and innocent to keep a conversation going that was dwindling off.

"Hard land, very unforgiving."

"Geronimo is the unforgiving one," Sam said.

"Do you feel the Apache are still a danger out here?" Abby asked, having forgotten about the Indian threat.

"We have Geronimo on the run," the lieutenant assured her.

Sam snorted. "The good old military, always take care of everything, don't they?"

"I take it you, sir, do not think highly of the military."

"I don't think of them period."

Abby gave him an exasperated look.

"From where do you hail, Ma'am?" the lieutenant asked.

"I've lived many places. My father and I moved a lot; now I live on the Circle R."

"With your husband, of course," Gardiner said, giving Sam an enigmatic smile.

"Of course."

Ralph Reimer came to join them, a cup of some liquid in his hand. "Sam owns one of the biggest spreads around here, but runs the least cattle."

"That's interesting," the lieutenant said. "Why is that, Mr. Ryker?"

"You just gave one reason. Geronimo. I've been away a lot, not about to leave a lot of cattle around to be rounded up by anyone."

Gardiner smiled. "Busy off courting."

"I did have to leave the ranch to get a wife." Sam's smile was ironic.

"With us here now though, we can increase the herd, can't we, dear?" Abby smiled recognizing how little Sam appreciated her addition to the conversation by the stormy look in those intense blue eyes.

"You in the market for cows?" Reimer asked.

Sam shook his head. "I'll build up what I have," he said, drawing on the cigarette again.

"Well, I gotta say, you're not a man to build up your herd at the expense of others. You always send ours back."

"I try so long as it's not a maverick."

"Maverick?" Abby asked.

"Calf what lost its ma. No way to identify who it was," Reimer explained as he lit a cigar and took a satisfied draw. "We all get a few of those."

"Rustlers claim more," Sam said with a smile that only Abby recognized for what it was.

"Well you been a good neighbor to me. I see how you're operating and approve. Slow but sure. Build up good stock. Take care of your grass. Doesn't leave a lot of gewgaws for the ladies though," he added thereby reminding Abby she wasn't exactly dressed like the other women present. It didn't bother her unless it humiliated Sam in some way. She actually felt more free in the leather skirt and blouse than she ever remembered and smiled gratefully at Sam as the one who had given her that freedom.

Reimer chuckled. "Don't look like she begrudges you none, seeing that look on her face just now."

Before Sam had to respond to that, several other men had joined the conversation with suggestions on preferable ways to build up herds. Uneasy with being the only female, Abby excused herself to help Margaret.

CHAPTER 15

Abby had thought only Sam heard, but the lieutenant smiled and said he'd come with her. She didn't take the risk of looking to see how Sam took that, but for the rest of the afternoon, she had the lieutenant at her heels. Since he knew she was married, she hardly understood why he was following her, and finally said as much.

"You shouldn't feel you have to entertain an old married lady," Abby said. "There are several young women here, who I'm sure would appreciate your time."

"As you don't," Gardiner said with a grin.

"It's not that," she said trying to be polite.

"You underestimate the value of your company. Not many women or men can intelligently discuss Lew Wallace's book about the conquering of Mexico."

She wished she'd never begun to discuss literature because obviously Mark Gardiner was an avid reader and an equally avid conversationalist about books. In another setting, she might have enjoyed such a conversation but not with Sam glowering at her from a distance.

Able to stand it no longer, Abby asked the lieutenant if he

could get her a glass of lemonade, and as soon as he was gone on his mission, she went to Sam. He was leaning one broad shoulder against a cottonwood tree, his eyes on her as she walked up.

"You're not having fun," she said as she stopped in front of him. The two other men still discussing cattle were paying no attention to her arrival.

"It's my fault. Remember," he said through his teeth.

She remembered her own curt warning as they'd left the ranch. She wished she hadn't said that. "Do you want to leave now?"

"No."

"Why not?"

"You're having fun. So is Sandy. First time I've seen him with a gang of kids his own age. He looks happy."

"But you're not."

He shrugged and looked over her head. "Your lieutenant is looking for you."

"He's not my lieutenant." She felt her own temper rising.

"He's hanging on you like he'd like to change that. Young, clean-looking fellow like that, you could do worse."

"I have a husband," she hissed.

"In name only," he responded almost under his breath.

"Does my husband want to be more than that?"

"It wasn't me set up the rules."

"And I did?"

He scowled, then looked over her head. "Here your suitor comes."

Maybe it was time to change the rules. Instead of turning toward the footsteps she heard approaching, she leaned into her handsome husband, saw his eyes widen with surprise as she put one arm around his waist, while the other reached up and with no gentle grasp pulled down his head.

With a sense of satisfaction, not caring what anyone thought, she had something to prove to everyone at this party and to Sam most of all. She smiled widely, brought his lips closer to hers, then reached up and pressed hers against his mouth. His mouth was wide with surprise and before she could think more on it, she delved her tongue into its soft, wet warmth, as he had hers so long ago. She felt the impact through her whole body. He didn't put his arms around her, but his lips moved, his tongue mated with hers and when she stepped back, they were both breathing heavily. Her breasts felt heavy, her whole body on fire.

"What was that for?" he whispered.

"Did there have to be a reason?" With that, she spun on her heels and walked past the lieutenant on her way to find Margaret.

The lieutenant looked after her, then to Sam with an abashed smile. He held out a glass of lemonade. "Want one?"

The ride home in the buckboard after dark was filled mostly with Sandy's talk of the friends he'd talked to, the enjoyment he'd had, and his gratitude that Abby had insisted he come. Sam said little, and Abby wondered more than once what he was thinking, but if he was thinking anything, he didn't share it.

At the house, Abby went in while Sandy and Sam unhitched the buckboard. It was fifteen minutes later when he walked into the kitchen.

"Husbands and wives usually discuss an evening afterward," Abby said coming out of the darkness and surprising him sufficiently that for once his face showed it.

"Is the evening over?" He grinned wickedly as he put his arms around her.

"You tell me."

His smile was sensual and promising, his kiss equally so. Now that she knew what she wanted, she opened her mouth for his kiss, felt him exploring her warmth. She leaned more heavily into him, felt her breasts against his chest. She needed him throughout her whole body, all the way down to her toes.

His hands moved over her, first down her back, to her buttocks, cupping them, pulling her hard against him. She felt his hardness, knew what it meant. One of his hands slipped around front to cup her breast. She felt the nipple pucker and wanted him to do more. She sucked in a breath, wanting that touch, wanting it against her bare skin. But was this all she wanted? All she could have? She had to know.

"Did you have as bad a time at the Reimers' as you expected?" she forced herself to ask when all she really wanted was for those hands to keep exploring her body.

"It had its moments," he said, nuzzling her neck. He needed a shave as usual at the end of the day. The bristle against her skin added to her excitement. She sighed.

"Like with Lieutenant Gardiner?"

She pushed off his hat as she ran her hands through his hair.

He looked ruefully down at the hat on the floor. "You know how much that Stetson cost?"

She heard the smile in his voice. "I'm sorry," she said. "Can I find any way to make it up to your hat?"

"I doubt it."

"I could pick it up and put it properly on its rack."

He shook his head. "Not a good idea because to do that, I'd have to let you go, and I don't want to do that."

She smiled, taking his hand into hers and nipping one finger. "You really had a good time?"

"It had its moments," he repeated, his eyes teasing.

"Couldn't you see yourself living like that--like Ralph Reimer for instance?"

"Maybe for some men that's all right, but for others it won't work."

"And which ones are you?"

"Abby, quit trying to change what is. Life is how it is. Sometimes it's too late to change."

"You can't believe it is for you. You are a young man. You can change what you want. You have to know you cannot go on as you are."

"For awhile."

"And then what?"

"There are no guarantees in life."

She felt the passion draining from her body. "Why did you marry me, Sam? What did you want?"

"What do you think?"

"If it had been just sex, you'd have taken me the first night. You could have. I couldn't have stopped you."

"I don't rape women."

"We both know it wouldn't have been rape, not then or now."

"I did want you. Still do, but not if the terms are my pretending something I know isn't so. I am who I am. Is that good enough for you or not?"

"Are you saying you might want a life with me? A forever kind of life?"

"If I did, would it change anything?"

She couldn't answer that. She had never thought she'd stay with Sam, never imagined a real life here. Or had she? "Well, whatever I want," she said, "it wouldn't be for much of a life if you go riding off all the time to rustle other men's cattle. Someday you will get shot or caught and then what?"

"I could go riding out in the hills here and have my horse fall and break my neck."

"It's not the same."

"Isn't it?"

She felt angry and disappointed. She had hoped so much that things would change. She had told herself this was all for the moment. In her heart she had known from the beginning, from the time she had seen him in Tucson. She wanted more than she could ever have. It wasn't to be. He didn't want what she did. She felt so disappointed that tears welled up. She would not cry in front of him. She also couldn't risk making a baby with a man who wouldn't want forever with her. She wouldn't leave herself a child to raise alone.

"Good night, Sam."

She wished he would say something to stop her, would promise her things that could make it work, but he didn't. He just let her go.

～

The next morning was unnaturally quiet as Abby realized neither she nor Sam had anything to say to each other. They were tiptoeing around the things they should have said, perhaps out of fear that once said the words would be impossible to take back.

He was gone for half the day. When he returned, it was with a horned cow with a good sized udder on a line tied to his saddle and a crate of squawking chickens over the pack horse. Abby ran outside to see the acquisitions, suddenly encouraged again. He had wanted to please her. He wouldn't have gotten the cow if he hadn't wanted their ranch to become their home. She had to believe that.

He stepped down from the saddle, his gaze steady on her.

She smiled up at him. "You remembered," she said, throwing her arms around him, receiving his hug with gratitude. They'd had their spat, maybe now they could make up. She knew just how she wanted to make up.

"Kind of an odd present for a woman," he said, "but you did say you wanted them."

"Where did you get them?"

"I asked Reimer yesterday. He remembered a widow woman living near Harshaw that said she was getting rid of some. I didn't say anything because I didn't know if somebody else'd already bought them."

She smiled more broadly. "What's the cow's name?"

The other men had come to see what Sam had brought home. There were a few guffaws as he said, "Tildy, but I expect you can call her whatever you want."

"I love her." She looked at the pretty face and then had a doubt. "Will those horns uh be dangerous?"

"Lady said not. She's got a nice personality and they make it handy to hold onto." He grinned.

She looked at the full udder and thought of all the things that could be made with fresh milk-- butter, cream for coffee, ice cream. She only hoped Ollie knew how. Of course, now that she'd found recipe books, maybe she could figure it out for herself.

"You know how to milk her?" Sam asked, skepticism in his voice.

She nodded toward the pertinent end. "Well, I've never milked one before, but... I mean that is the right end, isn't it?"

Sam smiled again and looked toward the hands who'd gathered to watch the proceedings. "Any you boys know how to milk a cow?"

No one volunteered.

"How about you, Ollie?" Abby asked, looking at the skinny old man who was nearly holding his nose with disdain. "You know so much, surely you've milked a cow."

He shook his head. "Cowboys don't milk cows," he retorted. "They rope them."

"But milk would mean butter... sauces... ice cream."

Ollie stared more uncertainly at the brown and white cow, now torn between dignity and the promise of eating riches. "Reckon it could be figured out," he said finally.

"I've seen it done," Sandy offered, the only other wrangler to risk remaining.

Sam shook his head. "It'll take patching a few places, but you can keep her in the little pasture behind the barn, the one that has the creek running through it. Milk her in the barn."

"Is there a stanchion or something like that?" Abby asked, thinking vaguely such a thing would be required.

"Not too hard to rig one up."

"You brought me chickens too," she said, walking over to look at the crate in which at least ten hens and a rooster complained. "What kind are they?"

Sam looked at her as though she'd lost her mind. "How would I know? They're chickens."

Ollie looked in the crate. "Barred Rocks and Rhode Island Reds I'd say. Look to be young enough to lay good too, but it's going to take some doing to keep the critters around here from having chicken dinner before we get a single egg."

"What would bother them?" Abby asked.

"Skunks, badgers, weasels, foxes, you name it and they'd like a good chicken dinner."

"That means I have to bring them in at night." There was some chortling at that from the men.

Sam headed for the barn.

"Where are you going?" Abby called after him, afraid he was going to dump this problem in her lap.

"I'm going to build a pen, some perches, and a few laying boxes," he said. He nodded toward Sandy and Ollie. "One of you stay to help her with the cow." When both started after him, Sam stopped them. "Ollie, you help Abby. Sandy, you come with me."

Several hours later, Abby and Ollie had worked up a considerable sweat, but they had rigged up a stanchion, found a bucket and box to sit on. They had put Tildy out in the small pasture, which Joe had secured. The rope was still around her neck so that until she got used to being milked, she would be easy to catch.

All day Abby had heard hammering coming from the lower barn, but she'd not gone down to see how the work was coming. She was happy, pleased Sam had remembered what she had asked, that he was actually building a chicken coop. Her love for him was overwhelming her common sense. She knew she should keep her distance, that nothing had changed, but her heart wasn't listening. Yes, he was a man who wore a gun as other men wore a watch fob, but that too could change. Anything was possible.

It was nearly dark when Abby and Ollie led Tildy into the barn and tied her to the stanchion. The horns had complicated it but not to the point of stopping progress. The moment of truth was upon her. The cow's udder was so full it looked ready to pop. They couldn't delay. Abby had gathered some tall meadow grass to feed her while she was milked, hoping that would make her easier to handle.

The cow began chomping on the grass and waited; after all, she was the more experienced of the three. Unfortunately, all too soon, she would discover, she was the only experienced of the three.

Abby turned around and saw Sam standing against the barn door, one shoulder propped against it. He didn't say a word; his smile said it all. He was going to enjoy this, but he wasn't going to help. Sandy stood a few feet behind him, grinning widely.

Abby took a deep breath and moved the box to where she could reach the udder, trying to remember Ollie's instructions as to the proper hand motion to make milk come out. Stroke, squeeze... or was it squeeze stroke. Oh well, she'd learn by doing.

As soon as Tildy realized she was being handled by a rank amateur, which was the moment Abby touched her udder, the cow moved sideways, taking her attachments beyond Abby's reach. "We need to blockade her," Abby said to Ollie.

He went to stand on the opposite side and edged the cow toward Abby. For a moment, Abby thought she was going to go too far, but she stopped short of stepping on Abby's boots. She looked up grateful to see Sam had put his own weight into the effort of holding her in line.

"Did you warm up your hands?" he asked.

"Why?"

Sam laughed. "I thought everybody knew before you go touching any... uh udder, you need warm hands. Cold hands send... *any body* jumping." Abby's face flushed as Ollie snickered and Sandy looked mystified.

Before Abby could start to rub her hands together, Sam said, "Actually, it's best you wash them with warm water right ahead of the milking. Cows are real susceptible to problems like hardening, infection."

She looked up at him, then ran for the house. It didn't take her more than a few moments to return with a small pail of warm, sudsy water.

"Good," Sam said. "You want to wash down the udder too. It encourages letting down milk."

"Letting it down?" Abby repeated as she tried her best with the udder. Tildy was now less than pleased with her technique.

When she looked up at Sam, she saw his wicked grin. He bent low and whispered, "Stroke her like you did me the other night. She'll give you just about anything you want then."

She returned his smile. "You didn't," she reminded him.

Again Ollie chuckled, while Sandy was now the one who looked embarrassed.

Using a little more sure touch and pretending she had Sam Ryker under that soapy water, Abby stroked down the udder and teats, washing each, then drying them with a small towel she'd tucked into her belt. "Now?" she asked, looking up at Sam.

"Seems like you've got a relationship going here," he said, smiling again in a way that played havoc with her stomach. "Give it a try."

She took hold of two of the teats, stroked down and squeezed. Nothing happened. She tried it again and again there was no milk in the pail. She looked up at Sam again.

"Remember the stroke. It's all in that stroke and squeeze," he said, his voice almost a purr.

"You know more about this than you've admitted."

"Not about cows."

As Sandy and Ollie chortled, Abby felt like kicking him, but she took a deep breath and again tried with the stubborn cow.

This time she was rewarded with a spurt of milk. Not a large one, but proof that she could do it. She tried again, perfecting her technique as she worked and vowing Sam would pay for the way he was teasing her. She could feel his gaze on her back. It was as though she could feel his hands doing to her breasts as she was doing to the cow's udder. Her body grew hot and heated at the thoughts. She knew he was enjoying this. Someday she'd get her revenge, and she knew just how she'd do it, then she grew more heated at where her thoughts were going. She was grateful Sam wasn't a mind reader.

When she heard Snake Smith make a muttered comment from the barn door, she glanced over to see that most of the men had come to watch the new acquisition--or more likely watch her make a fool of herself. Well, she decided, with growing confidence, this wasn't so bad. That was the moment when Tildy kicked out and knocked the bucket that was a quarter full onto the ground. Abby came as close to spouting profanity as she'd ever come. She glared up at Sam as though it was his fault.

"Did I mention you got to watch out for kicking?" he asked with a grin.

"Thanks," she growled, righting the bucket and trying again, this time keeping one eye on her hands to make sure she was getting the milk where it belonged, but the other watching the cow's back leg, ready to jump up with the bucket. She did not know if Tildy did it deliberately or was innocently restless, but it happened twice more, both times Abby saved the milk.

Finally with a bucket almost full, Abby sighed with relief when she realized there was no more milk in the udder. She looked up at Sam. "Is that it?"

He nodded. "A little wash down at the end is nice," he said with that teasing smile, "lotion, back rub, and some sweet words are always good."

She glared at him, while Ollie chortled.

"I'll leave the back rubbing to you," she said, taking her bucket and heading for the house. "I think I should do something with the milk.

"Hey, you got to let Tildy here out of the stanchion and put her in the field," Sam called after her.

"You're the great lover," she called back, loud enough for everyone anywhere near the barns to hear, "you do it. After that kind of treatment, she'll follow you anywhere. I know I would!"

CHAPTER 16

Sam watched Abby walked away, the sway of her hips in those boy's pants a teasing temptation. He snapped at the men to return to work as Ollie unfastened the cow's head from the makeshift stanchion and led her out to pasture. Sam watched, leaning his arms on the fence by the barn, his thoughts going in circles.

"What you going to do about it?" Ollie asked when he walked back.

Sam didn't bother to ask what he meant. "What can I do?"

"You could settle down here and make a go of this ranch."

"You know I can't do that."

"Why not? You wouldn't be the first man to walk with the whirlwind a few years, then settle down and live like real folks."

"It wouldn't work."

"You figure you'd get bored?" Ollie asked.

"It's not that. It's just--" Sam had no answer for Ollie anymore than he had for Abby or himself. Everything had begun so gradually for him-- one step after another. All so easy and so irredeemable.

When he had first met Abby, he had thought... but only for a moment that maybe there was a way with her. He'd taken her with him, hoping for that. It hadn't been taking into account who he was-- all he had been. After awhile he had come to see there was no way out. If it wasn't Mexico, it'd be somewhere else. He would keep on until he stepped into a hail of bullets. He should have never brought Abby to the ranch.

Snake came up and watched the cow walk toward the little stream. "Milk cows. Ice cream. You're getting soft," he ridiculed.

Sam smiled at him, the darkness masking both of their faces. "I wouldn't count too much on that."

"We going out next week?"

"I haven't decided."

"If you don't lead us south, we'll go without you."

"You will, huh?"

"I've been talking to the boys. They're restless. We got that contract, and they want to fill it. We didn't get nothing off the last one."

"You don't have to remind me." Sam rolled and lit a cigarette, his mind on anything but returning to Mexico. He didn't want to go, had lost his taste for it. Was it Abby or had it happened before her? But what did he owe the men working for him? If he tried to run the ranch, he'd be lucky to pay two of them salaries to begin. If he backed out of this last deal, they'd be left with nothing. Had he gotten soft?

"I'll scout out the herds," Rock offered from behind Snake. "If we do this right, we shouldn't be gone long."

Sam nodded, not wanting this. Did he have a choice? He began to consider the possibility of not going. Let the men go without him.

"I'm going this time," Sandy said quietly.

Sam swung around to face him. "You are not."

"It's only fair. You said I could when I was a man. I am a man, Sam. You know it's true."

"You don't need this, don't need to start down a road that'll leave you with a stain you can never get out. You start down this road, won't ever be a girl like Cindy at the end of it."

"I want my chance," Sandy insisted.

"Chance for what? To die?"

Nothing he was going to say was going to change the boy's mind. Sam could see that even before he heard the youth continue his argument. "I want to ride with the gang like you promised I could when I was ready. I am a man now. I am ready."

"And when the herds down there run out, when the buyers quit wanting that, when the Rurales close in, and you have to give that up. Where else will you follow Snake? Robbing stages and banks?"

"It's not the same."

"I don't want you finding out that it is."

"You can't stop me, Sam. They said I can go, and I will. You can't protect me forever."

"I'll go instead, and you can have my share when we sell the herd. You can use it for a start." Sam saw no other choice. This was his fault. He had to fix it.

"I can't let you do that." Sandy's voice cracked. "Either I'm a man or I'm not. This is the proving of it for me."

"You don't have to steal to become a man."

"That woman's made you weak," Snake growled. "You're trying to make the rest of us weak too."

Sam wasn't sure he was wrong. Maybe she had. He didn't have a good feel for going south this time, but he saw no way out. He was ensnared in a web that he'd spun for himself. He had thought he could stop Sandy when the time came, but he saw he couldn't.

"Sandy," he said, trying one more time, "I haven't done much that matters in this life, but you... I've thought maybe you'd be that one thing. You go with them, and it's all for nothing."

"What a crock," Snake said. "You think he's yellow, think he's too weak to make it, and this is your way of keeping him safe."

Sam turned on him. "He's a kid. He should be riding and

laughing with young men like Rafe, not with the likes of you or me."

Sandy shook his head. "You can't stop me, Sam. I got to go. I got to know I can do it."

"You're a fool then," Sam said, glaring at Snake, who he knew had planted this in the youth's thinking. "All right," he said, taking a long drag on the cigarette. He wouldn't think further on this. "We'll send out Rock tomorrow morning to find the herds."

Sandy left with Snake, bubbling with excitement. Ollie stood at Sam's shoulder. "You tried."

"Too late."

Sam looked up at the house, thought of Abby waiting. He knew what she wanted, what she had been promising him all day. He wanted it too, but he couldn't take her now and go off. What if she got pregnant? What if he didn't return from this? He could feel black clouds gathering.

He wanted that woman with an ache in his gut. He knew she would feel rejected when he put her off, that she would hate him for going south again, but he had no choice. He couldn't let Sandy go alone, and he wouldn't take the chance of leaving another child to be reared without a father.

But maybe he was wrong. Maybe he'd come back. Maybe she would wait for him. Maybe they would have a future, could start a new life. He wished he could believe it was possible, but he didn't.

The parlor was lit with several lamps and Abby sat on the sofa, her feet curled under her after dinner. He had seen the looks she had given him all evening, not missed her mood of anticipation. He had no idea how he was going to tell her that he was heading south.

"I thought before dinner tonight we could read some poetry," she suggested.

"Poetry huh? Isn't that for sissies?" He knew that would get her dander up.

She gave him a mock scowl. "I know you said that deliberately. There's poetry and there's *poetry*."

"All seems the same to me." He knew it wasn't, but he liked arguing with her, getting her to convince him he was wrong.

"What kind of poetry would you like?" She smiled seductively, and he sucked in a breath.

"Bound to read me one of those dead poets, huh?" he teased, sitting on the chair across from her. He didn't trust himself to sit next to her.

"If some are dead, their ideas are not."

"I'll take your word for that." He thought of how much he'd like to be sitting next to her, taking her into his arms, dropping that book of poetry onto the sofa beside her and teaching her about live emotions, about her own body, but he wouldn't. Not tonight. Maybe never.

"I would like to read you something by Alfred Lord Tennyson."

"Sissy sounding name." He smiled at her look of annoyance with narrowed eyes.

"He wrote about a lot of *masculine* subjects--like war, fighting for a heroic cause, dying but yes, also about love."

"Can't believe any real man writes poems."

"Poetry is about ideas, Sam."

"The kind a man never experienced but likes to talk about what someone else lived?" he asked with a smile.

She gave him another look. "Tennyson wrote one about a true event during the Crimean war and it's called 'The Charge of the Light Brigade'."

He was not going to like that subject, but he couldn't afford to have her reading love words. He'd never resist what came next. Hell, even watching her milk a cow had had him hard and wanting. Likely so would listening to her read about war or whatever went with the charge of the whatever. He managed a smile and sat back, legs stretched out and crossed at the ankles, a pose as relaxed as he could force and listened to her melodic voice as she put feeling into her reading.

"Half a league, half a league, half a league onward, All in the valley of Death Rode the six hundred. 'Forward, the Light Brigade! Charge for the guns,' he said: Into the valley of Death Rode the six hundred. 'Forward, the Light Brigade!' Was there a man dismay'd? Not tho' the soldier knew Someone had blunder'd: Theirs not to make reply, Theirs not to reason why, Theirs but to do and die: Into the valley of Death Rode the six hundred."

Hell, Sam thought, it was worse than he had expected. He listened as the story went on. Cannons to the left, cannons to the right. He had been there. The words struck him like bullets. Was this a warning? If so, he couldn't yield to it. He was committed as surely as had been that foolish Light Brigade.

"What did you think?" she asked when she had finished the poem and closed the book.

He rose from his chair and walked to the window, staring into the night. He wondered what she hoped to hear from him. Did she want to hear that he saw them as words of heroism? Or what he really thought as he saw the story about a willingness to die for a foolish cause. He knew nothing of noble causes, only of survival.

"Nice poem," he said when he saw she was determined to wait for his opinion.

"That's it?" Her tone was exasperated.

"What do you want me to say? That I think like that. I don't." He turned to look at her. "I'm a simple man, Abby. I do what needs doing; don't think more than the day ahead most of the time."

"Is that true?"

"Did you want more? Want a man who could write poetry like that? A man who thinks in terms of honor?"

"It's about men. I thought you'd relate to it."

"Through a pointless, stupid death?"

"It was hardly stupid. They did what they had to do."

"Men do that usually when they got themselves in a spot never should have been in to begin." Certainly fit the situation he was facing. He had to go with Sandy. Couldn't let the youth go alone to Mexico, maybe have the others abandon him if the going got tough. He would go, but he saw no honor in it for him or anyone. He'd go because the alternative to going was worse.

It was how he'd lived his whole life. Looking at two choices, neither of which did he want, but he had to take one. He had, and he'd lived. He was responsible for Sandy, for the boy's choices. If not for Sam, Sandy could be living a normal life of a boy somewhere. No, that wasn't true either. Sandy's chance for a normal life had been ended when he was too young to understand the whys or wherefores of it.

She had moved to the window and put her hand on his shoulder. "It seems to have put you in a bad mood. I only wanted to show you that poets can write of men's events, of more than romance. I'm sorry."

"It's not your fault." None of it was her fault. She had given him good things. He wished he was better at words to tell her what she had brought into his life. No poems would be coming from him.

"Shall I read you something else? Something that might put you in a better mood?"

"You think a poem can do that?" he asked, trying to lighten his own darkness. Her poem had been prophetic. He felt it. Mexico would be a disaster this time. Even knowing, he couldn't change it. He ran his hand over his face, wishing he could erase the pictures that were always there.

"Some can." She picked up a different book. He heard her soft, sweet voice as she read again. These words he knew, had heard before, long ago. God was supposed to be a man's shepherd. Even in the valley of the shadow of death, he wouldn't be alone. Those words weren't meant for the likes of him.

He didn't need to hear them to know them; so instead he watched Abby, the fire reflected in her hair, the thick hair falling in tendrils that brushed against her cheek as he wanted to do. He watched her mouth, imagining it moist and wet with love for him, thinking of those lips forming other words, ones he wanted to hear. He closed his eyes to stop the thoughts. He couldn't let himself dream that way. Not now. Now he had to harden himself. When she had finished, the room fell silent with only the crackling of the fire as a sound.

"I have heard that one," he said finally opening his eyes and looking at her, seeing the questions in those beautiful brown eyes.

"Where had you heard it, Sam?"

He ignored her question. "It'd be good to have faith, I suppose. In something."

"God is there for everyone, Sam."

"You believe that?"

"Of course."

"I know the stories, Abby. Doesn't mean I buy them."

"Where did you hear them?"

He had not meant to tell her. Never meant to tell her, but he heard himself starting. "When you're a kid running around with nobody much caring, there are some who use what they see as your weakness for their own ends."

"What are you saying?"

"Where I heard the stories. There was a preacher in a church in Abilene. He pretended he cared about the boys who were castaways. He did it because... of what he wanted. I was young and stupid when I first heard his stories, didn't know what he really wanted until one day. I fought his hands and him off and ran for it. I learned then the value of those stories."

He saw the moment she realized what he was telling her. "What a monster. How old were you?"

"Maybe eight."

"Did you bring charges against him?"

He laughed with no humor. "You think anybody would

believe a street scruff against a man of the cloth. No, I felt lucky I got away."

"But then he kept on doing it."

"For awhile."

"For awhile?"

"Years later, he was shot. The law could never prove who did it, but the little kid he had that time, he was the last one."

She frowned. "Sandy was in Abilene..." She stopped.

"I shouldn't have told you about any of this. Just you asked where I'd heard the stories."

"In the worst possible way and probably distorted versions."

He shrugged. "Maybe so. Maybe there's no good way when the promises are all about fire and brimstone, about everlasting punishment if you don't do what God and the minister say. And somewhere down the road, I figured it out. Hell is just a word and more likely here on earth than somewhere else."

Abby was not sure she believed in some kind of eternal damnation herself. She managed a smile. "Well, maybe the man who tried to hurt you ended up finding out."

"Could be. In the moment he died, I saw his face, saw he was scared he was about to find out."

She knew she should not have been shocked but she was. "You killed him?"

"Murdered. You asked before how many men I'd killed. He was the only one that wasn't self defense. I could have gotten his last victim away from him without killing him, but I didn't."

"The boy was Sandy, wasn't he?"

Sam stopped resisting the temptation to sit beside her on the sofa. He ran his finger over her cheek, the touch so light it was like breath of a butterfly against her skin. "Does it matter? The skunk wouldn't fight me. There was only one way to stop him. That night I became judge, jury, even God, and I took him out."

She touched his hand, turned it against her lips and kissed the fingers. "That was not murder." She knew legally perhaps it had been, but not where it counted. "What you did was defense of another but moreover of future boys. You are most likely right. I wish you weren't, but probably you were. It's sad to say that our legal system would fail that way but." She stopped and shook her head. "Without that, he likely would have kept right on."

"Maybe and maybe I just wanted and exacted revenge."

She had no answer for that. Perhaps he had. It would have been only human. "And now Sam, what do you want now?" She knew she was ready for him, for whatever he wanted with her. She felt so much desire that it filled her heart, her whole body. She desired the man he was, but something else was there. She wanted to salve over every pain he had suffered. Making love would solve nothing for them, but she was past caring about that.

"I don't know."

It wasn't the answer she had wanted to hear. She felt hurt. He didn't want her after all. She shouldn't have been surprised.

The day Rock returned with his report on the lay of the land, Sam knew he could delay telling Abby no longer. He and she had skirted around a lot of issues. He wanted to make love to her, had seen her hurt that he hadn't already done it. He knew from her soft yielding in his arms that she wanted him. He couldn't take her. Not as it was. He forced himself not to touch her and struggled with the temptation to take the release he was sure awaited within her lovely body.

Walking into the house, he could hear Abby in the parlor humming, the sound of her soft, earthy voice cutting into his heart.

"Good afternoon," she said when he walked into the room. She put down the feather duster and walked to him. "You're in early. Is something wrong?"

Her intuitive ability to read his thoughts never ceased to

amaze him. Sometimes it scared him, sometimes he cherished it, but today he dreaded it. "The boys and I are heading south tomorrow. I'm leaving Joe here to look after you and the place."

"South? You don't mean to get cattle, do you?" She dropped into a chair and looked up at him, disappointment in her big eyes.

He nodded. "We made an agreement for one more herd before I ever met you. The boys lost out on the payment for the last herd. They need this stake."

"You can't continue rustling. It's wrong."

"I can't not go." He wouldn't burden her with the knowledge that Sandy would go no matter what he did. He had tried several time to change the boy's mind and been unsuccessful. It didn't matter. The truth was simple. He was going, and he knew what that would say to her.

He could try to justify his actions as he had done for himself before. Tell her how the longhorns in the area from which they'd be rounding up were unbranded, that they belonged to dons who lived hundreds of miles to the south, who didn't even know their cattle were there, but none of that mattered because the cattle still didn't belong to him.

"You can't do this."

"I don't have a choice."

"There is always a choice."

"Sometimes it's already been made."

"It's not only wrong, it's dangerous. How can you take such risks?" Her dark eyes grew even darker. "If you're leaving Joe, what does that mean about Sandy?"

"He's going."

"I can't believe you would take that boy on such a dangerous venture."

"He's a man now. He makes his own choices."

"He could be killed."

He nodded. "Rock saw a large herd only sixty miles or so south of the border. Nobody was around. I don't think we'll have any trouble." He knew that wasn't the truth. No one could ever know if there would be trouble. Sometimes it was simple. Round up the cattle, drive them north and collect the money. Other times they had to fight their way north, every mile marked with blood.

"Don't go." She reached up, putting her arms around his neck. "You can have more now. You know you can."

"I know you will not understand this. But I have to go. The men are counting on me. I can't let them down." He would not promise there'd never be another trip, even though he believed it. He had no right to try to soften her heart with such a promise. Once he'd met her, he'd begun to think differently, to want to make the ranch into a home, to have all the things she said she wanted, except he hadn't dared plan for that even to himself because things had a way of not working out. He'd seen so many of his dreams smashed that he wouldn't promise her something he didn't know he could deliver.

She pulled his head down, her lips soft and pliant as they pressed against his, then her tongue darting out and filling his mouth, teasing his tongue, kissing him as he'd taught her and with devastating effect. He felt his body turning hard, his need for her so strong it was all he could do to pull her arms away.

"You don't want me?" she asked, hurt in her eyes.

"I want you," he said, swallowing. "I just can't take you this way, not when I'll be leaving."

"You want the excitement of it all. You want that more than me," she accused.

He almost laughed at her naivety, except the anger in her voice, the full lips pressed so tightly together, the stiff line of her spine made this anything but funny. She didn't understand. He couldn't expect her to, didn't want her to know all he faced when he rode south.

He'd made his choices years before. It wasn't for her to pay for them by his trying to wheedle her down, convince her he was right when deep inside he also knew he was wrong. The wrong though had happened so long ago, he couldn't even remember when. People talked of second chances, but Sam more than most knew there was no such thing. A man chose a road, or sometimes it was chosen for him. From that time on the next choice was made.

"If you go, I won't be here when you come back. I won't live with a thief."

He clenched his jaw. He had expected that. It was why he'd decided to leave Joe Fox with her. Joe had his instructions to see her safely wherever she wanted to go.

"You can get that annulment," he said. "There is cash in the box in the bottom desk drawer. Take it with you. I'll see that your father gets back what was stolen."

She frowned, staring at him. "You'd do that?"

"I'll see it happens." He would leave the instructions for that also with Joe. Joe knew where it was, could retrieve it. If Abby went home, she could take her reward with her. He had never touched it and thank god not her. It was all he could give her.

"Don't go," she said again, tears in her eyes but not attempting this time to touch him.

He shook his head, unable to find the words to tell her what she'd meant to his life in the short time she'd lived with him. He managed a smile. "Whatever you do," he said, "I hope it works the way you want. I wanted to make you happy, Abby. I really did. I'm sorry I made you cry instead." He reached out with the vague thought of touching her hair, then let his hand drop. It wouldn't make the tomorrows any easier for either of them.

CHAPTER 17

Sam and his men left before daybreak. He had hoped he would see Abby if just for a moment, but if she rose to watch him ride off, she didn't show herself. There were no tender good-bye kisses, no second thoughts. He had to believe she had meant what she said. She would be riding to Tucson as soon as he was gone. The thought brought pain, but it had only been a matter of time no matter how it had ended. Nobody stayed.

Angling south, then west, they rode into Nogales in the late afternoon. For the men this would be an opportunity for fun. For Sam, no town meant much of anything, except that somewhere on the ride he'd decided to buy Abby some pretty clothes, even knowing it was a fool thing to do for a woman who'd told him she wouldn't be there when he got back.

Sam ordered the men to meet him south of town in the morning and to be sober, then he let them go. He had half expected Sandy to stay with him, but either the youth was still angry for not wanting him along or he decided he'd have more fun with the men than with a sober Sam.

Stabling Satan for a good brushing and feed, Sam walked up the street, looking for the right kind of establishment. The buildings were mostly of thick-walled adobe, some with brightly painted designs on the walls or awnings to cover the doors.

Having been propositioned several times in a block, once by a pretty girl and twice by men who promised him that their beautiful sisters would be eager to meet him and knew just how to bring a smile to his face, Sam found what he wanted in a dimly lit store.

A heavy-set Mexican woman came from the back. Sam spoke Spanish well enough to communicate his needs. He pointed to a pile of brightly colored skirts and asked how much. She named an exorbitant price. He grinned and started for the door. She called him back, asking what it was worth to him and serious dickering began.

When he'd finished, Sam had purchased a turquoise skirt with a richly embroidered hem, a red skirt that was plain and two simple white blouses, one long-sleeved, the other cut to allow it to be worn off the shoulder. Sam doubted Abby would ever wear the shoulder and breast revealing blouse, but a man could dream. A dream was his only excuse for buying such things for a woman who'd promised to be gone before he returned--that and the fact it fit with his own dream, one that was harder to kill than he'd expected. He'd never bought a woman clothing. He would have the joy of that, even if he would never know the joy of giving them to her.

"You buying these for your woman?" the Mexican woman asked as she wrapped the purchases in heavy paper.

He nodded.

"You make her very happy."

"Maybe." Adding to his foolishness, in the next shop Sam bought leather sandals and a silver Concho belt, then added a pair of silver hoop earrings and another of turquoise, with a necklace to match. The jewelry was not elaborate or fancy. They would look beautiful with her coloring.

Some lingerie was next on his fantasy list, a silky nightgown, silky underwear, and finally some colorful silk scarves. Maybe he'd find a way to send them to her, not giving his name, of course-- if he lived to do so.

With his shopping finished, he stopped at a café where he knew the food was good and ordered a plate of frijoles, tamales and enchiladas. He rolled a cigarette after he'd polished off the meal and drank a cup of strong Mexican coffee as he smoked it.

"You all alone, mister?" the waitress asked in Spanish, coming to sit across from him.

"No."

"You look alone. Lonely too. I get off early. Want some company?"

The girl was dark-haired and pretty, but she held no allure for him. He didn't want company. He shook his head and smiled faintly as she got up and walked away, her rounded hips swaying to give him one last temptation, except it wasn't a temptation, not when he could only think about one woman.

Walking out of the restaurant, he saw what he hadn't seen walking in. A poster with a drawing of Abby, her name, and description. He tore it from the wall. The likeness didn't look a lot like her, but close enough that if his wolves saw it, they would know. The $500 reward for information for her whereabouts would be enough to tempt some to sell out their own mothers. The added reward for the capture of her kidnappers might slow them down if they couldn't figure out a way to get the reward without incriminating themselves. The probability was the posters were around town, so he could count on at least one seeing them. If Abby was already on her way to Tucson, it wouldn't matter.

He thought about getting a hotel room, but he'd not sleep well if he did. The noise of the town, lumpy mattresses were not for him. He picked up Satan and rode a few miles, finding a protected spot, off the road, with a little grass where he hobbled the stallion. He spread out his blanket, and then sat back against a tree, his mind on anything but the setting sun or the job ahead. He rolled and lit a cigarette, staring at the rich purple and red colors as they slowly turned to black. She wouldn't be there when he got back. He believed what she said. There wasn't anything he could do about it.

～

Abby rose before first light, determined she would leave that day. Sam didn't deserve her. He didn't deserve her waiting around to pick up the pieces of his broken body if it even returned. The way his life was going, he'd end up dead on a desert somewhere with the coyotes to pick the bones apart. It would be no more than he deserved.

"You want me for anything, Miss Abby," Joe Fox asked, coming around to the kitchen door.

"There's fresh coffee," she said in a sour mood. She knew by the careful way the wiry little man looked at her that she had to have snapped her invitation, but he took the cup and sat at the table.

"Sam told me to do whatever you needed doing... or take you wherever you want to go."

She stared moodily into her own coffee cup. "He did, did he?"

"Yes, ma'am, he did."

"Have you done any new drawings?" she asked, not dealing with the issue at hand. She was going to leave. Just didn't have to rush off right away.

His smile barely showed under his big, handlebar mustache. "I did one of Sam. Want to see it?"

She almost said no, but then nodded. She was mad at herself as he went off to get the sketch. Why in blue blazes was she letting him show her a drawing of Sam Ryker? She didn't want to think about him. He didn't deserve her thinking about him, caring for him, worrying over him.

When Joe came back, he opened a sketch book and flipped

through the pages, then handed her the book. He'd captured Sam on one of the broomtail horses he'd been breaking several weeks earlier. His legs were wrapped around the barrel of the horse, his arm flung high, his body stretched taut. The smile on his face was not what she'd have expected to see. Breaking horses was hard work, yet Sam looked in that quick sketch as though he was a man doing what he'd been born to do.

"This is very good, Joe, one of the best drawings I have seen. So much feeling and life to it," Abby said. "May I see your others?"

Joe nodded and she began at the beginning, seeing the men doing various tasks around the ranch, the horses in a pasture eating grass, even one of her hanging up a wash on the line out back. With his pencil, Joe had captured the essence of this ranch.

"You already know you are very talented," she said. "You could sell these in town. Have you thought of doing that?"

"I've sold my work before," he said, "but it wasn't the same for me. I found myself trying to draw things or paint something just because somebody would buy it. It wasn't the same. The work wasn't as good as when I just drew whatever I saw, whatever I wanted."

"Do you have training as an artist?"

"I studied some. I thought that's what I'd do... but then things happened."

"Do you want to talk about it?"

He took a sip of his coffee, then looked at her. "I don't know. Maybe. You might be somebody that would understand."

She sighed. "I don't seem to understand much these days, but I'll try." She got up to refill his coffee cup. Outside the birds were making a racket as the light brightened with the sun rising enough to silhouette the ranch with an intense glow.

"I come from New York--up the Hudson River Valley. I'd met quite a few artists coming through our little town, had seen their work, gotten the idea of doing it for myself. My father was a banker, a practical man. He didn't think much of me studying at any art institutes, didn't think drawing was any vocation for a man. My mother disagreed.

"When the Civil War came along, I was not really old enough but jumped at the chance to join up. Maybe that sounds crazy, being an artist--then being a soldier, but it was a way to prove myself to my father, I guess."

"I can understand that," Abby said, thinking of the many times she'd gone out of her way to prove herself to her father and what a failure it had always been.

"I was wounded at a battle that doesn't have a name, didn't amount to much, except it made me a prisoner of war, put me in a Reb hospital. By the time I got out, I didn't care for much of anything, cared even less when I got home and found out my father had died, my mother remarried. So, I started wandering, hit the bottle too much, drank myself from one end of this country to the other and spent about ten years drifting."

"How did you end up with Sam and begin..." She stopped.

"Rustling?" he finished with a grin.

She smiled back. "For wont of a better word."

"There is no better word. I am another of Sam's walking wounded. I met him in New Mexico. I was still drinking heavily. He was foreman and hired me on. We weren't rustling to begin, but the ranch owner desired a larger herd, and he'd done it before, taught us the ropes. After the first trip, it was easy to make another."

"A textbook example of the life of crime," Abby said bitterly. "Do you still drink too much?"

Joe laughed. "Blunt and to the point. No, I don't. Equally blunt. No, after I had a few friends, began to feel better about myself, crazy as that might seem. I didn't need the bottle so much. I started to draw again, that helped too."

"I'm glad you found that out, Joe. You do have talent. Did Sam say you used to paint in oils?"

He nodded. "No time or money for that now."

She studied the drawings. "If you have as a good a feel for

color as you do line and shape, it might be worth giving that a try again."

"Thank you, and now Mrs. Ryker, where do you want to go today?"

Abby walked to the sink and threw out her tepid coffee. "I know where I should go."

"Home?" Joe asked.

"Not sure where home is at the moment," she admitted with a little smile.

"How you going to find out?"

She laughed. She heard the cow bellowing down by the barn. "Not sure of that yet... I guess I should milk Tildy at least."

"From the sounds of it, she'd like that."

"I can't stay here with a man who rustles cows," she said, unsure of whom she was trying to convince, as Joe didn't argue the point.

"You never know. Sam might not keep doing it."

"I had hoped that but there he is, off again."

"He had limited options this time. Sandy was determined to go whether Sam went or not. You can thank Snake for that."

"Sam didn't want to go?"

Joe shook his head. "I can't say he confides in me, but I heard him try every way he could to talk Sandy out of it. Even offered to go instead and give him his cut. No, I'd judge he didn't want to go."

"I wonder why he didn't tell me that." That made her about as angry as his going had.

"I have no clue. Sam is a proud man. Maybe that was it. Maybe he figured it wouldn't make any difference to how you felt. Would it have?"

"I don't know." She reached under the sink for the milk pail. "I better take care of the cow."

"Need help?"

"I can handle it." She wanted time alone to think.

"Shall I saddle two horses?"

"No."

At the barn, Abby got Tildy into her stanchion, following the ritual she'd learned the cow liked best. As she was milking, she tried to think through what she ought to do. She couldn't make her thoughts link together in a logical sequence. A + B = ... What was A... or B?

As she washed down the cow after the milking, she heard a faint mewing from the corner of the barn. She put Tildy outside, then went to see if one of the barn's feral cats had gotten hurt. There in the corner was a gray-striped kitten. It looked up at her, its tiny mouth opening and closing with almost no sound coming out.

"Who are you?" Abby asked, picking up the tiny mite. "Where's your mama?"

As she stroked its soft fur, the kitten began to purr. She could see by the sunken little belly that it hadn't been fed recently. Had something happened to the mother or was this one of the kittens she'd decided to abandon? Holding the kitten against her breast, she picked up the milk pail and headed for the house.

In the kitchen, she poured a small amount of milk into a bowl and put it in front of the kitten, but the little one didn't seem to know what to do with it. She sat on the floor, dipping her finger into the warm milk, then put her finger to the kitten's mouth. This time with sharp little teeth and tongue, it sucked at her finger. Repeating the process, Abby finally showed it the source and in moments it was licking at the milk with a fair degree of messy success.

Leaving the kitten to its riches, Abby took care of the milk--a task that was becoming more and more difficult. Tildy provided more milk than all the men and Abby together could consume in sauces or butter. With just Joe and her at the ranch, the problem would grow worse. Certainly the kitten wouldn't use much of the supply. She decided cheese was the answer, except her only guide for making cheese was a cookbook with rather vague instructions. When she saw Joe at the back door, she asked, if he knew anything about cheese making and wasn't surprised when he shook his head.

"Who's that?" he asked, pointing to the kitten that had rolled into a contented ball in the corner and fallen asleep.

"I haven't decided on her name, but she's the new house cat. We have had a few mice."

"She doesn't look big enough to take on a mouse."

"She will be. Think Sam likes cats?"

"I have never seen him with one, but that doesn't mean he doesn't."

"Do you know how to tell if it's a male or female?"

Joe grinned and picked up the sleeping kitten, earning a squeak of protest for his troubles. "I think," he said after his examination, "you've got yourself a little lady here."

"Uh oh. I don't suppose that will please Sam, what with more kittens and all."

"So," Joe asked, "what are you going to call her?"

Abby considered a moment. "Let's see we could name her after one of the Greek gods... or a character in a Shakespearean play or... a Bible character. I know, let's call her Rahab."

"Who's Rahab?"

"A harlot with a heart of gold."

"You going to name a kitten after a prostitute?" Joe asked, clearly aghast.

"Well, that particular woman was a Biblical heroine. She saved some men's lives, taking a grave risk herself."

"Hmmmmm. Seems like a lot of name for that little mite." Joe looked at her thoughtfully, then at the kitten. "All right if I sketch her?"

"Be my guest." She decided she would get some paints for Joe first chance she had. She'd love to see what he could do with them. Her thoughts then turned to the problems of cheese making. She knew she'd made her decision regarding leaving right away. Who would milk the cow? Maybe the Reimers. For today she'd try to make cheese. Tomorrow would be soon enough to decide whether to go or stay.

~

Ollie rode beside Sam. "You look like you had a hard night."

"I didn't."

"You look like you did," Ollie said. "Want to talk about it?"

"If I did, I would."

"Might. Might not. We could still turn around."

"We could if I wanted to kill Snake." Sam looked ahead at Sandy riding beside Snake. "I might have to do that anyway if he keeps leading the boy the wrong way."

"Sam, the kid's needy, got a weakness that lets Snake get away with it."

He couldn't deny that, but he didn't trust Snake's motives in befriending the youth, who was eating up the attention. Sam had given him less of his own since Abby had arrived. Was Sandy that weak-willed? Some of it was youth, but was it also a character defect, one a damaged childhood had made impossible to overcome? He couldn't do anything about it for now, except to hope the boy's commonsense would help him see Snake's true character before it was too late.

The sun almost overhead, they stopped for a noon break to water their horses. Sam sat on a rock near the edge of the waterhole, not wanting the biscuit he was eating. When he saw Sandy was alone, he called him over.

"What do you want?" Sandy asked in a surly tone.

"What do *you* want?"

"To be treated like a man," Sandy retorted. "You've treating me like a baby, Sam, and I don't like it."

"Is that what you think or what Snake thinks?"

"There you go again. Just avoiding what's going on. I'm a man now. I want you to treat me like one."

"I've been treating you like a sixteen-year old," Sam said. "That's not a boy or a man."

'You're wrong, and I'll prove you're wrong. I'm as much a man as any of you. The trouble is you can't forget how you found me..." He stopped then, gritting his teeth.

"That's not true. I can't forget you need a chance to grow up; and if you keep listening to Snake, you won't get it."

"You done?" Sandy asked, stalking off without waiting for an answer.

Ollie walked up and put his hand on Sam's shoulder. "He's just feeling his oats. You're like a pa to him. He's gotta rebel a mite," he said sending a stream of tobacco spit a few feet to one side.

"Listening to Snake, he won't live to seventeen." Sam rolled and lit a cigarette.

"Maybe so, but you can't change that. Every man has to grow up his own way. You've done what you can for the boy. Now he has to do for himself."

Sam gave a snort. "And what did I do for him? Teach him to be a rustler?"

"You tried to keep him clean of this. The boy just has to learn for himself."

"I should've gotten out of this a long time ago." Sam watched the smoke waft upward. "If anything goes wrong this trip, it'll be my fault."

"Can't live his life for him, Sam."

"I set him on a road."

"And while I'm at it, let the past go," Ollie said, his tone sharpening. "Not just Sandy has something he needs to deal with. You could have a future if you take it."

Sam looked up at him. "Can I?"

"You know you could."

"You didn't think much of me bringing her."

"Didn't know she'd get you to give her a cow." Ollie chortled, and Sam had to laugh too. "Gotta admit, I like her. She's spunky, going to make things over some, but ain't that just a woman's way."

"She won't be there when we get back."

"Then you can go after her. Bring her back."

"She'd never come."

"She did once. She'll come again."

Sam shook his head. He was not so sure. He watched as Sandy laughed at a joke of Snake's and shook his head.

"Sam, just gonna have to let it be. The boy will be all right or he won't. You can't protect him forever. It's his time to test his wings. Take care of your own life when ya get home."

Sam said nothing as he drew the smoke deep into his lungs. He felt fatalistic. Words weren't going to change what was to be. He rose. "Let's just get this over with."

The next days were long ones for Sam and the men as they reached the area of the herd and began cutting out cattle to drive north. From this time on, they had to watch the horizon, sleep as little as possible as once the herd went north, they would move slowly, most likely camp three nights before they reached the border and such safety as was ever possible for wolves.

With the herd bunched and the men edgy with the most dangerous part of the drive ahead, Sam sat on the edge of camp, smoking the last cigarette of the day. He felt trapped as he finally lay back on his blanket. Nothing was turning out as he had planned. Life was full of traps. As he saw it, the problem was a man didn't see them until he'd walked into them. Then it was too late.

~

Abby had sat on the porch until the sun sank into the west; the sky slowly turned a brilliant combination of crimson and purple. It seemed to last with those jewel tones late into the night.

"That is one beautiful sunset," Joe said, walking up from the bunkhouse.

She nodded, absently petting Rahab who'd curled onto her lap.

"It seems that little mite knows a good thing when she sees it," Joe said, sitting on a bottom step, his eyes on the distance. The first star was visible just above the horizon.

"She's good company," Abby said. "I'll miss her."

"You're not going to keep her?"

Abby shook her head. "I don't see how I can take her to Tucson."

"Sam said I should take you wherever you want to go. You going tomorrow?"

"It's what I *should* do."

"Is it?"

"Isn't it?" She looked at Joe, tears in her eyes. "I can't stay with a man who rustles cattle. It's dishonest... It's illegal. It's..."

"Wrong?"

"Yes."

"And how do you know what's right or wrong, ma'am?"

"Some things just are. Stealing is one."

He smiled. "Ah yes, stealing is wrong when it's rustling cattle but all right when it's a bank cheating someone with a higher interest rate than they had told them or a store where the owner tacks a little something extra onto the bill."

"That's stealing too. I don't justify things that way. Wrong is wrong wherever it is." She didn't like the priggish tone to her voice.

"Life isn't so simple. When life hands you a bowl of cherries, it's easy to eat them. When it gives you nothing but pits, your options change."

"Sam has made choices," she said clinging to her old sense of right and wrong.

Joe laughed. "Very true, and when he was a child, he could have starved to death rather than steal bread."

"Did he have to do that?" She saw the answer on his face and felt her belly constrict, but it didn't change today. "Even if that is so, he's not a child anymore." The more she talked, the angrier she got but it was surprisingly at herself. What had she expected when she ran off with him? She had wanted to escape the strictures of a life with no freedoms. She had taken her chance with a man who she saw as a total free spirit. Outlaws. What could be freer? The world had turned much more complex since then.

"Growing up as Sam did, with no parents, he could have been a stage robber, a killer, a thief, a liar, but you'll never know a more honest man than Sam Ryker. When he shakes hands with someone, his word is as good as a contract would be to another."

"He steals cattle," Abby repeated, feeling like a child who was being chastised and resenting it. "He's off stealing cattle right now."

"He's more truly off trying to keep Sandy alive; so the boy has a chance to grow up."

"Sandy would not have started into this without Sam." She knew that was not likely true. Given Sandy's beginning, he well could have ended up worse than he was.

"You think Sam should have let Sandy go alone?"

She felt annoyed. This was all so confusing. There was right and wrong. She knew it, but she also did know this wasn't all about the rustling.

"You want to leave him," Joe said, "I'll help you, but I think the day will come when you'll regret it as much as I would bet right now Sam's regretting ever rustling in the first place."

Overhead the sky was black, the moon not yet risen. The stars spread in sparkly gems across its expanse. Bats swooped down by the barn. "You can't know that."

"I know this. Sam's the kind of man who does what he has to, what he believes is right, even when it costs him personally."

"You make him sound like a hero, not a rustler," Abby said, making her tone deliberately caustic.

"He is to me. He gave men like me a chance. He'll always be a hero to me." Joe rose. "What time you want me here in the morning, Miss Abby?"

She swallowed, petting Rahab. "No hurry. After breakfast, I guess. I... I'll let you know."

When he was gone, she stared at the black sky. Somewhere, south of the border, Sam was lying beneath this same sky. What was he thinking? Did he have regrets? If she left him, would her life be filled with them?

She walked into the house, still undecided. She cared deeply for Sam. Did she love him? Sam was a rustler, an outlaw. Did she want to love such a man? No, she had to leave before it was too late. In the morning. She had to do it whether she wanted to or not. She had no choice. Whatever she had thought when this began, she wasn't up to living with a man who led such a reckless life.

CHAPTER 18

Although Sam normally enjoyed working cattle, this time he was tired, dusty, and ready to head north finally to have this drive behind him. These longhorns were an anchor, which would now slow their pace and make them targets. He didn't like it. He kept his eyes peeled for danger, but he saw nothing out of place.

"Snake says herd ain't big enough to head north yet," Ollie said, riding up to pull in alongside of Sam.

Sam's smile was as cold as his heart. "You have Snake come tell me that to my face."

Ollie chuckled. "I'll tell him. So we go now?"

"Now."

Sam heard no complaints, and the men began the trek, moving the cattle as fast as they could. Sam set Sandy and Ollie to point, thinking the older man would spot any trouble. If it came, he wanted those two as far out of it as possible. He put Bull and Rock to swing positions, and Snake on one flank. Short one man, after letting Buck go, Sam took drag and watched the other flank, eating dust and keeping his gaze pinned to the south, the direction from which he most expected trouble.

The day was scorching with no breeze to cool them. The cattle, not used to being bunched tight, were spooky and irritable, making constant breaks for freedom. The work was hot and hard, not leaving Sam much time to think about what he was doing or what might be waiting for him at the ranch.

When Sam saw the canyon ahead, he felt a fist tighten around his belly. They had to go through it. Although he saw nothing, the dust of the cattle would've made it hard to see anything in the distance. The dust of the cattle also would have alerted anyone around to their activity. If there was going to be trouble, this was the place. He repositioned the men before they entered, sending Ollie and Sandy to the rear, while he himself rode point. When Sandy rode past him, he yelped boyishly, "Looking good, huh, Boss?" He was smiling; his eyes alight with joy.

Sam sucked in a breath. Nothing looked good to him. If they could get through that canyon, maybe he'd change his mind. Right now, he felt as though doomsday had come and was waiting for him somewhere in the shadow of those rocky cliffs.

"Men want to take a break," Rock said, as Sam passed him.

"When we're on open ground." They were all tired, but there was no choice for it. In his mind, the deep canyon loomed as a portent of disaster. He wanted to be through it as fast as possible. As he brought the first of the cattle into the canyon, he pulled his rifle from its scabbard, checking its load, loosening it for trouble, trouble he could taste. He hoped he was imagining too much.

He saw the opening of the flat ground beyond and began to think it was going to be all right when the first rifle shot rang out. Sam shot his own rifle in the air to make the cattle run and ensure the men knew what was coming. He heard more shots coming from behind. He wheeled Satan to ride back.

A rain of bullets was coming from the west rim of the canyon, and he cursed himself for not having seen the hidden shooters. Whoever it was had waited until the bulk of the herd and most of the men were beneath them to unleash their lethal fire.

Sam spurred Satan, feeling the large horse surge between his thighs, picking up speed as Sam yelled at the men to get the cattle running. It was their only hope. He was almost to the rear of the herd, when he saw the bullet hit Sandy, saw the boy reel in the saddle, clinging to the pommel.

Sam didn't know how he managed it, but he was there, catching Sandy before he fell, grabbing the kid's belt, flinging him by sheer muscle onto the front of his own saddle, dropping his rifle in the process. Ollie rode next to them, trying to steady Sam's grip on Sandy.

"Ride for it," Sam yelled at his old friend. "Forget the cattle, head north. I'll try to catch up to you." He knew, even with Satan mighty strength, carrying extra weight, he wouldn't be able to keep up with the others.

"No," Ollie yelled, keeping his own horse even with Sam's. Sam slapped Ollie's mount on the flank, saw the frightened horse surge forward, racing down the herd, heading for the mouth of the canyon.

Now, Sam could concentrate on keeping Sandy on his horse, on getting them out of there, though it meant riding right through a hail of bullets. The dust and running cattle made visibility nearly impossible, and he hoped it would help him as much as it had hidden the shooters from any effective retaliation from his men.

Sam saw the mouth of the canyon, thought for a moment he would make it safely when the bullet struck him, nearly throwing him from the saddle. He reeled but kept his seat, got his boot back in the stirrup. No way to assess how badly he'd been hit. No time to do anything but kick Satan into a full gallop.

He felt dazed, only half aware of where he was heading. He let his horse have his head. He had to hold onto Sandy, stay in the saddle, or the cattle running beside and behind would kill him as surely as maybe the bullet already had.

Then the cattle were gone. He and Satan were riding through the chaparral, the brush tearing at his shirt, the wind whipping through his hair, his hat hanging from its cord from his neck. He didn't know where he was going, where it was safe to go. Ahead he saw a rider, wondered for a moment if it was enemy or friend, then through a growing dimness recognized Ollie, who'd waited despite his command.

"How's the kid?" Ollie asked before his eyes went to Sam's own bloody left side. "You got hit."

"Head northwest. Don't stop," Sam managed, having to gasp for the words.

"You're bleeding like a stuck pig, Sam. We have to stop and bandage that hole."

"You want a hangman's noose?"

Ollie would've argued, Sam saw it in his eyes, but Sam kneed Satan to a faster pace. They had to keep going until dark. Darkness would be their friend. He wondered vaguely where the rest of the men were, but for now he couldn't worry about anyone else. He had to ride and keep riding. It was his and the kid's only hope-- if there was one. The boy hadn't moved since he'd gotten him across his saddle.

When darkness settled around them, when they seemed far enough away from the shooting, Ollie said, "Stop here." Sam didn't know where here was, was beyond coherent thought, but he reined in Satan.

He realized when Bull reached up to take the kid from his cramped hold that the others were there. Rock was lying on the ground, a bloody scarf tied around his leg. Bull had a blood stained rag wrapped around his head. Only Ollie and Snake hadn't been hit.

Dismounting, Sam swayed. He looked to where Ollie was tearing apart Sandy's shirt and saw all the blood. The boy was so thin. How could so much blood come from such a skinny body?

"Not good," Ollie muttered.

Sandy's eyes opened, the pupils so dilated, Sam didn't think he could see anything, but then he looked straight at Sam.

"It hurts."

"I know," Sam said.

"Am I going to die?" the boy asked, his lips blue.

Sam wanted to lie to him but he couldn't find the words.

Sandy swallowed. "Don't want... to die...."

Sam dropped to his knees. He smoothed the boy's hair. "Anybody got some water?" he asked and in moments a canteen was put in his hand. He lifted the Sandy's head; put the canteen to his lips. A belly wound usually meant no water, but it wouldn't matter this time. Sam had seen the gaping hole. They could do nothing. It would have been no different if it had been in a town with a doctor down the street.

"I didn't think it'd be like this. Thought..."

"I know." Sam stroked Sandy's forehead, wishing he had words to soothe him.

"That preacher," Sandy whispered, "remember...w--what he said about... hell? He said I'd go there... Reckon he was right."

"No," Sam said, his own side hurting so badly that it was all he could do to keep his words straight. "That son of a bitch wasn't right about anything."

Sandy's eyes closed, and then opened as he looked at Sam. "I am going to die, aren't I?"

"I don't know."

"You believe in God, Sam?" the boy asked, coughing with blood in the froth.

Sam would've done anything to give Sandy comfort at that moment, but he couldn't lie to him—not at a moment like this. "I don't know."

"I think... maybe I do... Seems like... someone is with me... Maybe... it's..." And then he was gone.

"You can't do anything more for him, Sam," Ollie said as he half lifted, half dragged Sam from the boy's body. "Now's time to take care of your wound."

Sam didn't care, didn't care about anything anymore, but he lay back, let Ollie tear open his shirt, heard the old man's groan, felt a pad being pressed against the wound, a bandage being wrapped around his torso. He didn't have much more chance than Sandy.

"The bullet didn't go through. It's still in there," Ollie muttered as he tied off the bandages. He held the canteen for Sam to drink, then ran his fingers through his thinning hair. "It's gotta come out."

"Back at the ranch," Sam said. "Have... Bull bury the boy. I won't leave him for the vultures."

"Sam, you can't..."

Sam interrupted. "I have to. Ollie?"

"Yeah?"

"Light me a cigarette."

Ollie retrieved the makings and roughly rolled one for Sam, putting it between his lips, then lighting it. "You shoulda took up chewing. Cuts down on a lot of this."

Sam managed a smile. "Right, like spitting would be easier." The cigarette was helping at least as much as anything could. "How is Rock?"

"He'll make it... Not sure he'll want to. Bad wound in his leg. Hard to say what that'll do later."

"Damn."

"Least the bullet went through. Don't have to take it out like I will with yours." Sam saw the sick expression on Ollie's face. He knew how little the older man liked blood. Not much anybody could do about that either.

"When the moon comes up, we'll head north," Sam said. "We need the light, can't have the horses breaking a leg now or we're all done for."

"You shouldn't ride 'til we get the bullet out."

"You know we have to." Sam swallowed hard against the nausea. "Ollie?"

"Yeah?"

"You say words over the kid?"

Ollie frowned. "I reckon I'll have to but I don't know none."

"You'll think of something. Just... he'd like it. Something about heaven... not hell."

"All right."

Sam lay gathering his strength, letting the others take care of what had to be done. He knew what lay ahead for him. It was going to be at the least a hell of a ride to the ranch if he even made it. Maybe he would. He wouldn't give it odds.

~

Abby watched the dust rising up to the south. Was it men on horseback? She walked out into the yard and saw Joe come from the bunkhouse. "Can you tell who it is?" she asked.

He shook his head. "Shouldn't be our men. They're not due back for almost a week."

She stood mutely alongside Joe as figures became distinct. It was them, but from the way they were riding, it was not all right. When they turned their horses into the ranch yard, Abby had eyes only for Sam. He was slumped forward in the saddle. Ollie was holding the reins to Satan and brought the horse to the hitching rail, slowly dismounting, near exhaustion himself.

"What happened?" Abby asked as Ollie reached up to cut Sam's wrists free of the saddle. He and Bull were there to catch him as he fell. Abby stepped back as they carried him into the house. She saw that Snake and Joe were doing the same thing for Rock. She looked then again at the horses. "Where's Sandy?" she asked.

Snake looked at her, his eyes cold as his namesake. "Buried," he said gesturing, "back there."

She bit down on her lip, suppressing a cry. No time for tears. She ran into the house to where Ollie and Bull had laid Sam across the kitchen table.

"What are you doing?" she asked as Ollie pulled off Sam's shirt.

"Bullet's still in there."

She saw they were carrying Rock into the house. "Put him in the front bedroom, I guess." A crude bandage around Sam's torso was blood soaked. He needed a doctor and then she realized there would be no doctor close enough. Even if there had been, men with bullet wounds gotten this way, could ill afford to ask for help. She stroked the damp hair from his forehead, felt the heat of fever in his skin.

"Are you going to take it out?" she asked looking up at Ollie.

"Have to. Wouldn't let me do it on the trail."

She bit her lip. "What about Rock?"

"Bullet went on through. He's lost a lot of blood, but since he's still breathin', I figure he'll make it. Joe can take care of pouring whiskey on it and bandaging his leg."

She nodded, running her finger lightly along Sam's jaw, then feeling of his forehead. "How can I help?"

Ollie looked at her as though he was surprised but told her to boil water, then find the narrowest boning knife and throw it in.

Abby stoked up the fire in the stove. There was hot water ready. They would need more. She dug through the drawer and came up with a thin, wicked looking knife. Ollie added a long piece of wire to the pot.

"I don't see how you'll get it without hurting him worse," she said, trying to concentrate on what had to be done, not think about the man lying across the table, about the amount of blood he had to have already lost. How much more could he lose and stay living.

"If I can't get it easy, maybe I'll have to leave it there, but it's better getting it out. Soak a thread and needle in alcohol."

She reached into the cupboard for the whiskey bottle. Besides being the only disinfectant she could think of, it was also the only thing they'd have as a pain killer-- if Sam was unfortunate enough to regain consciousness before the bullet was removed.

Ollie began carefully washing his hands at the sink. She saw his whole body was shaking and realized he was near to exhaustion. "You can't do it now," she said, pointing to the tremors.

"I have to." Ollie looked down at his hands, tried to force them to hold still and couldn't.

"Maybe in a few hours, you'll be less tired, then..."

"Sam can't wait. You felt the fever."

"But..."

Ollie sucked in a breath and looked up at Joe who had returned after putting Rock in bed. "What about you?"

Joe paled. "I faint at blood."

"I forgot about you and your missishness." Ollie cursed creatively, then looked at Abby. "You can do it."

"Me?"

"I could tell you how, just like the cooking."

"This isn't like cooking..." She swallowed back her urge to vomit. "I can't." She looked over at Sam and saw his eyes were open and watching her. She went to him. "You weren't supposed to do this," she said with a tremulous smile.

"You... weren't supposed to be here."

"Did you want me to be?" Instead of answering, he gritted his teeth against the pain, suppressing a groan. She took his hand to her lips and kissed the dirty, bloody fingers. "I thought I could go," she said, tears running down her cheeks onto his skin. "But in the end I couldn't."

"I'm... glad."

"The bullet has to come out. Ollie is too spent to do it. Joe can't handle blood." She took his hand and kissed it.

Despite the pain, he managed a half smile. "Don't tell me."

"I'm afraid so."

"You can't even cook."

"I'm a lot better at it these days." She decided not to mention the failed batch of cheese. "I can do it, Sam."

"You shouldn't have to." He grimaced.

"Somebody has to."

"Maybe you... want to," he suggested with another faint smile.

"How dare you joke at a time like this?"

His smile became more real. "You know, I'd do damned near anything to get you to smile."

"Don't you dare do anything like this again. Not ever, you hear me."

"You're a stubborn woman."

"Too stubborn to let you die."

Ollie cleared his throat. "Everything's ready."

"God," Sam said with a groan. "Wish I could enjoy this more."

"Ain't none of us going to enjoy it, but we'll get 'er out." When Sam saw the cords in Ollie's hand, he protested, but Ollie was adamant. "We got to tie you down. I know you don't think you'd move, but if you did, it could be the last move you make, can't afford to go puncturing no vein that ain't already. None of us are strong enough to hold you down when you got a notion to move."

Sam sighed, but yielded to them, hating the rope that tied his wrists to the table legs, the one that secured each leg and even more the one that went across his chest just below the armpits.

"You got me strung up like a stuck pig," he grumbled when they'd finished.

"Just about." Ollie then unbuttoned Sam's pants.

"What the hell are you doing?" Sam asked with more energy than he'd yet shown.

"Just got to push them down a little. Relax."

Abby lifted his head and put the whiskey bottle to his lips. "This will help," she suggested.

He couldn't stop the flow of whiskey, but when she took it away, he said, "No. It'll just make me sick later."

"Want me to sock you in the jaw then?" Joe asked, blanching as he looked at the wound Abby was uncovering as she removed the bandage.

"I remember your help," Sam muttered. "Get out of here... before you fall and hit your head like you did when the mare gave birth out in the yard."

Joe, visibly paling, backed from the room. "I'll just be in with Rock," he said, then was gone. Bull came in. "Rock's doing all right. Need me?"

"You keep your hands on his shoulders," Ollie suggested, peering at the wound. Abby saw that it entered high on his side, an ugly hole, bleeding sluggishly now. Where had it gone? If it had gone into his stomach or ripped through his intestines, he wouldn't live long. She felt the blood drain from her face, a coldness in her own belly at the thought. She refused to lose him this way. If will power was enough to make him live, she would provide it.

Ollie fished a wire from the boiling water, let it cool a moment, then wrapping a cloth over one end, handed it to Abby. "Probe with this," he said. "Follow the path of the bullet as best you can, go slow, gentle, until you feel something solid."

"How will I know if it's the bullet?"

"By the size and whether it moves. Go gentle. Bout the only other thing solid there could be spine or rib. Don't feel to me like it shattered a rib, so..."

She met Sam's gaze then. She saw no doubt in his eyes, just that steady look he had given her so often. She clenched her jaw, forcing her hands to steady as she began to do as Ollie directed.

Knowing she was probing in Sam's flesh, that she was causing him pain, made her feel lightheaded. The only thing, which kept her on her feet, was knowing the bullet had to be removed. She was the only one who could do it. She concentrated on going slow, letting her now blood covered fingers sense what the wire was touching. she didn't look again at Sam's face until she heard a groan and looked up to see his eyes roll back in his head as he went limp.

"Don't stop. It's okay. Now he don't feel it," Ollie said. "Just don't you do the same thing, gal."

"I won't," she said with more assurance than she felt. She kept probing, until the wire touched something solid. "I think... Yes, there," she whispered. "I've found it."

"Where you figure it is?" Ollie asked, looking closely at the depth the wire was in the wound.

She swallowed hard. "There, I think." She pointed with her other hand on the trajectory as to where it lay. It was below the ribs, maybe high enough that it wasn't going to kill him or was it? She felt near to tears with her feeling of helplessness. They could do so little.

Abby never could remember how she got out the bullet, but she knew she had when it bounced out onto the table, bloody and frightening with how small it was and yet lethal. Ollie poured alcohol into the open wound, but she felt barely aware of anything. She was numb, forcing her hands to follow Ollie's instructions, her mind devoid of feeling or thinking. She did what was needed with no energy for more. When it was over, she slumped into a chair. Ollie put the whiskey bottle to her own lips and coaxed her to take a couple of swallows. She coughed as the liquid burned her throat.

"You done good, gal. He's a tough one. He'll make it," Ollie said, washing away the blood, then putting a clean pad over Sam's wound that he tied in place. "I'll make a poultice for it later, but for now, we'll let it and him rest."

They picked Sam up and carried him into his room, laying him on the bed. Abby watched as Ollie and Bull pulled off his pants and covered his nakedness with a sheet. She sat in the chair beside his bed, her mind as numb as her body. She tried to respond to Ollie's questions. She didn't suppose she was making much sense because her only thought was to stay with him.

Gradually she became aware of the sounds of the house, of Sam's restless movements on the bed. Little by little the world became real. The hazy feeling, in which she'd felt wrapped, receded. Color returned to the room and with it her awareness of Sam's needs. She felt of his skin. It felt dry and hot. Out in the kitchen, she found water and a cloth and brought it back to wash him, to fight the fever the only way she knew.

Infection was inevitable after a bullet wound and such crude medical care, not discounting the grueling ride he'd made. During the night as his fever rose, Sam began to mumble; his words those of delirium, of other times and places, sometimes of her, of a dream, other times of enemies, then of Sandy, of the time in the canyon.

As he muttered out his fear and pain, she learned more than she wanted to know about what it had been like for him as the bullets rained down from the canyon rim. She heard him talk about his reluctance to go, about his feelings of impending doom and she wept for and with him as he relived the moments again when Sandy died.

When he pushed off his blankets, she let him, sponging his skin to aid it in cooling. At first, she was almost unaware of his nakedness, but then she couldn't resist looking but felt guilty for it. It seemed unfair to look at all his parts, to see the fine workmanship of his chest, the flat belly, the sinewy thighs, and irresistibly to his maleness.

She had never seen a naked man, although from art books she had a good idea of what to expect. Well, she had thought she had a good idea. A real man was much larger than she had expected. Although Sam's penis lay slack in its nest of dark curls, it looked remarkably potent. When they had kissed, she had felt his hardness against her, knew it didn't stay soft and flexible, but it seemed so large now, she wondered how relations between a male and female were possible. How could she be large enough to take that within? Babies came out of women. Obviously females stretched. She pulled the blanket back up, lingering to kiss his bristly cheek.

She dozed in the chair, only waking when she heard his voice. "Cold so cold." It was a hoarse whisper. She got another blanket but he still shook with the cold. Finally she got into bed with him, curling her own body against his uninjured side, wrapping her arms around his naked body and giving him her warmth in the only way she could.

Through the night he alternated between hot and cold,

between delirium and lying almost comatose. She talked to him, told him how it could be with them, that he had to get well. In the hours just before daybreak, she began to doubt he wanted to live. Perhaps in his fevered thoughts, it seemed easier to let go. Perhaps it was a way to avoid the hard facts of his life, of a marriage that wasn't yet a marriage, of Sandy's death.

She remembered then her Tucson dream of the wolf that had changed into a man, a wolf who may have not wanted to live. Did Sam want to live? Was he fighting to let go or to be saved? She remembered how in her dream when the woman had realized only the wolf/man could heal himself. Could she do what the woman in the dream had been unable to do—give him a reason to live.

"Try to live," she begged. "Live for the future... our future." What else she said she barely remembered, but she kept talking.

Ollie came in at dawn to put a hot herbal poultice on the wound. "You get some rest," he said when he'd rebandaged the wound.

"I'd rather stay here," she said, sitting by Sam's side, holding his hand.

"Not goin' to do him no good if you get sick," he argued.

"He rests easier when I'm touching him. I think... I give him energy somehow. I won't leave him."

He looked at her before he said, "Maybe so. I'll get you some breakfast." When he returned with coffee and toast, she forced herself to eat because he was right. She had to keep up her strength, but nothing would convince her to leave Sam. She couldn't let go for fear she would return to find he'd let go. Her will that he live might be the thing that kept him with her. She realized, in facing the fear of losing him, that she did love him. She wondered when it had happened. Maybe the first day she saw him in Tucson, the day her heart had recognized who he was to her. She had no barriers left against that love.

The day seemed to stretch into an eternity and yet Sam lingered in fever and pain, not seeming cognizant of anything around him. She took his hand and stroked the long fingers. "I love you, Sam," she whispered. "You have to want to get well; so we can make a life together."

"No," he'd muttered and she was unsure of what he meant, of how much he understood of her words. "Doesn't work."

"Just goes to show how much you know, you renegade, you," she whispered against his cracked lips.

The sky had darkened again when she bathed his skin and felt for the first time it was cooler. His fever was dropping. She closed her own eyes, and for the first time since he'd come home, slept soundly. When she woke, she was nestled against his good side, and the sun was shining through the window. She moved to look up at his face and saw his eyes were open and watching her.

"Are you really here?" she asked, reaching up to touch his face to see the fever was down.

"Seems so." His glance flicked down at the small furry ball sleeping at the foot of his bed. "I've been laying here trying to figure it out. What the hell is that?" he asked.

"A kitten."

"That much I got. What's it doing here?"

She smiled, not remembering when Rahab had come to sleep on the bed. "It's going to be *our* cat. She was abandoned." She moved to stretch the kinks from her back.

"She?" He raised skeptical eyebrows, and she felt like laughing. If he could notice a cat, if he could react to the undesirable fact that it was a reproducing female, he was truly on his way to healing.

"Her name's Rahab. I hope you don't mind taking in another waif."

He shook his head, then winced. "Funny name, but... no, it's all right."

"Are you hungry?"

"No. Thirsty though."

She got the water glass and lifted his head to help him drink. When he'd had enough, he growled. "I feel as weak as that kitten."

"You've been sick."

"I remember that much."

"But now you're going to get better."

"Looks like." He didn't look pleased at the prospect.

She bit her lip. She didn't know if Sam remembered Sandy was dead. She didn't know if he was strong enough to absorb the blow if he didn't. "Rock is in the front bedroom," she said. "He's doing better."

"Good." He closed his eyes. "Maybe I'll sleep awhile."

"After you get some broth in you," she said, heading for the door.

"Not hungry," he grunted.

"You need sustenance."

He didn't open his eyes, but his lips quirked upward. "Suste--what?"

"Food."

In the kitchen, she found Ollie stirring a delicious smelling chicken broth. One of the hens had been sacrificed to the cause. She told him Sam was awake. "He said he doesn't want anything," she added, filling a mug for him and one for herself.

"Don't much matter what he wants," Ollie said with a grin. "Sam's about the worst patient I ever saw. I'm warning you now, Miss Abby. Whatever you want him to have--he won't want. What he wants, won't be good for him. You just thought the last two days were rough."

"I had a feeling about that. We'll get him on his feet though."

Ollie chuckled. "Won't take nothin' to do that. He likely got on them the minute you walked out of the room."

"You don't mean that," she said, aghast at the very idea.

"Might be a good time to tie him to the bed."

"He wouldn't like that."

"Nope, but the threat of it might keep him in there long enough to heal. Tell him me and Bull will do it for you." He chuckled again as he turned to kneading bread dough.

Abby hurried down the hall, uneasy that Ollie might have

been right about Sam's ploys and sure enough in the room, he was sitting on the edge of the bed. He grabbed the blanket and pulled it over his groin.

"What are you doing?" Abby asked, her voice as stern as she could make it.

He sucked in a breath. "I had figured I'd get up."

"Did anywhere in your reasoning it occur to you that you almost died?" She put down the two mugs and walked over to him, pressed against his chest and easily forced him flat on the bed. Before he could do more than grunt, she had his legs levered over and the long length of him tucked under the covers.

"I can't stay in this bed, Abby." He couldn't believe the amount of effort it had taken to get upright and how she had undone it all in a moment with a tiny push.

"Yes, you can and you will."

"I don't like lying around."

"Well, then you better eat," she said, propping an extra pillow under his head, then retrieving the mug and a spoon.

"You're not going to feed me."

"I'm not?"

"Don't think you got me at your mercy here." She stuck the spoon into his mouth.

"Of course." She got in another spoonful before he could complain again. "It so happens that I do."

"I am not going to stay here all day," he grunted, frustrated at his weakness and at the knowledge that he would have to do exactly that if he didn't want to end up flat on his face.

"You nearly died," she said, her lips pinched together in a stubborn way that made him want to kiss them soft, except now he felt too weak to do so much as hold her. If he tried anything more, he'd probably faint dead away, and so he let her feed him, then wash his face and hands. As she worked, he began remembering things about his illness. The feeling of her touching his body, washing him, touching him--everywhere. The memories were vague and dreamlike. Maybe they hadn't really happened.

"Where are my clothes?"

She sipped from her own cup. "You'll get them when you need them." She gave him one of her sassy smiles.

"I need them now. You want me to walk around here buck naked?"

Intending to shock her, he frowned as her smile widened. "I wouldn't mind. For one thing, it will be easier to get you back in bed when you faint, which you will about three steps away from your bed."

He glared at her. The worst part, about what she'd said, was the probability that she was right.

CHAPTER 19

Tucson

Drago Sinclair watched from the shadows as Jacob Spenser puffed his way down the boardwalk toward the tall marshal. "Marshal O'Brian!"

Knowing that Tucson was suffering under a sweltering heat wave, the rainstorms that should have come, should have cooled off the city were still lingering in Mexico or hitting only the mountains, and despite that Spenser wore a proper suit, Drago smirked. This would not be a difficult man to fool.

"What can I do for you, Mr. Spenser?" The marshal's laconic drawl came with a touch of impatience.

"What about the stolen shipment? What about my daughter? What are you doing to get Abigail back?"

"We've got the notices up all over the territory. If it's going to work, we should hear something soon."

Spenser moaned. "You know she can't still be alive. She was--I mean--is a delicate flower. Being in the hands of men like those, who took her, will destroy her spirit if it hasn't destroyed her body."

"We don't know what men have her," O'Brian said. "My deputy and I running all over the county might satisfy you, but it isn't going to get her back. You stopping two, maybe three times a day to ask the same thing isn't helping either."

"The squeaky wheel gets the oil," Spenser muttered.

"What?"

"You have never been a father or you'd understand my concern."

"I'm trying to figure out what's worrying you most--the lawsuit the Montoyas are threatening or your daughter's disappearance," the marshal said cuttingly. "And I am a father."

That stopped Spenser but only for a moment. "You don't have a daughter here."

"She's with her grandparents in Kansas."

"You left her?"

"Mr. Spenser, you have a way of pulling my strings," the marshal said with a tight smile.

"Well you pulled mine too. How dare you imply I don't care about Abigail."

"I'm not." The lawman took off his Stetson and ran his fingers through thick, black hair. "I understand how you must feel, but I'm doing all I can."

Another man walked out of the dry goods store and nearly into them. "Ah Marshal O'Brian and Mr. Spenser, I'm so glad to catch you both together. What is happening with the disappearance of Miss Spenser?"

O'Brian sighed with the look of a man whose day had not been good and was growing worse. "We are working on it, Pastor Ryan."

"I've been on my knees day and night," Ryan said, his face breaking out in a pious smile. "I'm sure we'll hear good news soon."

The scene grew more amusing as Spenser turned toward the pastor with a frown. "I didn't realize you were so concerned with my daughter's well being."

"You are members of my church. Although it seems I haven't seen you there since her disappearance. Is it possible you blame God for this tragedy?"

"I haven't felt well," Spenser protested.

"My sister and I are both quite concerned about Miss Spenser's falling into evil hands," the pastor said with a sigh. "Doubtless your daughter had told you that I'd asked her to dine with us."

"No, actually she hadn't."

The pastor nodded. "Just a few days before her disappearance." He closed his eyes a moment, then looked at each of the men in turn. "Do you think her disappearance was a sign from God?"

"To whom?" asked O'Brian.

"Why to me, of course. I've always felt I should stay a bachelor. Perhaps my seeking to become better acquainted with Miss Spenser led Him to have her kidnapped."

"Wouldn't there have been easier ways?" O'Brian suppressed a laugh. Drago had to resist the same temptation.

"I'm quite sure my daughter wouldn't have been in the way of any plans the Lord might have had for you," Jacob snapped. "Abigail was all but engaged to Martin Matthews."

The marshal looked thoughtfully at Spenser. "Perhaps she staged her own disappearance."

Drago didn't know this Matthews yet, but clearly, the marshal had no use for him.

"She would not have done such a thing. How dare you suggest it? You just want to distract from the fact that you have done nothing to get her back."

Believing himself to be a shrewd judge of men, Drago saw the marshal curb the urge to throttle Spenser. The lawman was not the kind of man to provoke, but Spenser seemed oblivious to that fact.

"When I have something concrete to go on, you can believe I will move on it. But frankly so far it's a man with intense blue eyes. Even I have blue eyes. I suggest you spend some time talking to Matthews. Every time I question him, he pretends to faint, and that little nurse of his shovels me out the door."

"Of course, we're all concerned about Martin's health. Cannot be too careful about how he's tended," Pastor Ryan said.

The marshal snorted derisively. "Martin Matthew wasn't wounded enough to put a man off his feet two days, let alone two weeks. You go over and make him dig into his memory. He ought to be able to give us more identification about the man he saw. Ask him to try to remember if any of them called each other by name. Even a first name would give us something."

Spenser sucked in a noisy breath. "All right, but while I'm doing your work for you, what will you be doing?"

The marshal's smile was cold. "Little things like arresting murderers, putting old Mr. Benson in jail again for near beating his wife to death, keeping the drunks off the street. Little things, Mr. Spenser." With that, he stalked off.

"I'll walk with you on your way to Wesleys," Pastor Ryan said. "I really do think we need to talk about this bitterness you feel toward God."

"I do not feel any bitterness to God," Jacob said, apparently too emphatically because Pastor Ryan smiled, the smile of a bloodhound on the scent of something particularly tasty.

When the men had all gone their way, Drago thought about what he had learned and how he could profit from it. Who should he be to accomplish his goals? The game. It was always the game that was the fun.

Circle R

"Sam, you have to stay in bed," Abigail argued as he wrapped the sheet around his loins and managed to get to his feet.

"Can't stop him, Miss Abby," Ollie said, his own voice disapproving. "Man's goin' to make a fool of himself, he's going to do it."

"I'm not making a fool of myself," Sam muttered, waiting while the lightheadedness passed. He would not let them keep him flat on his back. Bad enough Abby had had to shave and bathe him. He felt disgusted with his body's failure. Only getting up would help him regain his strength. Besides, lying in bed gave him too much time to think and thinking was more painful than the wound he'd sustained. Abby had tried to get him to talk about Sandy's death, but he'd refused. The nightmares he suffered were bad enough. He didn't want to give them added reality by voicing them.

Three steps from the bed told Sam that they were right. He managed to turn and make it to the mattress, collapsing on it as though he'd just run a mile.

Abby untangled the sheets, adding to his feeling of frustration and tucked him into the bed like a baby. He laid there, his eyes closed, wishing they'd all go away. When he opened them, he knew she was still there, even though Ollie had at least had the decency to leave.

"We need to talk," she said, her hand resting on his chest as a temptation and a reminder of all he would never have.

"We've been talking."

"Not about what matters. We need to talk about Sandy. It's like a poison eating at you. I see it going deeper day by day. Talk to me about it, Sam."

"Talk won't change anything."

"You can't hurt worse than you do now. You're blaming yourself for Sandy's death, and that wound is healing slower than the one in your side."

"You told me it would happen. You have to be blaming me too."

"No, I don't blame you. Sandy made his own choice in going to Mexico."

"If it wasn't for me, he'd be sitting on the porch, whittling a gewgaw for that girl of the Reimer's."

"If it weren't for you, he'd have died even sooner." She stroked the dark hair from his forehead. "Sandy was at that age where youths feel they have to prove themselves. You were like a father to him. He was going to show you--one way or another--that he was his own man. You know I'm right. What happened once he did that was just bad luck."

"Yeah right," he muttered, the pain of talking about Sandy's death worse than the pain in his side.

"Sam, you can't change what was. You just have to let it go."

"I'd like to, but..." He stopped, angry that he was talking about this despite his certainty it would make it worse.

"But what?"

"At the last, he was afraid he was going to go to hell. Maybe he did."

"That's what's worrying you?"

He turned away. "I told you. I don't want to talk about it."

"You are carrying that burden, and you don't think you need to talk about it?"

"No, damn it."

"I have to confess something to you."

He looked uneasily at her. "What?"

"I don't believe in a hell."

His smile was involuntary. "I thought you were one of those believers."

"Well, I believe in God. I think the Bible has good stories with wisdom in them, but if I have to believe in hell to be a Christian, I am not one."

"Preachers talk a lot about it."

"To scare people, I'd guess."

"Well it scared Sandy at the last."

"I am sorry for that, but you didn't teach him that, and you didn't send him anywhere. He made his own choice, isn't that so? And if there is no hell, he didn't go there."

He looked away from her. "He was still a boy, and now he'll never be a man."

"Sam," she said, brushing her hand along his bristly jaw, "the Bible says there's a time for every man to die, a time to be born and a time to die. A time to plant, and to sow."

"And that comes from God?"

"More just how it is—not about a god or anything but just reality. Sandy's time came sooner than we would wish. You didn't cause that. You gave him love that he'd never have known otherwise. He made a mistake in who he trusted, in what he did. You tried."

"Not soon enough.

"You know this better than I ever will. You can't go back, and you can only take responsibility for your own mistakes. You can't make others follow what you dictate. That was how it was with Sandy. You gave him a chance. You could not dictate what he did with it."

"Let it go, Abby."

"Can you?"

He looked away, and she bent to kiss his lips. "Forgive yourself, Sam for whatever mistakes you feel you made with him. I think that if Sandy was here, he'd be asking you to forgive him for forcing you to go on that last trip, which could have well killed you too, a trip I know you didn't want to make."

"How do you know that?"

"Wasn't it true?" He didn't look at her. "What happened to Sandy was not your fault. Quit beating yourself up over it."

"You should leave, go back to Tucson."

"You can't mean that."

"It'd be the smart thing."

"And I'm so good at doing the smart thing." She gave him a saucy grin. "Sam do you want me to leave?"

He clenched his jaw. It didn't much matter what he wanted. A man never got what he wanted. He got what he deserved, and he knew what that would be. Certainly not his lady.

"All right," she said reading the pain on his face, "we can talk about this some other time, when you're feeling better."

"Good."

She smiled. "You think I'll forget."

"I could hope."

"Don't count on it."

"A man is a fool to count on much of anything in this life."

"Lord, you are in a dark mood. Well, there are some things a man can count on."

"Like what?"

"My love is one." The words were out before she'd realized it. She had told him she loved him when he was unconscious but not since.

She had hoped when she said the words, he would be pleased, but he wasn't. "You don't want my love?" she asked hurt despite her best intentions.

"You don't love me. Pity maybe, but not love."

"There isn't much reason to love you, is there?" she retorted, knowing he wasn't feeling well enough for an in-depth conversation. She needed to let it go and wished she hadn't gotten it started.

"I'm a bad bet."

"If a woman was a betting woman that might be true."

"I took you by force."

She laughed at him, this time with genuine amusement. "Uh who took who by force?" His scowl deepened. "Did I ever tell you what I thought that day when I saw you in Tucson?" she asked, knowing she hadn't. It was a time to give up her secrets.

"Probably disgusted or scared to death."

"Oh, I was shaking but not with fear." She ran her finger over his stern lips. "Even with that beard covering a lot of your face, you were the best looking, most exciting man I'd ever seen." When he would have argued, she pressed her fingers against his mouth. "I envied you the power and freedom I saw in you, and I felt a surge of something I didn't recognize then, but I know now. Want to know what it was?"

"No." His breath was coming more quickly. She saw what he might deny to his dying day with his lips, he would never be able to hide in those blue, darkly rimmed eyes. He did love her whether he would admit it or not.

She smiled. "Desire. Pure and simple. I started dreaming about you after that day, but I knew I'd never see you again." Before he could put together a reason she shouldn't feel that way, she bent and pressed her mouth against his, tracing his lower lip with her tongue until he opened to give her access to deepen the kiss.

"I dreamed about you," she whispered, pulling away just a little, "but I never could have dreamed what you were really like, never could have imagined kisses like the ones you gave me because I didn't know. I didn't imagine you'd be the kind of man to bring a woman a cow and chickens just because he remembered she'd asked. So much about you, I didn't know."

"Like removing bullets, men dying, stealing, and killing."

"I learned about killing all by myself, remember. I'd seen dying though. My mother and then myself. Oh yes, I was dying inch by inch, Sam. And now... Now, life has never seemed so... alive to me as it does today."

"You don't know what you're saying."

"I know more than you think. I know you're not ready for all of what I'm thinking right now."

"There's more?" His voice was heavy with irony.

She smiled. "Could be."

It was his dream but he couldn't have it now. Not the way he was, the way his life was. He put his forearm over his eyes. "I'm tired, Abby, real tired."

"I know, but things are going to get better, Sam."

"How can you know that?"

"Inside me. I know it like I knew you that day in town before I had any idea who you were."

He turned to stare out the window. "I can't talk about this anymore."

"All right." She stroked his forehead with her cool fingers, soothing him when he didn't feel he deserved to be soothed. "Just remember one thing."

"I'm afraid to ask what that is."

She smiled. "I do love you."

He said nothing, closing his eyes and she saw by his even breathing, eventually he slept. He would heal and come to know that she loved him. She just had to give him time and surely it would all work out. It had to. She felt the tears running down her cheeks as she thought about how empty her years would be if it couldn't.

CHAPTER 20

P ropped up by pillows, feeling a little stronger because he'd made a tour of the room, albeit wrapped in the sheet, Sam watched as Abby walked into the room a tray in her hands.

"More broth?" he questioned with a grimace.

"No. This time you get solid food."

He looked with more interest at the piece of chicken and mashed potatoes on the plate. "One of our chickens?" he asked with a faint smile.

"To a good cause," she smiled as she set the tray on his lap. He ate as she sat on the edge of the bed; then he noticed her bedraggled clothing and remembered his own seeming foolishness.

"Where are my saddlebags?" he asked between bites.

"You don't want to get dressed," she retorted with narrowed eyes.

He managed a smile. "I have to sometime, but for now, no. I bought some things for you in Mexico." He took a sip of the coffee and pushed the kitten away from his supper.

"Some things?"

"My saddlebags didn't get lost did they?"

"I don't think so."

"Then find the bags."

She was gone a few moments, then returned with the worn leather bags. "Open 'em," he said, breaking off a tiny bite of chicken for the kitten.

As Abigail untied the laces, she said, "Rahab seems to approve of that chicken."

He looked at the tiny little mouth tearing up the chicken viciously. "Kind of a fancy name for a plain cat, don't you think?"

"I like it." She had the bags open now and drew out the wrapped packages. "All of this?" she asked, when she'd spread them on his bed.

He nodded and she untied a string, carefully folding back the paper. She hadn't received a lot of gifts and found herself delighted at one from him, even if it turned out to be towels. Then she saw three skirts, one brilliant red, one turquoise with embroidery and a white one with a ruffle, skirts such as she had envied on the Mexican women a lifetime ago. She felt her eyes fill with tears. "Sam, they're gorgeous," she said, holding the white one up to admire.

He resisted the feeling of pleasure at watching her unwrap the items and praise each one. Even though she didn't comment on the fancy lingerie, he saw the way her fingers slid over it that she liked what he had chosen. He'd enjoyed buying it all for her, thought he was a fool because she'd be gone, hadn't dared to believe he'd be able to watch her face as she unwrapped them.

"It's like Christmas," she said as she spread her booty on the bed, admiring each item again. "I love the earrings." She bent then and kissed him.

"You going to wear them?" he asked, pointing to the white blouses that would show the tops of her breasts, and could bare her shoulders if she chose.

"Yes," she said, looking up at him and smiling. "I'm going to wear them all in time but for now..." She began unbuttoning her worn blouse.

"What are you doing?"

"I'm going to put on the clothes you bought me."

"Here and now? What if somebody comes in the door?" If he'd been a gentleman, he'd have turned away, but he wasn't and so he watched as she slid her old blouse off her shoulders, revealing more silky skin that he'd thought to see, but with the chemise still in place, also a little less than he might have hoped.

"Nobody will without knocking," she said with a smile, then reached for the buttons at the back of her riding skirt, shimmying out of it to reveal long, slender legs beneath the pantalets. She picked up a white blouse and slipped it on over her head. Then came the red skirt. When she was dressed, she held out the skirt for him to admire. She'd kept the sleeves of the blouse on her shoulders, but he knew how easy it would be to slide them down and the thought caused the blood to pulse to his groin in a way he hadn't felt since he'd been injured.

"You are beautiful," he said, smiling with a feeling of relinquishment. If only this could be real. If she could be his wife in all ways, but it wasn't going to be. He more than anyone understood why that was so. Pretend. He could pretend for this moment that he was a man like any other. That he hadn't killed, that he hadn't stolen, that he wasn't responsible now for a young man's death. She bent to kiss him for the moment taking away his gloomy thoughts.

"Thank you," she whispered against his lips. He could see down the front of her blouse, the dark forbidden cleft between her breasts, the milky tops of creamy round orbs. It gave him a warm glow to realize she was wearing something he'd given her, something that he realized revealed more breast than he wanted seen by anyone but him.

"Did you see the scarves?" he asked, trying to keep his voice casual.

She nodded and picked a bright flowered one up, tucking it into the front of the blouse and covering that which he wanted covered when she left this room.

"Is that better?' she asked, amusement in her eyes and he knew he hadn't fooled her for a moment.

"Whatever you want," he said, but when she would have loosened the scarf, he took her hand in his and kissed it.

"Would you like to go outside?" she asked as she brushed her fingers over his jaw.

"With this?" he asked, holding up the sheet.

"I think you might be ready for some clothes of your own," she said. "No boots though and a shirt would probably be painful. Just pants--for now."

"You're treating me like a kid," he protested but agreed as he wanted to be up, to be outside.

"I'm treating you like my husband who was seriously injured," she amended as she went out of the room and returned with his pants.

He swung his legs over the side of the bed and sat a moment swaying. "Lying here has made me weak," he grumbled. She held the pants and helped him put his legs into them. When they were at his knees, he said, "I can manage the rest."

"You're not shy, are you?" she teased. "You know I've seen all you've got." She smiled more broadly. "Handled it too."

"Abby!"

"Hmmm?" she asked, all innocence in her tone. "You are my husband, Sam."

He ignored the provocation as she helped him stand, then pull up the pants, despite his own embarrassment at the service.

When he was covered, she said, "You will be my husband in all ways, Sam, if it's what you want." She met his questioning gaze. "I want to be your wife."

"Even knowing all there is to know about me?" he asked, as she put her arms around him to help him walk to the porch.

"Well, I'm not sure but..."

"What do you mean?" He felt his heart grow cold.

"You are... uh awfully big."

He looked quickly at her and saw the flush on her cheeks. He smiled despite himself. "I am?" he said with a broader grin.

"I don't, of course, know much about that kind of thing, but it did seem that way to me."

"We'll talk about it another time," he said realizing this kind of conversation was going to leave her more evidence of his size than he wanted anyone to have at the moment.

Outside, sitting on his own porch and feeling a breeze against his skin, he felt as happy as he'd been in days. He felt Abby fussing with the bandage at his side, but there was no fresh bleeding. He could hardly believe how good it felt to be out of the house. Rahab jumped onto his lap. She'd taken a fancy to him and seemed to be underfoot wherever he was. "How'd you come to name her Rahab?" he asked as he petted the kitten.

Apprehensive about the name for the first time, Abby considered not telling him who the first Rahab had been, then she realized he would find out. "She was a Biblical heroine," she said and told him about the harlot who had saved the lives of two spies who'd been sent ahead by Joshua to scout out Jericho before his conquering of it, and then whose own life had been spared when the city was taken.

Sam didn't say anything for a moment, just looked at her through narrowed eyes. "Is there a moral to this story?"

"There usually is."

"And I don't suppose there's any way I'm going to stop you from telling it to me."

"She is praised for her courage and faith. She was later married to Salmon, who some might be one of the spies she saved."

"This is beginning to sound like a fairy tale."

She smiled. "All love stories seem that way."

"Maybe. So you decided to name this little one after a whore. You are a strange woman, Abigail Spenser."

"Abigail Spenser Ryker," she corrected.

"That can still be changed at any time."

"I suppose... if I was so inclined, unless you were so inclined to make it impossible," she said with a note of irritation. "I'll get you something to drink."

The glass of water came with Ollie, not Abby. Sam didn't question it, deciding she'd said more than she wanted and was going to avoid him, hoping he would forget her words.

"I sent her off to take a nap," Ollie said.

"Did I ask?"

"Nope, but you were wondering, and I wanted you to know. She's wearing herself thin, taking care of you."

"I didn't ask her to do any of it." Sam heard the surliness in his voice. He didn't like it but felt unable to force it away.

"You don't need to, her being the kind of woman she is."

"She'd take care of a dog, in other words," Sam said, freeing his finger from the kitten's tiny teeth. Strays, that seemed to be Abby's specialty.

"She loves you, boy, stupid as that is for anybody," Ollie snapped.

"She feels sorry for me."

"The main one feeling sorry for you is you. Talking to you is like barking at a knot. A man wants to make a fool out of himself, a smart man steps back and lets him do it."

Sam's scowl deepened as Ollie left him. Rahab nipped particularly hard on his finger, her little paws kicking his hand as fast as she could go. "You too?" he asked, teasing her round little tummy with one finger.

Tucson

"Now, you have to think. There must be something you're not remembering about the day Abigail was kidnapped." Jacob

Spenser stared at Martin Matthews, the pointed gaze causing Martin to move uneasily in his chair.

Martin didn't want to think about it, didn't want to be in the office where the heat was sweltering. He wanted to be with Priscilla, sitting on her patio, having her bring him lemonade, and bathe his forehead with lavender water. He looked at Jacob and resented everything about what had brought him to this moment. "I told you all I know," he said.

"Are you sure you want to get Abigial back?" Jacob asked, his voice equally resentful. "Perhaps there's something about that day you're afraid she'll reveal."

"Ridiculous." Martin jumped to his feet, and then held his head as though it hurt. He glanced sideways at Jacob Spenser and saw no sympathy on his stony face. "Remember I had asked Abigail to marry me," he said defensively.

"But what was her answer?" Jacob asked.

Martin sunk in his chair. "You know what it was. She said no."

"Perhaps there never was a little man," Jacob said, his voice rising. "Perhaps you took my daughter out onto the desert and killed her, burying her in a secret grave."

"That's insane."

"I've seen how you're making up with Miss Wesley. Perhaps you never wanted to marry Abigail."

"I refuse to stay here and listen to this."

"Anybody here?" A voice called from the outer room.

"Come back here," Jacob yelled.

A tall, thin man filled the doorway, his suit neatly creased, his hair slickly combed back, a small mustache, neatly trimmed beard, and wire-rimmed glasses giving him a look of somber consideration. "I'm looking for Jacob Spenser."

"I am he."

The man held out his hand. "I'm Fred Graves with Wells Fargo. I'm here to investigate the theft last month."

Jacob had been wiring back and forth to them, had expected

that they would send someone but hadn't expected it so soon. "Have you talked to the marshal yet?"

"This is my first stop."

"There has been nothing since I sent the last telegram," Jacob said. "This is my assistant, Martin Matthews. He was with Miss Spenser when they tried to retrieve the stolen shipment."

Again the man shook hands, looking at Martin. "I heard about that. It was a foolish thing to do. I hope you know that now."

"I knew it then," Martin said, "but I couldn't let Abigail go alone."

"I see. Well, let's go through all of what you do know again. I'm sure you're tired of telling the story, but you never know when something new will come to you. A little piece you didn't remember before." He smiled.

"I'm willing," Martin said. "So far nothing has helped." That wasn't the literal truth. He'd remembered most of the events of that fateful afternoon; and he had no desire that it all come out. He had no choice but to appear helpful. He went through the story again, more or less stopping it at the point where he was shot.

Graves sat in a chair, crossing and recrossing his legs as he listened. He glanced down, saw a scuff on one shoe and frowned before he looked at Martin. "One thought has come to me, as I listened and tried to piece this all together. That day when the man led you to what he claimed was the stolen mails, did you see the bags, any sign of the shipment?"

Martin thought a moment. "No. He seemed upset that they were gone, became quite agitated."

"Hmmm. Interesting, and do you believe he was pretending?"

"Why would he have needed to?"

"To me," the Wells Fargo man said, "it sounds as though we could have two separate gangs. One man who planned to be there. Others who may have been there by coincidence. The question is who was either one? Any honest cattlemen would have long since contacted the marshal."

"I never thought of that."

He smiled and took off his glasses, cleaning them carefully. "These things have a way of surfacing."

Martin felt himself start to sweat. If Priscilla ever knew what a coward he'd really been, there'd be no more bathing of his head with lavender water. No more sweet times in her family's garden. He looked up and met the questioning gaze of Fred Graves. He felt like a man proverbially between the devil and the deep blue sea. He couldn't hide much from this man without his becoming an object of suspicion, but if he was fully honest, the truth just might come out. He couldn't afford that. He rubbed his forehead, this time because of a real headache.

∼

Circle R

Abby sat beside Sam on the porch swing feeling the most relaxed and happy since she'd come to the ranch. Sam had been growing in strength, and the fever hadn't recurred. Day by day he was stronger. Although he didn't talk much, he was trying to be pleasant, at least he had been since the day Ollie had--as he'd described it--taken Sam to the woodshed.

The stars shone overhead, the moon was still low on the horizon, and she and Sam sat in darkness, a warm feeling of comfort in the air. Behind her in the house she could hear Bull and Ollie having a checkers game, Ollie winning from the sounds of his laughter.

She teased Rahab with a string, giggling at the kitten's antics.

"You look like a little girl tonight," he said with a smile.

"I feel like one."

"What kind of little girl were you?" He took her hand in his, stroking the fingers, bringing them up to his recently shaven jaw.

"I don't know. Cosseted, over protected, I suppose. My parents only had me. My mother was sick a great deal; so life was pretty quiet."

"I'll bet you were a pretty little thing."

"I was gawky and anything but pretty."

"I don't believe that. You're beautiful now. Do you know that?"

She shook her head. "Not really. I see it in your eyes though."

"Wouldn't have had much use back then for a little kid who swabbed out the saloon, would you?" She felt his smile against her fingers.

"I'd have ordered you to take a bath."

"With good reason. There weren't a lot of chances for a kid like me to take a bath... or a change of clothes if I'd wanted to wash them."

"Then I'd have been rude to you, but inside I'd have been envious because you could run free, and I couldn't." She teased her fingers into the hair that was long on his neck.

"And I'd have known even then I couldn't even touch the hem of your skirt without getting strung up."

"Take a bath, little boy," she said, taking the string and teasing it down his cheek, alongside his neck, then wickedly letting the end drop inside his shirt. "Now what would you have said to me? Would I have learned some words I didn't know."

He was very aware of the end of the string as it tickled his skin. God, did she have any idea what she did to him with her little games. It seemed she did more and more teasing. Sometimes he thought he'd go crazy if she didn't quit, other times he knew he'd die if she did.

"Might be. How hard would shocking you have been?" He smiled.

"Not very. I didn't know hardly anything."

"And you do now?"

She flicked the string at him, a wicked little smile on her lips. "Maybe a little more."

"Like?"

"Well... I know... uh. Let me think." She let the string tease the sensitive lobe of his ear, the side of his neck.

He grinned. "Better you don't know."

"I guess we all get taught what we need most."

"Life'll do that," he agreed.

"What were you taught as a little boy?" she asked, "besides how to survive."

"Hmmmmm, trying to think if there is anything for polite ears." He tensed his muscles as she followed the string with the tip of her finger, trailing it lightly down his cheek, to his jaw, then turning to stroke across his lower lip.

"Lady," he warned.

She grinned. "Yes?"

He opened his mouth and took her finger into it. He held it with his teeth, aware that she held every part of him within the crook of that little finger. She could do whatever she wanted to him, and he'd let her. It scared him to realize how completely she had taken him over and without yet having made her really his. He was half afraid to take that last step. He knew she was teasing him into it, trying to bring about her will totally over him and maybe it would happen. He wondered when it did if any part of him would be left free.

"Were there any special women in your life?"

"Special? Like how'd you mean that?" He asked with a grin.

"Have you loved anyone?"

Damn, how was it a woman never was satisfied to stay on the easy stuff. "I don't know if I even know what love is."

She ignored his answer as she took his hand in hers, felt along the fingers, then the palm. "You work hard," she said. "Your hand is callused, your skin toughened."

"I do work the ranch here when I'm home and even rustling isn't easy," he said, feeling his body come to life as she thoroughly explored his palm, her fingers gentle and probing as she felt of a ridged scar.

"Where did you get this?" she asked. "Were you attacked?"

"More or less." He wasn't sure he wanted to tell her the story, then decided she'd keep asking questions until she got it all and he might as well give up now. "I was about thirteen, working at a bar in Witchita, cleaning up after everybody left, which was like maybe three or four in the morning. A cowboy came in, drunk as a skunk. He wanted a whiskey. I told him we were closed, the bartender had gone home. He didn't like the answer. I tried to stop him, a bottle got broken. I ended up with this and he ended up... a little worse."

"How much worse?"

"He bled to death." He grimaced. "Dumb thing, huh? Bleeding to death over a shot of whiskey."

"That's terrible. Were you blamed?"

"It was an accident, but the sheriff didn't think much of me, for which I can't say I blame him. He threw me in jail for a couple of weeks, for which I do blame him. Maybe he was thinking he was doing me a favor, scaring some sense into me. I suppose it worked, but I also met a couple of guys who knew more about ways to make money than I did. It was the start of my... for wont of a better word, outlaw ways."

She kissed the scar. "Kansas, Texas, New Mexico. You've lived about as many places as I have."

"Not likely the same ends of towns. Like in Tucson. I've seen the inside of saloons, the street but never anyone's home."

"How about Maiden Lane?" she asked. "Have you been inside any of those establishments?"

There was a long silence. "What do you know about Maiden Lane?"

"That is Tucson's--how do you say it--tenderloin district."

"Well, you're not supposed to know about that."

"Why do they call it the tenderloin?" She looked up from behind her lashes.

"Lord, lady. You expect an answer to that?" He gave an amused laugh.

"You're my husband. Who else should I ask?"

He didn't much like the idea of her asking anyone else that was for sure but to explain would bring him to an arousal.He couldn't afford that right now. "Ladies don't need to know things like that."

"Oh they don't, huh? I think you're wrong about that too."

He shook his head. "Maybe." His smile turned wicked, and the light in his eyes was so sensual she could barely stand the sensations that just that look sent shimmering through her whole body. She could feel him in every part of her body.

"All right, I'll let that go for now. You were going to tell me about the women in your life."

"You think this is a proper conversation for us to be having?"

"I'm curious, of course. You know about the men in my life."

"I don't count that Martin as much of a man."

She thought about telling him about the pastor's attempted advances. He had enough grievances against so called holy men. "So it's your turn," she argued. "There has to have been someone."

"There were a few when I was young and stupid enough to think a woman could care for me. They would meet me in the dark, the pleasures we found were always forbidden, and then the next day they wouldn't admit they knew my name."

"That's not very nice," she said indignantly.

He smiled, pulling her hand back to his lips, kissing the tender palm. "And will it be any different with you, lovely lady?" He worked to keep his tone light. "When you get to Tucson, if I go riding by, won't you turn your head as though you've never seen me?"

"If you go riding past me in Tucson, like you did before," She smiled and brought his hand to her breast, felt the shock throughout his body. "If you do that," she said, turning in his arms and reaching for the buttons on his shirt, unfastening them, brushing his skin as she undid each one, until she could pull the shirt apart.

"Well, when you do that," she said, bending to kiss the skin she'd bared, "I'll run out into that street and order you to stop.

Accuse you of deserting your wife." She pushed his shirt more widely apart and shocked the hell out of him when she took one of his nipples between her teeth.

"Good God, do you know what you're doing?" he asked, sucking in a breath.

She smiled against his skin. "Maybe not. I think I need instructions."

"And maybe you don't."

"You're almost well," she said with a teasing smile, then dropped her hand down and let it brush across his groin.

"Woman," he said with a little laugh. "You want to get those lessons right here with the boys coming in and out?"

"Mmmmmm, let me think."

He couldn't repress the laugh, then felt the humor disappearing as she nuzzled against his throat, her fingers tangled in his hair. He knew it couldn't be, that none of it was possible, but he pulled her onto his lap, ignoring the squeak of protest from Rahab and the jolt of pain it cost him.

He kissed the soft indent at the base of her throat. She opened to him like a flower with the petals opening to the sunlight, and he brought her head to him, kissing her lips, the kiss deepening as he claimed her with lips and hands and felt her brand him with her loving caress. He wanted to pick her up, carry her into his bedroom, but his physical condition made that impossible. Instead, he kissed her again. "I don't know the why of this," he whispered, "but I've learned not to throw away good things when they come to me."

She smiled against his lips. "Am I a good thing, Sam?"

"The best that's ever come to me."

"I want to be yours in every sense," she whispered against his mouth. "Now."

"This is mighty cute out here," the nasty voice came from the darkness.

Sam shifted Abby to one side. "How long have you been

watching?" he asked, looking toward where he knew Snake had to be standing in the darkness.

"Can't blame a man for watching when a couple is going at it the way you two were right in public." Snake stepped onto the porch.

Abby gripped Sam's arm, held him for fear he would attack Snake. Not yet recovered from the wound he'd received, there would be little question as to who would get the better of such a fight. It was the only reason Snake would dare say the things he had.

"Please, Sam," she said, feeling his biceps swell beneath her hand. She could never hold him if he made up his mind to lunge forward.

"Yeah," Snake slurred with a chuckle, "please, Sam."

"You're drunk."

"True. I drink too much. Drink to forget. Drink to remember."

"Whiskey will be the end of you someday."

"But not tonight," Snake said, moving closer to them. "That's real nice the way she's holding you. Maybe she's scared you'll get hurt again."

"No chance of that," Ollie said from the doorway, a shotgun cradled in his arms. "You move any closer, and I'll let you have it right in the chest. We've had enough trouble here without you adding to it."

Snake's laugh was ugly as he looked at Sam, then Abby, sending a shiver down her spine as the light from the kitchen gleamed in his eyes, giving them the reddish glow of the serpent for which he was named. "Another time," he said, stumbling off the porch and heading for the bunkhouse.

"We fire him," Ollie said.

Sam shook his head. He didn't want to tell Ollie the reason in front of Abby, but he knew if Snake was let out of their sight, it wouldn't take him long to find out about the reward for Abby's return. He would turn them in, and then they'd have a worse problem than just Snake's treacherous personality.

Whatever promise the moment had had, Abby saw it was gone; and she felt cold and cheated. He told her goodnight, and she knew if Snake hadn't interrupted them, their tonight would have been together. She felt frustrated but resigned to waiting once more.

In her room, Abby stripped off her clothing, put out her lamp and started to get into bed. She could hear Sam entering the hall, knew the rest of lights were being blown out. Soon he would be stripping naked, then lying on his big bed. It was a warm night and he'd be on top of the sheets. Would he fall asleep immediately or remember the things she'd done to him, the things he wanted to do to her?

She'd gotten used to spending the night beside Sam and liked it. Now that he was nearly healed, that wasn't necessary, except she didn't want to sleep apart from him. She'd had enough being apart. And she had had enough of something else. Of having men rule her life, make all the decisions. Even when that was a man she loved.

Moonlight filled the room as she sat on the edge of her bed, reluctant to lie down. She remembered then the blouse Sam had bought her and smiled. Stripping off her underwear, Abby picked up the blouse that was meant to be off the shoulder, low on the breast but that she'd worn more modestly. Tonight was no time for modesty. She slipped the blouse on, then the red skirt. She went to the mirror and looked at herself in the moonlight. She fluffed out her hair to fly wildly around her face. She pulled the blouse a little lower, revealing more of her breast, then bit her lip to redden it before she walked out into the hall.

CHAPTER 21

S am's room was illuminated by the moonlight. She closed the door softly behind her. He was lying on the bed, just as she had imagined. She didn't think he was asleep, but he said nothing as she walked to the bed. His eyes were open, looking up at her.

"Do you know what you're doing?" he asked, his voice hoarse as his gaze skimmed over the blouse, down her hips, then back to look into her eyes.

She put one knee on the bed, leaning toward him. "Some of it," she said with a nervous giggle.

"You're sure about this?" he asked, his eyes heavy lidded, a faint smile on his lips. "What have you got on under that?"

"I suppose you'll just have to find out, won't you?"

"God, are you sure?" he repeated

"You said I'd have to beg. Is that what you want?"

"There's no going back from this."

"And you want freedom?"

"It's not about me, Abby. It's about you. You can never give this night to another man."

"There will be no other man to give it to."

He smiled then and pulled her down beside him. "I thought

about you in that blouse when I bought it, imagined how it'd look with nothing but your breast under it." He cupped her breast in his hand, teased the nipple into the tight nubbin, and then did the same to the other breast. "God," he whispered, "you are more beautiful than I imagined."

"I want to be for you," she said, leaning over him and letting her breasts hang loose for his pleasure. He slipped the blouse from her shoulders, down her arms, and soon had it at her waist. She lay on the bed beside him as he caressed her, his lips teasing against hers, his hands stroking her breasts and then down her belly to the line of the skirt. She felt herself catch fire. She was alive with wanting. Desire seemed to be swallowing her in its hot womb. This was better than any dream.

She thought then of his nudity and realized she wanted to touch him as he was her. Tentatively she reached out to touch his nipple, felt it tighten under the touch and she bent to nibble on it, teasing it with her tongue. Heard him suck in a breath and knew she was doing something right.

He had bought the skirt and should know how it unfastened, but his fingers fumbled with the strings. He wanted this too much to go slow, but he had to go slow for her. He would make this take all night; he'd touch her everywhere, all the secret places that would leave her quivering for him. And he'd somehow keep from exploding from his own need.

Finally he got the damned skirt off and pushed it from her silken skin. "Oh yes," she whispered as she pushed herself against his hand, felt the calluses graze across her skin, bringing her to a feeling of yearning that left her insides like jelly.

"You want me, baby?" he asked, his voice low and soft, the tones like honey brushing over her soul.

"Yes. Oh yes. Just you." She gasped as he delved between her legs, touched her where she hadn't ever been touched.

"You're wet with wanting me" he said, teasing her with his light touches.

"Oh God, Sam. Don't..."

"Yes."

"Aaahhhh, yes. Yes." She reached out then and felt of his manhood, felt how hard he was. It felt swollen and large and again she wondered how she could take that into herself at the same time she wondered how she could live if she couldn't.

He moved over her, spreading her legs apart but instead of entering her himself, he pushed his fingers into her, touching her where she hadn't imagined a man should and yet where she wanted so much to be stroked. She realized then that he was stretching where he would go, and she yielded herself to his ministrations; let him do with her as he would. She knew it was wanton to be sprawled as she was before her lover and yet it was so right. This was what she wanted. What she had to have.

"You are so ready, baby," he whispered. "Ready for me." And then he was leaning into her, pushing that large shaft of his into her, filling, gradually stretching her even more. It was hurting some, but it felt so right to have him there.

She moaned her assent, her need.

"Just be patient, little one. Soon." When she knew she couldn't take more of him, he let his weight drop onto her just a little.

"Your wound?"

"Is fine."

"Are you sure?"

His lips closed over hers, his tongue pushing her lips apart, pressing within her, teasing her mouth and tongue, until she felt herself pressing up against him. She as finally his. This was it.

Sam began to move and she discovered that hadn't been it at all. "Oooohhh," she moaned as she felt the sensations growing within. "What are you..."

"Move with me, baby. Thrust up. Come on, that's my girl."

And she let her hips begin to do what they wanted. She reached up then grasped his buttocks as she had been wanting to do. When she heard him gasp, she hesitated but he said, "Yes, do that. Touch me, grab me."

She smiled then against his lips as he kissed her soulfully, made her feel alive from her head to her toes. She let her hands stroke down his buttocks, felt the muscles shifting in his back under her hands as he moved, and she felt the sensations growing, seeming to be filling her and yet at the same time making her want something so badly that she couldn't imagine living if she didn't have it.

Just when she thought there could be no finer feelings, a kaleidoscope seemed to burst within as she felt an explosion of sensations in her groin, radiating outward and throughout her whole body. "Oh Sam," she cried, feeling as though she might faint with the bursting feelings.

"Yes." She felt his body seem to convulse into her. He collapsed onto her, twisting to the side to spare her his weight as he went down. She lay feeling as though she had died and been born again.

He started to pull out, but she held him to her. "Not yet."

"You'll be sore."

"I don't care. I don't want this to end yet. I never..."

"Never what?" He brushed her hair aside kissing the lobe of her ear.

"Never imagined this was it."

"Well, it was the beginning of it." She could hear the smile in his voice.

She felt suddenly so sleepy. "Is it okay to sleep now?" she asked, hearing the slur in her voice.

"Very." She liked it that he was holding her. She worried for a moment that maybe he had hurt himself with his exertions, and then she thought of nothing more as she fell into a sound sleep, wrapped in his arms and his body still part of hers.

When Abby woke in the morning, she was cradled in Sam's arms. She stretched, more content than she ever remembered being. She looked up to see his eyes on her.

"Did you hurt yourself last night?" she asked remembering her last coherent thought of the evening.

"Do I look like a man who hurt himself?"

"No, actually, you don't. You look like the cat that got the cream."

He grinned. "How about you, are you sore?"

She thought about that and surprisingly found she wasn't.

"You're not sorry?" he asked, a faint frown between his brows.

"Do I look sorry?" She ran her hand up his arm.

"No."

She looked up. "Sam, don't think because of last night... that you owe me anything... I mean if you decided--"

She didn't get out the rest of her words before he pulled her into his arms and crushed his lips against hers. "What do you think I am?" he asked, when he gave her breath. "Crazy? Last night was the best night of my life. When I bought you that outfit in Nogales, I never dreamed it was a gift for me."

Sighing with contentment, she cuddled against him, enjoying the feel if his skin against hers. "If I'd known this was what they were talking about, we wouldn't have been talking that first night."

He laughed. "It wasn't the time for it."

"Maybe but... we've waited a long time. How long do you think we'll have to wait before--"

"Before we can do it again?"

She nodded, watching him eager to find out if it would be as good a second time.

"Maybe... about five minutes," he said, his lips claiming hers in a kiss that told her everything she wanted to know.

The sound of the door opening, startled them both. Sam threw the blanket over Abby, using his own body to shield hers, then looked into Ollie's startled face.

"I was just going to see how your wound was--" Ollie stopped and stared at Sam, then beyond to Abby, then he grinned.

"Reckon I'm in the wrong room," he said with a chuckle. "Pardon me." With that, he backed out, slamming the door.

Abby began to giggle. Sam looked worriedly at her. "This is place is impossible to get some privacy. I'm sorry." She giggled more. "You're not embarrassed?" he asked.

She bit her lip and smiled impishly at him. "Are you?"

"Well, we are married," he said.

"I know, but that was *your* mother."

He laughed. "He'll get used to it."

"I think he already has." She pulled him down into her waiting arms. "Now I want to get used to it."

Tucson

Walking into the darkened cantina, Martin Matthews and Jacob Spenser, ordered beers and sat at a small table. "Where's the detective?" Martin asked.

"Who knows? The man has been no help anyway. Noses around, looks at everyone but other than clean his glasses, what does he do?" Jacob grumbled, swallowing a healthy slug of the beer. "What does Wells Fargo care about the theft? I'm the one being sued by the Montoyas. They'll have my house, everything if I don't find that shipment."

"And Abigail," Martin reminded him.

"And Abigail." He shook his head. "I don't want you to say a word to anyone, but I'm half ready to believe she ran off with a man. Maybe she had the whole thing plotted. Steal the booty, leave me hanging to dry, and run off."

Martin almost laughed at the preposterousness of the suggestion, until he remembered Jacob's last farfetched idea was that he'd murdered Abigail. This was at least an improvement over that one.

Marshal O'Brian entered the bar. When his eyes adjusted to the dimness, he looked over the room, saw them and headed for their table, snagging a beer for himself on the way. He threw his hat on the table, wiped the sweat from his forehead as he took a long drink. "Nothing. So far the reward notices have brought nothing. I've had the weirdest suggestions from people as to what happened to her with the idea they might get the reward for the suggestion."

"Like what?" Martin really disliked the tall, handsome marshal. Something about his arrogant demeanor reminded him too much of the man he was sure was an outlaw. Two of a kind— badge or not.

His mood of irritation hadn't been helped when Priscilla put him off rather than saying yes to his offer of marriage. The look on her face had told him that she wouldn't be saying yes when she found a way to not hurt his feelings. Two women had rejected him in one summer. He had to think that meant something. Unfortunately he couldn't decide what.

"A witch down in Tubac said Abigail Spenser is living in Boston now with a fat

merchant. She'll send you a telegram tomorrow... or maybe yesterday." O'Brian pulled out a cigar from his pocket, bit off the tip, and lit it.

"That's not so farfetched," Jacob said, waving the bartender over for another beer. "She might be with a fat merchant some place.

"Any man that has bought a piece of jewelry or a gewgaw for his wife is suspect," O'Brian said. "Your daughter's disappearance and cock and bull stories about it are about all I hear. The Wells Fargo detective isn't helping. He has stirred up people all over Tucson with his questions but no answers." He looked at the two men through the smoke of his cigar.

"This is going to cost me my home, my business."

O'Brian's eyes narrowed. "I thought you were worried about your precious little girl."

"I am. Of course, I am, but she could come home anytime. I mean she might be off cavorting with a blackguard for all I know."

You said your daughter is a lady." O'Brian's voice grew cold.

"She is... I mean. Of course, she is. I'm just desperate with the situation."

Still looking at him suspiciously, O'Brian said, "I've done what I can. I don't know what in the Sam Hill has happened to her or the shipment."

"Sam hill?" Martin asked, sitting up suddenly in his chair.

"So I swore," O'Brian snapped. "A man's been through what I have over this situation deserves a good curse once in awhile."

"No! It's that I remembered the name of the man."

"Not Sam Hill," O'Brian said. "I've heard enough about witches and the likes. I'm not going to believe the devil took off with Miss Spenser."

"No, not Sam Hill. Just Sam. His name was Sam."

O'Brian ran his fingers through his hair. "So now we have a man with blue eyes, called Sam. Do you know how often men use their first name in this country?" He raised his eyebrows.

Martin sank in his chair, not knowing if he was disappointed or relieved. In the excitement of trying to figure out where Abigail and the shipment were, he'd forgotten he had reason to be glad she had disappeared. "Well, they were unusually intense blue eyes."

A man sitting at a nearby table rose and stood over theirs his hands leaning on the table surface. "You looking for a Sam, maybe a big man with blue eyes?"

"Who?" Jacob asked. "Where?"

"Might be I know a man like that. Might be I don't. This worth any money?"

O'Brian looked up at him, his own intense blue eyes going

glacial. "Might be it's worth staying out of jail. I know you, Reese. You got anything, you better spill it now."

Reese glared at the marshal, but then looked at Jacob. "I'm a good citizen. Don't want no trouble. Might be the man I know ain't the same one, no how. What do you want him for?'

"That important to you?" O'Brian asked, lightly running his hand over the butt of his Colt .

Reese's eyes flicked from the marshal's hard expression, to the gun, and back again. "The man I know's a rancher east of me. Over in the San Rafael Valley, down near the border. Comes to Tubac now and again for supplies. Now you going to tell me what you want him for?"

"What's his full name?"

"Ryker. Sam Ryker."

"At this point, we just want to talk to him," O'Brian said.

"What do you mean?" Jacob said. "He kidnapped my daughter, maybe stole the Wells Fargo shipment."

O'Brian took a moment to find a smile. "We are looking for a man named Sam purely as a possible witness to a disappearance. We don't know this Ryker is the same person or has anything to do with your daughter or the robbery. Don't go off half cocked, Spenser, and cause yourself and this town a lot of trouble."

"What do you mean?" Jacob asked resentfully.

"I mean that you could get a lynch mob going with that kind of talk. Ryker might be no more than a rancher." He gave Reese a hard look. "What else do you know about him?"

"Ryker?"

O'Brian's face darkened. "Who else do you think I could mean? Saint Nicholas?"

"Yeah... uh, well, he's tall, keeps to himself when he's in town. He's got a rough bunch that ride for him, but then in that country, who don't?" Reese chuckled, saw that no one else was amused and sobered.

"What about a family, things like that?" Jacob asked.

Reese laughed again. "Man'd be a fool to ask questions of that one."

"Ryker spelled with a Y?" O'Brian asked.

Reese nodded.

"I will see if there are any posters out on him, but the name doesn't sound familiar. I can wire the sheriff in Tombstone and see what he knows about him." O'Brian rose polishing off his glass of beer.

Jacob sighed. "Is this man--" He looked Reese directly in the eye. "Do you think he'd be the sort to kidnap a woman? The woman who disappeared is my daughter."

Reese rubbed his bearded jaw thoughtfully. "Reward on that, wasn't there?"

O'Brian swung around and took hold of the front of Reese's shirt. "You holding out on me?" he asked, raising Reese up on his toes. "You tell the law what you know, or you'll be finding yourself spending a night in jail and that's not a fun place to spend a night--especially when I don't want it to be."

Reese paled. "I told you what I know. As to whether he'd kidnap a woman. Damn it all, how's a man to know a thing like that? He's a hard case. I know that. Wears his gun like he knows how to use it, but I ain't never seen him shoot nobody. People walk a wide circle around him. He's the kind tough enough to spit in a rattlesnake's eye."

"How recently have you seen him?" Martin asked, finally finding his own voice.

"Not for maybe six months. I haven't been to town much though myself. So he might've been in and out."

"How many men ride with him?" O'Brian asked.

Reese considered. "Ten maybe. Hell, how would I know?"

"That would require a very large ranch," Jacob said. "Either that or Mr. Ryker is involved in something more than ranching."

"Or," O'Brian said, skeptically, "Mr. Reese here doesn't count too good." He watched as Reese sunk into his seat, then said, "I'll go see what I can find out," and was gone.

The three men sat. "I'll buy another round," Jacob offered, hoping no one wanted anything.

Without waiting for a further word, Martin headed for the bar and returned with three beers, setting them on the table. The thought of finding the big man who had looked at him so menacingly was not one to fill Martin's heart with joy. It didn't seem there was any way out though without proving himself to be a coward in front of all the people of Tucson. He might know it to be true in his heart, Abigail knew it to be true, but he didn't want it confirmed to the general populace.

As he'd remembered the name of the big man, he also remembered the way the man had looked at Abigail, the returning glint of interest in her own eyes. It was just possible Abigail was where she wanted to be. Martin hoped that Sam could never be found. If the marshal decided to check him out, was it possible he'd be expected to ride with the posse, ride with them to identify a man who would spit in a rattlesnake's eye? He took a healthy swig of his beer and stared into the glass.

"You know," Reese said, staring into his own beer, "I really don't know that man. Don't know him at all... Don't want no truck with him. No siree. I'm thinkin' I was due home yesterday. Shouldn't hang around here at all."

"There would be a reward if my daughter and the stolen booty are recovered," Spenser reminded him.

Reese laughed with no humor on his sour face. "Reward don't do a dead man no good." Martin's sentiments exactly. He looked at the man more hopefully. Maybe he could yet find a way out of this.

O'Brian walked into the bar, straddling one of the chairs. "No posters and nothing on him in Tombstone. He either hasn't caused any trouble there or hasn't been in the territory long."

"Then that's that," Martin said with relief.

"It can't be," Jacob protested.

"We'll have to go down and check him out," O'Brian said, looking at Reese. "Think you can find the ranch?"

"Never been there. Just heard," Reese said uneasily, his eyes shifting from the marshal back to his beer. "Dangerous thing to do in that country. Identify a man. Get a bullet. That's the way it works sometimes."

"Dangerous up here not to," the marshal said coldly, lifting Reese's chin so he was forced to meet his hard gaze. "You will lead us to the ranch. I'll get together a posse, and we'll leave in the morning." His smile was glacial. "If--by chance--you leave town before that time, I will find you. I know you're afraid of Ryker, but you'll find I'm a man to fear too."

"You will protect me," Reese said, "not let him know I'm the one identifying him?"

"Don't worry about it. You aren't identifying him as a kidnapper," O'Brian said, reaching out and slapping Martin on the shoulder. "Matthews here'll be along to do that—if he turns out to be the one."

Martin swallowed hard, nearly choking on his beer. He knew--short of leaving town--he had no choice. He'd have to ride with them and pray this Sam Ryker wasn't the man he'd seen.

"My wound," Martin started to say but was cut off by the marshal.

"Is luckily healed."

"Uh yes." Martin wished he could disappear. No hope. He was the only witness. He'd have to go. Then he thought of a bright lining to this. Perhaps it would make Priscilla become more passionate again in her attachment to him. Perhaps she'd be upset when she thought of him riding into danger.

"I have to say good-bye to someone, but I'll be ready in the morning."

"Good," the marshal said grimly.

Outside, Martin headed straight for the Wesley's. He would have the chance to be the first person to tell Priscilla about the possibility of finding Abigail. That should impress her.

At the house, the sun shone on Martin once more when

Priscilla herself opened the door at his knock. "Martin," she said, stepping back to allow him to enter. She was dressed in a confection of pink ruffles, and he thought the color was perfect on her curvy little body and sweet face. He wished he had the right to kiss those full lips good-bye. Perhaps she'd yield him that favor too when she realized the danger into which he was going.

He told her his remembrance of the name Sam, about the man Reese, about the ranch in the San Rafael Valley, about the possibility that this was the place Abigail was being held.

Priscilla's face grew more animated as he spoke. "Oh I hope so," she said when he'd finished. "If only they could bring her home. You can't imagine how much I have missed her."

"It's possible," he said. "I'll be going with them."

"That's wonderful. It makes it more likely they'll be bringing her back." She moved around the little table in the parlor to look out the window, then back at Martin.

Martin nodded. "It could. I have to identify the man... if Abigail isn't with him."

"I can't bear to think that. This has to be the one, and she will be all right."

"It could prove quite dangerous," he said, trying to make his voice sound brave and determined, "but anything is worth bringing Abigail home."

Priscilla looked at him strangely.

"Not for myself," Martin added, hoping she was jealous, "but for her father and herself."

"I think of her everyday," Priscilla said. "She's my dearest friend."

"If she's there, we will bring her back," Martin said, trying to add another degree of determination to his voice. He wasn't very good at playing the hero, didn't really want to, but if heroes were what ladies wanted, he was willing to give it a try.

"Good."

"May I kiss you good-bye?" Martin asked, moving to stand near Priscilla, but not too near.

She looked at him thoughtfully, her luscious lips looking so ready to be kissed, but she shook her head. "No, Martin and I have to tell you now that I won't marry you."

Expecting it or not, he was still disappointed. "Won't you think about it? "

"It would be wrong to let you think it would change. It won't."

As he walked out the door, he wondered how he had managed to lose out again.

CHAPTER 22

Circle R

Abby dangled a piece of grass over Sam's mouth. She brushed his lips just enough to hopefully make him think a fly might have landed there. Looking at his closed eyes, she was disappointed he was asleep or ignoring her. Smiling, she made the teasing blade move a little faster, a little stronger. He reached up to bat it away but still didn't open those cobalt blue eyes.

She considered the situation a moment, looked down at the small stream, the cottonwoods that were shading them, then at the lean man lying beside her, his hands now under his head. They'd gone for a short walk with the intent of building up Sam's strength, but she'd been the one to suggest they stop at the stream, that they lie down and take a nap. Of course, she'd had more than a nap in mind when she'd made the suggestion. The joys of the marital bed were a delight of which she never tired. Exploring her husband's hard body was a delectable experience. She did know he needed his rest though. Perhaps the walk had tired him more than he'd admitted.

"You're looking for trouble," he muttered not opening his eyes.

She smiled. "Am I going to get it?" She put a hopeful tone in her voice.

"It's just possible."

She dropped the grass and kissed his cheek, enjoying the smoothness of his jaw. "How come you don't wear a beard like so many men?" she asked as she teased along his skin with her lips, then her tongue.

"Want me to grow a beard?" he asked, still not opening his eyes.

"No, I just wondered why you didn't follow the fashion of the times."

"Maybe I don't know it."

"Maybe but you could follow what other men do."

He smiled. "Why?"

She giggled. "No reason I can think of."

"Me either."

"Hmmmmm." She nipped at his full lower lip. "Well, not that I always approve of rebels, in this one instance, I do like you going against tradition."

"And why is that?"

"Without all that facial hair I can see your whole handsome face and all its expressiveness."

"So I expect you'll be wanting me shaving twice a day just for you?"

"Well actually." She laughed. "I kind of like the bristle too, the way it rubs against my cheek, my lips, my..." She laughed again before she pressed her tongue against his mouth and encouraged it to open.

"Abby," he warned.

"Hmmm." She slowly undid the buttons on his shirt--her second favorite thing to do. Sam had such a wonderful chest, muscular, sculpted with strength and grace, the skin bronzed.

"What do you want?" he asked.

"Your shirt off would be a good start." She pulled the material apart so she could see the whole breadth of his chest, spoiled only by the white bandage. His eyes opened then, the clear blue as startling to her as it had been the first time she saw it. "You are so beautiful," she said, running her finger along the edge of his jaw.

"I think that's my line," he disagreed, his lips quirked just a little.

"I've seen pictures of Greek sculptures," she said, kissing the point of his jaw and leaning her breasts against his bare chest, "and you're more beautiful than they."

He swallowed caught up in the sensations she was inciting. She stripped his shirt from him, then bent to unfasten his heavy leather belt. She pulled it from the loops. It was a unique experience, as until Abby, he had never allowed a woman to undress him.

"How far you going with this?"

"How far could I go?" She slipped the first metal button from its cloth loop, then the second, until she had them all undone. She pulled the pants apart then just far enough to reveal the dark curly hair arrowing down his abdomen to the jutting proof that what she was doing was not without effect.

"Do you like this?" she asked, slipping her hand inside the jeans.

He pulled her head down to where he could kiss her lips, the kiss drawing her into him, making her feel as though their very essences were flowing together. Taking their time, they undressed each other, playing and touching until his hard body was levered over her.

"I want you," he rasped, his voice not much more than a whisper.

"Then take me. Take me now." To be outdoors, under the blue sky, to feel the breeze against her skin and to see above her lover, powerful and potent as he came into her with force, brought a primal rhythm to her. It was one she rose to meet; that she felt throbbing in her veins making her want to give him all, as she took all into her.

Afterward as they lay, limbs entwined, she kissed his chest, letting her fingers tease his nipples. She wanted to hear him say he loved her and she never had. She wanted to ask him. Surely he loved her. It couldn't be like this if he didn't, but why didn't he say the words? She knew she shouldn't ask. Someday. Someday he would tell her.

He went to the stream and sluiced up water to wash. Then returned with a smile and washed her skin with leaves and fresh clear water. After their skin dried in the sunlight, they dressed.

Reluctantly she realized she had to talk to Sam about something else. She had put it off as long as she could. "Sam, I think I should make a trip to Tucson." She saw him stiffen, wasn't surprised that he had. "I feel so guilty," she said, wanting him to understand, "because I'm so happy, and I know my father must be frightened as to what happened to me."

He buttoned his shirt without saying anything. If she went to Tucson, she would not return. It was that simple. Once she got back with her people, she would begin to forget what they had had. This would be a moment in her life. She'd remember it fondly, if she thought on it at all, but she'd never return to him. He couldn't go with her, not farther than the edge of town.

If he arrived with her and the stolen mails, the authorities, and her father would decide he'd been the man who robbed the stagecoach. The trial would be for appearances. They would hang him no matter what Abby tried to say. Besides she didn't know that he hadn't been the thief. She knew he would steal cattle. How much of a reach was that to stagecoaches? Worse, if she tried to defend him, they might decide she had been part of the plot from the beginning. Sam knew how the law worked, and it wasn't always fair. He wouldn't take the chance, not with her precious life.

"You want to leave?" he asked finally.

"Not leave but visit."

"You've always been free to go when you want."

"I didn't say go."

"It's what it amounts to."

"I worry about my father. Isn't that normal?"

"So, you make love to me; then you tell me you're leaving."

"That is the most ridiculous thing you've ever said," she snapped, eyes flashing.

"You wouldn't be the first woman to do it."

"I don't use people that way. I don't sell myself, Mr. Ryker. I don't know what kind of people you've been around. Wait, I suppose I do know. Well, I want you to know everybody doesn't live that way!"

He ignored that. He knew people better than she did. "You can leave whenever you want."

"I told you that I don't want to leave," she said. "I want to stay and make a life with you. I want us to be together in a normal life, like everybody else, but I don't know if I can stand your suspicion, the way you never really trust me."

"So what are you going to do about it?" he asked, not wanting to hear the answer.

"I don't know," she said, stomping down the trail toward the house. "When I do, I'll let you know."

∽

Martin rode with the posse, exhausted at the long trek they'd made down the valley, camping once, and then moving on at daybreak. He wasn't cut out for this sort of thing, but he saw the steely-eyed determination in Marshal O'Brian's eyes and knew nothing short of finding Sam Ryker would satisfy him. Martin could only be grateful that if that did happen, and he imagined now it would, at least he rode with eleven other men.

Of course, looking at those men, Martin was unsure how many were any better with a gun that he was. He had no idea how many hard-cases they would face, if Sam Ryker was the man who had stolen Abigail away. These men were for the most part ranchers and storekeepers. Two had talked of fighting in the Civil War, probably the only ones besides O'Brian who had used a gun for more than hunting or an occasional target practice.

Martin felt sick, as at a little before dusk, they rode over the ridge that according to Reese would take them to Ryker's ranch. He had hoped O'Brian would wait for morning for the confrontation, but the marshal was in no mood to wait. Reese had spent the better part of the morning cadging his bets every direction he could by claiming to be unsure where the Circle R was, and even more unsure about who Sam Ryker was. Martin recognized Reese as being of the same stripe as himself, which was anything but reassuring and had done nothing to improve the temper of the marshal.

The day before they had stopped at one ranch, another that morning. No one at either admitted to knowing anything about the Circle R, other than a ranch south of them. They never heard of Abigail Spenser. O'Brian then had pulled his horse beside Reese's and said, "Either your memory improves or we'll be taking a little ride--just the two of us."

"That way." Reese had swallowed and pointed south. "Uh... after I point it out to you, can I go?" he added in a weaker tone.

The marshal's smile held no humor. "You'll leave us when we've talked to Ryker." Reese's face had fallen, but he'd not tried again to convince O'Brian to let him leave. Martin felt certain the delay was over. The ranch house he saw in the distance would be that of Ryker. He could only pray Ryker was not the Sam he'd seen.

Riding into the ranch yard, several men came from the bunkhouses to watch the armed men riding into their yard.

Martin felt his stomach turn over when he saw a tall man walk from the house, a gun low on his hip, tied down to his thigh. The man didn't leave the porch. He watched as the riders rode up, stopping their horses by the hitching rail.

"You boys need something?" he asked lighting a cigarette. The smoke drifted up. Martin wished it was thick smoke. Thick enough to cover the reality before him. This was the Sam.

"Your name Sam Ryker?" Marshal O'Brian asked.

The tall man took a drag on his cigarette and nodded. His blue gaze scanned over the men in front of him, passing over Martin and Reese, then back to the marshal.

"I'm Tucson's Marshal O'Brian."

Martin saw then that two men from the bunkhouse had come up and were lounging near the lower side of the porch, both armed. Two more came out from the house to stand behind their boss. To Martin, they all appeared to be tough customers.

"This all your men?" O'Brian asked, his eyes flicking over them.

The tall man nodded. "Pretty much. I got a man down with a broken leg, but otherwise what you see is my crew."

O'Brian looked at Reese. "This the Ryker you seen coming in for supplies?"

Reese nodded.

"That now a crime, Marshal?" Ryker said with a derogatory laugh. "Last I heard a man could still go to town. Maybe the law's changed."

"We're looking for a kidnapped woman, Abigail Spenser. A man named Sam was last seen with her."

Sam Ryker glanced over the men on horseback again. "And you all came along to bring her back?" he asked with a hard smile.

"We came to see if the Sam Ryker who lived here knew anything about her." The marshal now looked at Martin. "Is this the man you saw that day?"

Martin nearly choked. He knew, if he said it was, guns would blaze. He saw it on Ryker's face as he watched him, the cigarette dangling from his lips, his hands loose at his side, not far from his gun. He knew it from the equally stern expression on Marshal O'Brian's face. He would be in the middle. Even though the posse outnumbered the men on the ground more than two to one, it wouldn't be enough to save him.

Ryker's eyes were cold as death. "So," he said, "you think I'm someone you know?"

"No," Martin said, aware his hands were shaking, his whole body cold. "Never... uh saw you before. You couldn't be him. Not the same at all. No way. That guy was uh shorter. Yeah definitely shorter." To identify Ryker would be a death sentence. Martin swallowed against his dry throat. Maybe Abigail was already dead. What good would more people dying do?

O'Brian looked at him, must have read the fear in his face, because his expression was one of pure disgust.

"Reese said you had more men riding with you," O'Brian said, turning to Ryker, his eyes looking beyond him into the house.

"I had three more. Like I said, one of them has a broken leg. Ranches go up and down in number. You ought to know that," Sam said, the tone of his voice friendly, the expression in his eyes anything but.

"Mind if I search your house?" O'Brian asked.

Ryker threw his cigarette to the dirt. His lip curled in what could never have been mistaken for a smile. "No man searches my home without cause," he said, his voice level and calm.

"There is cause. A woman is missing."

"Your man told you I'm nobody he saw before. What more do you want?"

"You got something to hide?" O'Brian asked, his own smile hard.

"Every man who's grown has something to hide. The point is do you have the right to go into my home without my say so. I'm betting, without some kind of legal paper, you don't. If you want to try it anyway." He moved away from the post he'd been half leaning against, his legs now spread, his hand loose but so close to that gun. "Well, we can see who walks away from this."

O'Brian seemed to consider. "You know a fair amount about the law for a *law abiding* man."

Ryker's teeth flashed white against his swarthy skin. "I've had a few--unfortunate experiences with lawmen who were less than honest. It pays a man to know his rights."

O'Brian sucked in an angry breath. Martin could feel the marshal's rage, his urge to challenge Ryker, to draw his own gun, but the law was the law. Martin knew Ryker was right and so did O'Brian. Without a warrant or permission, they had no right to search the house.

"Well," O'Brian said, matching his smile to Ryker's, "I do want you *law-abiding* citizens to know that if you meet up with Miss Spenser, there's a reward of $500 for her return and more for the Wells Fargo shipment that was taken at the beginning of the summer."

"We'll for sure be on the look-out," Ryker said. "You be careful on your ride home, you hear marshal. There's outlaws in these hills."

The tall man's haughty smile was pure deviltry, and it irritated even Martin. He could imagine how it was infuriating the marshal to see the man standing so tall, his legs spread wide, his stance one of pure arrogance. He was the man. Martin knew it, and he guessed the marshal did too. It didn't matter because Ryker had more nerve than Martin did. Irritated or not, he wasn't willing to stand against him, not even behind the marshal.

"I'll be looking out for you," the marshal said, his eyes still on Ryker. "You know that, don't you?"

"Well, that'll make me feel a whole hell of a lot safer at night, Marshal," Ryker said. "Nothing like law and order to help a man sleep like a baby."

Martin heard Ryker's men laugh and knew Ryker had won. He'd won because of Martin's cowardice. It wasn't too late. He could still tell the marshal that he knew this was the man, then he looked at Ryker, saw those cold blue eyes watching him with calculation. He knew he'd be the first one blown out of the saddle.

"I think we ought to go," Martin said, trying to keep his voice from shaking. "We do have a long ride to Tucson."

The marshal was all but ready to chew nails, but he had no choice but to wheel his horse and ride out. Martin knew the man would grill him on the way back. He had to stick to his story. He was a coward. Ryker knew it too, but he didn't want anyone else to be sure of it.

As they rode north, Martin felt sick at his spinelessness. It didn't matter. Under no circumstances could he face Ryker. A thought came to him. Maybe there was another way. Jacob had spoken of hiring a detective. There were bounty hunters, ruthless men. That's what they needed. Tough men who would be a match for Ryker's own toughness.

Martin remembered a couple of names he'd heard when the subject had arisen before. Men little different from Ryker. He would convince Jacob to spend the money. If he had to, he would spend it himself. He had no choice if he ever wanted to hold his head high.

"You think they'll come back?" Ollie asked.

Sam shook his head, staring at the kitchen door. When Ollie started to follow him inside, he said, "No, I need to talk to her alone." Ollie nodded and followed the other men to the bunkhouse.

Opening the kitchen door, Sam wasn't sure what he'd expected. It wasn't Abby sitting on a chair with a rifle across her lap. "They're gone," she said her gaze meeting his.

He nodded.

"Will they be back?" She rose, laying the rifle on the table. Her hands were shaking.

"Your boyfriend won't dare change his story. O'Brian wanted to make a stand here but without that coward's word, he couldn't." He smiled at the memory of the rage he'd seen on O'Brian's face. "They won't be back soon if ever."

"He was never my boyfriend. There's a reward for my return.

Did you know about that?" She turned to look at him, her gaze probing.

"Yes."

She sucked in a breath. "You talked about my not being someone you could trust. Don't you think you should have told me about that?"

"I found out about it in Nogales. When I got back here, it wasn't the first thing on my mind. I didn't think about it later. To be honest, I didn't know it would matter until you asked to go back."

"I told you; it was just a visit," she retorted as she walked to the counter. He watched as she measured out coffee, then filled a pot with water, putting it on the stove.

"I half expected you to come out while they were here," he said, sinking into a chair. He felt tired, so tired he was having trouble thinking straight.

"And watch you get yourself blown to kingdom come?" she asked, a sarcastic twist to her voice. "Is that what you honestly expected? It's not as though you would have gone peaceably. Do you think I want you shot or at the end of that rope you claim is waiting? If you did, then you don't believe I love you, do you?"

He met her disappointed gaze. He couldn't protect himself by lying to her, and the truth was he didn't know what he'd expected. "If you wanted to go back, you missed your ride," he said.

"Oooh!" She swirled around and stared at the coffee pot, willing it to begin to boil.

"The men know about the reward now."

"And what does that mean?"

"It means that at least one of them will be interested in claiming it--one way or another."

She turned to look at him again. "Snake?"

He nodded. "I wasn't sure if they'd seen the poster in Nogales. Likely they hadn't or were too drunk to pay any attention to it.

O'Brian made good and sure they know about it now." His smile was sardonic.

"I thought..." She stopped and wrapped her arms around herself to stop her shaking. "He believed it was you, didn't he?"

"He was pretty sure but couldn't prove it. He left here one mad hombre."

"I was afraid there would be a gunfight."

"It looked that way for a minute."

"Would you have killed innocent men to keep my presence here a secret?"

"It's not that simple."

"You know we have nothing to be ashamed of. We're married. No one would claim you kidnapped me once that was told."

"If you were so sure of that, why didn't you come out?"

"Because I wasn't sure of it," she snapped. "By the time I realized what was happening, it was all so tense, I was afraid anything could ignite a spark and blow it up."

"If O'Brian had seen you here, there'd have been more questions. Even if he'd believed we were married, he'd have figured I had something to do with that stage robbery. One of us would've left here only over a horse. He's half convinced me and my men were the ones who not only took you but robbed the stage."

"How could he think that? They know there were only two men who robbed the stage."

"Because it would be tidy, and marshals like tidy cases. If we had you, we were there with the shipment. We must have been in on it. It's the way he'd think. The worse is he might think you were involved too."

Despite his having mentioned it before, she still was aghast. "How could he think that?"

"If you're with me now, who's to say we weren't in this together from the beginning."

"My father would know better."

"Would he? Would it even matter what he thought? The point is we do need to get that shipment to Tucson, but we don't want either of us connected to it. We don't want O'Brian to have an excuse to come back."

"I can't hide forever. There are others, who know we're married. Someone's bound to say something--especially if there's a reward poster."

"That's possible. Maybe if we can get the shipment back, wait awhile, then it will be less linked together when you show up."

"This all seems so complicated. Can't we just take it back?"

"If you want to see me hanging from a tree, it's not a bad idea."

"You know I don't want that. This is terrible. All confused."

"Since when isn't it. You'll just have to trust me about this and--" He stopped and gave a mocking laugh. "I don't know how I can ask for that when I can't do it myself." He glanced at the rifle now on the table. "Who was that for?"

His gaze met hers, and when he saw the tears in her eyes, he wished he hadn't said anything. "How can you ask? How can you even ask? I'm not proud of it, but I would do anything to keep you safe." Tears ran down her cheeks. "Does that satisfy you or is it just another truth you won't believe? But then why should I waste my breath trying to tell you anything. You prefer to believe there's no one trustworthy because then you don't have to take the risk of trusting yourself. Isn't it safer that way for you, Sam?"

He couldn't explain the pain in his heart when he thought about letting her down, about being let down by her. If he ever told her how weak he was where she was concerned, she would have power over him. He'd once vowed no one would ever have that kind of control again. The only trouble was he wasn't sure that where it came to Abby it wasn't already too late.

She knelt in front of him, her eyes large and luminous in the fading light. "There is a violence in you sometimes. Maybe you wanted there to be shooting. Maybe you hoped a bullet would be the easy answer to your problems."

"You think I wanted to get myself shot?" he asked with disbelief.

"Did you?"

"No." Even as he said the words, he wondered if they were true. Did he want to die? Did the last bullet somehow seem like an easy answer to the web in which his life seemed to have become enmeshed? Whichever road he took was the wrong one. Every path doubled back on itself. He didn't like thinking Abby would kill for him, didn't like thinking he could put her in a position where that might be necessary. What kind of monster was he?

She took his hands in hers, holding them to her cheek. "We can work anything out, Sam, if you'll just give it time."

He knew that wasn't true. Knew sometimes there was no road back, but he couldn't bring himself to tell her that, not when she was rising and coming up into his arms, not when her lips were against his. He wanted to believe she was right, wanted to believe it even if only for that moment. The trouble was--he couldn't.

"I truly appreciate your visiting me, Margaret," Abby said, handing the older woman a cup of tea as they sat on the sofa in the great room. Although she didn't have in this valley the silver tray and china that her Tucson home offered, she found it unimportant. Mugs and a plain wooden tray were less important than enjoying another woman's conversation over a cup of tea.

"I'm glad to have a neighbor close enough to visit without being gone all the day long," Margaret said, sipping the tea and smiling. "It's been a long time since I've enjoyed goin' visitin'."

Abby smoothed down her turquoise skirt, glad she'd had a moment to change into it and the white, long-sleeved, high-necked blouse when she had seen Margaret drive up in her buckboard. She wished for a moment that she had her things around her--her Hepplewhite chairs, the pianoforte, but those things weren't important either.

"That good looking husband of yours didn't look too pleased to see me though," Margaret said with a smile that said it didn't matter. "That man scowled at me like I was some kind of spy, sent to infiltrate the enemy camp."

"I'm glad you didn't let him scare you off," Abby said, not denying Margaret's assessment. Sam had been moody and his dark expressions enough to scare off all but the heartiest souls. Even the men had been complaining about his quick temper in the week since the marshal had made his late afternoon visit to the ranch.

"I thought you might want to talk to me," Margaret said her gaze on Abby. "We had us a visit from the Deputy U.S. Marshal."

Abby should have expected it but hadn't. "When?" she asked.

"A week ago, I expect. He asked about an Abigail Spenser. We told him we didn't know such a woman, then played dumb about Sam too. Out here, men mind their own business, don't mess much with each other unless they find out the other is stealin' from 'em."

Abby sipped the cup. "He came here too."

"It looked like a hanging posse to my Ralph, and he said we don't have no truck with town folk comin' out here, doing a lot of damage, then runnin' back to town. Your man's never been a problem. He's even rounded up some of our stock what wandered down your way and driven them back. I wanted you to know there wouldn't be no problems coming to you from us"

"Thank you." Abby swallowed back tears.

Margaret's gaze was sympathetic. "You don't need to be telling us anything. It was obvious when we saw you two together how much you loved each other. No way you was taken off by some man if you weren't wanting it."

She managed a smile. "That is true."

"Well, just figured it'd be good for you to know," Margaret said, reaching over to pat Abby's hand. "That husband of yours is a right good looking man, reckon it makes up for his surly ways."

"He's not always like that. We've had a few problems to work through. He doesn't trust people easily." She smiled up at Margaret. That was certainly understating the case but more or less true.

"My boy and I were looking for Sandy when we came in. He rode off someplace?"

"Sandy's dead," Abby said, biting her lip, wishing there was some easier way to say it. "He was killed in a cattle accident about a month ago."

"Oh my." Margaret's face showed her shock. "It comes quick out here, but when it comes to someone young like that, it's a right shame."

"It--It's been hard on Sam."

Margaret sighed. "Now I see why his mood's so poorly." She shook her head. "I'm always a fool, judgin' folks when I know that's the Lord's business, not mine."

"You've been a friend to us, and I won't forget it."

CHAPTER 23

Martin walked into the Wells Fargo office, startling Jacob who looked up at him wide-eyed. "Well?" Jacob asked, then looked beyond to see the man who had followed Martin.

"Who is this?" he asked, his gaze scanning over the tall, wiry man. "Do I know you?"

"Nope," the man said, a faint smile on lips almost hidden by a big mustache.

"This is Drago Sinclair and his partner." Martin looked at the second man. "What did you say your name was again?"

"He didn't say, and you don't need to know," Drago answered, sitting in the chair in front of Jacob's desk and putting his scuffed, dirty boots up on the desk.

Martin nodded. He looked at Jacob. "These are uh detectives I want us to hire to get back Abigail and the stolen Wells Fargo shipment."

"Detectives?" Jacob Spenser snorted as he looked over the two men, his expression derisive. "Martin, we need to talk."

Drago's smile was mean. "Anything you've got to say, you can say in front of me. I don't like secretive partnerships."

"Partnerships?" Jacob squeaked. He glared at Martin. "We need to talk.

"Your partner offered me a deal," Drago said. "I'd consider that now makes me your partner too. You trust me or the deal's off."

"Partner?" Jacob said looking uneasily at Martin.

Martin turned to the bounty hunter with a placating smile. "Just give me a minute to explain this all to Mr. Spenser."

Drago dropped his boots with a thud to the wooden floor. "All right. I'll be in the bar down the street." With that, he and his partner walked out of the office, slamming the door.

"Martin," Jacob said as soon as they were gone, "you are my employee not my partner."

Martin resented that—true or not. "I had to say that to give my offer more clout."

Jacob shook his head. "That's neither here nor there. Do you know what kind of men those are?"

"I know exactly. I asked around town, found the right man for this job. I was told that they are the kind who can find Abigail and the stolen shipment. It'll take men like them."

Jacob shook his head. "You make a deal with the devil, and you're his bondsman. Those men are devils."

"Don't be ridiculous. They came well recommended."

"By whom?"

Martin looked away. "Jared Smithers."

"He's a gambler."

"Not only that. He's also an astute businessman, and you know it. He said Sinclair can do what we need."

"I am beginning to wonder about you, Martin. I don't like any of this." He hesitated, drumming his fingers on the smooth wood of the desktop. "How much do they want?"

"A thousand dollars."

"That is twice the reward."

"It's what they say they must have. We don't have a choice, Jacob. The marshal hasn't been able to find out anything. He has to operate within the bounds of the law. These men don't." Martin felt an anger deep within at the way he had felt humiliated by Sam Ryker. There was one way to get revenge.

Jacob sighed noisily. "What are we becoming, my boy?"

"Desperate," Martin answered. "Don't you want to find out what happened to Abigail?"

"You know I do."

"Then Sinclair and his partner are our best chance. We have to hire them."

"What makes you think they'll be any more successful than the marshal?"

Drago, who obviously had not gone to the bar, threw open the door, his eyes narrowed, his smile ugly. "I know the territory, and I know the kind of man you're looking for." Clearly he'd listened to every word they'd said. Martin knew the man couldn't be trusted, but he was desperate. He couldn't stand against Ryker, but he could hire someone who could.

Spenser stared at Drago, then to Martin. "I don't like it, but I suppose since we've had no response, increasing the reward makes sense."

"Five hundred up front. The other half when I have done the job," Drago said, rocking back on his chair. His small partner stood in the open doorway, his gaze darting from one to the other.

"Nothing up front," Jacob corrected. "If we give you five hundred dollars, we'll never see you again."

"You calling me a liar?" Drago asked, his dark eyes showing how quickly the situation could turn nasty.

"Of course not. The question though is what would we get for our money? The reward should be sufficient."

"I told you my terms. Take them or leave them." He shrugged as though it was nothing to him either way.

"Where would you start looking?" Jacob asked with a sigh of relinquishment. Martin knew he would go with the bounty hunter because he had no other options.

"Somebody's seen something or knows more than they've

said. I'll get it out of them. I got a few connections might help me more than the marshal." Drago smiled as he looked at Martin.

Martin cast his gaze at the floor. He hadn't dared to tell Drago Sinclair that he had recognized Sam Ryker. If he had, the man would have had him in his control. He'd told him only what he'd told everyone else, but he believed Drago could dig up what the marshal couldn't, because Drago wouldn't care what methods he used. It was no more than Sam Ryker deserved--to send a wolf after a wolf.

∾

Circle R

"What did Mrs. Reimer want?" Sam asked he ducked his head under the pump and held it there under a stream of cold water.

"Just paying a social call." She decided it wouldn't hurt Sam to know that his neighbors were more dependable and trustworthy than he thought. "Margaret did mention that the marshal had been to their place asking about you and me."

He looked up, shaking the water from his head, then taking the towel she handed him. "When?"

"Before he came here last week."

"What did they tell him?"

"Nothing. Mr. Reimer believes you've been a good neighbor and didn't have any interest in giving out information to outsiders." When he sat at the table, he handed him a cup of coffee. "Margaret also asked about Sandy. I told her he'd died after a cattle accident."

He sipped the coffee looking darkly into space.

"I fixed a corn chowder for dinner. Hope that sounds good to you."

She wished she hadn't brought up the subject of Sandy. It was an unhealed wound to Sam. The meal she had planned was a simple one--potatoes, a white sauce and dried corn. She hadn't felt up to any more complicated attempts, especially since most of those still ended in failure.

"Sounds fine."

"I invited Ollie and the other men to join us tonight." She wished Sam would tell her what he was feeling, share his pain, but that wasn't his way. When he hurt, he closed down around himself, and nothing could get him to pry open the wound.

"Fine," he said, his mind on anything but supper.

"Talk to me." She sat beside him, putting her hand on his where it rested on the table.

"Nothing to say."

"You sure you don't mind having the men here tonight? I thought I could read aloud. It makes for kind of a nice evening."

"It's your home for as long as you want it that way, Abby. You can invite anybody you want."

"My father?" she asked, raising her eyebrows.

"Sure. Invite the marshal too while you're at it. A hanging party's always popular."

"Sam!"

He rose. "I'm sorry. What time you figure supper for?"

"Six."

"I'm beat. Just think I'll lie down a bit."

When he was gone, she felt more worried than ever about him. Sam never admitted to weakness, never took a nap when someone wasn't forcing him. She didn't know how to reach him, but she had decided to give it a desperate try in what she had chosen to read. Somehow he had to realize that all men had second chances.

When they'd eaten supper, the men settled into the great room, as ill-at-ease as their boss. It took all the courage she possessed to walk into that room a Bible in her hand.

Snake snorted when he saw the black book with the gold cross on its cover. "Might've known."

"Shut your mouth," Bull said. "My ma used to read to us. I like a woman reading at night. Seems like a good thing."

Snake gave him a gimlet-eyed glare but said nothing more. Sam stood by the door, one shoulder leaning against it, his eyes hidden in the shadows from the lamplight.

She had already opened the book to the section she wanted to use. She knew in some ways she was being manipulative to use a story that suited her purpose, but she read it anyway about the man losing a sheep and leaving all the rest to go back and find that lost sheep. It was a story of redemption and forgiveness. She hoped it would speak to Sam. When she finished, she looked up and saw the men looking at her with mystified looks.

"Sheep?" Ollie said with a sneer. "What man wouldn't shoot a sheep before it got the chance to be missing. Dumbest critters on the face of this good earth."

"Well what if it was a cow," Abby said, managing a smile. "Supposing it was a prize Hereford cow, newly brought in from New Mexico and it wandered off."

"Wal, shore you'd go after it," Rock said from his place on the sofa, his bad leg propped on a pillow.

"Would you if it was a scroungy longhorn?" she asked unwilling to give up. "There are so many. If one just wandered off, nobody'd maybe care at all."

Ollie shook his head. "Not so. A good cattleman don't want to lose none of his stock."

"That's why rustling's so unpopular," Sam added acidly.

Wandering cattle wasn't going to work much better for her purposes than sheep, but she had to go ahead with it because she'd run out of examples.

"All right then," she said, "in this story the teacher was talking about sheep because that's what the men he was speaking to understood, but supposing it was a cow. He'd come home and there'd be rejoicing right?'"

She looked at the laughing men and tried to decide what was so funny. "Miss Abby," Ollie said, "a cowboy coming home thataway, braggin' about bringing' home a measly cow, when that's his job to do everyday, would get laughed off the ranch."

"I suppose a cowboy wouldn't normally brag to everybody, but if that cow had been lost and nobody could find it. If everybody else had given up, had said, it's probably been eaten by wolves, well, then, maybe he'd come home and be proud about it."

They considered that, all their expression thoughtful except Snake's. He looked at her with a sneer and something in his eyes she didn't like. She suddenly wished she'd worn her boy's clothing instead of the Mexican skirt and long-sleeved blouse. Although she knew the blouse wasn't revealing, Snake's near ogle made her feel it was.

"A man might brag in a situation like that," Joe said, smiling. "I've been known to gloat a time or two when I've been right and everybody else is wrong."

"Well, it's not exactly gloating," Abby said, "but more joy."

"Joy over a stinking sheep?" Rock asked, a frown on his face as he had been unable to release the original story.

"Parables are just stories with a message, and that's the way this one is." She knew she was floundering and wished she'd never thought of using the Bible to do this.

Ollie chuckled. "Why not just say it straight out then?"

"Don't pick on Miss Abby," Bull growled at Ollie, a frown on his big face. "She's reading us from the Good Book. My Mama used to do that. You dimwits oughta be grateful to her, not finding fault with it, even if it don't make any sense."

"Thank you, Bull," Abby said, smiling crookedly. This wasn't nearly as easy as it looked when the pastor got up to do it. She was determined though and tried again. "The Bible says people are a lot like the sheep Ollie was talking about. They're not remembering anything, wandering off, getting lost, then not knowing how to get home."

"If God compared people to sheep," Rock said with disgust, "I don't guess he's wanting us back."

Abby sorely regretted this whole idea. She glanced over to try to see what Sam thought about it and noted the smile on his face, then wondered if it came from the message or the mess she'd gotten herself into with it.

"The point is," she said, trying again, "there is always a second chance for people. God never gives up on us."

"And," Sam said, moving out of the shadow, the faint smile still on his lips, "that word repent, what does it mean?"

"Well, being sorry, I think," she said.

"Just being sorry? Or does it also mean paying for what you've done wrong?"

She looked away from Sam because when she looked at him, she felt lost in her desperate need to make him see he could begin again. "It's easy to love your friends," she said, "but to love an enemy, to die for him. How many do that?"

She made the mistake of glancing at Sam. "Not any still alive," he said the expression in those blue eyes sardonic.

"Well, it isn't easy for men to love the way God did," she said, knowing with a sinking feeling that she wasn't going to convince him. She suddenly wasn't even sure she understood it that well herself. These stories were so simple, so easy and yet how did they really apply to the things life threw at some people as it had Sandy and Sam?

Sam dropped into a chair but said nothing. She didn't know whether to be grateful or frustrated. He, of all the men, was the best at punching holes in her story. Looking at the men's blank faces, she decided the next time she'd try to find one out of something like Aesop's Fables.

"I'd like to read from stories like this or others now and then," Abby said, stubbornly standing her ground, even when she realized it was being pulled out from under her, "but I don't want to force any of you to listen if you aren't wanting it."

"Does it mean we don't have to eat your cooking?" Bull asked, and the others laughed.

"Definitely," she said, "Well except for Sam." The men

chuckled again as they left, most saying they'd be glad to return. Too bad they had to add that it was at least something to do in the evenings to avoid losing all their wages to Snake.

When they were alone, Abby looked at Sam, saw the thoughtful expression in his eyes. "What about you?" she asked. "Will you listen to the stories?"

He nodded. "For sure any time Snake does."

"What does he have to do with it?"

"You saw how he was looking at you. If he comes back, it won't be to repent," he said, rising and stretching with a grimace. "I can't believe how hard it is to dig up dirt."

"Dig up dirt?"

He looked chagrined. "I didn't mean to tell you yet. Guess there's no point in hiding it though. I'm working up that vegetable plot you said you wanted. I don't know why because anything you plant's going to be eaten by the birds, deer or coati, but if you want it, I figured it'd be a good way to get my strength back."

She smiled. "Sam, thank you." She bit her lower lip. "I... I'm very appreciative."

The gleam in his blue eyes was a welcome sight to her. "How appreciative?"

"How tired are you?" She walked to him, putting her arms around his waist and hugging him as tightly as his still healing wound permitted.

"Not any--anymore."

Splitting wood, his shirt on the stump beside him, gloves on his hands, Sam worked methodically to split the pine chunks into stove sized pieces. The work was hot but satisfying. Sometimes, if he moved too quickly, he could feel the pull on his scar but he could work without thinking which suited him perfectly.

He took hold of half a log, set it squarely on the block and swung to cleave it neatly in half. He didn't trust Snake and hadn't liked the look in his eyes when he watched Abby. There was a glow about her since they'd begun to make love, a full voluptuousness and moist warmth to which he thought Snake was reacting. It was, of course, possible it was just the reward. Whatever the case, Snake was someone that he wished he could shoot and be done with. Unfortunately, that wasn't his way. So he waited. At some point, Snake would make a move and give Sam a chance to clear his Eden of the snake who threatened it.

Setting another quarter log onto the block, Sam almost didn't hear the little shriek, which was quickly cut off. Knowing it came from where Abby had been hanging out clothes, Sam grabbed his Colt from where it lay under his shirt and ran. With the men out rounding up strays, no one from the ranch should've been around. Maybe it was another mouse, but he was taking no chances.

When he saw them, Snake was holding Abby, his lips pressed against hers. Sam felt a red haze of rage to see that Abby was beating ineffectually at him with her hands. Sam was on them before he had any idea of what he was going to do. Grabbing Snake by one shoulder, he spun the man around, slamming him alongside the head with the gun barrel. Instantly he wished he hadn't done that as Snake crumbled to lie still in the dust. Sam had wanted to kill him, not disable him. He'd just lost his chance.

Breathless, he turned to Abby. "Are you all right?"

Tears were running down her cheeks, but she managed to nod.

Sam bent and pulled Snake from the ground, holding him half suspended by the front of his shirt. "You're out of here," he snarled into the dazed man's face.

Snake's eyes blinked open. "Just a kiss, man."

"Pack your gear. Get off the place. Just give me one excuse, any excuse, and I'll kill you."

Snake's eyes looked dazed. "You're making a mistake."

"I made one. Now I'm correcting one." Sam let go of his hold on the man and rose to stand above him, still shaking from the conflicting emotions of anger and fear. Snake struggled to his feet, stood looking at Sam a moment, wavering on his feet before he managed to walk off unsteadily in the direction of the bunkhouse.

Sam turned to Abby, drawing her into his embrace, needing to hold her and feel her as much as he thought she could ever have needed his support. "You're sure you're all right?" he asked to reassure himself as much as anything.

"I'm sorry," she said, tucking her head against his chest. "I should have handled it better." He heard the sob in her voice and felt angrier than ever at the man who'd caused it.

"You have nothing to be sorry about. I should've gotten rid of him. Any man touches you; you scream the roof off. I'll always come."

"Always?" she asked, tightening her arms around his waist.

"I won't let anyone hurt you so long as I'm around," he said, knowing he could promise nothing more. He picked her up in his arms.

"Sam," she protested, wriggling. "You might hurt yourself."

"Don't fight me, Abby. I'm going to carry you to the house, and you can make it easy on me or hard."

Abby gave up and wrapped her arms around Sam's neck. "Just so you know if you open up that wound after all the trouble I went to closing it up, I'm going to be real mad," she threatened, nuzzling his neck.

"It's healed. That won't happen."

"He didn't hurt me."

"I'm doing this for me."

At the house, he saw Joe come riding up. Sam set Abby on the porch and called Joe to him. "You sure you're all right?" he asked Abby.

"I'm fine. I'll just start supper."

"Joe, you stick around, huh?"

Joe nodded dismounting and tying his reins to the hitching rail. "How long?"

"Not long." Sam looked at Abby. "You should lie down."

"I'm not hurt, Sam. I'll start supper." Then she saw the look in his eyes. "Where are you going?"

"I need to settle up with Snake. I'll be back."

"What does that mean?" she asked frowning.

"Talk a little."

"Talk, that's all?"

His smile and the hard look in his eyes didn't reassure. She couldn't stop him and could only watch as he strode off.

"What in blazes happened?" Joe asked her, looking after him.

Abby told him briefly.

"Snake is lucky he walked away."

"But what does Sam want to talk to him for now? He told him to leave."

"He might need reminding."

"About what?"

"Snake's the kind'll go the marshal and name Sam as the one who robbed the stage. He'd turn you in alongside him if he thought it would increase the reward."

"But Sam didn't rob that stage, you know that."

"And who would ask my opinion?"

At the barn, Sam smoked his cigarette as he watched Snake unsteadily saddle a horse. "You're making a mistake," Snake threatened as he mounted.

"Likely," Sam agreed, knowing he ought to kill the man, but reluctant to do so without proof that it was necessary. "You remember which way you were riding?"

Snake glared at him. "I'm heading south for Nogales," he snarled.

"Don't stop this side of it. and remember this country's unhealthy for men who grab women."

"It was just a lousy kiss."

Sam felt his rage mount again. "My woman, Smith."

Snake cursed as he looked down at Sam.

"One more thing," Sam said. "It isn't healthy for men who talk. You do know what I mean?"

"You think you're so tough," Snake retorted. "You ain't all that fast. I seen you."

Sam's smile was easy and confident. "You want to test that out?" He rested his hand lightly on his revolver in its holster.

Snake scowled, but shook his head. "I'll see you in hell," he said and put his spurs to the side of his horse, heading south.

"You reckon he's heading for Nogales?" Ollie asked, coming to stand at Sam's side to watch the horse and rider disappear in a cloud of dust.

"No."

"What you going to do about it?"

"Go in and talk to Abby a little." He looked at Ollie. "Then I'm going to count on you to keep an eye on her in case Snake doubles back."

"You know I will. The boys are back too."

"Then I'll do what needs doing."

"I oughta go with you. Joe and Bull'll watch Abby."

"No. You and I both know I need to do this alone. You just keep her safe. If anything goes wrong, get her and that shipment she's so worried about to her father in Tucson."

"Anything happens to you and that shipment, and Tucson's going to be the last thing she's worried about."

"Maybe. Maybe not. You just see to her." He stared into the sky. "I might not be back tonight. If I'm not, keep her from worrying. If I'm not back by tomorrow night, well you know what to do."

CHAPTER 24

Riding Satan after a long spell of idleness took a steady rein, physical strength and some concentration even when Sam was fit. The loss of blood he'd suffered had taken a lot out of him, even more had been stolen by the long spell of inactivity. By the time they'd ridden five miles, the kinks were out of the horse but just beginning for Sam.

Talking to Abby hadn't eased his mind. She was shaken by Snake's attack but more upset that he was riding off and not telling her what he was doing. He'd consoled himself that it wasn't a lie because he wasn't sure. If Snake rode south, he'd be at the ranch by dark; but if he was heading for Tubac as Sam figured, he'd follow him.

The sign wasn't difficult to follow, as Snake did not attempt to hide his trail. Either he didn't believe Sam, because of his recent wound, would follow, or it was what he wanted. He passed through the first settlement without stopping, which left Sam little doubt about where he was headed and what his goal was. Hard riding took Sam to the outskirts of Tubac with Snake not far ahead of him.

Tubac on the Santa Cruz River south of Tucson, was a small

community of adobes and a few businesses. At one time it had looked as though, because of the beauty of its setting, it might become a real town, but the Apaches had burnt it to the ground. Now with the Apache danger having lessened with Geronimo at least for now supposedly on the reservation, the community was again growing. A small but convenient supply center, a few whites, Mexicans and Papago Indians were the main inhabitants.

If Sam was right, Snake would head for the small cantina in the center of town. He'd go there to get information on the reward and try to work out a way to collect it without incriminating himself. Snake's plan suited Sam because he wanted plenty of witnesses when he confronted the traitor.

When Sam saw Snake enter the cantina, he rode Satan to the corner of a nearby building and dismounted.

"I watch your horse, mister," a small, dark-haired boy offered.

Sam smiled down into his dark eyes, remembering how many times he'd asked just that question. "How much?"

"I do it cheap, but I do it real good."

Sam reached into his pocket, pulled out two bits, and flipped the coin to the boy, who caught it and grinned.

"I water him too for this much."

"No, you stay back from him." Sam tied Satan's reins to the corner post. "This horse is mean. Eats little boys like you for lunch."

The youngster took a step back and looked up into the eyes of the big, black stallion. Sam grinned. "He'll be fine. You just make sure nobody tries to take him." Not that he figured anybody with sense would try.

The little boy nodded. "I do that real good for you."

Sam lit a cigarette and leaned against the hitching post smoking it. When a man started into the bar, he called him over. "You mind telling the man who just went in, that someone's out here, waiting on him."

The stranger stared at him before nodding.

A few moments later, Snake came out of the cantina, a smile

319

pasted on his narrow face. "Funny you didn't tell me you'd be coming this way," he said as he walked out onto the boardwalk.

"Funny--you didn't either."

"Just getting a beer."

"And if I walked into that bar would that be all I'd hear you were after?" Sam asked taking a drag on the cigarette.

Snake swallowed. "Man can ask for information. Don't mean he's goin' to do nothin' with it."

"That's true, but I'd consider it a right unfriendly thing to have done."

Snake moved farther into the street, positioning himself so the sun was at his back, his gaze not leaving Sam's. "We could talk about this," he offered.

Sam accepted the disadvantage of the sun in his eyes. "Talk won't fix this."

"I did figure it'd come to this," Snake said with a reptilian smile. "After I see you lying in the street, gut shot, I might go back to the ranch, see that little gal of yours. Reward's nice and tempting, but so is a hot little thing like her."

Sam waited, knowing Snake was talking to enrage him hoping it would give him an edge. It was fine with him. He needed the traitor to draw first and for there to be witnesses.

"Funny thing about her," Snake said, "first time I saw her, I figured her for--" Sam saw Snake's hand dip for his gun. Snake had his pulled and almost brought to bear when Sam's bullet caught him square in the chest. A look of shock crossed Snake's face as he staggered back, tried again to bring up his gun as he was struck by Sam's second bullet.

Jaw clenched, Sam walked to the fallen man and knelt at his side. Snake looked up at him, his eyes filled with hate, then the expression faded, and there was nothing. Sam felt for a pulse but knew there would be none.

Death came sudden. No matter how many times he'd seen it, even the few times he'd dealt it out, it was nothing he took lightly. He sucked in a breath, wishing there'd been another way, but almost from the moment he'd met Snake Smith, they'd been on a road to this moment. More than ever Sam saw the inevitability of destiny--of not being able to escape fate.

People came from the buildings to look at the dead man, then at Sam as he slowly rose. One man, obviously as much authority as Tubac had, said, "I'll have to notify the marshal."

"Fine by me. Be sure and tell him what you saw."

The man nodded. "It was a fair fight."

Sam pulled a double eagle from his pocket. "This enough to see him buried?"

The man nodded. If he thought it strange that a man would kill another then pay for his burial, he kept any comments about that to himself.

"Have them put Bill Smith on the marker."

"He wanted for anything?" the man asked with his first sign of interest.

"If he was, you won't find out what now," Sam said, heading for the cantina. He felt a powerful thirst, one he knew alcohol wouldn't satisfy.

"I'll need your name," the man called after him.

Sam told him, then entered the dark cantina. "Tequila," he ordered, throwing two bits onto the counter as the bartender filled a small glass, even salted the rim. Sam heard a sharp exhale and looked at the other man who had been leaning on the bar. Sam smiled. "Reese, isn't it?"

Reese's smile was sickly. "I didn't know you were out there."

"I imagine you didn't."

"I didn't mean to cause you trouble the other day."

"That right?" Sam took his tequila and a slice of lemon with him to a small table.

Reese followed with his beer. "Lucky you weren't the right man. I mean not wanting to see trouble and all, I was real glad of that."

Sam looked at him as he bit into the lemon then swigged

from the tequila. "That so? You didn't hear what old Snake wanted just now, did you?"

"Not a thing," Reese said, the lie showing on his face.

"That's good. A man knows too much in this territory, it can be dangerous."

"I seen that myself," Reese agreed.

"Good."

"Yeah, I don't want no trouble. Not none. Nope, never have."

"Might be good to stay away from temptation for awhile."

Reese nodded emphatically. "Don't much like big towns anyway no more anyway. Since the railroad's come, Tucson's just plain too big. Hardly ever go there."

Sam nodded, downed the remainder of the tequila, and ordered another. "And another beer for my friend," he said.

Back on Satan, a bottle of whiskey in his saddle bag, Sam decided not to head straight for the ranch. He felt a dark depression settling over him. One way or another he had to put an end to this thing, and the first step was retrieving what had been stolen.

When he and his men had seen what was buried by the weasel, they'd taken the leather satchels and reburied them nearby. Close enough to find, but not be found unless a man knew where to look. He'd ordered them left because to possess them was tantamount to a confession of guilt. From the moment he dug them up until he got rid of them, he would be a marked man. If found with the goods, no sheriff or marshal would ever believe he hadn't been the one to rob the stagecoach.

He rode hard, got the bags not long before sunset, and decided he wasn't going to have any choice about spending a night out. Even though he had told Ollie to reassure Abby, she would worry, but he was near exhaustion, not discounting that riding on such a moonless night in this rough country would be asking for a broken leg for his horse and broken neck for himself.

He'd brought no food with him; so his Spartan camp was

made up of a small fire, the water in his canteen, a few swallows of whiskey. The air was warm enough that he barely needed the single blanket he had brought. Trying to sleep and finding it impossible, he lay watching the coals of the fire and thinking about Snake and Sandy. Indirectly, he blamed himself for both deaths. One he'd killed, the other he'd put in a position to be killed. Had he sent them to heaven or hell--or were they no more?

All the talk Abby had been putting out about a God who cared brought back memories of the pastor who'd spoken of hell-fire and damnation, but who had then tried to use those threats to force him as a boy into doing things that were unspeakable. Man was no one to judge God by, but since that time he'd done just that. Now he had someone else--Abby. Her belief made him wish he could also, but he'd gone past the point of being able to accept something like that for himself.

Redemption. People threw out the word, but unless he missed his guess, someone like Abby had very little from which to be redeemed. Her sins had been the little transgressions that people he knew would consider virtues. It was different for Sam. He'd killed men. Murdered one. He'd been a thief.

There was no possible way any kind of god could overlook what he'd done, and it was only a matter of time until the I.O.U.'s were called in and his own life forfeit. He would not see Abby caught in that with him.

The answer was to get the stolen goods to Tucson and Abby with them. He would never be able to have her for his own. His punishment while he was alive would be the loss of the thing he now wanted more than anything he'd known. He had called down the vengeance on himself, along with his own verdict-- guilty.

Night settled around him, seemingly stilling the very air. At first the quietness was unbroken, then he heard the tiny sounds of the night creatures as they went about their business, some not so far from where he laid. Rustling in the grass was either a snake or lizard, then it was gone. In the distance he heard an owl, then another answered.

The crescent moon was coming up in a corner of the skies, the sky overhead bright with stars. In the blackness, everything looked pristine and pure. That wasn't where men lived. He reached for a handful of dust, let it trickle through his fingers. Dust to dust. Wasn't that what the Good Book said. Man was made of dust and to dust he would return. So far as Sam could see man also spent his whole life working in that dust, living it, eating it. If there was a place that was different, Sam would never see it. Snake was right. Someday he'd meet him in hell.

He must have dozed sometime during the night but didn't know when as it felt he had lain there awake all night. Eventually he was aware of light beginning to grow in the east. He saddled Satan; feeling like his own body was past the point of tiredness but determined to get to the ranch. With nothing to eat, he took a few more swigs from the whiskey bottle. It went straight to his head and did nothing to give him the energy he wanted. He rode, half asleep in the saddle, not keeping a tight rein on Satan as he knew he should, but for once the big horse seemed calm and let Sam get away with the laxity.

At the ridge above the ranch, Sam stopped Satan to look at his land as he was his wont. Sitting loose in the saddle, he didn't see the snake slither across the road until the big black horse reared back, bucking twice. Before he realized what had happened, Sam was on the ground, flat out, the wind knocked from him. He cursed himself and the evil minded horse that was now running pell-mell for the ranch. He tried to get up enough air for a whistle, but by the time he managed, Satan was out of earshot, not that he probably would have stopped anyway.

Pushing himself to his feet, Sam winced as he put his weight down on his right leg. He cursed again as he realized he'd twisted his knee in the whole fracas. He didn't think he'd done it any serious damage, but it was going to make walking the three miles to the ranch house a less than pleasant experience. If Ollie noticed Satan coming in, he'd probably backtrack to him. Sam held onto that thought as he began to limp his way down the road.

He had gone a scant half mile when he heard the horse coming fast from the ranch. Looking up, he saw with surprise that the rider was Abby on her mare, her skirt flying in the wind. He almost smiled when he saw she was riding bareback, a definitely pleasurable sight, until he remembered that she would want to know where he'd been.

"What happened?' she asked as she pulled Belle to a stop a few feet from him.

"Fell off," he said, thinking the answer should have been obvious.

"I've been worried sick."

"I told Ollie I might be out overnight."

"Where have you been?"

He smiled, unsure of why he did so as he found his situation anything but humorous. He didn't want to tell her about Snake but could not think of a way to avoid it at some point. Before he could say a word, she had slid off Belle and walked up to him, the horse's reins in her hands.

"You've been drinking," she said as she got close enough that the whiskey on his breath would have been obvious to anyone. "Is that why you fell off your horse?"

"Where's your gun?" he shot back.

"Where's yours?"

"On the saddle." He had made a mistake in not wearing it, which didn't make him pleased to admit. "You though rode out here not knowing what you'd face."

"When I saw your horse come racing in, it did occur to me you might be lying in the road, wounded or with a broken neck," she snapped.

"And if somebody had been standing over me, you'd have been the next target, wouldn't you?"

She glared at him. "You're deliberately trying to distract me from your drunkenness."

"I'm not drunk."

"You've been drinking."

"I've had a couple of nips from a bottle that is now hopefully safely in the barn. On an empty stomach, it left a little more glow than usual, but not enough to be drunk by any man's definition."

"What about a woman's?"

He grinned. "There would be a difference, would there? Does that mean a woman only cares what it looks like while a man cares what it is?"

Her eyes narrowed into angry slits and she looked mad enough to spit nails at him. He thought about then he was probably lucky she hadn't brought a gun with her. "You are a hypocrite," she finally said.

"Just like a woman to change the subject."

"That is the subject. You tell me I'm taking a risk by riding out here without a gun, yet you ride off to face a man you know wants to kill you, who probably wouldn't mind ambushing you; then you get drunk."

"So you knew where I went."

"It would take an idiot not to guess."

"Well, to start with I'm not drunk, and Snake won't be ambushing anybody."

Her mouth snapped shut. "How do you know that?"

"Because I killed him."

"Did you have to?"

He nodded, doubting she would believe him.

"Will the law be looking for you because of it?"

"It was a fair right with witnesses."

She looked away. "Were you hurt?" she asked, still not looking at him.

"No."

"Then why were you limping?"

Damnation. He'd thought he'd stopped walking soon enough

326

that she wouldn't see the limp. She had eyes like an eagle. "I twisted my leg when I went off Satan," he admitted.

"Do you think if you changed that horse's name, maybe he'd behave better?"

He suppressed the smile. "He saw a snake. I didn't-- in time."

"Are you all right?"

"Fine." As fine as a man could be who had faced some hard truths. There would never be any end to the killing, and he had to find a way to let go of the only woman he'd ever loved, the only one he was likely ever to want.

"Can you get on Belle or should I ride back for some of the men to help you?"

"I don't need any help getting on a horse," he said through his teeth.

"No saddle," she reminded him.

"I didn't hurt my eyes when I fell, just my dignity."

She smiled then. "If you helped me get on her first, I could pull you up," she suggested. As soon as the words were out of her mouth, she felt his hands on her hips, lifting her onto Belle's back. She settled the horse, then reached for him.

"You really think you could lift me?" he asked, half amused despite his determination to stay aloof from her.

"If I had to."

Using his good leg, He gave a twisting leap and was on Belle.

She lifted the reins and turned them slowly toward the ranch. Her soft buttocks were pressed against him, the rhythm of the horse moving him and her. He tried to shift away from her. Making love to her again was not part of the plan. She scooted back and soon was pressed against him again, that soft little butt doing things to his body that made him forget for a moment why it mattered. He felt more heat surge into his groin.

"You sure you're all right," she asked, leaning against him, now touching the whole length of his torso. He'd never experienced anything like this riding with her and realized they needed to make this a quick trip if he had any hope of keeping either his determination or sanity.

She twisted to look into his eyes, her own eyes alight, then dusky lashes went down in a movement as old as time so seductive he felt his senses reel. If he had thought she was innocent in her movements, he realized he'd been wrong. His arousal swelled against his jeans.

"Abby," he warned.

"Mmmmmmm?" She moved her legs enough to push against his thighs.

"What are you trying to do?"

"Well, I'm not sure, but am I succeeding?" She put the reins into his hands. "Go slow," she ordered.

"And if I don't."

"We might both fall off." She twisted then and brought her lips against his, her arms entwined around his neck.

"This isn't going to work," he said beginning to see what she had in mind.

"Are you sure?" She moved a bit more. "Hold Belle steady," she ordered as she lifted her leg and scooted around, and in less than a moment was facing him her legs over his thighs.

"Good God," he muttered. Then his lips were sealed by hers. He knew anyone could come along, that this wasn't really possible even given Belle's steady even gait, but he couldn't stop her. No longer wanted to.

"Do you think we can?" she asked pressed so tightly against him that the horse's movements were making him think he was going to go off before they could find out.

"No," he managed finally but he felt her fingers on the buttons of his pants. Soon, she'd know his body wanted to try. She finally got the pants apart and he realized she was wearing nothing under her skirt as he felt her skin against his.

"I want you," she whispered.

He groaned as he felt her settle over him and they were one, the horse's movement building onto theirs. He began to shift to try and satisfy her and himself, felt her moving against him. She moaned, her face showing all that she was feeling, the passion, the building sensations. He could feel her body swelling, the moist warmth, echoed by her full mouth, now teasing and kissing his face, his lips, doing all the things a man might dream of in a fantasy but never imagine experiencing.

The moment seemed to go on forever and yet might've lasted only a few moments as he lost track of time. He felt the sensations building, his own control going. There was only this woman and him. Nothing else existed. He'd be able to hold off his release no longer. His whole body was ready to explode. Gratefully he heard her cry out, her body begin to contract, and he knew she'd found her own fulfillment and not a moment too soon.

He held her as sanity returned to him. God, what the hell was he doing? At this rate, she'd be pregnant, and he'd never be able to set her free. He felt her warm and willing in his arms, a woman he couldn't have. He had to find a way to set her free... but not just yet. For now, he'd hold her; he'd stroke her and whisper how beautiful she was to him. He'd say all that while in his heart, he knew their time together was ending.

"We can't ride into the ranch like this," he said with a smile as he saw the buildings looming ahead.

She groaned against his chest. "You sure?"

"Pretty sure."

With his help, she shifted around; so she was riding forward as both readjusted their clothing to respectability. "Can't shock Ollie, I guess," she muttered.

"Nope, can't do that. Maybe anyway." He chuckled.

"Sam, what do we do now?" she asked with a sigh as she settled against his chest, let him continue to hold the reins.

"With what?"

"Us?"

"Don't ask."

"Why not? Don't you think I have a right to know?"

"How could I tell you what I don't know."

"What do you want?"

"God, woman, is this the right time for this conversation?"

"Is there a right one?"

"No."

"Well, when we get back, you can rest and then..."

"Then what?"

She laughed.

He knew he couldn't resist her. If he was near her, he would take whatever she offered him. He had to see her safely to her home, safely away from him.

CHAPTER 25

"Tell me what happened in Tubac," Abby said as they sat in the parlor, Sam's foot propped on a pillow. The quietness, the sounds of the crickets and frogs outside the window were disparate from the conversation she was apparently determined to have.

"I told you," Sam said. He didn't want to talk about it, didn't want to admit his knee hurt nor tell her what he'd stowed in the barn after he'd gotten to the ranch. What was it with this woman, always probing, never satisfied? Is this what he thought he'd wanted before he knew what it was?

"Did you have to do it?" she asked, her lips pressed tightly together.

"If I hadn't believed it needed to happen, I'd not have gone after him."

"I suppose I knew but wanted to hear you say it."

"Maybe you're trying to find a justification for being with a man like me."

"Is that what you think?"

"I'm asking."

"I don't need a justification. While I'm unsure of a lot I used to think I knew, at least where it comes to being with you, I did the right thing the day I asked you to take me with you. I also still believe it's good to talk about things after they happen. It's what husbands and wives do."

He laughed. "Ah yes, the usual conversation about how your day went and did the cattle rustling go well, dear, and oh yeah, how many men did you kill today?"

She glared at him clearly not amused. "Well, maybe you can change some of your habits."

"And maybe I can't."

"Maybe you don't want to."

"I think we've had this conversation."

"We should share things." Her jaw jutted stubbornly. "When we decided to be married, we made a vow that said we were going to be like one person."

"You didn't even understand what we were saying when we got married." He tried to think back to how this conversation had begun and decided it was a safer subject than the state of their marriage. "All right, you want to hear about how I killed Snake. You want every last bloody detail, you can have it."

"That's not what I want."

"Isn't it? Then I don't know what you want." He rose and limped to the fireplace, staring into the black ashes. "I've never understood what you wanted not from the minute you said you wanted to come with me." He turned to face her. "So, let's start with Tubac. As soon as I saw where he was heading, I knew what I was going to do. I let him draw first, let him take the advantage of the sun behind him, but I knew none of it would matter. I was faster, and I'd kill him."

"Just like that?"

"Yes."

"And you're saying it didn't bother you to kill him?"

"Sometimes there is no choice. You want me to say it bothers me now? I won't. I did what I believed I had to do. I have no regrets."

"There was no other way?"

"There always is. I could have let him ride on into Tucson. By now we'd have a posse and the marshal back with a warrant this time. At that point people probably would have died, me at the least."

"Because the marshal would have accused you of the stage robbery."

"I won't be locked up, Abby. I won't go to that hellhole of Yuma for something I didn't do."

"Good lawyers--"

He cut her off with a sharp laugh. He thought about what he had hidden in his barn now, the proof that was all the marshal would need. "We can't win talking about this. We've lived different lives. Seen different worlds. You'll never understand the way I have lived, how I think, and I'm damned glad of it."

"I want to."

He shook his head. "No, you don't. Give it up, Abby. We're a mismatched pair of mules, trying to pull a wagon, but it won't work."

"What are you saying?"

"I'm saying you need to think about what you want, about what's good for you in the future. I don't think it's me." He limped out of the room, knowing she was following, and he wouldn't turn her away.

Sam walked down to the bunkhouse before first light, his mind made up as to what he had to do. Ollie was yawning and putting on the coffee when he walked into the long, narrow room.

"You're up early," his old friend commented needlessly.

Sam straddled one of the chairs by the long table. "We're short some men. I'm going to Tombstone in a couple of days to hire what we need."

"Need for what?" Ollie asked, frowning.

"To move a herd. We've lost the last two--one way or another. It's time to make up the difference."

"I thought we weren't going back," Joe said, crawling out of his bunk. "It's been good, working the cattle, building fence."

"Any of you want to quit, that's your choice," Sam said, his voice cold and emotionless, his heart shut off from what he was doing. It had to be this way. He wouldn't let himself consider anything else.

"Miss Abby know about it?" Bull asked.

"Miss Abby isn't part of this ranch."

"She won't like it," Ollie said.

"I'm not asking her permission. You boys think about what you want, but this ranch is mine. I don't want to work it. If you aren't interested in picking up cattle in Mexico, you can find something else. It won't be here."

Ollie cursed. "I don't like it. Them wide open days down there is done. You know it. What are you're really sayin' here?"

"I'm telling you what you need to know." Sam rose, in no mood to argue. "Don't say anything to Abby until I do."

"I know what this is about. I never took you for a coward, Sam."

"No man but you could say that," Sam said as he walked out the door. At the stable, he moved Satan from the stall and threw the saddle blanket over his back.

"I'm sorry, Sam," Ollie said from the doorway.

Sam turned to look at him. "Maybe it is cowardice, but she doesn't belong here. The one way to convince her of that is when she finds out I'm going on with the rustling."

"Are you? Or is that just a dodge?"

"It doesn't matter."

"There are easier ways to commit suicide. You know this country's getting too civilized to keep going the way we were."

"I hear you." Avoiding the stallion's attempt to take a nip at his arm, Sam adjusted the bridle over his head. "I won't ask you or any man to go with me."

"I just wish you'd tell me what's going on. You ain't never been a man to use up all your kindlin' makin' a fire, but it seems lately you been closing up tighter than a clam." When he saw Sam throw the saddle over Satan's back, obviously not going to reply, he said, "You know if you go south, I'll go with you."

"We'll see about that when the time comes," Sam said, tightening the cinch. Mounted, he said, "I won't be back 'til late. You can tell *her* that."

Ollie stared up at him. "She deserves more from you than that. She loves you, boy."

"Does she?" Sam spurred the stallion into a hard run and left the barnyard in a cloud of dust. He felt a reckless need to ride and fast enough to leave behind the devils that tormented him—if that was possible. The big horse was eager to give it a try.

He rode across the open grasslands, heading south. Because the land had been grazed lightly over the last five years, the grass was high and thick--rich land for cattle, good country for a cattleman. It lay in undulating hills, surrounded by higher land, forested land, but the valley itself was wide and free of restrictions. As far as Sam could see, the land was his. The cattle grazing here and there were his.

Heading up into the low-lying hills, into the scrub oak country, Sam halted the stallion at a vantage point and turned to look at his home. He felt his heart swell with the feeling of pride at knowing this piece of ground belonged to him or maybe him to it. There hadn't been much in growing up that he'd been able to call his own. This land was the first concrete thing. It wasn't that the ranch was so huge--not by Western standards, but there was still room around him to expand, then he cursed himself for what he was thinking. Foolishness. It wasn't possible. There were no second chances. A man couldn't change, couldn't turn around after he'd gone too far down certain roads.

He dismounted and put a rope around the big horse's neck, securing him to a juniper where he could graze. In the distance, Sam saw the thunderheads building up and hoped they'd come his way. The land was dry. It needed rain. He needed rain. He sat on a ridge of rock and stared out at the mountains in the far distance.

Trust. She kept talking about trust. Trust was for fools. This business of love was throwing him for nearly as big a loop as all the other things Abby talked about. He hadn't seen many examples of love in his time, even less of trust.

Use, convenience, lust. Those things there'd been plenty but not love. Abby claimed she loved him, but it wasn't possible. How could a woman like her love a man who couldn't read, who was ignorant?

Even the feelings she did have for him would be easy to turn and twist until they became hate. He'd seen her anger, knew how easy it would be to arouse that again. He would use that knowledge to do exactly that. She would leave him in Tombstone. He couldn't walk away from her, but he could make her leave him when she saw him for all he was.

He heard the bleating calf then. At first he thought the mother would see to it, but he heard nothing but that calf. No answering bellow. Irritated at having his bout of admitted, self-pity interrupted, Sam slipped the bridle onto Satan's head, winding up the rope and securing it to the saddle.

He rode toward the sound of the distressed calf, convinced that when he saw it, it would be fine with its mother nearby grazing and ignoring it. The sound led him farther into the hills, to a rocky ravine. Overhead Sam saw the vultures, not a good sign. He found the mother's bloated body by the smell, but the calf wasn't beside her. He dismounted and examined the dead animal, deciding it was something internally that had gone wrong. The only outer marks were those of the scavengers.

Back on Satan, he no longer heard the calf. Great, finding it without its crying would be near impossible in all the rock and brush. He kept the big horse quiet. Nothing. Was the calf dead? That didn't seem likely, as its cry had sounded strong moments before.

He headed in the direction from where he thought the

bawling had come and heard a rustle of rock. Dismounting, he walked to the edge of a narrow ravine and looked down. There in a natural hole was the calf.

"And they say sheep are dumb," Sam said staring at it, knowing the smartest thing he could do would be to put it out of its misery. He almost got his rifle, but instead tied Satan to a scrub oak and reached for his rope.

He secured one end of the lariat to a large tree not far from the lip of the crevasse and let himself down. Rock, dislodged by his boots, bounced from the wall, bloodying his forehead with a sharp slap. Now he knew he'd gone crazy.

At the bottom Sam looked at a week old heifer. She made a protesting sound, not seeming to regard him as any savior. It was probably right. There was no way she could survive without her mother. He nearly pulled out his Colt, but then the calf looked him in the eye.

"So," he growled, "you think you've fought to live and deserve a chance. I don't know why." It would be a female causing him trouble again.

The calf bawled. Still looking for an excuse to end its existence, Sam ran his hands over its legs and found nothing broken, nor any blood. However it had gotten into this spot, being in a virtual hole had protected it from predators.

Getting the little critter up the wall of that cliff wasn't going to be easy. He could carry it, but it looked to weigh a good sixty pounds. Hefting it on his shoulders would make them both vulnerable to falling if Sam lost his grip on the rope. The best way would be to tie the rope around the little one, climb up himself, then pull the animal up after him. It would also leave the calf most vulnerable to rock slides and being hit as Sam had been.

He debated a moment. The baby already had a lot of strikes against her for survival. Without considering it further, he tied the calf's legs together and put her over his neck to rest against his shoulders. "You lay still," he ordered, not expecting his command to carry much weight, but as he worked his way up the rock fall, the little one didn't move.

On the top, untying her legs, he lifted the protesting calf to his saddle, ignoring Satan's skittishness. Mounting he headed for the ranch, knowing he was going to feel like an absolute fool riding in with this worthless scrap of flesh over his saddle. Big tough man, real outlaw type. He only hoped Abby wouldn't see him.

Ollie looked up as Sam rode into the yard below the barn. Sam had hoped to see no one, but he guessed that was wishing for too much.

"What ya got there?" Ollie asked, obviously able to see what it was.

"I picked up this mountain lion cub," Sam said, putting his right leg over the pommel and sliding down. "Who's milking Tildy these days?"

"Most of the time Miss Abby. Sometimes Joe or me though. Why?"

"Why? Because if this thing is going to have a mother, it'll have to be her. Does it look big enough to you to be eating grass?"

Ollie chuckled. "Reckon not. Tildy will feed it?"

"She'd more likely kick it to death. It'll take rigging a kind of bottle from one of you to keep it alive."

"On her excess milk?"

"More likely all the milk before it's finished," Sam said setting the calf on the ground. She shook herself, and then looked with big expectant eyes up at Sam.

"Reckon she figures you're her mama," Ollie said. Sam saw him suppress another chuckle and was grateful for small favors.

"You think we can keep Abby from seeing it?" Sam asked, knowing he had no right to ask favors from Ollie after the way he'd talked to him before he'd ridden out. Ollie grinned and looked past Sam's shoulder.

"Not too likely," she said from just behind him.

Damnation. He turned to face her, knowing his expression was probably chagrined.

"It's cute," Abby said, kneeling to lift up the head of the calf. "What happened to its mama?"

"I am not sure. It happens that way sometimes. She looked to be a first timer."

"Its legs are scraped up." She glanced up at Sam and saw the dried blood on his forehead. "Did you two get into a fight?"

"Not quite. She was in a hole. I had to go after her."

"Had to?" Ollie asked with a wider grin.

Sam ground his teeth together. "Are you two going to stand there and laugh or get this squirt some milk?"

"Laugh first, then milk," Abby said, running off with a giggle.

Sam watched her go and felt his heart go with her.

"I'm looking for a woman," Drago Sinclair said looking around the dirty, little Tubac bar.

"This ain't the place," the barkeep said with a smirk.

Drago felt what little patience he had begin to fray. "Don't get smart with me." He pulled from his vest pocket a by now worn picture of Abigail Spenser and showed it to the bartender. "Seen her?" He bit off the end of his cigar and lit it as the barkeep looked at the picture.

"Nope."

Drago cursed. "Give us a beer."

"Us?"

A small man walked into the bar, dusting off his pants.

"Find somebody to tend to the horses?" Drago asked.

Monk nodded.

The bartender set two beers on the bar, resuming wiping

down the other end of the badly scarred bar surface. "What you want with the woman anyway?"

"A man with too many questions doesn't last long out here."

The bartender smiled and glanced toward his shotgun, which lay on the shelf behind the bar. "I've noticed that."

Drago had been aware of a man sitting at one of the three tables but had paid him no mind until he heard him clear his throat. "Mind if I look at the picture?" Drago shrugged and tossed it to him. The man smiled after looking at it. He was large, his body seemed to fill the chair in which he sat. "What you want with her?"

"What's it to you?"

"That was my next question."

Moving to sit at the man's table, Drago signaled Monk to bring the beers over. He set a double eagle on the table. "What'll this get me?"

The man laughed. "That's just burial money around these parts."

Drago took a swallow of his beer. "How do I know you have something worth more?"

"You want the reward, don't you?"

"If you know that much, why haven't you claimed it?"

"Reasons."

"Craven ones?"

The big man straightened in his seat. "I been up against him. If I go back, I'm a dead man."

"Him?"

"Forget I said anything." Almost before the words were out of his mouth, Drago had him by the front of his shirt. He lifted him almost from his chair. For a wiry man, Drago was strong, and the big man's eyes showed his fear.

"Now, we can talk," Drago said dropping him into his seat.

The bartender had his shotgun in his hand. "I'm not having no trouble in here."

"There won't be. Will there, whatever your name is," Drago said with a smile.

"Buck Russell." When the barkeep was gone, Russell managed a grin. "It'll take three of those."

Drago pretended to consider. He looked at his partner. "You think this scum knows anything, Monk?"

Monk's smile was nearly toothless. "Don't make no never mind to me."

Drago put two coins on the table. "That's what it's worth to me; and if you don't know anything, you'll find I'm a man who doesn't take to game playing well." Actually, Drago thought smiling to himself, he did like game playing when he set the rules.

"I was riding with some fellas two months ago. We were the ones that woman rode off with."

"Rode off?" Drago questioned. "I heard she was kidnapped."

Russell laughed. "Not hardly. She was hot after the boss, and she got him. Bad luck having a woman on a ranch, having a woman ride with a crew. I tried to tell him, but he wouldn't listen. That's when we split."

"What's your boss's name?"

"Sam Ryker."

"Ryker? What's the man look like?" He'd come close to finding him before. He would hear the name, but then it'd be someone else. He felt a surge of elation that maybe his search was at an end.

"Big man, black hair, Jesus, I don't know. What the hell does it matter?"

"It matters because I asked." Drago puffed on his cigar, his thoughts turning over again and again. Maybe this was the one. "And the woman is with him? At this ranch?"

"Hell, she's his wife."

Drago hid his surprise. "What would you want to take us there?"

Russell gave a snort. "Not doing it. Ryker's a gunman."

Drago smiled and blew out the smoke. This was sounding promising. "He got blue eyes, kind of unusual ones?"

"Maybe. Guess so."

"Want that other double eagle?"

Russell signaled for a whiskey. When the shot glass was in front of him, he swallowed in a gulp. "Money don't do a dead man no good," he said wiping his mouth.

"A lot of men talk a good line," Drago said. "Most don't walk it." Monk chuckled.

"It's more than that with Ryker. He just killed a man in Tubac. Snake was going to claim that reward."

"Snake, huh?"

"Real name Bill Smith-- maybe. You know how it is."

"Fair fight?" he asked although he knew what the answer would be. If Ryker was his man, it didn't matter if he let a man draw first. No fight with him was fair. Not for *most* men anyway.

"So I heard. I didn't see it or I wouldn't be alive to talk about it. Guy who did said Snake was dead before he hit the ground. Ryker's fast, and he don't mind killing."

Drago stared into the distance. "I'll make it worth your while. One way or another, you will go with us."

Russell stared at him seeming to be assessing before he nodded. When he left to get his gear, Monk sighed his disapproval. "I hoped you'd let that go."

"Not when I'm this close," Drago said remembering the different identities he had used in Tucson, the watcher, the Wells Fargo agent and finally his own. It had all been a game then. If this was the Ryker for whom he had been looking it would all be worthwhile. He smiled.

CHAPTER 26

Circle R

"I don't see why we have to go to Tombstone," Abby said, all the while stuffing clothing into the saddle bags Sam had handed her. "That town is wild and full of saloons, outlaws and gunfights and--" Rahab leaped onto the blouse Abby was attempting to pack and tried to get hold of it with her teeth. Sam scooped her off and onto the bed.

"And men. I told you, I need more men," Sam said. "You don't have to go if you don't want. You can stay here with Rock and--" He considered a moment. "I'll leave Joe. Milking that cow and feeding the calf isn't something Rock's leg is up to yet. Two's plenty to take with me."

"I'm glad Ginger is doing so well on Tildy's milk." She didn't like thinking about Tombstone. Sam hadn't said why he wanted more men, but it wasn't hard for her to guess. How could she deal with his continuing to rustle cattle, to risk his life? She had believed that it would change. What if it wouldn't?

"I told you not to name that calf," Sam said. "Cows aren't pets."

"I know, but how can I give her a bottle when I can't talk to her?"

"Just don't forget she's going to grow horns a foot long. When she swipes her head sideways and says howdy, you'll know you've been greeted."

'You have a point."

"So does she."

"Your jokes are terrible." She shoved the last item she could fit into the saddlebag. "I think I need a bigger bag."

"You can buy what you need there."

She looked up. "I don't know if I'll feel like shopping." What if she ran into someone who knew her? It seemed that keeping a low profile in Tombstone would be essential. She wondered again why Sam even offered to let her come.

"You'll have to. You need other clothes."

"Why? What is really going on?"

He frowned, and she knew with certainty that he was hiding something. She popped down on the bed and stared up at him. "Well."

He walked to the window. "I didn't tell you before, but after Tubac, I dug up that shipment of your daddy's. We'll be taking it with us to Tombstone. We'll find a way to get it back from there."

Her first thought was pleasure. Then she felt something cold clutch her heart. "Isn't that dangerous?" She remembered what he'd told her about those mail pouches--that with the marshal already believing he was the robber, if he was found with them, there would be no way to prove it wasn't so.

"It's the only way." Absently he squatted to pet Rahab who had followed him and was rubbing around his legs. "If we don't return it, there'll always be somebody coming after us. We go to Tombstone, ship the mail back. I put it in sacks. Nobody will know what it is 'til they open it in Tucson. If you make a trip home from Tombstone, everything is cleared up."

"A trip home? Why would I do that?"

"You said you wanted to."

344

"Well, yes but... sometime. Not now."

"Until you go back, the reward posters will be plastered around maybe with increasing numbers on them. There is no way to get this straightened out short of that."

"But this all sounds dangerous for you."

"For awhile."

"What if someone recognizes me from the poster too soon?"

"It's a risk we have to take, but you don't look much like that picture anymore and it's been out for long enough, probably not many looking at it anymore."

"I don't look like it?" She smiled, pleased by the thought. She had never much liked how she looked.

"No."

"What do I look like now?" She liked having Sam tell her that she was beautiful. She wasn't sure she believed him, but the words always left her warm and glowing. And the expression in his eyes made her body turn to a flame, ready to yield up all her warmth.

"Hair loose like that, flowing all around you. Lips full and lush, those eyes that say everything without a word." He grinned. "Nope, unless a man knew, he wouldn't recognize you." Her hope the words would lead to something else were dashed when he stood to look out the window. "Besides, you can't stay in hiding forever."

"I could send my father a telegraph, explaining everything is all right. Maybe that would take care of it."

"How would he know you hadn't been forced to send it?"

She stared at him, trying to read beneath the mask. There was more to this trip than he was telling her. She would not get it from him now. She moved across the room, putting her arms around him, beginning to unbutton his shirt. She felt his reaction to her touch and smiled as she centered her interest where she most wanted it.

~

Riding horseback through the Huachuca Mountains was pleasurable for Abby. Although the country was dry and barren, especially as they climbed into the mountains, it had a quiet, pleasing beauty. Scrub oak dotted the hills, and the canyons were dry and dusty where streams ran once or twice a year, when at all. Twice they came upon bands of coatimundi as they scurried for cover, surprised at having been interrupted on their foraging. "With those long tails, they are so cute," Abby said.

"No more pets," Sam said as he rode along side of her. "Those cute little critters bite something fierce."

'You are not going to tell me you've been bitten by one," she said with disbelief. She could see their long snouts would allow for vicious teeth, but she couldn't imagine being attacked by something so teddy-bear like.

Sam shook his head. "Heard about it though. Woman, took one as a pet, had her nose bit clean off."

"You are kidding?" she said horrified, then looked over and saw that wicked grin that turned her stomach inside out. "That's not funny."

"You sure?"

She giggled.

They came to the bluff above the San Pedro River at near dark, the shadows lengthening as the sun reached for the horizon. "We'll camp here," Sam directed. Abby was relatively sure that if he'd been riding with only his men, he'd have ridden on without stopping.

"I can keep going," she said.

"You could. No reason to get you saddle sore. We've got time."

As the sun headed toward the horizon and the sky began to turn mauve, Sam found a protected campsite with a sufficient view of the surrounding country and cottonwoods to shelter them. It was far enough from the banks of the river that even if a thunderstorm were to hit the distant mountains and send the shallow river into flood, they would be safe.

If Abby had fostered any hopes that she and Sam would have time alone there, time to talk, time to work out whatever was troubling him, he dashed the hopes when he said the men would have to take turns watching. When she looked at him skeptically, he said this was outlaw country. The battles between the lawless elements and the law-abiding had been fought in Tombstone and were still being fought in the surrounding territory with various outlaw settlements like Charleston continuing to supply men for robbing, killing and general deviltry. Add to it Geronimo was rumored again to be in the hills somewhere, and it was nowhere to take for granted.

Watching the ranch house through binoculars, Monk smiled with satisfaction. He climbed down from the promontory. "Looks good, Drago."

"How many?"

"All I seen is two. If there's more, they're in the house but not moving around."

"So where did the others go?" Drago mused. Something about this didn't seem right.

He turned to Russell. "Thought you said there'd be six or seven men there, not counting the woman."

"Maybe they left. I don't know. Can't read their minds from here."

Drago smirked. He could read the big man's unease. "Tell me again about the trouble you and Ryker had?"

"Does it matter?"

"Yeah, tell me."

"We had a fight."

"That was all?"

"I hate him. Want to see him get knocked down a peg or two. That's all."

Drago sneered. He knew a lie when he heard it. "You're scared of him," he said and read it on the big man's face. "I want the truth about what happened. All of it. I don't ride with men I can't trust."

Russell let out a gusty breath. "All right... I'll leave. No need for money for bringing you here."

"Try again."

"All right. All right, I took a shot at him."

"You got off a shot at a man you say is so fast you're scared to face him." Drago smiled and pulled out his own gun, pointing it at the hapless man. "How'd that come to pass?"

"I brought you to the ranch. Why would you pull a gun on me now?" He made a failed attempt at innocent confusion.

Drago cocked his pistol but said nothing more, just waited. A coward would always yield, would end up giving whatever it took to keep him alive. Patience was all it would take to get those things from this man.

"All right, I shot at him after a disagreement. I... I did it without thinking." His voice dwindled off as he saw the expression in Drago's eyes.

Drago laughed. "You took a shot at his back."

Russell nodded, staring at the ground.

"I don't ride with back shooters," Drago said.

"What do you mean?"

"I'll give you a chance."

Russell pulled on the reins to turn his horse.

"Russell."

He waited. "What?" he asked.

"I don't ride with 'em. I don't trust 'em to ride behind me."

"What does that mean?"

Drago had holstered his pistol. "It means get your gun out or die trying."

Russell tried, but two bullets hit him so quickly together they were as one. Russell fell hard form his horse.

Drago dismounted and walked over to him. "Any last words?"

"Boots off," Buck begged, choking on blood. "Don't want to die with my boots on."

Drago laughed and fired again, directly into his head. "Too late for that."

"What now?" Monk asked as though nothing had occurred.

"We'll wait a bit, then go on down and see who's at the house." He reloaded his gun. "If it isn't Ryker, we'll find out where he and the woman are."

They rode slowly into the ranch yard, not wanting to concern the men who'd come out onto the bunkhouse porch. "Mind if we water our horses?" Drago asked with a smile.

A man with a crutch nodded his head toward the trough. "Help yourselves. You ridden a long way?"

"Far piece. Is this ranch hiring?"

"You don't look much like cowboys," a second man said as he stood to one side of the door, a rifle in the cradle of his arms.

"Man does what he needs to do. Boss around?"

"Not here."

Drago let Monk take the horses to the watering trough. "Where'd you say your boss was?"

"We didn't," the crippled man said. He kept his hand close to the gun on his hip.

Drago stroked his mustache, familiar with men like these. They wouldn't be easily taken off guard, but then nothing was impossible. Although if required he could track the horses. It would be more amusing to get what he wanted from these two.

"You got any grub to spare?" Monk asked, walking up onto the covered porch where the two men stood, placing himself now to their far side, making it difficult to watch them both simultaneously.

"We can give you a little."

"We ain't been real friendly," Drago said. "I'm Drago Sinclair.

This is Monk Jones. What'd you boys say your names were?"

The one man looked at the other, then the cripple said, "I'm Rock. This is Joe."

"You got any coffee?" Drago asked knowing it was a request that could not be turned down.

Joe considered a moment before he smiled. Drago knew he didn't trust them. Good. He liked it that way. "Sure. Strong enough to put hair on your chest, but you're welcome to a cup."

Drago and Monk walked ahead of the two hands into the bunkhouse positioning themselves at opposite ends of the room with their hands near their guns. Monk poured the coffee. Drago felt a surge of excitement at the nearness of action. He saw Joe clench his jaw. He debated whether he would kill these two after he got what he wanted.

"No reason for us to have trouble," Drago said, smiling as he sipped his coffee. "We're just looking for work. If your boss is hiring, we need to talk to him. Tell us where he went, and we'll be gone."

"Wait around here," Rock offered, his tone sounding amiable enough to anyone who didn't read men as well as Drago did. "They'll be back in a few days."

"That right?" Faster than the two hands could react, his coffee cup was gone replaced by his six gun, which was now pointed at Rock's chest. "You know, Joe, if you put that rifle down and step away from it, I'd consider it right friendly."

Joe moved away from the rifle, holding his hands out from his sides. "What's the matter?" he asked. "Thought you just wanted a cup of java."

Drago laughed, the sound piercing in the small room. Monk, who had now drawn his own gun, chuckled too.

"I'll tell you what I want," Drago said, "then you give me the answers. If it all goes well, you two might just survive 'til tomorrow morning."

"We've got nothing to hide," Rock said.

"We'll see about that. Now, no fooling around. Where did

Ryker head?"

When neither Joe nor Rock said anything, Drago said, "See if you can convince the cripple."

Monk walked to Rock and kicked away his crutch. Rock grunted, tried to move away, but Monk was fast and landed a solid kick at the leg. Rock collapsed groaning to the floor.

"Now, Joe," Drago said, coming to stand in front of him, using the barrel of his gun to force Joe's chin up. "I can trail the horses that rode out of here. It'll take me longer, put me in a bad mood, but it won't stop me. The thing is, you can save me some time. You can save your friend some pain, maybe you too. Monk there." He gestured toward the smaller man, "He likes hurting people even more than I do. Show him your knife, Monk." The knife appeared almost instantly. "He's good with it too, Carve your friend up and keep him alive a long time. Think that'd do your boss any good?"

Drago could see Joe thinking through his options. He could almost read the man's mind as he decided he had no choice but he would ride ahead to warn his boss. He smiled as Joe said, "All right, he's going to Tombstone."

"Why?"

"He's looking for hands."

Drago grinned. "I was told there's a woman here. Where's she?"

When Joe didn't respond, Drago drove his fist into his belly, knocking the air from his lungs and doubling him with pain. When he could again straighten, he looked into Drago's eyes. Drago knew how close Joe was to death and wondered idly if he also knew.

"It's his wife," he managed, gulping for air.

"What's her name?

"Abby."

"What's she look like?"

"Beautiful. Dark hair. Hell, I don't know. Good figure."

"Where'd she come from?" Drago asked.

Joe grimaced. "How would I know? He courted her, brought her here. If you knew my boss, you'd know a man don't ask questions when he brings home a woman—not if he says she's his wife." Joe managed to sit up but didn't attempt to stand.

"All right," Drago said. "I appreciate you boys being loyal to your boss and all. I respect that, but I can't have you following us." Smiling, he stepped back, lowered the barrel of his gun and shot Joe in the right leg. "I figure two men with bad legs won't be riding anywhere. I don't kill men unless I have to... unless they're the kind the world's better off without."

Joe groaned as Drago again took hold if his chin and lifted it. "You're a lucky man," he said. "You'll heal from this, but you try to follow us to Tombstone, a tombstone is all you'll find."

Drago turned to Monk. "Take what supplies you can find. We'll drive off the horses, just in case either of these two get the idea they can ride after all."

Drago knelt then beside Joe. "There's a man up in the hills." He pointed off to the west. "Vultures going to start circling in a day or so. If you're of a mind, you might see if you can get up there, bury whatever's left." He grinned and left Joe writhing on the floor. Just the way he liked it.

At first light, Abby munched on a dried biscuit as she watched Sam and the men saddle the horses. When they started out, Sam rode beside her.

"Have you been to Tombstone often?" she asked after a long silence.

"When needed." He pulled out his Colt, checked its load, and then dropped it in its holster.

"Why'd you do that?"

"Habit."

"You need a gun in a town where there's a sheriff?"

"Especially then," he said with a grin. "If there's a no-carry law, I take it off, keep it in a bag nearby, and don't stay long."

"What is this town like?" she asked more for wanting to get him to talk than a genuine interest in Tombstone. He was withdrawing from her and there was a glint in his eyes she didn't like.

"A silver camp, grown into a mining town. Maybe ten thousand living there right now. Rocky barren place with no reason for being other than silver, and when it's gone, that'll be it."

"Is it dangerous?"

"Not more than others."

"I heard there is a kind of sophisticated district."

He laughed. "I wouldn't know. I go for supplies. In and out as fast as I can."

"I'm going to look pretty strange there." She glanced down at her worn riding skirt, the boy's shirt and over-sized jacket she was wearing.

"Not in my end of town."

"Was that supposed to make me feel better?"

"We'll buy you new clothes right after we get the horses stabled."

"I'd like that. A real dress and clean underwear. What a luxury." She smiled at him, wishing he'd answered her smile with a real one of his own.

As they neared Tombstone, Sam told her he needed to ride the restlessness out of Satan before he stabled him. He said he would be back before they entered town and with that he was gone in a cloud of dust. Abby's apprehensions grew as she watched him ride that big stallion out across the ridge. She wondered who needed that wild ride, the horse or him. Any hole and they'd go down, but none of those fears could've been in Sam's head as he let the stallion have his head.

Not having been in any town for some time, she would generally have looked forward to the shopping and restaurants. Instead she could only feel fear for the man she had married.

Ollie brought his horse alongside hers. "You want company?"

"You are a friend to know it."

"You doing all right?"

"Not so much." Riding over a ridge, below her she could see the town laid out. To her left was a cemetery. She felt a shiver go down her spine at the sight of the lonely, rock-heaped graves and plain markers. The setting was barren and rocky, removed from the life of the town below. Such a forlorn place for a life to end. Dust to dust.

Ollie looked over at her. "Now don't go looking that way," he admonished. "it's just Boot Hill."

"They call it that?"

Ollie chuckled. "Not hardly. More likely they call it Tombstone Cemetery, but boot hill's what it is. Lawless towns like Tombstone, men don't tend to live long enough to die with their boots off."

As he gave her a brief history of all he knew about Tombstone's burial ground, listing off gunfights, accidental deaths, hangings, and murders, she couldn't decide if he was trying to distract her from her upset, or if he thought she'd want to know all the violent ways a man could die.

"The Earps put Billy Clanton and the McLowery brothers under that ground. A gunfight that nobody that day saw the same way. I heard more versions of what happened than there are days in the month. The only ones who know and are still here is them buried over there, I reckon."

She put words to her own fear. "I'm afraid Sam's going to end up in a place like this sooner than need be."

"Worries me too," Ollie agreed, when she wished he wouldn't have.

"What are we going to do to see that doesn't happen?" she asked, stiffening her spine with determination. She had let others dominate her life for too many years. She was done with that. Sam would not end up there, not if she had anything to say about it.

CHAPTER 27

R iding down Fremont Street with Sam again on one side,
Ollie on the other, and Bull riding protectively behind,
Abby tried though not to worry, to let herself instead enjoy the
town. It was impressive with all the wooden-fronted businesses,
the number of people on the boardwalks, the horsemen in the
street, the heavy ore wagons lumbering past.

Sam turned them into the stable where they left their horses
at what Abby felt was an exorbitant price. Putting the two saddlebags, one innocent one not, over his broad shoulder, he told Ollie
and Bull, "You two have fun but remember I came to add men,
not lose them. I'll meet you at the Oriental tonight."

"Want to clean up first or buy those new clothes?" he asked
when he turned back to her.

"Clothes. Then when I bathe, I will have something to change
into." Abby took his arm as though she was the finest and
proudest lady in Tombstone, which if Sam hadn't seemed so bent
on hiring more hard cases and being reckless, she guessed she
would have been. He led her up Third Street to Allen where so
long as they stayed on the south side, he told her there would be
shops that would have what she wanted.

"What's wrong with the north side?" she asked, looking at it more critically.

He smiled. "Remember Tucson's Tenderloin?"

She nodded.

"Welcome to Tombstone's."

"Oh." She looked again. Other than the usual saloons and restaurants, little told her this street was anything but an ordinary one. "What would happen if we walked along it?" she asked, giving him a saucy smile.

He patted the butt of his gun. "Likely nothing much."

'You mean you might have to fight?" She frowned.

"Unless I was interested in turning a little money myself."

"Sam!"

"You asked." He grinned and steered her into a shop where dresses hung on racks and there were stacks of ready-made clothing. Abby headed for the dresses while Sam stopped to pick himself up a shirt. His took little time. With curiosity, he headed to the back of the mercantile. She was holding up a dress, trying to decide on color. It was his first time with a woman shopping. She whirled to look at him, having seen him in the mirror. "What do you think?" she asked her eyes aglow.

The dress was a plain one, but the gold color caught the gold of Abby's hair. "Nice," he said, sinking into a chair which he guessed had been provided for such viewing.

She held up a blue wool gown that looked very sophisticated, tailored, the perfect lady's dress. Then a white one of light and filmy cotton, no ruffles but a starched white collar and cuffs. "Which do you think?" she asked frowning as she tried to decide between the two, having obviously discarded the gold.

Caught up in the enjoyment of watching her with new things, he pointed to a russet red dress on the rack. "How about that one?"

She held it up to herself. "It's pretty bright, don't you think?" It had a scooped neck and fitted bodice with straight skirt.

"We'll take all four."

"Four, but I don't need four dresses."

"You will eventually."

The saleswoman, recognizing authority when she heard it smiled. "You've made excellent selections." She scooped up the dresses to wrap. "The red came in only yesterday."

Abby felt uneasy at all the purchases. "A lot of money and I still need--."

Sam smiled. "Whatever you want," he said and pulled out a roll of bills that looked to Abby as though they could have purchased the whole shop. She didn't miss the increased subservience of the saleswoman.

It took almost an hour to complete all the purchases, piling up lingerie, shoes, stockings, and a nightgown. Abby was still ill at ease at all the money Sam had spent. He could have used that for ranch purchases. She didn't want him ruining his chances of making a success of the Circle R because of his generosity to her.

Outside, under the hot Tombstone sun, she said, "We should return half of this."

"Nope."

"You won't have enough for food or other things."

"There's more in the bank if we need it."

"Bank?"

He smiled but she wasn't sure he was amused. "Where did you think I'd keep it?"

Stolen money?"

He stiffened. "You know what I've done, but there are other ways I made money. I worked for several ranchers, invested in cattle instead of daily wages. When I sold them, I had a good profit; then one winter I panned for gold—and actually found more than I expected. Annie left me a little. I didn't want it then, but it's drawn interest, but yeah," he smiled, "livestock trading has been... profitable. Think I'd have been doing it if it wasn't?"

He stopped in another store and she stayed with him as he made purchases of boxes of various sizes of ammunition and a new rifle that caught his eye. Daydreaming, she thought it would be easy to forget for what he'd come, forget the wildness she'd seen in his eyes earlier.

"Come over here," he said, drawing her to a display case. The gunsmith handed her a tiny gun.

"What is it?" she asked.

"Derringer. Ladies like them because they fit in a pocket. Two shots and you can stop most any man who gets too close, which is the only place this gun is truly effective," the proprietor said.

Abby felt the grip, then handed it back.

"We'll take it too," Sam said, "and a box of shells for it."

She frowned at him, but said nothing until they were outside in the glaring sun. "Why do I need that? I have my gun."

"It's too big to fit in the pocket of one of those frilly things you just bought or a little bag. I want you to have protection, especially here."

"You think the town is that dangerous?"

"I have to leave you alone, and I don't like that with nobody looking after you."

"I'm not a child."

He grinned. "Which only makes it worse."

She glared at him, but decided she wouldn't refuse the gun.

At the Cosmopolitan Hotel Sam registered them as Mr. and Mrs. Ryker. He requested a room that fronted onto Allen street. As he and she walked up the stairs, a boy helped them with bags and her new purchases. "Won't it be noisier?" she asked.

"And safer." She did not try to argue because she'd never actually traveled alone. Their room was number fifteen. She was surprised at the luxuries it contained, including fluffy towels, a bar of French-milled soap in a porcelain soap dish, a wide bed with a brass headboard and foot board, a soft mattress that bounced nicely when she tried it, two over-stuffed chairs, a rosewood dresser, gaslights, and as a final touch--a small desk equipped with paper.

"This is wonderful," she said. "I don't think Tucson has anything finer."

"Where there's money, there are people helping you spend it," Sam said as he laid the saddlebags in a corner of the room.

"Are you sure it's safe for you to have them?" she asked looking with concern toward the bag she knew held the stolen mails.

"Not much, but safer here than in the stable and maybe stolen again." She pulled the blind close as he turned up the lamp. The glow lit his face, shadowing the hollows, the cheekbones and revealing the tired lines beside his mouth. She went to him, putting her arms around him.

"Do you really have to go out tonight?"

"I told the boys I'd meet them, and I'd better do that."

She didn't release her hold, tilting her body so she pressed against him in the way she knew elicited a response. She saw it in his eyes, felt it in his body, but he broke the embrace and moved away to sit on the bed.

If she'd had a mind to, she could have felt angry at the rejection, but she felt happy, pleased he'd purchased her so much clothing and even the gun. Surely that proved he did love her. She whirled around the room while he leaned against the metal rails and watched her. She unpacked her dresses, hanging them to remove the few wrinkles from their short time of being folded. She put away the undergarments in a drawer.

The knock at the door startled her, and she almost reached for the derringer which she'd put into the pocket of her riding skirt, but when Sam didn't seem alarmed, she relaxed.

He opened the door and ushered a young man carting a small hip tub and a large pitcher of warm water. Abby smiled as Sam handed the boy a coin, then turned to look at her as she poured the water into the tub.

He had known he would have to sacrifice his own desires if Abby was to have any chance for happiness, but he realized how hard this was going to be as she began to unbutton her blouse. To avoid watching her bathe, he walked to the window and stared out. He gritted his teeth as he heard her splash into water.

To avoid imagining what was behind him, he said, "I'll take you to dinner at the Chinaman's tonight."

"Sounds lovely," she said and he heard the smile in her voice. He could almost see the cloth and the soap slick up her skin, moving over her rounded breasts and down her belly as she would wash her soft skin. He wanted to help her, to stroke all those secret places with the soft cloth and then his tongue but he was determined on how it had to be. No more intimacies. He would not increase the risks that he might leave behind a bastard as his father had. He knew if he turned to look at her, he would be finished. He was not about to leave her to take the risk of bathing by herself; so he had to stay, endure the torture of knowing what he was forsaking and keep his eyes focused on the street.

"The water feels wonderful, Sam," she murmured. He heard a louder splash, knew she must have stood. He sucked in a breath, barely able to breathe. He had no time to prepare himself, to stiffen his resolve before he felt her hands on him, her wet body pressed against his back. He felt her fingers on the buttons of his shirt. "Abby," he warned.

"Mmmmm?" she asked, pulling the shirt open, baring his chest and shoulders as she pulled it down his arms, leaving the cuffs buttoned. She was gone a second and he thought he could shrug it back up. When he felt the washcloth on his skin, he knew his resolve was for nothing.

Later, lying in bed, limbs still entangled, he whispered, "You missed your dinner."

"I'm so disappointed," she replied, her lips against his damp neck.

"You make me weak."

"That's funny because you make me strong."

"You're sucking my power, is that what you're telling me?"

"Am I?"

He had to go. Tonight was the night to convince her to leave him. He had to make sure it went as he planned.

"I'll be back late," he said. He walked naked to the dresser and unwrapped the new shirt. When he had pulled on his pants and tucked the shirt in he turned to watch her on his bed. Her hair fanned out across his pillow. He hated putting a disappointed look on her beautiful face but it had to be this way as he pulled on boots and finally added his gunbelt.

"Lock this door when I go out and don't unlock it for anybody except the room clerk bringing you your dinner in about half an hour, and even then, keep that little gun handy." He rechecked the load in his own gun.

"I don't see why you have to go tonight." She felt like a fool, she kept hoping he'd change his mind, kept hoping he'd want to stay with her, but she apparently didn't have enough to offer. "I don't know how to use the new gun," she said, irritated that her voice sounded weak in its complaints. This was no way for a mature woman to behave.

He took the gun to her, showed her the trigger and cocking mechanism, then loaded it. "If you have to go out, keep this with you. Tombstone can be pretty rough at night."

"I won't go out. When will you be back?"

"Late. Don't wait up."

He pulled on his hat and left her with no good-bye kiss, nothing but one last fiery look as their gazes met before he turned his back on her and shut the door. She got up and locked it, then leaned against it. She should dress. If the room clerk was really going to bring her a tray, she didn't want to open the door in a nightgown, but she felt too numb to move.

The street was growing noisy as she heard loud voices and laughter, a piano tinkling somewhere up the street, then a gun shot pierced the air. Sam was going out into that. Why? Was it to hire men or was his plan darker than that?

The image of the cemetery came into her mind. Boot hill Ollie had called it, because men went there so suddenly they didn't have their boots off. She jumped at the sound of a nearby gun shot. Was that Sam? She could so easily see him falling to the ground, crumpled on the street, his blood draining into the dust. Who would tell her? She imagined his body, still and white, in a black hearse, a horse pulling it up out of town to that lonely little knoll.

"God, stop this," she harshly ordered herself. To erase the images, she pulled on undergarments, her new gold dress, the gun in its pocket, and then sat, wishing she could go out and look for him and knowing that would be the most foolish thing of all. Whatever he was doing, he would do. She wondered then if she could live this way, waiting for him to return, hoping he would, and then one day facing the empty doorway. Was this a way to live a life? And what if she became pregnant? She felt of her belly, knowing that she hadn't been pregnant, but it could still happen. Maybe this time, it had. How would that be with a man like Sam for a father? She sucked in a breath, unwilling to think further.

When the food tray came, she sent it away. Any appetite she'd had was gone. She didn't know how long she sat. There would have been times she'd have stood in the window to watch the red sky in the west, to admire the beautiful colors as the sun set and the show began. This sunset brought no pleasure as she wondered if it would be the last for Sam. God, why had she let herself fall so deeply in love with a man where every day could be his last?

Finally she pulled off her clothing and put on a nightgown, but when she lay in the bed she didn't sleep. She stared at the ceiling, blindly looking at the ceiling, at the reflected lights that seemed to dance there. The sounds of the city closed in around her.

Walking into the smoky atmosphere of the Oriental, Sam felt torn in two. Part of him wanted to be with Abby in their room, make love to her again. Part of him argued he was no good for her. He had to free her one way or another.

Before he could reach the polished bar, a woman came up, her hand grasping his biceps. "Hi, big boy," she said, "remember me?" He looked down and knew he'd never seen her before.

"Nope." He removed her hand.

At the bar, he put a boot onto the rail and ordered whiskey. He didn't want that anymore than he'd wanted the strange woman. On all sides of him men were leaning and talking while they drank, the smoke was heavy in the air. At the back of the long, narrow room a piano was being pounded to death. Maybe another day he would have appreciated the bouncy tunes, but this night he was in no mood for music, especially not *Camptown Races.*

The bartender poured him a shot glass of whiskey setting the bottle beside it. "Looks like it's been a long day," the man said with a smile.

"You don't know the half of it," Sam muttered. He put the money on the bar for the bottle and took it to a table where he could be alone. He sat, staring at the people having fun, and wondered if he ever had in a place like the Oriental. He thought then about the nights with Abby, nights when she'd read to him, tried to teach him to read, the times they'd made love or laughed over her cooking. There had been peace with her he would never know elsewhere.

He refilled his glass and slugged it. The whiskey was his answer. It would give him the oblivion he sought but moreover send him back to her drunk enough that she would see him for what he was.

His third glass almost turned his stomach, but he forced it down. On an empty stomach, it was having a powerful effect on his body, but not the one he'd sought. Instead of oblivion, it seemed all he found was an increasing awareness of what he would be losing when she left him. If he had been a selfish man, he would have kept her with him. The cost would be high for her. There would come a reckoning, and when it happened, what would he be leaving her?

"You look like you up and died but don't know it yet," Ollie said, plopping into a chair at his table.

Bull sat on the other side of him. "Drinking that rot gut is pure suicide, boss. didn't nobody warn you about that?"

"Two mamas," Sam said, feeling the whiskey starting to kick in. "What did I do to deserve this?"

Ollie chuckled. "Don't worry about us. We'll just stick around to chuck you back into Abby's bed when you pass out. What she'll want with you, is beyond me, but that's the way women are."

Bull brought back two glasses and poured himself a drink. "Not as bad as I thought," he said, taking it in one swallow.

"Don't you go getting soused too," Ollie warned. "It's bad enough I got to figure out how to get this one back to his woman. Picking you up, would be pure out of the question."

"I don't get drunk," Bull retorted. "Man my size can handle a lot of liquor." He hiccupped.

"I can see that," Ollie said with a snort.

Sam managed to swallow one more shot of whiskey; but his stomach was turning on him, making him regret his plan with a passion. Returning to her drunk had seemed a good way to convince her she was with the wrong man. Being drunk meant a hangover, meant the room was beginning to move. He rose, swayed, and put out his hands to steady himself, finding his two friends under his arms.

"Don't need any help," Sam retorted, irritated that his voice sounded slurred even to him. A few shots of whiskey shouldn't put a man under the table. Just goes to show what a mistake it was to lead a sober life-- couldn't drink when he needed to.

Outside, Sam looked down the street realizing he'd lost the hotel. He looked up the street, but nothing looked familiar.

"What you looking for, boss?" Ollie asked having followed him out.

"They move the Cosmopolitan?" Sam asked, frowning and trying to see through the hazy movement of everything.

"Not last time I noticed," Ollie said and he and Bull again took hold of Sam's arms over his protests.

"We're getting you back to her. Not for you but for her," Bull said, not letting go when Sam would have pushed him away.

Bull was too big to argue out of anything; so Sam let them help him to the front of the hotel. "I can handle it now," he slurred, thinking the night air had cleared his head a little.

"Sure you can," Ollie said, loosening his grip enough to show Sam that without them, he was going to stumble.

"All right, help me in, but that's it," Sam said, looking toward the stairs that seemed to have grown in number since he'd walked down them. "I can make it," he repeated, and pushed them away. He knew they would watch him go up them and made a concerted effort to climb up without falling backward--only had one near call.

At the top, he realized he had another problem. He couldn't remember the room number. Couldn't very well knock on all the doors, and the room clerk had looked decidedly unfriendly as he'd walked past him. No help there. Then he remembered he had a room key in his pocket. Squinting, staring at it, he made out the number and directed his steps accordingly.

Putting the key in the hole was another obstacle. After three misses, he connected and turned the lock, satisfied that he wasn't as drunk as Ollie and Bull thought.

He opened the door, hoping Abby was asleep. The light was off, but when he looked toward the bed, he saw her sitting in the center of it, legs folded under her, the derringer pointed at his chest.

"You can put it down," he said as he closed the door. "It's me."

"It is, is it?" she asked. "How do I know that? It's dark in here. I didn't have a drunken sot for a husband, but you look like one."

He half smiled even though he knew she didn't intend her comment to be funny. He eyed the bed, wishing he could collapse across it, but with her centered in it, the gun still pointing at him, he guessed he was more likely to sleep on the floor.

"Now, Abby," he said, then stopped. He wasn't supposed to explain himself to her. The whole idea was for her to get mad. She was mad. Success. Except, why didn't he feel successful?

She put the gun on the nightstand. "I've been worried all night. Every gunshot has been you falling dead. I've had to listen to drunken louts on the street yelling and laughing, a man rattling my door handle, and then what happens? I thought you were supposed to be out conducting business--nefarious though it was."

"Sort of." He was too far gone to ask what that word meant, wouldn't remember it in the morning if he had.

"Do not lie to me. Please give me at least that much credit," she snapped. "You were out getting drunk!"

He moved away from the wall that had been supporting him. "I could sleep somewhere else," he said, unable to think of anything else he could offer her.

"You will not," she snapped, jumping up, grabbing his hand, and tugging him to the bed. He felt her unbuckling his gun belt, pulling at his clothing, pushing him flat, pushing blankets over him, then he knew no more.

CHAPTER 28

L ying in bed, sun shining in the window, Sam felt as though his head was going to blow apart. The light blinded his eyes, hurt his head.

"Awake are we?" Abby asked, her voice unnaturally loud as she pulled the curtain open to let in more light.

He squinted his eyes open and nodded, regretting the movement. A hangover was no fun. This was no way to win his point with her. Death would have been more merciful.

"How long you been awake?" he asked, noting that she was dressed.

"Awhile." She sat down on the bed beside him, bouncing the mattress enough to set off the pain in his head again.

"Uh, baby, don't do that." He put his hand to his aching head.

"Man who sets out to get drunk, deserves what he gets," she said without an ounce of sympathy in her voice.

"I'm feeling... fine," he lied.

"I can see that. Why don't you get up then and we can go get some breakfast--maybe bacon, eggs, fried potatoes, how about some sausage?"

He tried to smile and knew it probably looked weak. "Maybe later."

She shook her head. "I didn't eat last night. I'm starving."

"You are a hard woman." He made what he considered a superhuman effort to move and levered himself to a sitting position. "You were kinder when I was shot."

"I was afraid you'd die then. This time I know you won't die, not that you might not want to."

"How do you know so much about hangovers?" he asked, forcing himself to stand. He was naked and guessed he'd gotten that way with her help. He couldn't imagine himself doing anything more than falling into bed. That must mean she still had some feeling for him. He ought to say something crude to crush that, but he couldn't bring himself to do anything more than stand there and look around the room for his clothing.

"My father has had a habit of over indulging now and then," she said, handing him a glass of water.

"What's that for?"

"It has a headache powder in it, which the room clerk kindly got for me, and the water is because alcohol tends to dehydrate the body."

He drank the glass down; unsure of how much he liked her sarcastic manner even when she was supposedly helping him. Knowing he deserved it, he suppressed his own sharp retort.

Somehow he managed to get dressed, his head feeling a little better either from the powder or just from getting his circulation going. He began to think he could manage breakfast. If he could just get a cup of coffee, that would help.

When he buckled on his gun, she frowned. "Do you need that?"

He nodded, tying it down to his thigh. "You think people only get wild at night?"

"From my admittedly limited experience, it's been the most common."

He ignored that, taking her hand, appreciating for the first time her thick hair pulled into a loose pile on top her head, the pretty, gold dress that hugged her curves in a most flattering manner. "You look beautiful," he said.

"I wish I could say the same." He took a look in the mirror and grimaced at the bristly jaw, sunken eyes, uncombed hair, and conceded her point with a faint nod. She had water on the dresser, a comb and shaving equipment, which made it relatively easy to tend to his ablutions. At least he didn't cut his throat with the razor, even if he did nick his jaw twice.

Outside the town was bustling. Different people, different noises from the night, but no less activity. They ate breakfast at a small cafe where Sam found after coffee and a piece of toast he began to feel halfway human. He wasn't sure Abby was pleased with that. He thought she'd have liked to see him suffer a little longer.

"Do you do this sort of thing often when you come to town?" she asked, the wet squirrel look still on her face.

"Eat breakfast?" he asked with mock innocence.

"You know what I mean, Samuel. Do you get drunk?"

"No."

"What brought it on last night?"

"Actually, it doesn't take all that much for me. Goes right to my head."

"Did you find men last night? Can we go home?"

"Didn't look."

She pursed her lips, her eyes narrowed. "Isn't that why you came?"

"I'll do it tonight."

"And get drunk again."

His smile was wry. "I don't think I need to repeat that."

"That's some comfort."

"Last night should have shown you that you need a better man." He nodded to the waitress to refill their coffee cups.

Abby looked at him for a moment, then around the room with a considering eye. "Like that one?" she asked, motioning her head toward a portly salesman eating across from them. "I've seen him eyeing me. Could be he's a possibility?"

"Not good enough for you."

Her smile was cool and calculating. "Are you going to be the arbiter of my new swains?"

"Swains? What the hell is a swain? Is that anything like a swine?"

She smiled deliberately at the salesman who smiled back.

Sam glared at her. The thought of another man, any other man, in her bed was almost enough to drive him back to the bottle. When the salesman rose and started toward their table, Sam gave him a look that turned him around in mid-stride.

"Interesting. You don't want me, but you don't want any other man to have me either." He gave her that look. "Well, aren't you trying to get rid of me?" She slammed down her coffee cup.

"Why would you think that?" He reminded himself that he wanted her mad enough to leave him. Except, whenever he got it near that point, he backed off and tried to placate her. His mix of emotions weren't helping him.

"Isn't that what you are up to?"

"Nope." Not working right anyway.

She sipped her coffee, and he could see the wheels turning in that lovely head. He didn't have long to find out which way. "Are you going to send back the uh... You know?"

He nodded. "Right before I leave town."

"But what if someone finds it?"

Although no one near them could understand what they were discussing, he still would have preferred it not be verbalized. She was a terrible conspirator. "Hopefully that won't happen," he said, unable to come up with a good answer for her as to what they'd do if it did.

Out on the boardwalk after paying for their meal, she suggested they go for a stroll. Although he still felt under the weather, he didn't refuse. Her hand on his arm, they strolled up

Fourth Street. The morning air was pleasant, with a surprising scent of roses in the air.

"Sam!" He turned to see Bull coming down the boardwalk. "You feeling all right this morning?" he asked with a grin.

Sam nodded.

"He will be fine *this* time," Abby said. "Next time he'll find his head split open."

"Felt like it this time," Sam said.

"I meant by me."

Buck chuckled. "Sound just like my ma." He scratched his head. "Almost forgot what I was going to tell you. Last night Ollie and me went over to the Crystal Palace and a couple of guys come in. We got to talking, and they sound like maybe somebody you oughta talk to."

"What did Ollie think of them?" Sam asked, not wanting to hire anybody. He wanted to get to the ranch, wanted to keep Abby with him, wanted to be selfish, and pretend would work out.

"Don't know. He didn't say, but they were real anxious to talk to you. We said you'd be around tonight. That all right with you?"

Sam nodded, even though it wasn't. He was tired of seeing the sad expression on Abby's face whenever they talked about adding men for only one purpose. He stared past Bull to the rocky, desolate hills north of town, his mind a hundred miles it needed to be.

Abby walked a little ahead to more closely examine a red, climbing rose. "What were their names?" Sam asked, his gaze on her as she lifted a rose to her nose, sniffing of it delicately.

"Sinclair and Monk something. Sinclair's the one with the brains, but Monk's all right, I guess."

"You tell them anything?"

Bull shook his head. "No, figured it was up to you. Me and Ollie already said we'd be satisfied to run the ranch and forget the rest. You know we said that."

"I know."

"You decide you want to talk to them, they said they'd be at the Crystal Palace tonight."

An old lady came out of the adobe that was behind the rose and smiled at Abby. "You like roses?"

"You keep them blooming even with the heat. I admire that," Abby said.

"My name is Jane Grainger," the white haired woman said as she extended her hand.

"I'm Abby Ryker. Your roses are wonderful. I tried to grow them in Tucson but never succeeded."

"In this climate, it does take patience and careful nurturing."

"I guess I didn't know enough."

"Experience makes all the difference-- that and trying again and again. I brought this rose here as a cutting when Tombstone was a tent city. I didn't know if it would live in this rocky soil, but my son brought me some better earth from the hills. The first winter I thought I'd lose it, but part of it lived, and I didn't give up on it. That's the way it is with roses you know, my dear. You can't give up."

"Mine shriveled up in the torrid heat."

"Maybe it was the type. Some are heartier than others." She smiled and looked at Sam as he walked up to them. "This your husband?" she asked. Abby nodded. "Strapping fellow. My son's a strong man too. Works in the mines."

"I've heard that's difficult work."

"It is that. Well, if you want a cutting, feel free. This isn't the best time of the year, but later in the fall or even next spring, why don't you come back and get one, take several."

"I would like that very much. Thank you."

When Abby and Sam walked on, he asked, "What was that all about?"

"About sticking to things," Abby said with a smile as she put her arm around his waist.

"Some things aren't worth sticking with."

"But you never know ahead of time, do you?" she asked, her eyes bright with unshed tears, the love in her eyes something from which he couldn't run.

As they walked, he considered his situation. He couldn't leave her. He hadn't been very successful at driving her away mostly because he didn't want to do it. How could he protect her? He felt empty of ideas. There had to be a way, but he didn't have the answer.

"I know I've been acting strange," he said.

"An understatement."

"I've had a lot to think about."

"I did gather that too."

He smiled. "Would you mind if I took some time--by myself?"

"No." She wished she meant it. In a way, she did. She wanted him to be happy; and if time alone was what he needed, she would accept that. "I could go back to the hotel," she said.

"You don't mind?"

"I think I already answered that." She stopped, stopping him too. "I'd like it if you could talk to me, but if you can't, I will try to understand," she said as honestly as she could.

He walked her to their hotel and saw her safely inside their room with Bull and Ollie on the porch, drinking coffee, and committed to keeping an eye on her if she needed to go out. Then he began to walk out of town. At first he didn't know where he was heading. Nothing out that way but then he saw that there was—the cemetery.

It was quiet on the lonely rise, the only human reminders those of wooden markers. Beneath a scraggly juniper, barely recognizable as a tree, he lowered himself to his haunches and stared at the town in the distance. Birds chattered, the wind blew with almost a physical presence, but there was nothing to distract him from his ponderings.

Mind blank to why he was there or what he hoped to work out, he looked at the weathered, wooden marker to which he'd ended up next. J. Martin. d. May 1881. Not much of a statement left to represent a man's life. What would be on his own marker —assuming he didn't die out on the desert and leave behind nothing but bleached bones?

He wasn't sure when he realized another person was in the cemetery. Someone was walking down the rows toward him. He rose as the tall man approached extending a well-shaped hand. "Hello." Sam took the man's hand mostly because he had no good excuse not to. No miner-- there were no calluses. The man wore a dark suit, string tie, crisp white shirt, and no gun.

"We haven't met, have we?" the stranger asked. He looked down at the marker. "You a relative of John's?"

Sam shook his head. "Just came up here to think."

The stranger chuckled. "Figured it'd be quiet, huh? And then along come I."

"About that."

"Want me to leave?"

"It's a big country."

The man eyed Sam with a touch of curiosity. "You a rancher?"

"Sometimes."

The man smiled, his cleanly shaven face handsome in a dark, almost saturnine way. "You look like you've known trouble, friend. Like you're trying to find a way out of it."

"Did I say we were friends?" Sam asked, eyes narrowing.

Instead of being offended as Sam had expected, the man smiled. "Actually, you didn't, but then aren't we all brothers when it gets right down to it."

Sam frowned with wry recognition. "You a preacher?"

The man nodded and laughed. "John Damian, sky pilot. I take it from the expression of disdain on your face that my being a pastor doesn't endear me to you."

"Should it?"

"Not particularly." The man sunk onto his haunches and looked up at Sam. "Mind if I sit here with you awhile?"

Sam lowered himself. "Depends."

"On what? Sermons are out, I take it?"

"You figured to preach one?"

"Actually, I have a funeral this afternoon and will be doing just that. I came out to get my thoughts together." He smiled at

Sam, who ignored the attempt at friendly convesation. "Do you believe in coincidence--what did you say your name was?"

"I didn't, but it's Sam Ryker."

"All right, Mr. Ryker. Do you believe in coincidences?"

Sam smiled then. "Pastors and their trick questions."

"You've known a few pastors well?"

"One."

"I see by the expression on your face that the knowing wasn't to your benefit."

"Nor to his," Sam said coldly. "I killed him." He expected the pastor to pale and move away, but the man only looked at him.

"A particularly bad sermon?"

When Sam didn't smile, the pastor's own face grew somber. "Sorry. I didn't take that as seriously as I should have. Taking another's life can be a terrible burden. Bother you much at night, Sam?"

Sam pulled the makings from his pocket and rolled a cigarette, struck a match and using his hand as a shield, lit the cigarette, drawing the smoke into his lungs before he answered. "Not that one. Should it?"

"Maybe, maybe not."

"I expect I'll pay for it someday in hell; but if I had the choice to make again, I'd repeat the favor; so no, I don't repent of it, if that's the next question."

"You're a hard man."

Sam nodded, taking a long drag on the cigarette. "I did try to call him out, wanted him to fight me, but he laughed at me." He didn't add the crude suggestion that had accompanied the laugh.

"You're not asking for absolution."

"Could you give it to me?"

"No."

"Then I'm not asking."

"The only man who can give that to you, Sam, is yourself."

Sam snorted. "Nothing like a double talking pastor. You been in the trade long?"

"Awhile."

Sam looked at the glowing tip of his cigarette and decided that for a reason he couldn't have explained he wanted this man to know why he'd done as he had and so in simple words, he told him, ending with finding the naked boy and the pastor's sorry attempts to explain what he'd been doing.

"You dispensed divine retribution," the preacher said showing no shock.

"Depends on how you see it, I suppose."

"That is how I see it," Damian said, his dark eyes probing, seemingly into Sam's very soul--if he'd believed he had one. "There is more, isn't there?"

"Could be."

"But you don't want to talk about it?"

"No."

"Words don't always help. There are many words I could say to you now, but you're not ready to hear them."

"How do you know that?"

"I work for someone who is very discerning. Occasionally he passes along the knowledge to me."

"You talking about God?" Sam snorted. "A lot of people say they hear from God. Most are crazy."

Damian chuckled. "I won't intrude on you longer, Sam Ryker, but if you ever need me, I'm preaching at the small church off Safford Street. Welcome is over the door. You come talk to me when you are ready."

"I won't be."

"Maybe maybe not."

Sam shook his head. "That's what I don't like about pastors. Always that secret little smile that tells you they know something you don't."

"From what you've told me, you've only really known one well, and I'd put my chips on that one having a different master than I serve."

"Chips?" Sam raised his eyebrows.

Damian rose to his feet. "I will see you again, Sam Ryker."

"I doubt that."

"Time'll tell."

"It has a way of doing that."

Walking into the Crystal Palace Sam felt about as undecided as any man could. He had told Abby before he left that he would not come back drunk. He knew he wouldn't find any answers to his problems in the Crystal Palace, but he'd told Bull he'd talk to the two men. It was about the only clear direction he had when he was a man who still had the taste of her kisses on his lips. She was giving all to him and asking nothing unless he counted the expression in those big eyes. He didn't remember ever feeling so out of focus.

With the entertainment on the small stage, the loud voices and the clapping of hands and laughter, the Palace was no place for a conversation. Sam picked up a beer as he looked around and saw Bull and Ollie at a table toward the back of the room. "They ain't here yet," Bull said. Sam hesitated a moment before sitting as it would put his back to the room, but then he did it anyway.

He looked at Ollie. "What was your take on them?"

Ollie shrugged. "I don't like any part of the idea, but I already told you all that. I think you ought to take that little wife of yours, set her up on her horse, and head for the ranch."

Sam was feeling much the same way, but he still had the problem of getting the stolen shipment to Abby's father. He wondered how she'd respond if he mentioned again how it would be good for her to visit her father, taking the stage to Tucson.

When he saw Bull look over his shoulder, he knew the two

men had arrived and the crawling feeling on his spine made it hard to resist turning around with gun in hand, but he waited.

Bull brought them over. "Sam this is Drago Sinclair and Monk... Don't think I ever caught what the whole name was."

"Don't matter," Drago said, sitting down at the table. He signaled one of the girls and soon he and Monk had beers. He sipped his then smiled at Sam. "I hear you're looking for men."

Sam shrugged. "It's been talked about."

"They said you got ranch down by the border."

"Who said?" Sam asked, rolling and lighting a cigarette.

"Somebody must've said something. So, you looking for wranglers?"

"No."

Sinclair's gaze was hard, his smile somehow familiar. Sam thought he'd seen him before but had no idea where. "Do I know you from somewhere?"

"Don't think so," Drago said. "You work much in Texas?"

"Some a lot of years ago."

"A lot of years ago I was in Kansas."

Sam considered that, debated where he might have met the man, but the memory was elusive if it existed.

"Well, sorry," Sam said, "but I changed my mind. There'll be no new hires."

"You think it over." Sinclair smiled with a glint of anger in his eyes as he rocked back in his chair, his hand resting comfortably near his gun butt.

"Don't need to." Sam knocked the ash from his cigarette.

Drago shrugged and took another sip of his beer. His eyes were kind of a yellow color again reminding Sam of something or someone. "I keep having this feeling I met you somewhere," Sam repeated.

"I been a lot of places. Could be," Drago said.

Sam took another draw on his cigarette. "Maybe you look like somebody."

"Well, if you figure it out, let me know."

378

"Likely I won't."

Drago smiled. "You sure you don't have a job?"

"No jobs for you."

Drago took a deep breath, seemed to be contemplating something, then suddenly rose. He started to walk away, then turned. "Most likely see you around."

"Possible."

When the two men had gone. Ollie let out a whistle. "Good choice, boss. When we going to the ranch."

"I don't know." Sam felt confused, his decisions being tossed back and forth as if by the wind. "Just because I didn't hire those two, doesn't mean I have decided against anybody."

"Sure. Sure," Ollie said with a grin, "but either way, it's good we don't take on them two," Ollie said, shaking his head and looking at Bull. "Don't know how you ever found 'em to begin with."

"Didn't," Bull said, sipping his beer. "They found me."

"Kinda strange," Ollie said, tapping his finger on the table. "What do you figure, boss?"

Sam rose. "I figure I need a good night's sleep for once."

"Never used to go to bed so early," Bull said with a grin.

"Never had a pretty little wife either," Ollie chortled.

Sam ignored their laughter and left the bar, grateful when he was in the fresh air. Maybe he was getting old. It just didn't feel the same to be in that crowded, loud, smoky establishment.

Out on the street, he stood a long moment watching the sun setting in the west. The colors of rich purple and deep maroon deepened against the Whetstone Mountains. He had never felt so undecided and fatalistic. Life was winding down just like the day. Was it almost over for him?

When he got to their room, Abby was lying in bed, a book she had borrowed from the small downstairs library, propped on her knees. "You're back early," she said as he settled on the edge of the bed.

"Uh huh."

"Did you hire men?"

"Uh uh."

"You're not too talkative tonight."

He bent and kissed her, her lips soft and inviting under his, and he let the kiss deepen, allowed himself to fall into the feelings she engendered in him. Maybe he was crazy to let himself care so much, to trust her, but if he couldn't trust her, he'd rather be up in Tombstone's boot hill.

The knock at the hotel door woke them both. Outside it was barely light. When Sam asked who it was, the knock was repeated but no answer. Abby slipped her nightgown back on.

"Who is it?" Sam repeated.

"Message," the voice said.

Sam growled to wait and pulled on his pants. Abby pulled the covers up to her neck and began to think what they might do with the rest of the morning. Several intriguing possibilities quickly came to mind all of which got Sam's pants back off him. When he opened the door, his arm stretched across it to bar further access, Abby saw a man standing there with a piece of paper outstretched.

"Wire," the stranger said, "figured it might be important when I saw it was for your wife."

"It could've waited, Sinclair," Sam said. He looked down at the paper, a puzzled expression on his face and Abby realized he couldn't read it. She knew how that made him feel, saw the expression of embarrassment.

Let me see it, Sam," she said.

"Too bad about her father," Drago said.

Abby gasped. Sam, who had started to shut the door, turned to her sound of dismay. The door was shoved hard against his hand, and Abby saw something come up and down across Sam's head.

She shrieked as she watched Sam fall to his knees. Almost simultaneously the man pushed his way into the room and slammed the door behind him. When Sam tried to struggle to his feet, the gun lifted again, but this time Abby was off the bed and had grabbed the attacker's hand, putting all her weight into deflecting the blow, which even glancing, sent Sam flat out.

The gunman gave her a shove, sending her to the corner of the room. She scrambled to her feet and looked at the gun now pointing at her. "Who are you?"

The man's gaze went over her body, telling her without words that the thin nightgown wasn't hiding anything from his piercing gaze. She felt frightened but then the sight of blood on Sam's head, drove all fear from her. She crawled to his side to examine the wound. "I have to bandage this."

The man smiled but stepped back. "If it makes you feel better."

"Who are you? Why did you do this?" She opened a drawer widely; so he would see there was clothing in it. Taking one of her handkerchiefs, she made a pad to stop the bleeding and tied it in place with a silken scarf. Not all she wanted to do, but all she would be able to for now. She then looked up at the gunman. "Now what do you want?"

"First you tell me your name."

"I'm Abby Ryker."

"Spenser Ryker?" he asked

"Yes."

"I'm here to take you home."

"To my father?" She felt confused. Everything was happening too fast. Who was this man? "I had planned to visit later."

He frowned as if this wasn't going quite as he had expected either. "It needs to be now."

Abby swallowed. "What about my husband?" She looked down at Sam's still form.

"Him?" He shrugged. "He's a dead man."

CHAPTER 29

A bby tried to stop her shaking. This couldn't be happening. "Why would you say that? He hasn't done anything wrong." "He kidnapped you. That's enough in this country."

She had to think, not panic. There would be a way to save Sam and herself. She had to be strong. She managed to smile as she shook her head. "We eloped. You know how that is."

"You're lying."

"Why would I?"

"Who knows? When it comes to women, figuring out the why of something isn't worth the trouble it takes."

"Just go now. No problem if you leave now."

"No way. There's a reward, and I'm taking you to Tucson to collect it."

She tried to think, but her mind was blank. She had to get this man away from Sam. That was the only thing clear to her. "Then leave Sam here."

His sneer was ugly. "I planned on *Sam* staying here."

She saw his intentions in his eyes even before he took out a long knife from its sheathe. "If you kill him," she said, swallowing hard, "I'll scream and tell everyone you attacked us."

"I could kill you both," he said with a smile that said he was capable of that.

"Not soundlessly. You take one more step toward either of us, and I will scream this roof down before you can kill me."

He believed her.

"Leave Sam here, alive, and I'll go with you." When he seemed undecided, she added, "I know where the stolen shipment is. You can take that back too. It will increase whatever reward you've been promised."

Drago rubbed the tip of his knife along his chin. "Maybe we can work something out."

"I'm sure we can, but it doesn't involve hurting Sam Ryker. He's done nothing to deserve that." Abby forced herself to smile again. She knew it had to be shaky, but she had to disarm him and would use whatever weapons she had.

"Ma'am, you don't begin to know but all right. We'll play the game your way. We have to tie him to the bed though or he'll be following us. That wouldn't be healthy for him or you." Drago's smile deepened. She was a lot more desirable looking as a woman than he'd been expecting. He wanted revenge against Sam Ryker, but he wasn't worried that he would lose his opportunity to kill him if he left him here now.

Ryker would follow as soon as he was able, and Drago would be waiting. He would disarm him because he had his woman; and then he could take his time before he finally killed him. Drago knew a lot of ways to kill a man. Ways that would take days. He would use Ryker's woman in all the ways he could imagine right in front of the helpless man. Yes, the more he thought about it, the more he wanted to have Ryker out of town, and she would help him do it.

"Help me get him to the bed," Drago ordered, enjoying the view of her feminine curves through the thin nightgown. He began to feel aroused. Between a beautiful woman and killing, it was hard to say which was best, but he would have a chance to do both before this was finished. The beauty of it was he could still get the reward after he did things to her she'd never dare tell.

Abby looked warily at the knife, but Drago reassured her. "Don't worry. I'm only going to use it to cut up the sheet to tie him. We'll leave him here nice and safe just like you want."

Abby swallowed, seeing no choice, at least not for now. She helped Drago wrestle Sam's body onto the bed. He ordered her to stand in a corner where he could see her. She watched as he ripped the top sheet into long, wide strips, using them to tightly bind Sam's hands and feet, spread-eagled, to the brass bed. He forced the unconscious man's mouth open and shoved in a length of sheet, tying it in place with another strip effectively gagging him if he didn't choke on the wad of cloth.

When Drago had finished, he looked down and chuckled. He wished Ryker was conscious; so he could enjoy the helpless look that would be in the man's eyes when he realized what was happening. Drago knew he didn't have long. Time was already running out. "Get dressed," he ordered the woman.

Abby couldn't look at Sam. She was about the play the most dangerous game of her life. She had to concentrate all her efforts on keeping them both alive and deceiving Drago sufficiently that she would get an opportunity to break away, but not here, not when he had Sam helpless.

"I always have admired a winner," she said huskily, looking him up and down with a smile.

Drago grinned, not deceived but willing to play along. "You're a smart lady."

"I've been told that."

For a moment Drago considered not waiting but instead taking her right there. She would do whatever she was told to keep Ryker alive. Maybe Ryker would regain consciousness. That would be the ultimate punishment to have to lie helplessly and watch him spread the legs of his woman. On second consideration, he knew he couldn't afford the time. Ryker's men might show up, then what was simple would become complex. Besides, he had no doubt he'd get a second chance at the man. Ryker would follow like a dog on a scent.

Abby went to the cabinet that held her new dresses. She had left the derringer in the pocket of the gold dress. It would have to do and she would have to distract Drago sufficiently that he would not notice its weight. *Be calm*, she ordered herself. *You know what to do.*

She swallowed down her nausea and reached for the neck of her nightgown, unbuttoning the buttons as he watched. Slowly she worked, revealing more and more of her skin. She saw the desire growing in his eyes but that was not enough. When the opening was wide enough, she let the gown fall to the ground in a white pool at her bare feet. Naked, she faced him and somehow managed to smile. She felt frightened and humiliated but she let him look at her body without an attempt to cover herself as she reached for the chemise she had worn the night before. She stepped into it, bringing it up to cover her breasts, then the pantalets. She didn't rush. She knew her hands were trembling, but if he noticed, he wouldn't care that he was scaring her. His mouth had dropped open; his eyes narrowed as he watched each movement. She felt as though his gaze had raped her, but she was not finished. There was more. After tying the slip at her waist, she took her stockings to the nearby chair and sat. She rolled each one up her legs until she secured them with garters.

Now came the most dangerous part, that which could end any hope and make all she'd endured for nothing. She had to get the dress on without his noticing the weight of the derringer. She took it into her hands, let it drop over her shoulders. "I'll need help," she said, turning for him to fasten the buttons up the back.

She felt his hands against her skin, felt the touch as though something unclean against her, but resisted the instinct to pull away. With the dress in place, she turned to him.

He was smiling. "You're a lot more woman than I'd figured."

She knew she wasn't the same woman she had been in

Tucson only short months before. "The mails are there," she said pointing to the larger of the two saddlebags.

When he bent to get the bag, checking its contents, she put on her jacket. With the saddlebag in his hand, he put away his knife and reached for Abby, pulling her into his arms. Afraid he'd feel the gun, she threw her arms around his neck and lifted her lips for his kiss, pressing against him in a way that profaned what she had with Sam. She'd do whatever it took to save the man she loved. Even if that had meant having sex with this monster, she would do it. She prayed she would not have to go that far. She would get free. She'd learned a lot in these last months, not the least of which was she could kill if necessary.

She broke off the kiss, unable to bear being touched by him one second longer. She felt like throwing up but managed to smile. "Not here," she said, keeping her eyes shyly downcast so he wouldn't see the repulsion in them.

"All right, lady," he said, patting her buttocks as though her body already belonged to him. "Let's go. We've got plenty of time."

Drago opened the door, watched her go through it and looked at the bed and directly into Sam's dazed eyes. Saw him try to move only to find he was bound and gagged. Life was too sweet. He grinned and raised his hand in a half salute just before he slammed the door.

Walking down the hotel stairs, Abby considered her options. If she used her gun too soon and wasn't effective, Drago might go straight back to where Sam was helpless. If she waited too long, a man much more familiar with guns would easily overpower her.

Drago stopped at the desk. "Mr. Ryker isn't feeling well. Please don't clean his room today.

The clerk frowned. "Does he need a doctor?"

Drago winked. "Not that kind of sickness, son."

Abby grimaced at the clerk's understanding smile. "We'll give him complete peace," he promised.

On the street, she saw three horses, one of them ridden by a small, dirty man "That's Monk," Drago said, putting his hand on her hip. "He's my partner."

"You were pretty confident I'd agree to come," she said gesturing toward the horse intended for her.

"In myself at least," he said with a smirk.

Before she could say anything, Bull yelled from down the boardwalk, "Hey there, Miss Abby." He walked up to them and looked suspiciously at Drago, then to Abby. "Where's Sam?"

Abby saw Drago's hand hover near his gun and knew from having seen the speed with which he'd pistol-whipped Sam that he could kill before Bull so much as got his gun out of the leather. She smiled. "I thought he said he was meeting you and Ollie somewhere. Wasn't that what you remember, Drago?"

"He change his mind about hiring these two?"

"Sure," Drago said with a grin. "We're good men, and he figured it out for himself."

Bull looked again at Abby. "You sure you're all right?"

She nodded and smiled. "You go on and look for Sam. Maybe the Oriental." She used the name of the only saloon she knew as she looked up at Drago. "Do you think that's what he said?"

"I didn't hear, but there or the Crystal Palace are good places to start."

Bull left, but not without another backward glance. Drago grinned. "Smart thinking, baby. I think you and I are going to get along just fine."

Struggling against the bonds that held him, Sam raged at his helplessness, then at Abby's duplicity. She'd led him to believe she loved him, but that kiss she'd given Sinclair seemed to say she'd meant none of her words. She had turned to another at the first sign of his weakness. Her betrayal didn't come as such a surprise to him, but why a man like Sinclair? Was she so naive that she didn't know what kind of man he was?

He had regained his senses in time to see her willingly go into the man's arms. She had walked out the door without so much as a backward glance. Sinclair's gloating smile had been his last glimpse of them.

He twisted his wrists, pulled at the strips of sheeting that held him, but nothing gave, except his skin as he began to rub his wrists raw. The gag left his mouth dry, made him feel as though he was choking on the wadding that had been shoved into his mouth. He couldn't make more than a grunt. Spread-eagled on the bed, he couldn't kick out to make enough noise to get noticed. Sinclair had been thorough; he'd give him that. Struggling was getting him nowhere. The rough friction was only hurting, but he couldn't stop himself. Like an animal caught in a trap, he thought he'd probably have chewed off a paw, except with this trap he couldn't even do that.

At the thought of Abby's betrayal, he felt tears come to his eyes. He wouldn't cry. Hadn't cried, not when his own mother died, not when Sandy died, but he'd wanted to, and he wanted to now. Despite Abby's deceitfulness, he loved her and knew she was stepping into a situation with Sinclair that was beyond her experience. He tugged on his bonds again. The bonds couldn't be that strong but somehow they were.

This whole mess was his fault. He put her in a place where it could happen and now he was helpless to help her. His head hurt, felt it was splitting in two. It was hard to think clearly but he knew one thing. She didn't deserve what Sinclair would do to her. He knew the kind of man he was. Abby didn't. Somehow he had to get free. He closed his eyes, then opened them again, concentrating on keeping the room from spinning as he again pulled against the bonds that kept him from going after her.

Abby walked to the horses with Sinclair at her side. When she saw him throw the saddle bags over his horse, she drew the gun from her pocket, cocking it as she said, "This is far enough."

He turned to see what she meant and looked straight into the barrel of her derringer.

"They tell me it has two shots," she said smiling, "and that at close range it's quite deadly. Do you think this would be considered close range?"

Sinclair glared at the gun, then at her. "What are you trying to pull?"

"Warn your friend to stay on his horse and keep his hand away from his gun. I would shoot you first if he made me nervous. If you take one step toward me, that's what I'll do. Now unbuckle your gun belt and let it drop to the ground."

Sinclair gritted his teeth but did as she ordered and Monk settled watchfully into his saddle.

Not taking her eyes from Drago, she said, "You too on the horse." When she heard the sound of his gun dropping, she told him to pull his rifle and Drago's from their scabbards. Again a satisfying sound. "

Now," Abby said, "my suggestion is you take the stolen shipment to my father. Tell him that you left me in good condition with my husband. You can then pick up your reward and keep riding."

"You won't get away with this."

"I won't? You do one thing I don't want, and I'll shoot you dead as I start screaming that you're trying to kidnap me. My husband unconscious and tied to that bed upstairs will be all the witness I need."

He sneered at her. "You wouldn't do that."

"I've killed before, Mr. Sinclair."

He stood still as a rattler waiting to strike as she backed a step from him to stand on the boardwalk. "I don't believe that," he retorted, scorn on his face.

"Are you willing to bet your life on it?" she asked with a faint smile.

He was infuriated. She felt the anger radiating toward her, like a red aura of hate and was surprised she didn't feel afraid. Fear seemed to have fled from her. She had decided she didn't need to watch them both, just Sinclair as the other would do as he was told.

"Now get on your horse and ride out of here. Leave the guns. I'm glad you were reasonable about this. I didn't want to kill anyone this morning. It is a terrible start to a day."

"You won't win," Sinclair hissed. "I will see you again."

"I understand your feelings, but if you and your partner are wise, you'll get that reward money and forget the rest. It's not worth dying for, and if I do see you again, I will be watching you die."

She watched as Sinclair mounted and wheeled his horse, with his partner at his heel, to gallop down the street. She then gathered up the revolvers and rifles and walked into the hotel.

She stopped at the desk and smiled at the room clerk. "Did you notice the man who was with me a few moments ago?"

He nodded, looking curiously at the guns in her arms.

"I don't want him upstairs, and if he or the one with him come in, could you immediately go for the sheriff?"

"They cause you trouble?"

"They hurt my husband and tried to kidnap me. I'm going up to check on him now. If he needs a doctor, I will ask you to send for one."

The clerk paled. "Hope there's been no serious trouble in our hotel. We're a quality establishment."

"I know. Just one of those dangers of life in our times, I fear." She walked toward the stairs

"Well, if you need him, Dr. Goodfellow's one of the best in the territory ma'am, and I'll be happy to send for him."

"I'll let you know."

He shook his head. "I don't like knowing there's been trouble in our hotel. I think maybe I ought to call the sheriff now."

She considered a moment. "I don't think my husband would want that, not yet anyway. Not if they don't come back." She smiled again and was relieved when the man smiled his agreement. Bad publicity wouldn't help either of them.

∼

When the door to the hotel room opened, Sam looked toward it. When he saw Abby and not Sinclair, the relief was so great as to almost cause him to lose consciousness again.

In angry frustration, he watched as she glanced only once at him before she locked the door, put a pile of guns on the dresser, and only then came to sit on the bed. He stared up at her, torn between anger that she'd gone, that she hadn't already started to untie him, and a relief that she was there so intense that he could barely think straight.

She reached up and began undoing the gag in his mouth. It took her awhile, but she finally got it loose. He spit it out and tried to say her name but all that came out was a croak. She went to the dresser, poured water in a glass, then put the glass to his lips. When he'd had a few sips, she took the glass away and set it on the bedside table, all without saying a word. God, what was she thinking?

"Untie me."

She folded her hands on her lap "How do you feel?"

"Uncomfortable."

She unwrapped the bandage she'd placed on his forehead and dipping a cloth into water, began washing carefully around the wound, her expression probing but giving nothing away of what she was thinking, of why she hadn't already freed him. Her touch was both soothing and painful.

391

There were quiet steps outside the door, then a knock at the door. "Room clerk, ma'am. Does Mr. Ryker need that doctor?"

She looked questioningly at Sam. "No, he doesn't," he said.

"Very good." The steps retreated.

"Cut me loose," Sam ordered, yanking at the unforgiving strips of cloth that held his wrists above his head.

"I don't think so, just yet."

"For God's sake, why not?"

"If I cut you free, you'll go after him." She rested her hand lightly on his bare chest.

He stared at her. "You want to protect him?"

"That blow to your head must have loosened something important," she retorted, continuing to bathe his forehead with the cool water.

He gritted his teeth. "Abby, I'm losing patience here."

"Not good since we both know you don't have a lot to begin."

"No more games."

"No, no games."

"Then?"

"I won't untie you until you promise not to go after him."

"You are trying to protect him. I saw you kiss him." He knew he sounded distrustful, angry, and he couldn't hide it.

"I think he was a bounty hunter. Did you know that?"

"No."

She stroked the hair from his forehead. "He wanted to kill you." Her voice was little more than a whisper, tears in those big dark eyes. He wanted to wipe them away. He wanted...

"He... had a knife too."

"You're not going to cry, are you?"

"I think I am." A tear trickled down her cheek, then her face crumpled and she lowered her head to lay against his chest. "I thought he was going to kill you. He's got the stolen shipment though... so maybe he'll go away."

"All right." He took that all in, tried to assimilate what she was saying. She had kissed the man because she was protecting him.

Somehow it didn't make sense but then women rarely had to him. "Cut me loose now. I have to go after him, Abby, and the sooner the better."

"No."

"He will be back."

"You can't know that."

"Yes, I can."

"You've been hurt. You might have a concussion. You can't go after him now."

"Now is when he won't be expecting me."

"He'd kill you," she argued.

He felt frustrated in trying to reason with her. Okay, he'd try a different angle. Get her to talk, make her think logically and maybe then she'd see he had to go after Sinclair. He forced his voice to sound reasoning, far calmer than he felt inside. "Tell me what happened."

She did, leaving out how she had deliberately set out to titillate Sinclair. She didn't want to talk about that, was not sure she ever would. The thought, of having to use her naked body that way, still left her feeling unclean. She knew under those circumstances she'd do it again, but it was a painful moment to remember.

"You did good, Abby. Now finish it up and cut me loose," he said, as firmly as a man spread-eagled to a bed could say it.

"No."

"Damnation woman. You can't keep me here forever."

"I don't need to, just for long enough that you can't go after him."

He lay back, breathing hard in his anger. Reasoning with her never seemed to work. He knew he was right. A man like Drago Sinclair wouldn't take lightly being bested, even more so by a woman. The man would shadow their trail until he was killed.

He felt her fingers tracing a pattern on his chest. He looked down as she kissed where she'd drawn. She bent, her hair was long and loose and it brushed across his belly as she bent to sip at his nipple, sucking a little.

"Abby, what the hell are you doing?" It didn't take much to arouse him although he'd have never imagined under these circumstances it could happen. He had gone from believing she'd betrayed him, to understanding she had saved him, to feeling she was trying to make his decisions for him, and his mind was too beclouded by the blow he'd taken to make sense out of any of it.

She kissed his shoulder, running her tongue lightly over his skin. "I like this."

"What?" he muttered, then felt her lips against his. Without thinking, he opened his mouth to her, felt her tongue dart within, tease his. The sensations traveled down his body and increased his hardness. God, the woman would make him crazy.

"You are always so powerful. I like this... this being in control," she whispered as she put her hand over his growing bulge.

"Abby--" Again she planted her lips on his, the kiss so filled with heat and passion that it took his breath away and left him wondering why he wanted to be free. There would never be any freedom for him. Whether he was tied to her bed or not, he was bound to her in all the ways that mattered. Ways he could no longer deny.

"I love you, Sam," she whispered as she peppered kisses across his face, then down his neck and chest.

He was having a hard time controlling his breathing now for another reason. "What are you doing?"

"I am not sure, but do you like it?" She lost her train of thought as she again kissed him. To be able to touch him, stroke his muscular body, and make love to him was a heady drug. She dipped her fingers below the line of his pants-- almost, but not quite, touching his growing erection.

"So it would seem," he managed, his voice husky, his eyes dark with passion as his body showed how much he liked it.

"Now, about what I want from you. I want it all, Sam. I want everything you've got, and I want to give all that back to you."

He closed his eyes. It was hard to believe how quickly he'd gone from losing everything, to knowing he'd won more than he'd ever imagined existed. He opened his eyes, met her gaze. "I do love you. You know that, don't you?" he whispered.

"I've hoped it." She bent and kissed him again. "And I've so much wanted to hear you say it."

The knock at the door, bold and loud, startled them both. "Who is it?" Abby asked reaching for the gun and wishing she had cut Sam free. Maybe he was right. Maybe Drago Sinclair had returned immediately for his vengeance.

"It's me, Bull. I couldn't find Sam at any of the saloons. I got to wondering if everything was really all right."

"It's fine," Abby said, stroking a hand down Sam's torso. She smiled and unbuttoned the second button on his pants.

"But Ollie ain't seen Sam either, and I thought maybe--"

"Quit worrying," Sam growled. "I'm right here. Now get lost."

Bull chuckled. "Gotcha, boss." Then they heard his footsteps recede down the hall.

"Think you can cut these ties now?"

"What about Drago?"

"Abby!" His tone said he was losing his patience with her all over again.

"I mean it, Sam. You were hurt more than you think. I will not lose you."

"You won't." He shook his head, wincing at the pain. He knew she was probably right about his head. He wasn't in any shape to go riding off. "You know I could have had Bull come in and untie me," he reminded her, not wanting to have to capitulate completely but realizing he was close to it.

"But you didn't want him to see you like this, did you?" she asked with a little smile, as she undid the next button on his pants. "I personally think you look particularly appealing, spread out across this bed, all those muscles in tension, so ready for me and all I'd have to do is pull down your pants for... but I expect

Bull might think it was funny--at least, after he knew you weren't seriously hurt."

He gave up. "All right, what do you want me to do?"

"Take me home."

He closed his eyes as the pain slid over him. Had he misunderstood what she had been saying? After all this, she wanted him to take her to her father. He couldn't go with her. Tucson was no place for him, but he would take her. "When do you want to leave?" he managed.

She smiled. Kissing him before she went for the knife. "As soon as we can. I want to check on our chickens, how the calf is doing, and hope Joe didn't forget to give Rahab milk."

"You mean the Circle R?"

"Of course. That's home for us, the only home for me now. A place we'll fill with children and have a real family including your gang who can be wranglers and maybe even find women of their own. You do want that too now, don't you?"

He opened his eyes then and saw everything in hers that he'd ever wanted. "Will you marry me?" he asked, as she began sawing at the bonds holding his right wrist.

"We are married."

He felt his wrist fall free, and with effort brought his arm to his side, wincing with pain as the circulation returned with a vengeance.

"If we're going to do this right, we ought to do it when you understand the words and we both mean them." With his other wrist free, he began to rub his hands. As soon as she'd cut his ankles free, she took over the task.

"I know my father would probably like to see me married," she said, chewing on her lower lip.

"You mean go to Tucson. I'm still not sure that would be such a good idea for awhile even if Sinclair does what you told him to do." Which he doubted.

"You're probably right, and a trip here would be too hard on him." She felt the tears start again when she saw the raw spots on his wrist.

When he saw the tears, he said, "If you want to wait and go to Tucson, that's all right with me." He didn't mean it, but he would make it be all right. Whatever she wanted, he wanted. When he realized how far gone that meant he was, he didn't even care.

She shook her head. "No, just... I can't help but think how close I came to losing you." She bathed his wrists with the cloth, washing away the blood. "I need to get some salve."

"I'm fine," he said, trying to sit up and finding that his head felt like it was splitting open and the room spun when he moved too quickly. He settled for pulling her into his arms. Maybe he couldn't feel much in his hands yet, but he could feel her against his body, and it was right.

She curled against him, fitting her body into the hollows of his. "I should send the clerk for Dr. Goodfellow."

"Uh uh. I don't need a doctor. I just need you."

"I could go get you something to eat."

"No. You go no place in this town without me." He kissed her to soften the gruffness of his words. They had not seen the last of Drago Sinclair, and he wouldn't take the chance that she would again have to face the man alone. "I'll feel better soon," he said, "then we can go down to the hotel dining room for something."

"And tomorrow," she suggested, teasing his nipple into an erect nubbin, "you can make good on your promise to marry me again. Maybe we can do it later in Tucson with my father. We could do it every year."

He lifted his head and looked at her with concern.

"Just teasing," she said, smiling impishly.

"Well, just in case you weren't--I'll marry you wherever, whenever and however you want." He pulled her down for a claiming kiss.

"I don't suppose it'd be good for you to... well, you know," she said with one of those smiles.

"There are ways. Take off that dress."

CHAPTER 30

D rago's fury knew no bounds. He'd been deceived, made a fool of by a silly chit of a woman. Homely to boot. He didn't know why he'd ever thought her beautiful. He remembered the poster, remembered the pulled back hair and knew he'd been wrong about any beauty he'd imagined.

Monk and he rode to the edge of town, turned south and circled to a gunsmith's where they purchased new weapons. Better guns, Drago told himself. He said nothing to Monk about any of it his mind revolving round and round with plots for revenge. The game was not over.

"We going to collect the reward?" Monk asked as they rode north out of town..

"Not yet."

"But--"

"Shut up. I do the thinking, and I say we aren't leaving yet."

"But where are we going?"

"We'll camp outside of town. That's all you need to know."

"I think we oughta get what we can out of this like she said."

Drago snorted. "You think I'd let her get away with pulling a gun on me? You think I ought to let her do something like that, then go to her lover and laugh about it?"

"Well--"

"Shut up! You know what this is about."

"You think it'll make it better for your brother?"

"And you think it won't. I've been looking for this man a long time. My brother's blood cries out from the grave. Nothing will be right until Ryker pays for what he did. The law won't punish him. I will."

"You can't bring your brother back"

Drago swung his arm from the shoulder, knocking Monk almost from the saddle. "And so I should let that bastard get away with it."

"I suppose not." Monk rubbed his cheek.

"Then you know I have to nail Ryker. I want him to know when I do it too. His bitch can watch and then..."

"That guy said he's fast, Drago. Real fast. I think we oughta take the reward and forget him." He ducked away when he thought Drago was going to slap him again, then straightened when Drago laughed.

"I'm fast too or did you forget that?"

"No, but--"

"We'll take the new guns into the hills and get the feel of them. Then we'll come back and wait for our chance."

"We going to ambush him?" Monk asked more cheerfully.

Drago smiled, his lip curled. "We'll see." Only humiliating Ryker as he'd been humiliated would satisfy the raging hunger Drago now felt. Only seeing the man on his knees, begging for his life would be enough to cover the degradation the woman had heaped on his head. Somebody had to pay for that. First Ryker, then her. They'd both learn what it meant to come up against Drago Sinclair.

Abigail Spenser had promised him something with her eyes, her lips, her body, and he meant to have it. He'd teach her to respect him, teach her what pain meant. Only when she knew all that would he discard her. Maybe she would live for awhile and maybe not. It depended on whether she learned to please him. He smiled more broadly.

~

Sam knocked on the door to Pastor Damian's small house, unsure if he wanted the man to be there or not. Reluctantly he'd entrusted Abby's safety to Bull and Ollie as she went from shop to shop picking out something to wear for their wedding assuming Pastor Damian could bring himself to bend his principles enough to do that. Sam knew he wasn't a prime bargain, as any pastor would see him.

"Sam Ryker," Damian said as soon as he'd opened the door. He waved Sam into a small, sparsely furnished parlor. Sam took a straight chair while Damian sat on the only stuffed chair.

"Sorry for nothing to offer you, but I haven't been here long. I'd like to offer you a cup of coffee or something, but I forget to shop and right now there's not much in my cupboards except a little tea."

"No problem. I'll get straight to the reason I'm here." He tried to think of the right words. He expected to be refused, and he didn't want that. What could he offer this man to make him willing to marry an outlaw and a lady? Even taking into consideration that the outlaw wanted to turn to mend his ways it would look like a bad bargain for the lady. Sam rose from the chair and paced to the window. Beyond the parsonage was a rocky slope, nothing living except some yellowed grass.

"I suppose some would say that's not much of a view," Damian said.

"Maybe."

"It keeps me humble."

"How so?"

"Rock. Not much more basic than that. I look out there and remember how this faith of mine was founded on a rock, nothing fancy but something basic and solid."

Sam didn't say anything for a moment. "I don't know how you'll feel about this, but I've come to ask you to marry me."

Damian smiled. "Do we know each other that well?"

Sam laughed. "I mean--me and Abby."

"You did say you had a wife."

"And it's her, but we got married sudden. We were married by a Spanish priest, and Abby didn't understand the words. I want to get married when she and I both know what we're doing, and we're figuring to make it work."

Damian leaned back in his chair and grinned broadly. "Sounds like a solid plan. Normally if I'm going to marry a couple, I ask them to come for several meetings to discuss marriage and what it means, but in your case, where you're already wed, I think we can skip that."

"I appreciate this, parson. You know, I have a ranch down by the border. Maybe sometime you could come there and visit. Don't get me wrong. I have no intention of converting but I have a strange feeling we might have more in common than that."

"Might be and I'd like that. Well then, when do you want to do this recommitting ceremony?"

"Nine tomorrow morning if possible. It's a long ride to the ranch," Sam said.

"No honeymoon?"

Sam hadn't thought of that. Maybe she would want a trip, but it would have to wait. "I have reasons to get back to the ranch." Sam wanted Abby safely there with his men around her, and then he'd deal with Drago Sinclair. There would be no peace until he did that, no hope for a real future. That kind of man would not be safe to leave walking around. Sinclair would hunt them and find them when they least expected it. Sam only hoped he could get her to the ranch before that happened.

~

Wearing the off white dress Sam had bought her when they first came to Tombstone, Abby walked to the church with Bull and Ollie. Her long hair was piled loosely on her head, held as much in place as her unruly hair ever was by a small feather hat she'd found in one of the shops she'd dragged the two men through. Outside the church, their horses waited, packed for the ride to the ranch. Inside would be Sam, the pastor, and Jane Grainger, the only person in Tombstone who she had known well enough to invite to the wedding.

At the thought of what lay ahead, Abby felt nearly overcome with joy. Sam loved her, was going to marry her in a church where they both understood and meant the words. They would be able to live a life like other couples, work for their needs, raise their children, love each other. There was nothing more for which to wish.

Entering the sanctuary, she saw that it was a simple, straight-forward structure, wooden walls, plain pews, with a rustic cross at the front. Her white haired elder friend sat on one of the pews and smiled at her, handing her half a dozen red roses. "You can take the cuttings later, my dear," Jane said, patting Abby's hand, "but for now I'd love it if you would carry these."

Abby smiled her thanks, then looked at the tall handsome man who was standing at the front of the church. She felt her insides grow heated and aching with need, as she saw his heavy lidded gaze. She walked to the front of the church, barely aware of the man at Sam's side, the one she knew must be the pastor. She knew Sam introduced them, saw Ollie and Bull seat them-selves, but her own eyes were flooded with tears. Sam was wearing a new white shirt, a black string tie, black pants, polished boots, and no gun on his hip. She smiled up at him as she knew the latter was his real gift to her. She hoped it was a harbinger of their new life.

Standing beside Sam in the front of the chapel, juniper and sage boughs in large baskets beside her, the pastor in front of them, a Bible open in his hands, she heard him saying the words--words she'd heard at other weddings but that were now for her. Sam took a plain gold band from his pocket, and she smiled, tears running down her cheeks, as for the first time he put a ring on her finger.

When the pastor declared them man and wife, Sam's kiss was tender and sweet, and then she was being grabbed by Ollie and Bull, hugged again by Jane. The older woman thanked her for allowing her to witness their happiness. The pastor took her hand and offered his blessing and best wishes. The only thing that could have made it more perfect would have been her father attending, but maybe Sam wouldn't mind a third service someday if her father wanted that.

Walking outside the church, the air was fresh and clean, still cool and almost dewy, fragrant with the scent of the roses in her hands. Roses, sage and the scent of the desert. It was all perfect. She turned to Sam to kiss him when she heard the yell from the street.

"This is your hour of reckoning, Ryker!"

Abby looked up and saw Drago Sinclair standing in the street, a sneer on his lips, and a gun in his hand. She felt Sam stiffen as she tried to hold onto his arm, but he put her from him.

"Bull, I'm trusting you to hold onto her and keep her safe," he said. Without giving Abby so much as a backward glance, he stepped into the street, his hands held out from his side.

"You looking for something, Sinclair?" he asked. She was shocked to see him smiling.

"Could be a man. Could be I found him."

"What did you want him for?"

"Retribution."

Sam laughed. "Big word from a small man."

"You've got a right smart mouth. Could be it's all you've got."

"You want to find out? As you can see, I'm not heeled."

Sinclair chuckled. "I did see that. Kind of convenient, I'd say. You could go get it."

Abby saw Sam look toward his gun, which was hung over the horn of his saddle. She could almost see him calculate the distance and decide he would not make it.

John Damian stepped onto the wooden boardwalk, his boots unnaturally loud to Abby's ears. "Put down your gun," he said, his voice that of authority. "There has been a wedding here today." She felt a relief that someone would intervene, stop this before it was a murder.

"Wedding huh?" Sinclair grinned. "Thought you already married her or was that a lie too." He glanced at the pastor then, his gun still pointing at Sam. "Get back in your little church, sky pilot, or you'll be taking a bullet along with him. Monk, you keep an eye on Ryker's men. Anything stupid and shoot the woman first."

Abby watched as the pastor turned and walked into his church. Her hope disappeared. There wasn't anyone to go for the sheriff. She could not let it end this way. She looked up at Bull's face, saw his attention was focused on the street and not her. She wrenched her arm from his grasp. He turned to look at her, but she saw by the expression in his eyes that he was not going to stop her no matter what Sam had ordered.

"Now then," Sinclair said, "I think maybe it's time you know why I'm going to kill you."

"Always interesting to know a thing like that," Sam said. She watched as he edged sideways toward the horses.

"Not another step," Sinclair ordered as he swung his gun until it pointed at Abby on the boardwalk. "My first bullet will be for her."

She knew Sam would do nothing to risk her. She had to change that. He had to fight to live. "He won't shoot a woman. Do what you can, Sam. Running is no disgrace."

Sam didn't look at her. "Yes, he would."

"Smart man," Sinclair said. "And you're right."

"And now is where you tell me where I know you from."

"Not me but someone close to me."

"That explains it. I knew I'd seen vermin like you somewhere."

"You ever murdered a man, Ryker? Just shot him down like a dog?

Abby couldn't believe that Sam could smile, but he did. "Only time that happened, it wasn't a man but a cur."

Sinclair's expression turned from smile to snarl. "He was a pastor, you worthless scum. No man deserves to be shot down without a chance."

"There's times I'd agree," Sam said, the smile not leaving his lips. "Not with that one. He was worse than a dog."

"I been looking for you for a long time. That man was my older brother. I took a different name for my work so as not to embarrass the family, wasn't in Kansas when you killed him. When I got back, they said who they thought had done it but you'd gone and there'd been no proof. I knew I'd run across you someday, and when I heard the name in Tucson, I just hoped it would be you," Sinclair said, his voice growing more enraged as he spit out the words.

"If he was your brother, you know what he was."

"What did you mean by that?"

"You know what he did—likely you do the same when you get a chance."

Sinclair seemed momentarily nonplussed but shook it off. "Beg me for your life like he must have done."

"Oh he begged all right. He wouldn't fight. He wanted to crawl off like the worm he was to do it to another boy like the one I caught him on top of."

For a moment, Abby thought Sinclair was shocked; but if he was, he quickly hid it. "You're a liar and you will beg forgiveness."

Sam snorted. "If you're waiting for me to beg, it'll be a long time coming."

"Not so long." Sinclair smiled. "I've thought a lot about all the ways I could make you die but decided I want it to be slow." He fired his gun, the bullet striking Sam in the right arm, causing him to reel and clasp his arm. He straightened and again faced Sinclair, his jaw clenched.

"This is good," Sinclair said with a weird little laugh. "I've never shot a man to pieces before. Hell, this is so much fun I might not even kill you--just leave you a twisted piece of garbage. Handy it being that in Tombstone nobody pays any attention to a gunshot." Again he pulled the trigger, the bullet striking Sam in the left arm. Again it spun him around, knocking him from his feet.

Sam struggled to his knees then back to his feet to face Sinclair. Abby saw that with each shot, Sam had worked his way nearer to his horse. He needed a distraction. Her moving again led to Drago looking at her.

"Oh please," she pleaded, moving forward to the post of the porch. Her own gun was in the saddlebag on the back of Belle. "Please." She forced out what she hoped was a pathetic wail. "You can't do this to him. I know you're a good man."

Drago laughed, clearly pleased at finally hearing someone beg. "You're wrong. I'm not a good man. He threw another shot toward Sam, but this time the bullet missed as Sam shifted again a step closer to his gun.

"Stop this right here," John Damian's voice came from the church doorway. He held a gun.

"A pastor with a gun. Now that's something you don't see every day." Drago laughed.

"I can use it, if that's something you were wondering about," Damian said as he moved out into the street the gun looking very comfortable in his hand.

Now Drago had three targets to watch and seemed indecisive. The moment of indecision was enough as Sam was now at his saddle and somehow, hard to believe as it was for Abby, he had his gun.

Drago backed up but turned all his attention toward Sam and the gun pointed at him. "So we finish this another day?"

"You take me for a fool? There'll be no other day for you."

"You won't shoot me down in cold blood, not out here with witnesses anyway; so how do you propose to do that?"

"Easy, you let me put on my belt and we settle it in the street. That oughta be more what you want anyway."

"You're wounded," Abby cried. "You can't think..." She moved down between Belle and Satan not caring if Drago did shoot to stop her. She kept her movement slow, not wanting to distract Sam. She was determined she'd get her gun; and if she did, she'd kill Drago-- in cold blood if that's what it took. She had no moral compunction to prevent her doing it. Sam had said once that sometimes you had to kill. This was such a time.

"All right," Drago chuckled, eyes back on Sam. "Keep your dogs off me and I will leash mine. I can take you easy, could have even before you got shot."

"We'll see." Sam got the belt off the saddle and fastened it around his waist, dropping the gun into the holster. To Abby he seemed to be moving unsteadily. She moved down to her saddlebag to pull out her 38.

Damian fired a shot at Monk who dropped his gun and grasped his wounded arm. "He said stay clear of it."

Sam stepped out into the street. "Your brother was a coward and an abuser of children," he said. "You made out of the same cloth?"

"You lied about my brother," Drago snarled.

"When you meet him in hell, you can ask."

As they got in position, Abby clenched her jaw against the fear she felt. She saw the blood on Sam's sleeves. It seemed impossible that he could draw his gun fast enough to beat anyone to the draw. She wasn't sure though if she tried to shoot the bounty hunter that she wouldn't end up only distracting Sam enough to get him killed. She had to watch and hope he knew what he was doing.

When Drago went for his gun, two shots rang out. Sam stood with his gun still pointed toward Drago's chest as the outlaw staggered backward. He looked bemused but tried to bring his gun to bear again. Sam shot a second time, and this time Drago sank to his knees before falling forward, his gun landing at the tip of his fingers.

Abby pointed her gun toward Monk who seemed to be debating whether to try his luck. "Get out of town," she said. "Take the saddlebags to my father and then disappear. If we see you again and Mr. Ryker doesn't kill you, I will."

Monk grimaced as he looked at Drago's body. With three guns pointing at him, he spit onto the ground, and rode off.

Abby moved to Sam's side to assess his injuries. "How badly are you hurt?"

"Nothing much," he said sliding his gun back in its holster.

"I don't like this business of patching you up all the time." She managed a smile.

He looked down at the gun still in her hand. "Seems you are picking up some bad habits hanging around with wolves."

She smiled. "I wanted to kill him... If he had shot you again..." She left the statement unfinished, but he smiled down at her even though his eyes reflected pain.

"You're a pretty good shot," Bull said to the pastor. "Never seen no sky pilot shoot that good."

Ollie, belting his gun around his waist, looked at John Damian. "I seen you before?" he asked.

Damian shrugged. "Could be. I wasn't born a minister."

"Sit for a minute," Abby ordered Sam pulling him to the boardwalk. She then ripped open his shirt, pulling it from his shoulders to bare two wounds in his upper arms. Although they were both still bleeding, it was sluggish. Neither bullet had struck bone.

"Can you make a fist with both hands?" she asked.

Sam frowned, as he looked up, the expression in his blue eyes clearly irritated. She smiled. If he could let her know he was less than thrilled with her order, he was himself. When he made the fists anyway, she knew he had no serious nerve damage in either arm, which had been her greatest fear after she ascertained no vein or artery had been cut.

Frankly as she glanced at the pastor, thinking she might ask him to get the doctor, she decided he didn't look much better than Sam. Whatever it had cost the man to come out with a gun and use it, he was now upset by it. "I'll go get the doctor, dearie," Jane Grainger offered and hurried off at a surprising speed.

Dr. Goodfellow came quickly with his black bag and after a cursory examination, ordered them to carry Sam to his office to treat the wounds. Sam glared at him, then at Bull who had approached with the intent of carrying out the orders.

"I can walk," he said through his teeth and did so.

Abby watched in the small office as the doctor competently treated Sam's wounds as well as any big city doctor she had ever seen. When Sam had been disinfected, stitched, bandaged and had both arms put in slings, the doctor said, "I don't think you'll suffer any permanent damage from either wound, but watch that left arm. It's the deepest. After the stitches are out in ten days or so, if it seems to stiffen up, exercise it carefully, but do exercise it." He smiled as he patted Abby's shoulder. "You keep him in bed two or three days and he'll be just fine."

Sam, who had until that moment had said nothing, taking pain with his usual stoicism, snapped, "We're riding out--today."

"I don't recommend it," Dr. Goodfellow said. "There is shock attached with such a wound which could lead to dizziness."

"He's right," Abby said. "We don't need to leave immediately."

"We do," Sam said. "We are going home." Abby recognized the stubborn bent to his voice and knew further arguing was pointless.

"How you figure to ride," Goodfellow asked with a cynical twist to his words, "without two good arms?"

"Carefully."

"Then you ain't riding Satan," Ollie retorted.

"I will. Nobody else could anyway." He looked then at John Damian, who had been watching as his wounds were treated. "Thank you."

Damian smiled. "It's been awhile since I used a gun. I didn't think I ever would again."

"You could've let me die out there. Without your intervention, more of us would've."

"It helped make my decision."

"You will come to the Circle R?"

"I will."

"We'll talk more then."

"Many times, I'd guess," Damian said, managing a smile for the first time since the shootings. "Something told me to not get rid of that gun even though I wanted to. Today I know why." He looked up and saw the sheriff coming. With a wry smile, he went to head him off.

Abby caressed Sam's cheek, thinking how she'd never expected to do that to the living man again. While she had stood, watching him stand unarmed facing Sinclair, then the bullets hitting his arms, she had feared the most she could hope for would be revenge on his murderer. Now it was as though he and the promise of all they could have had been resurrected, brought back from the brink of death.

He looked into her eyes, his own warm with love. "It's time to go home," he said. For the first time in his life, he had one.

EPILOGUE

November 1884 Tucson AZ

"**W**ell, what do you think?" Abby asked, spinning around to watch Sam's face as he entered what had been her bedroom in the years she'd lived in Tucson. To see his muscular frame, hear the clomp of his boots on the polished floor and to know that soon they'd be making love in this room where she'd first dreamed of him, was heady stuff. She barely suppressed her smile.

"About what?" He sat on the bed to take off his boots.

"Everything tonight. You acted as though you enjoyed yourself."

"It was all right." She thought his smile was a bit tight.

"Just all right?"

"Marshal O'Brian is still looking for reasons to arrest me." His smile showed more humor.

"I can't believe that. Even with the Reimers coming into town and discussing what a wonderful neighbor you are?"

"Nobody is fooling him, but he's letting it go... for now at least."

"You are another rancher to him now."

"Think what you want." He stood and followed her to her mirror kissing the long line of her neck.

"You know, seeing you and the marshal in the same room, you could be brothers."

"Black to white?" he teased.

"You are determined to see what you want. At least you can't deny Father likes you."

"Now I know *you* see what you want. He still looks at me like I'm something the cat dragged in."

"He doesn't either."

"Yes, he does but it's all right. I took you from him. It's expected he'd not be thrilled with me."

"Do you like him?"

"He seems like a--uh good man."

She grinned, surprising him as she turned and gave him a push that sent him to the bed. She followed up immediately, pressing him to the soft mattress. "Pinned," she said with a grin. "Now tell me what you really thought." She began unbuttoning his shirt.

"Sweet Lord, woman, what do you think you're doing?"

"I'm taking off your shirt."

"Abby," he said warningly. "This is your father's home."

"And there are better places, my love?"

"Be careful--" His words were stopped by her lips in a manner she'd found most effective.

She lifted herself off him and headed back to her own task of removing her dress—something that her large belly was complicating. "Priscilla is becoming fond of Joe," she said as she reached behind her and managed to get the first two buttons. "She really liked the oil painting he gave Father of you and me. She and he talked all evening."

"I doubt that too but better him than Martin."

Abby laughed, pleased as he had come to unfasten the rest of her buttons. "You should not have given Martin that look," she said, giving him one of her own.

"What look?" Those intense blue eyes glittered with amusement.

"The one that stops most people in their tracks."

He chuckled. "Never you though."

"It's never stopped me because there was always another right along with it."

"You think, huh?"

"Mmmmmmmm." He finished with the buttons and she let the dress slide down her shoulders, baring them to his gaze. She knew he liked to take it slow and now she did too. Sometimes. Tonight though she just wanted him.

He moved back to the bed, leaning back against the headboard and watching as she slipped off the rest of her garments. She felt a shiver as in the mirror she could see his gaze moving down her body. She liked knowing he desired her. Still she was swollen with child. Perhaps he found her body less desirable.

"Do I look fat to you?" she asked.

He laughed and shook his head. "I've never seen you more beautiful." His eyes darkened with desire.

"You aren't getting undressed," she reminded him.

"I will."

She put her thoughts back to the evening with their friends as well as Pastor Damian. "Do you think John liked being here?" she asked thinking perhaps it was better not to probe into what Sam was thinking. She supposed it wasn't easy coming to Tucson, but he'd done it for her. She had hoped the dark moods had left him but being in Tucson may have stirred them back up.

"Maybe."

"He seemed to be happy."

"He's one to not reveal his own thoughts that readily," Sam said, finally removing his own clothing and slipping under the covers. "He pays a high price for it."

"You think that's why his church is not growing in Tombstone?"

"More likely it's because a lot of people are scared to find out he was a wolf himself."

"Not anymore."

"Folks aren't comfortable around those who can kill—past or present tense."

She smiled as she got into the bed and cuddled to him, running her hand along his muscular biceps. "Maybe he could come here to preach. It's a bigger town. I've heard that Pastor Ryan is leaving." She made a disgusted face. "We can hope anyway."

"John said he'll be heading north soon, maybe to Wyoming or Montana."

"We'll miss him."

"We'll see him again." Sam smiled, putting his hands under his head. "He said we would and I believe him."

She hoped that would be so. Without John Damian, she'd not be moving forward to take her husband in her arms. She did understand the man had his own troubles. She hoped he'd find some of what she and Sam had.

As she felt Sam's hands caressing her, his fingers lightly running over her rounded belly, she stopped thinking and let feelings take her to the oneness she always found with the man who was friend, lover, husband, and soon to be father to her first child.

The End

The characters and story line continue in "Tucson Moon".
(Introduction attached)

Love, Family and the uncontrollable desert.
Cord learns he's not a "Lone Wolf"... if he survives

-TUCSON MOON (ARIZONA HISTORICAL BOOK 2)

Priscilla Wesley has everything going for her with wealthy parents, beauty, a privileged life. The last thing she needs is to fall in love with a lawman. US Deputy Marshal Cord O'Brian makes his living with a gun, something she abhors. Attraction isn't enough—or is it?

Tucson Moon is about love, family relationships, the desert, and Arizona Territory in 1886-87. It's about choices and how one's character can be improved, or degraded one step at a time.

From this set of characters, three series of stories evolve connecting lineages into Western Contemporary stories. Look for them at
http://romanceswithanedge.blogspot.com